SOMETIMES IT IS WHAT IT IS

Copyright © 2015 by Biz-e-Bee Book Group

Beverly Hills, California

All Rights Reserved

Printed and Bound in the United States of America

Published by:

Biz-e-Bee Book Group

8549 Wilshire Blvd. Suite #139

Beverly Hills, California. 90211

www.bebpub.com

Library of Congress Cataloging-in-Publication Data

ISBN# 978-0-9817074-2-6

Cover Design: Biz-e-Bee Book Group

Formatting: Biz-e-Bee Book Group

First Printing, April 2015

10 9 8 7 6 5 4 3 2 1

Biz Nolastname

Publisher's Note

Author's Note:

Since my last book I've been through a Lot of shyt. I've been rushed again by a Task Force and been to more jails in more states. Because I can give you another novel from home is how I know that God has my back. God must've given me a lovable personality because he knew I would be in the world alone with no real family as a safety net.

Since my last book I've also had more new cars, trucks, girls and houses, even moved to Atlanta. I've gained a new respect as a great author and I've gained new friends. Life is still shitty and complex and good at the same time. I wouldn't trade it for anything else, lol.

Above all I try not to be too busy making a living or dwelling on things that haven't gone right that I forget to live my life.

My stories come from the fuzzy line in people where anyone can be a different way on a different day. I love everyone who loves me and none who don't, Fuck 'em.

I wanna thank everyone who supported my first effort as an author. I can only Apologize for making you wait longer than you thought you would for part two, life got in my way. If you wanna make God laugh just tell him your plans. To my boys and girls locked up, the hard copies are for yall. Everybody on the streets are downloading this shyt. I thank my children with everything in me for loving Daddy unconditionally.

It's still one thang for certain and two thangs for sure, either you gonna hate me or love me. And thank you to everybody who truly gives a fuck about me.

P.S. I wrote half of this book with my thumbs. Enjoy!

BE LIKE THAT SOMETIMES

Part Two

Sometimes it is what it is

A novel by

Biz Nolastname

PROLOGUE

Keno pulled into the alley to take a piss. He couldn't have been there for more than the time that it took to get out of the car, pull his dick out and drain about eight ounces onto the already piss-stained concrete behind a dumpster, when all of a sudden he heard a man's screams coming from over his head.

Then BOOM!

A body slammed onto the top of the dumpster he was behind. He pissed on his hand. Blood, dust, dirt, flies and stank flew into the air and engulfed him. Keno was immediately disgusted. He looked and saw a man splattered on top of the dumpster with his head hanging over the edge, eyes glued on Keno, no blinking, no nothing. The man let out a sigh and blood spilled out of his mouth and nose. Keno probably would've thrown up the Club Sandwhich he'd eaten for lunch had his attention not gotten diverted by the sound of an attaché case crashing to the ground and a shower of hundred dollar bills raining down over his head.

Keno quickly looked around and determined that no one on the ground was around or in earshot of what had just happened. He heard another sigh escape the man's mangled mouth. Keno's first thought was to scrape up as much money as possible and as quickly as he could and dash out of the alley and into the wind and that was exactly what he did. He started grabbing money and just stuffing it into his pockets until they were full then into his shirt until he looked fifty pounds fatter. He kept stuffing until it got ridiculous. There were too many bills. Still no one was coming so he picked up the wide silver attaché case and started stuffing money into it. After he gathered up all the money he jumped into the car and took off down the alley and around the corner.

Just like that he had come up on one million dollars!

The saying goes, "When somebody comes up, somebody else has to be coming up short."

Well, to keep it real, it wasn't really just like that. A lot of things had happened that put Keno in that alley at that time and the dude on the dumpster wasn't just a stranger.

Let's start from the beginning.

A Year and a Half Before

Chapter one

Before the last man could get into the Toyota Sienna van, a bullet pierced his forehead and dropped him. The other rear passenger reached back and grabbed the bag of money from the dead corps. Another passenger returned fire at random through the sunroof.

Federal agents seemed to be coming out of everywhere.

The bank robbery seemed to have gone perfect. Everybody had done what they were supposed to do and everybody inside had cooperated. They walked out with $1.5 million in cash.

It was almost perfect.

The van caught ten slugs in rapid succession. The driver slammed on the gas. They sped off. The van whipped around the corner. The rear end fishtailed. A black Dodge Charger police cruiser with its sirens blaring was right behind them. The three thugs were in the van sweating.

"Man! What the fuck are we gonna do?" the one in the back that grabbed the money bag said.

"It's only one thing we can do!" said the front passenger, exchanging clips on the Mac 10 semi-automatic machine gun.

Money Bag whimpered. "Ah man, this is fucked up. It's over. We're going to jail for life!"

He almost fell on the floor because the driver made a quick maneuver.

The driver yelled, "Shut up! That was my brother back there with a hole in his head! What we gonna do is… I'ma have to out run 'em!" as he ran through a red light narrowly missing a collision.

The feds ran the light too. The gunman looked back at the now five police cars on their tail.

The gunman said in a low voice, almost to himself. "Five against one. It ain't fair." as he popped up through the sunroof. "I gotta make it fair."

He let out a burst of shots and turned the first car's windshield into glass sprinkles. Bullets riddled all four cops inside. The car veered off to the left and crashed into a parked car. The same thing happened to the three cops in the next car except it veered to the right before crashing into a busstop bench full of people. Shots fired from the third police car and took out the van's back window. Several bullets flew past Mack 10's head. One grazed his cheek and one went into his shoulder and out of his back. He fell back down in the van as the driver made a sharp turn into an alley. Three more cars had joined in, so now six police cars shot down the alley behind them.

Mack 10, slumped and bleeding all over the seat, hollered for Money Bag to shoot back or pass him the pistol. When he got no response he looked back and saw Money Bag laid across the backseat, dead with his eyes wide open, staring at the roof of the van. He was covered in blood and glass.

KENO

"Ay Smooth, come 'ere." I said interrupting my homeboy Smooth. He was sitting in his car watching that bank robbery movie again.

"Hold up Keno, it's goin' down right now. The feds just killed the boy in the backseat!" he hollered out the window of his Lexus.

I stood up and looked in. Smooth was laid back on his tan buttersoft interior with both his eyes glued to the monitor in the dash.

"This is the third time I busted my fuckin' hand tryna put this rim on this bike and it still ain't tight. This lil worn out ass wrench ain't gonna work. We're gonna have to make a run to the rim shop to buy a new one." I yelled, complaining over the noise coming out of his speakers.

Smooth pressed pause on the movie and got out of his car. "Here, give it to me. You just gotta know how to hold it."

It was a Sunday afternoon and I was getting ready to enjoy the rest of my day on Crenshaw and some other spots on my Harley Davidson motorcycle with a few of my ridin' fellas. My government name is Keno Brown. The bike Smooth helped me put the wheel on was a '06 Fat Boy Hog, Tweety bird yellow in color. The seat was real alligator back. The rims were chrome and shined like new coins. I was working on the bike behind my apartment complex in a parking stall unofficially assigned to me. But there were no complaints, just like no one complained about the other two spaces I had confiscated.

Smooth followed my lead but he was smooth about it. "See I told you. You just gotta know what you doin'." said Smooth satisfyingly looking at the tightened rim.

"I'm still tryna figure out who sliced a hole in my tire in the first place. It might have been Crystal. But it's all good though, this bitch is back in action, new speakers too, and I got that new music by Jay Z.

Ay Smooth check it out. Why don't you go to the swapmeet and buy some fresh white T-shirts for today. I'm about to go take a shower and get dressed."

"Aight fa sho. You wanna hit this blunt first?"

"Hell yeah."

We smoked half of the blunt together then Smooth hopped into his car and pulled out the driveway pushing play on his movie. I heard cars skidding and gunshots booming out of his speakers.

I went inside the apartment. It used to be occupied by me and my girlfriend Shalleen. A big boned stallion, light complexion with jet black wavy hair she usually kept in a braided ponytail. Shalleen is a ghetto beauty and she just wanted to be spoiled by a hustler.

That's it and that's all.

But she had been in deeper than she knew from the beginning. I had already knew who she was and who her man was when I stepped to her in the club. My name had been ringing around town and I knew it. That was why she gave me her number. Her and her homegirls had even discussed me a few times before we met, that was what she told me later in the relationship. She said the word was that I didn't do any tricking but if you were my girl then you had it good. So we both had alterior motives when we made introductions like complete strangers. She was looking into upgrading. My motivation was to rob her daughter's father Big Will.

Crystal, my girlfriend at the time, found out about Shalleen and broke up with me. She was pissed. It gave me more time to concentrate on Big Will through Shalleen though. Shalleen's bad habit of pillow talking became my good fortune. We both got what we wanted and as a bonus the sex was crazy, so we ended up being together for a while. But my lifestyle got to be too much for her, things like the homies being sprawled out on the couch and floor in the mornings when she woke up, not to mention the blunt trash and empty alcohol bottles. She wasn't the square type but she was just tired of all the "senseless killings" as she called it, that surrounded us. She had already gone through the same things with her daughter's father.

The last straw was when the police raided our crib early one morning looking for cocaine and arrested everyone in the apartment. Shalleen's mother had to go down to the police station to pick up Shalleen's daughter Leslie. Shalleen was released the next day and hadn't spent a night since.

Now it was just me.

Smooth would be back soon. I cut the stereo up and blasted Snoop Dog while I did 200 push ups nonstop to maintain my toned physique acquired on a few too many stints in and out of the county jail.

I looked in the mirror at my chest and arms. I have a tattoo of a sexy female demon coming out of my skin on my left arm. She is a fine lil evil ink bitch. I needed more tattoos. I had plenty more room on my skin. Maybe I'll get an angel on the other arm. I did 100 more push ups then hopped in the shower.

CHAPTER TWO

SMOOTH

I was too quick for the Suburban when I maneuvered my Lexus on "Huneds" (that was what I call my four 25 inch rims) into the parking space ahead of it. The truck just sat there where I cut it off at. That's when I recognized it. It was Big Will and some of his homies. I peeped at them from the rearview mirror. They weren't budging so I hopped out the car with my 45 caliber Desert Eagle in my hand. They sped off.

Bitches!

About thirty minutes later I came out with three bags hanging from each hand. I got them new sneakers everybody was talking about. I don't know how the swapmeet got 'em first. They be on top of their game. With a push of the button on the keyless entry remote my trunk popped open. I threw the bags in and got in the car. I backed out and headed to the exit. The Suburban pulled up quick beside me and,

Pop! Pop! Pop! Pop! Pop! Pop!

I was caught off guard. Bullets punctured my body. The truck sped off, I opened the car door. My first instinct was to run. Where? Anywhere! Just run! Two steps into it I collapsed dead. Eyes wide open, gun in my hand.

KENO

I had just finished lacing up my crispy white Adidas when I happened to look up at the TV and saw a strikingly familiar Lexus with a body covered by a white sheet next to it and yellow tape around the perimeter.

"What the fuck!!" I said jumping up to raise the volume.

"Live at the Slauson swapmeet from Channel Two." some female news reporter was saying. "There has been a callous slaying. Apparently shots were fired from a SUV. We are not certain how many people were in the black Suburban. There was only one individual in the Lexus and he is deceased. The incident occurred subsequent to an alleged parking dispute. Just another chapter in the long running saga of nonsensical violence over trivial matters that plagues this city. The police are looking for a black late model Chevrolet Suburban with big gold rims and green Felix dealership paper license plates. If you have any information about the murder or if you spot the truck notify your local precinct."

I cut the TV off. I knew exactly who owned that truck. The hair on the back of my neck stood up. My heart pounded so hard it felt like it was trying to get outta my chest. A drop of sweat dripped from the tip of my nose.

Big Will was the enemy. Not only because I stole his girl Shalleen but me and Smooth robbed his stash house for a kilo of heroin and $75,000. The two workers who could identify us took that information to the grave. Big Will had his suspicions of who did it but he just could never get up on us.

Big Will and Shalleen kept in touch loosely for the sake of their daughter Leslie. So she knew enough about him that I could pillow talk what I needed to know out of her like I have been doing since day one. The scary thing about pillow talk is that it seems innocent when you're doing it but it has sent more people to the poor house and the grave than you know. I knew where all his spots were and I intended to go find Big Will before the coroner picked Smooth's body up off the hot tar.

I slipped my fingers into some latex gloves, then I changed my mind and went to the closet. I pulled out a box full of my different hobby projects that I never got around to finishing. You know, like toy airplanes and toy lowriders and stuff like that. I dug around until I found a bottle of Elmer's glue. Remember when you were in elementary school and you used to spread it around in the palm of your hand, let it dry then peel it off. Well that was my first lesson in concealing my fingerprints. One day when I was nine years old me and my friend agreed to keep the glue on until the

17

next day. We even scribbled something on each other's hand to make sure it was the same glue the next day.

On my way home from school I saw this car parked behind this strip club. It was a station wagon. It caught my attention because it looked just like my friend's dad's car. We used to get around in that car. His dad used to take us everywhere. I didn't think it was actually my friend's dad's car, especially at a strip club. Anyway to make a short story shorter, I had recently learned how to steal cars, especially General Motors cars, the steering column way. That day I said 'fuck the bus', stole the car and got chased by the police before I even made it home. I bailed out of the car and got away. Come to find out it really was my friend's dad's car. He said it got stolen from the supermarket. The cop's couldn't find my prints, I kept my mouth shut and everything was all good. That's why years later, I stood and waited for the glue to dry. By the way I double dip now. After I loaded up my AK 47, what I call my middle-east heat. I grabbed two extra clips. I took my ID out of my pocket and threw it on the table.

I held my gun up like a soldier about to let off a 21 gun salute, looked up to the ceiling and said, "I gotchu Smooth. I'm about to handle Big Will. Then you can get him once he get's up there."

When I stepped out back, I felt a tear drop from my eye.

Covered up in one of the parking stalls in the back was a stolen car. I pulled the car cover off. It was a dark green Toyota Camry with tinted windows. I laid the machine gun on the backseat and went on my mission. Motorcycle riding would have to wait until next Sunday.

CHAPTER THREE

BIG WILL

Me and my homeboys were maxin' and relaxin' in Inglewood at one of my spots. The Suburban was in the garage. That shit we did at the swapmeet was all over the news. The next day I would take the rims off and put the license plates on my truck.

We were sitting on the porch and laughing at how hardcore Smooth thought he was thirty minutes before his death. I had just made the comment that I wished Keno was there too when I saw a green Camry creeping up the street. I know what trouble approaching looks like. I said I had to use the bathroom and walked into the house.

All of a sudden the Camry screeched up on the curb. Rapid gunfire spit out of the driver's window. Nobody on the porch was spared. Their bodies released their souls with a gasp of breath.

I said, "Damn!!!" under my breath. Keno got out of the car and ran up on the porch as he exchanged clips. A couple of my boys bodies laid still and a couple twitched. I guess their nerves were still tryna figure out what was going on. When he saw that I wasn't one of the dead on the porch, he looked like he was about to come into the house. This kinda shit is why I keep a gun close at all times.

Boom! Boom! Boom! Boom! Boom!

Five shots from my .357 Magnum shattered the front windshield of the house as I yelled, "Suck my dick Mutha Fucka!" Every one of my bullets hit their target and stopped Keno's breath. The force of the impact tumbled him over the ledge of the porch.

The way I bust my gun. The way his body flipped. Ain't no question that he was dead. I started grabbing some things, personal things, identifying things, so I could get myself and my truck outta here. I heard some noise out front that spooked me. Instead of looking to see what it was, I picked up my pace and went out the back door. I drove the truck up the driveway, made a hard right and burned rubber up the street, gas pedal to the metal. I do know that I saw a car door on the grass and that Keno and the Camry was gone.

CHAPTER FOUR

KENO

I laid in the dirt in excruciating pain. The bullet proof Kevlar vest saved my life but I felt like I got hit by a truck named Rashad Evans, like we went a few rounds. No face shots, just all body.

I would've rathered not do any moving, just lay there but I had to get outta there before Big Will realized that I wasn't dead, plus I had four dead bodies on the porch.

I grabbed my gun and used everything I had in me to endure the pain and got in the car. I fell into the seat and pain ran through me so bad at first I saw white stars dancing then my vision blurred.

Instinctively, I put my hand where it hurt which was mostly in my chest, that made it worse. I was delirious and in so much pain. I thought the bullets had penetrated all my organs. I only knew for sure that I was alive and had to get away.

I stomped on the gas pedal. The door was wide open and my left leg was still hanging out. The engine kicked up but the car didn't move. I realized the transmission was still in Park. I jerked the gear shifter down into reverse and stomped on the gas again. The wheels spun, spitting up grass and dirt toward the house. The car sped backwards. I pulled my leg in right before I side-swiped a big palm tree sitting in between the sidewalk and the curb. It took the door off just as easy as knocking somebody's hat off of their head. I slammed it into drive and left a long black number eleven in front of the house.

I leaned awkwardly to my right. My lungs refused to expand enough for me to inhale. What I'm doing is closer to being trapped in an airtight closet and the only air coming in is seeping in through the keyhole. I could taste the blood on the back of my tongue. I started thinking that I was hallucinating about having a vest on and in reality I was dying. That shit was hurting too much.

I needed to stop at a hospital. Daniel Freeman was on Prarie, only about a half of mile up the way. But the puzzle pieces with the four murders could be put together too easily and going into Daniel Freeman could be my last taste of being a free man. Although the pain was killing me, I drove right past it. I even almost turned back but I pumped myself up and headed to the valley, at least a forty-five minute drive. I passed some kids up that were laughing and pointing at my missing door. Two blocks before I entered the freeway a police car crossed in front of me at a light. They didn't even look in my direction but my heart still stopped. When the light changed I tried to get the speedometer into triple digit numbers. I kept my RPM's up almost all the way there. I slowed down to the flow of traffic when I saw a Highway Patrol car in the center part of the road. Maybe not in time though because he pulled out behind me. I had been leaning in the least painful position possible the whole time but now I sat straight up like I was in the front row of the classroom and I knew the answer to the teacher's question. The officer eased up on my right side. I was sweating. He looked over at me. I had already put on my "innocent traveler's mask". If he would've looked at me good or for another couple seconds he would've noticed that he could see the car on my left a little too good. But he kept on moving at a slightly faster speed than I was going. Once he was about five car lengths up I leaned back over and stopped holding my breath. I exhaled what little air I was holding and the pain assaulted me again. It was getting harder and harder for me to breath. I felt my throat clogging. I finally got to the hospital and swerved into the parking lot. By the time I stumbled into the emergency room entrance I was coughing up blood.

A couple of nurses and a doctor rushed over to me and put me on a gurney. They assessed my condition on the way to the operating room. They removed my vest and found out that one of my ribs were broken and had punctured one of my lungs. I was suffocating on my own blood. They went to work on me and at the same time someone was questioning me about what had happened and who I was. I couldn't even breathe, so I couldn't talk, so they got no answers. Even if I could talk you know I still wasn't telling 'em shit. Right before I lost consciousness I heard somebody say, "He has no identification. He's a John Doe."

I woke up three days later. Chest pains were getting the best of me. From what I could tell I was in a long room made to accommodate a lot of recovering patients. There were tall curtains drawn around my bed. I could hear voices on the other side of my curtains. Not professional voices, more like somebody's loved ones visiting. I heard a whole lot of subtle electronical noises, beeps and tones like a musical. A musical nobody likes. There were a couple of communal TV's barely out of my line of sight. The pain struck me again. I found a button with a symbol of a nurse on it and pushed it and kept pushing it until a short, petite Asian woman with a painted on smile and a white uniform came to my rescue. She injected something into my I.V. and almost immediately the pain started to subside, and my consciousness too. I woke up the next day in pain. That shit was hurting just like the day before. I pushed the button for the nurse again and her smiling ass did something with my I.V. that sent me to La La Land again. The next day I laid in the bed for as long as I could take the pain before I called the nurse. I was tired of sleeping, I wanted to watch TV or talk to somebody or something.

They always say be careful what you wish for. About an hour after I woke up a detective walked through the curtain. A white dude about 5'7", bald on top, ponytail in the back, thick ass moustache like his follicles took a wrong turn from the top of his head to the top of his lip. His gut was a dead give away of late night meals and beer. He told me his name and what precinct he was from. He said it was evident that I was shot and wore a bullet proof vest for a shield. Then he pulled up a chair. He said they had me under a John Doe. He wanted to know my name and my story. There's never a good time for a conversation with a detective but this was about the worst. I made a quick move trying to reposition myself. Pain electrified me. He could tell by the expression on my face.

I pushed the button for the nurse.

He was tryna ask me questions. I'm groaning and cursing the pain. She came in and did what she does. I felt the pain leaving like the beach water receding after a big wave crashes. I pretended like I fell asleep instantly. I heard him trying to talk to me. A couple of minutes later I was out for real.

The next morning I woke up and just laid there and after a while my mind drifted onto Tanya, she was my first friend. We had played and hung out like she was a boy. Now that I thought about it, I guess she was pretty, she was forming a nice shape, something only God could have had a hand in at such an early age but back then I never knew. She was just my friend. In the same fashion I was genetically heading in the right direction. My arms, chest and legs made me look like a kid that was into all sports.

We lived next door to each other in Compton up until we were about ten years old. We were the same height and the same complexion just like we were siblings. Our parents got along pretty well, later I realized that it was because our parents enjoyed drugs together.

Back then we were just happy that our parents always had a reason to barricade themselves in the bedroom for long periods of time. Something fucked up happened to my friend, Tanya and nobody knows that I witnessed the whole thing through her window. I often remember...

As usual the electricity had been turned off after the final red notice was ignored. The one bedroom apartment the little girl and her mother shared was very tiny.

The little girl's stomach ached from hunger pains. There wouldn't be much food to find but she went to search. She got up from her small inflatable bed over in the corner of the living room. She made her way over the piles of dirty clothes and miscilaneous trash in order to get to the kitchen. The place was dark.

Remembering there were candles under the bathroom sink, she went and got one, lit it and took it to the kitchen.

27

The illumination from the candle exposed a huge gray rat running from behind the refrigerator to under the sink. If she hadn't been so hungry, seeing the huge rat would've ruined her appetite. She jumped back but after the rat disappeared she went back on her search. She reached for a glass as she peered into the cabinet, she went to pour some water out of the faucet.

Someone cleared their throat behind her. She jumped and dropped the glass. She knew who it was and she didn't like him and wished she could disappear. She was nervous so she just grabbed a rag and dropped to her knees and instantly began cleaning up the mess.

Meanwhile she was the object of the stares to her under developed butt and thighs in the pair of dingy white shorts she wore. No matter how hard she tried to ignore him he still found a way to encroach on her.

Arousal pumped blood into his dick. She was a pretty little girl. Her smooth mocha colored skin turned him on. He imagined how her young and pretty thighs would feel wrapped around his back. He wanted to sink deep inside her satiny walls. He watched her stand up. She was about four feet, eight inches tall and she had a nice booty for a ten-year old. Her mother was very curvaceous before the drugs and she inherited her mom's genes, even at ten she noticed that men in the neighborhood watched her sprouting shape. Perverts tried to lure her with candy and tarnished jewelry. And now another predator was at her. Although she was quite under developed in the breast area, those mocha colored thighs were nice to him.

"Come here, let me see whatcha workin' with."
"Please, get away from me!" the little girl begged.

Riiiiiiinng!!!!!!!!!

CHAPTER FIVE

Riiiiiiinng!!!!!!!!!

TANYA

The alarm clock sounded and I woke up in a cold sweat trying to catch my breath. I sprung up into a sitting position quickly. I usually didn't even have bad dreams. And this one was terrible.

Who was that? What was that about?
Whoa!

It felt so real. I felt the loneliness the little girl must've felt, and in need of protection.

I didn't remember the days when I was as young as the little girl in my dream. I only remembered two things. One, my own mother shipping me off to live with my grandmother in Memphis Tennessee, far away from Compton, Hub City.

Compton was known as Hub City because it was almost in the center of Los Angeles County. It was a place I was used to. In the midst of the 100,000 people, I felt at home.

And the other thing was Keno, who was my closest friend. Those were the only two things that I could remember about back then.

Cheryl, my mother and her husband, my father Ron Ron moved to Compton from Memphis and I was born six months later. Ron Ron was on drugs already but Cheryl hadn't tried any until I was a couple years old and from there every year her addiction got worse. Eventually, drugs took a front seat to everything in Cheryl's life, including me. To this day I still couldn't talk to my mother, although Cheryl supposedly had been clean for fifteen years I still had no words for her.

I sighed, threw back the comfortor, climbed out of the bed and stepped on a Mc Donald's napkin with a couple spots of ketchup on it. I picked it up.

The phone made more noise, the caller ID said it was Sahara, my sister. Had it been anyone else I would've treated her like a Jehovah's Witness but Sahara got nothing but love.

We talked for a while then I told Sahara about the dream. Sahara joked that I might need my head examined before we hung up. I thought the joke was not so funny. The dream confused me, scared me. I figured if I had another one like it then I might have to talk to somebody.

I went on about my daily morning rituals. I cleansed my face then turned on the shower to hot. After stripping naked I stared into the mirror at my naked frame. My breasts were big and saggy and a little disproportionate. My waist was hidden by my belly and extra large love handles. My thick ass, thick hips and thighs stared back at me. I wished I had an hourglass figure. I had started to spread early in life but never stopped. I put on more weight especially when I moved to Memphis.

An intense workout regimen and strict diet would probably slim me down but I didn't have the type of motivation for physical exertion.

My long, black locks were matted to my head. It reminded me of my hair appointment later on in the evening. Steam had begun to rise in the bathroom. I stepped into the shower and lathered up. The soap felt so good on my skin. I washed my hair. I could've stayed in the shower for much longer to wash away the ominous feeling from my dream but I had to get to work.

When I thought about my job, I smiled. At thirty years young I was the youngest investment broker at TSL Investments. On top of that I was the only black woman who worked there. Pretty impressive for a girl who came from Clementine Projects by the way of Compton. Compton, my love, my beginning.

I remembered the violence and bad name of my community in Compton and Memphis alike. I was determined not to be a product of my environment, when I went to live with my grandmother I worked extra hard and excelled in school, making mostly A's and B's all through middle school and high school.

I was accepted to a couple different colleges but University of Tennessee was my choice. Growing up around drugs and violence inspired me. There were many examples in my neighborhood of who I didn't want to be and how I didn't want to end up so I worked hard. And hard work will always pay off, right?

The phone rang again catching my attention and I reached over on the Travertine floor to grab the cordless phone off its base.

"Hello."

"Hey Child, whutchu doin?"

I smiled at the familiarity of the voice on the other end. My grandmother's southern drawl poured through the phone like honey. Thick and just as smooth.

"Hey Ma."

"Tanya I was callin' ta see if you culd take off early tamorra ta take me ta da docta. You kno I'm all out my blood presha pills an' I needs a notha perscripshun."

Explanations weren't necessary, there was no way I was turning my grandma down. Not now. Not ever. My grandma had done so much for me besides taking me in and showering me with love, the love my own mother refused to give me. After confirming the time of her appointment I told her I loved her and ended the call.

I was running late for work and this particular morning I had a very important Skype meeting with some new investors. They were investing in a project, an upscale Caribbean Resort and Spa, catering to high-end luxury clientele. I had worked hard on this deal. 60% of the timeshares were already sold by commitment and growing daily. 85% of the construction was completed. This was the last leg of the deal. They would be investing in the final 15% of the project today. I was also responsible for acquiring the certificates of occupancy on this day. When it was all said and done in 30 days $48,000,000 would be dispersed three ways.

I also dealt with (Forex) Foreign Exchange to deal with the fluctuations of the U.S currency. I facilitated in setting up offshore accounts in China where a client could invest money in trade with the Yuan currency.

I finished washing my body and climbed out. After taking a towel and wringing my locks dry I wrapped a dry towel around my hair and went to my huge walk-in closet. Sophistication was the look I was pushing for so after perusing through my closet I found the perfect black designer suit.

Expeditiously, I dressed and applied my makeup. By this time my hair had soaked the towel. I got another dry towel and wrung my hair as dry as I could. I pinned it up into a tight bun. Time was a ticking, money was awaiting and so were some very important people. I slipped my feet in a pair of three inch stilettos, grabbed my leather bag and matching attaché and hummed a catchy tune as I left my home for the day.

I stepped out of the house and strolled down the driveway towards my Lincoln, a mini SUV. Black inside, black outside. The paint was smooth as expensive liquor. It casted detailed reflections, with a mean grille. The black leather interior was soft and cozy like a living room chair. My music had the right amount of bass. The tweeter speakers gave it a fresh sound. Yeah, I liked my little SUV. I backed out of the driveway.

The neighbor's yard was beautiful with its wide array of flowers and plants, which made up the border of our property line.

Flowers were laced perfectly throughout the yard front and back. He tooted his horn as he pulled into his driveway. The neighbor is a tall white guy, low hair cut, handsome. He drove a silver Dodge. He had someone with him. He always did. He was a very sociable guy, I thought. I figured he had a ton of friends because I always saw someone

34

different in his passenger seat. At first I thought he was a major womanizing player because all he brought home were women. Then I saw him with a few guys and thought differently. One thing I knew was that they never came for a quick visit, once he pulled up, the car didn't move for hours, at least. I wondered if he was bisexual. But he looked like such a masculine guy.

You can never tell these days.

Traffic was kinda heavy so it took me a while to get to Crump Avenue from Lauderdale St. only to find out there was a wreck blocking Mississippi Boulevard.

Darn it! I cursed.

With great caution, I maneuvered my black Lincoln through the wreck and went through the Mc Donald's drive-thru and got a quick breakfast, then made it to my job.

I parked, cut the motor off and climbed out. I picked up my Gucci bag, it was a bag I bought for $50 on the street. I bought it because it looked exactly like the $400 bag I had in my closet. I couldn't believe the Chinese were so damn good at bootlegging and replicating stuff. Even the lining was perfect.

As I gathered my stuff and got out of my vehicle I could feel someone staring at me from the corner of my eye. I turned and was face to face with my only enemy at the company, Kimberly King, an average looking white girl with bags under her eyes and a bad attitude.

A few months earlier I had trumped Kimberly on a quarterly incentive and Kimberly hated me for it, but as my grandmother always told me,

"Kill your enemies with kindness, that will bug the hell out of them."

"Hello, Kimberly, how's everything going?" I spoke kindly.

Kimberly rolled her eyes, clicked her tongue and turned on her six inch heels. As she walked away I shrugged her rudeness off. I chalked it all up to jealousy.

Screw it!

I made sure I did what I was expected to do to be proactive at work but didn't forget that I couldn't satisfy everybody. I didn't care if Kimberly liked me or not, Kimberly would be the one with that problem.

Once inside the privacy of my own office I noticed multiple drops of water on my jacket shoulders from my hair. The longer the locks the longer it'll still be wet after you thought it was dry.

I began working on my project. Being that I'd been at the company for several years I knew the ins and outs of the company, the daily ritual, the accounts, the budget, everything was within my access.

My boyfriend, Malcolm was always trying to get me to steal from the company but I was too honest to steal a nickel. My grandmother didn't raise me to steal and I was an outstanding citizen. But I did entertain the thought of shopping everyday with it.

Giggle.

Never!

Never would I become a thief. I wouldn't embarrass my grandma like that. I believed in hard work and sometimes it really did pay off.

I knew Malcolm was using me because I made good money. Why else would such a fine brother want a fat girl? But because he catered to me, I allowed it.

Relationships were something I stayed away from. But one day me and Malcolm met by happenstance. He was walking through the lobby of the company and asked me if I knew where a Mc Donald's was located and I happened to have a Mc Donald's bag in my hand. Malcolm is 6'3"and has an athlete's body, built and toned. His skin was black and smooth and his low Caesar fade perfectly aligned with his beard and goatee. His facial features were ruggedly handsome and his teeth were so white he could be a star of a tooth paste commercial. He took great care of his hygienic responsibilities.

Lunch came swiftly, my meeting went fine and I rearranged my next day's schedule so I could take my grandmother to the doctor. Then I went down to the company's lounge and met up with my friend Jalisa Jeffers. Being that the rest of the women within the company were pretty shady, Jalisa was my only real friend.

Jalisa was a beautiful Hispanic woman with long black hair. Her red skin was flawless and she had a shape that Shakira would envy. She was about 5'7" and very curvy. For different reasons we were both hated on by the other women so we stuck together. Jalisa had a loving spirit. I could tell by the way Jalisa was towards me.

"What's going on Tanya?" Jalisa asked as we got our lunch and found an available table.

Kimberly King was at a table on the far right and her eyes never left me. Kimberly was watching my every move. So I wouldn't think it was only me imagining things, I asked Jalisa if Kimberly was staring at me.

"She watching you like you got the last piece of meat." she told me.

Laughter floated between us but I knew I had to watch a conniving and sneaky heifer like Kimberly. I didn't know what Kimberly was capable of. Also, being that I was the only black female at the company I was already on edge.

Fortunately, I was one of the hardest working women at the company so I knew I couldn't be easily replaced.

I talked to Jalisa about the investments with the Resort project that was at hand and the money that would be made and with the holidays coming up, things were moving. Lunch quickly passed and Jalisa walked me to my office. We made plans to have a few drinks the next day and I settled back at my desk.

I was hard at work and my face was glued to my computer screen when I heard foot steps aproaching. I looked up and met Kimberly's cold blue gaze. She just stood there.

Why is this woman always messing with me?

"What do you want?" I asked her, trying to be patient.

Kimberly was getting under my skin and pretty soon I wouldn't be able to control my anger.

"I wanted to talk to you." Kimberly said with an attitude evident in her voice.

"So, talk, because I have a lot of work to do."

"Why are you always trying to steal my shine?"

Kimberly was propped up on the wall with her arms crossed over her paid-for-breasts. I laughed at Kimberly's cockiness and arrogance. Kimberly had it twisted, I knew for a fact that Kimberly was never my competition. Kimberly may have had a better body but in brains she wasn't even on my level. I thought it futile to argue with the dumb blonde. I didn't have time for it.

You should never argue with a dummy. From a distance a person can't tell who is who. My grandma would say.

Shaking my head in confusion, I said, "Kimberly, get out of my office. I don't have time to play games with you. I fly above. I do have work to do and that's why I was promoted a few months ago. If you spent half as much time focusing on your work as you do picking on me perhaps you could get promoted too."

That last statement cut deep. I could tell by the look on Kimberly's face.

"We will see." Kimberly said, turning on her heels and clicking off.

I was so happy that Kimberly left. She was trying her best to get under my skin but I wasn't having it.

The rest of the day went by smoothly without any mishaps and I was glad. While gathering my things I was interrupted by the ringing of my cell phone. It was Sahara, my sister.

Me and Sahara shared the same father. He moved from Memphis right after she was born. Ma had us meet each other when we were young but Sahara lived in

Nashville on the other side of the state so we didn't see each other much. Recently, Sahara had moved to Memphis for a great job opportunity. When we met up as adults we got matching tattoos of a heart on the inside of our wrist, I had the left half of the heart and Sahara had the right. We were six months apart with her being the oldest. Our father was killed when we were young kids, while I was in Compton. He was what you would call a dead beat dad. He was in my life but not Sahara's, then one day he was killed, stabbed to death. It was his time. Around the same time Cheryl was focusing more on drugs than her child. Sahara grew up with her mom and they are close. I wanted that same closeness.

I put my earpiece in and continued to talk to Sahara as I gathered my things. I walked through the building as we made plans to have lunch together the following day and I ended the call.

The time we spent together was always cherished by the both of us because we'd spent so much time apart. I was anxious to leave the office and after ten hours I had every reason to be. My next stop would be to get my locks twisted up.

CHAPTER SIX

SHALLEEN

"Oh Daddy, oh Daddy!"

"Ugh, ugh, ugh, lift your leg up. Yeah like that. Ugh, Ugh, Ugh."

"Uh huh, ah, ah, ah, ouch! Will! We gotta scoot down. I hit my head again on the headboard."

"Ugh, Ugh, Ugh"

"Ouch! Will!"

"Shut up, I'm bouta cum."

"No don't cum yet!" I said wiggling his dick out of me. These are the games we played. He tells me to bring our daughter over so he can see her and give us some money. Then he stalls until she falls asleep. Then he says I can't get no money unless he fucks me. Then after he fucks the shit outta me and almost puts me in a coma, he cries broke and only gives me enough money for our daughter. So I played my games too. I let his greedy ass get all up in me and get all worked up, and when he was about to bust a nut I pumped the brakes. I understood the concept of not buying the cow when you can get the milk for free. But I separate the pussy from the milk. I run mines like a 'Got Milk?' commercial. I take him to the point of no return then leave him hanging. Fuck you Pay me. Don't get me wrong I don't go out prostituting myself. But the men I do fuck with gotta break bread. As the saying goes, "I ain't saying I'm a gold digger but I ain't fucking with no broke nigga." plus Cherise and Marijka wanna meet up at the Beverly Center mall tomorrow and there's this store in there that got this cute ass Michael Kors skirt and bag that I saw the other day that I just gotta have. They wanted $1,500 for the both of them and Will is gonna pay for them.

"Damn! Why you always fuckin' up my nut girl? Come 'ere." he said pulling me back in dick reach.

"Hold up, lemme me turn around." I told him as I'm getting up on my knees. He falls for it everytime. He loves to hit it from the back. Baby got ass if I do say so myself. Mo' cushion for the pushin'. And my big yellow ass ain't got no pimples on it or no shit like that. If I was a man, doggy style would be my favorite position too. But it's my favorite position because I can always move up on his backstroke and make his dick pop out. That's my money maker. Watch this.

"Oooh yeah, damn Shalleen." he said spreading my butt cheeks open so his nasty ass could see his dick sliding in and out of my pussy. After about thirty or forty good long strokes he picked up the pace.

Slap! Slap! Slap! Slap!

"Ooh Daddy, yeah!" They like that shit. "Fuck me with that big ass dick!"

Slap! Slap! Slap! Slap!

You can tell when they about to cum cause they're legs start stiffening and they're dick gets rock inside your pussy.

"Oops."

"Damn Shalleen, stop playin'!"

"You wanna cum in me Baby?"

"You know I do. Stop playin'." he said holding his dick like he held the cum in place.

"You gonna give me some money?"

"Yeah don't I always?"

"You promise?" I said backing my vanilla cream buns onto his ballpark frank. I can imagine how my hot juices felt on his thang. He grinded it up in me for a minute. Then the jockey was back in the race, riding his stallion.

Slap! Slap! Slap! Slap!

"Ugh, ugh, ugh."

"Oops."

"Damn you!"

He tried to lock me in by wrapping his arm around my waist but I was too quick for him. I rolled from in front of him and came down on my back with my legs open, knees up, pussy glistening.

"Give me some money now."

"Aight." he said trying to lay into me. I put my hands up on his chest and stopped him.

"Where is it at?"

"In my pocket." he gestured with his head over to his pants on the chair. I pulled my hand back slowly and let him ease down into my pussy. He beat it up for a good little while. You know if you fuck with their head enough their nut will go back and they'll have to start over. He fucked me so good I started cumming. He could tell by the look on my face. And he knows I like to come on top. We rolled over and changed positions. I hopped up and down and gyrated on his dick. I was in heaven. I rode it til I rode all my ecstasy out. Then I kept pumping on his dick til he was at the point again. Until he couldn't lay back playing cool no more. Until his dick got stiff as the bedpost and his eyes rolled in the back of his head. Then I jumped off of him and ran over to his pants. I pulled out a stack, had to be at least eight grand. He just laid there still on the bed trying not to cum without me. I had him at the edge. He meditated, trying to stay calm. He held his dickhead with one of his hands. I peeled off about three thousand, put his back in his pocket and put mines in my purse. He looked so funny laying there like that on the bed. I felt sorry for him. "Ohhh, let me help you out." I told him climbing up on the bed. I faced my ass towards him. I was on my knees. I spread my legs and laid my face down on the bed. He was on me like stank on shit. He mounted me and drilled me like a mutha fuckin' rabbit until he showered my walls. We both collapsed on the bed. He was breathing hard in my ear. I liked that. I have to admit, when the money is no longer an issue I'm a sucker for cuddlin' and snugglin'. After he got his heart rate back down and his breathing under control, we talked. I asked what happened the other day but he wouldn't give a straight answer. The news said Keno's homeboy Smooth had gotten killed by some guys in a black Suburban with gold rims. I knew that was Will's truck right off. Plus later on they said four guys got murdered. I knew they were Will's boys. I even had let one of 'em eat my pussy last year.

The police didn't make a connection between Will's boys and Smooth but I knew something was up. Mainly I'm worried about Keno. His lifestyle is dangerous but I still loved him. We're not together but I still loved him. And I hated that him and Will couldn't get along. I just hope Will didn't bury him somewhere or something.

Will was laying on his back. I rolled over on my stomach and put my head on his shoulder.

"Will, you sure you don't know where Keno is?"

"I already told you I didn't. But wherever he at, he ain't doin' too well."

Why he say that?

"When was the last time you seen him?" he asked me.

"I don't know, about three weeks ago."

"You still fuck him?"

"He used to be my man."

"He ain't no more. You ain't still gotta fuck him."

"You ain't my man no more either."

"Yeah but we got a baby together ."

He was rubbing on my butt while we talked. He knew I liked that. I was playing with the hairs on his chest.

"You see, you be with that bullshit. You love him huh?"

"Yeah, he always has been good to me."

"I heard he moved. Somebody was sayin' that. He still live on umm….whatchamacallit street?"

"What, on Hardy?"

"Yeah, and umm…"

"Myrtle."

"Yeah that's it. Good looking out… I mean you looking good."

I never even knew he knew where Keno lived. Anyway we talked for a while about stuff, general stuff until our daughter Leslie woke up. Then me and her left. The next day I met up with the girls at the mall. Cherise was with some bitch named Vallawn she had just started hanging out with. They met at the nail salon or something.

Vallawn stepped into the salon Cherise frequented. Five massage chairs for pedicures lined two walls. Eight manicure stations sat down the middle of the shop. All the women snuck a peek at Vallawn as she walked in. She was very very pretty. The décor of the place was a wine and peach color. Cherise is cute. Vallawn is gorgeous. Within thirty minutes her and Cherise were talking. Everything Cherise wanted to talk about Vallawn was willing to talk about. She made Cherise feel smart. Cherise ate it up. They exchanged numbers before they left. Vallawn got into a dark blue Tahoe with a man driving. He had a badge and a gun.

Marijka was doing her usual. Evaluating some guys worth that was trying to talk to her. She was the homegirl and she was pretty. Her father was in jail. Marijka always had dough but never had a job. And as far as I knew she wasn't hustlin'. When I got closer I realized her and the guy were arguing about the pronunciation of her name after she entered it and her number into his phone.

She said, "For the third and final time the J is silent. It's Ma-ree-ka!" He was telling her some shit about how J's are never silent in a name. That in Spanish names the J sounds like an "h" but they ain't never silent.

Finally Marijka said, "You know what, you right, let me take it out. She meant the whole thing. Not just the J. She deleted her info and outta spite she deleted some names

48

that were nearby. Marilyn and Mary. She handed him his phone back. He said, "Alright I'ma call you tomorrow Ma-ree-ka without the J." She was already walking away from him toward us.

Lame!

We stopped at an espresso shop for Marijka. She had a caffeine habit. Then we ran through the mall like we usually did and picked up some things, cute and sexy things. We judged our outfits by their ability to get the next guy to buy the next outfit and plenty more of course. Not meaning the next guy is gonna get some pussy mind you. I told you I ain't no hoe. To keep it real, it's really only two men that can say they been in this cookie jar in some years. But I do play.

I can't speak for Cherise. Her coochie be hot, especially while her babydaddy Mannish is locked up. Not sayin' she sees less dick when he's out though.

Marijka is worse than me. I couldn't say for sure but I think she's waiting to get married before she parts with the nookie. That's why she stays paid I bet. She be fuckin' with them kinda guys that keep her laced so when she decide to crack those legs they think they'll be that one. Ain't no telling how many men she has on line but they all think they'll be the one.

We hit a few more stores. Marijka tried on some jeans that looked so good on her that it made me wish my asss was a little smaller. Hers was in between an onion and an applebottom. I had that shit that you could see from the front. Cherise had a nice medium sized round butt with a gap that could only come from a large variety of dicks. That's my friend though. Don't think I'm belittling her or anything. That's just how she chooses to work with her stuff. She doesn't have to work a job. Mannish makes sure she's alright so that their son Taj is alright.

"Yall ready to go?" I asked.

We all agreed to eat at the Grand Lux. It was on the ground floor and attached to the mall but you could only enter from the outside. There's always someone famous around. I'm surprised we didn't see anybody in the mall, but when we got inside the Grand Lux Tyler Perry was eating with Spike Lee. Maybe a collabo is in the works. We ate and called it a day. It was a week after the shooting that I finally reached Keno at home.

CHAPTER SEVEN

KENO

When I woke up the detective was nowhere around. I pushed the button for the nurse. I told her to just give me some pain pills. She gave me a few Vicodins. I took them. When she left I tried to get up. I was weak. I laid back for a few minutes, then grabbed the rail on the side of the bed and pulled myself up. When I got to my feet my legs felt rubbery. I needed to get some blood circulation going. I could only move a couple of feet because I had tubes and wires connected to me. There was a wire connected to some kinda monitor. I snatched it off and the machine made a fucked up long tone like I had died or some shit. I punched a bunch of buttons at random until it stopped. An I.V. ran into the top of my hand. There was a tube leading to a plastic bag half full of some greenish, yellow fluid. I lifted my gown to see where the drainage tube was coming from. It was sticking out of my side below where the doctor had made an incision down under the left side of my rib cage. I didn't see anything leaking at the moment so I pulled the tube out and went for a walk. A very slow walk. I wasn't going anywhere in particular, just walking. I didn't know the layout of the hospital and I didn't read any signs. I was just walking, taking my time and trying to get some fluid motion in my

51

legs. My journey was stopped by a nurse, a little fat thing with a pudgy face and a waistline to match. She wore big glasses.

"Excuse me sir. Do you have a child in here?"

I looked at the sign on the wall. I was in pediatrics I.C.U. I walked over to a big glass window. There were like twenty to thirty babies in there. I saw premature babies in incubators, drug babies holding on for dear life. I put my hands up on the glass. I was paralyzed with sympathy. She was still talking,

"...you must have a visitor's pass. Are one of these children yours?" She said pointing a stubby finger. My mind wandered. I remembered one day on the block with one of my boys.

"Damn Keno you gonna sell that pregnant lady some dope?"

"Hell yeah, if she don't get it from me she gonna get it from somewhere else and all this shit I got in this bag is for sale. I'm even gonna give her some extras so she'll come back to me."

"Ay Keno you a savage homie."

"Yeah, all that and I'll beat a pregnant bitch ass too if that money don't be right."

I watched some nurses run over to one of the drug babies and try to resuscitate it to no avail. The baby went flat line. That will forever be burned into my memory. I realized I was standing too long when my legs started to give out on me. I needed to sit down. Pudgy grabbed a chair and slid it under me just in time.

When I got back to my room I asked the nurse for some more pain medication. Later on that evening I left the hospital. The car was gone. The stolen car I drove myself to the hospital in had gotten stolen from me. I wasn't in the hospital two hours when a car full of Mexican gangbangers pulled up next to it with one of their terminally shot homies. After they found out he was dead and left the hospital grieving, they noticed the door missing on the Camry. They didn't find the AK until they were back in their neighborhood stripping the car. Don't ask me how I know, I'm just telling you what happened.

I walked up to the first set of people I saw coming out of the hospital. It was a white couple, middle class. They walked over to a Chrysler minivan. I offered them a hundred dollars to take me to the hood. She immediately answered negatively. I could tell he had considered it for a second so I doubled it. She turned me down again. When I doubled it again he put the pants back on and went for the quick come up. After I paid the couple off and got to my apartment the first thing I did was peel off the hospital gown that was sticky from that shit leaking out of my chest.

Then I took the twenty-five ounces of cocaine I had in the closet and put them in the trunk of this 1967 Camaro

I had been planning on fixing up. I had no intentions on selling cocaine again but I didn't trash the ounces. I just put them in the trunk. They were left over from my last lick. That was part of the last kilo I had left. I had sold nine ounces out of it. As usual the weight was light. There should've been twenty-seven left. The whole kilo only weighed thiry-four ounces evidently.

I was half sleep and half watching 106 and Park when the phone rang.

"What up."

"Keno!?"

"Yeah."

"Thank God you're alright!" it was Shalleen. "I've been calling everywhere. The jails, the hospitals, the morgues. Last week Smooth got killed at the swapmeet and then four of Will's friends got killed at one of his houses. I asked him what was going on and he made me more nervous. I thought you were dead. Is anybody there with you? I wanna see you." she rambled.

"Naw, ain't nobody here. Come on over and bring me something to eat. I ain't ate in a week."

"Okay."

She came over, fed me, tended to my wounds and asked a whole bunch of questions about the murders that she got no answers to. I didn't answer the phone much neither. I mostly slept.

Shalleen walked around with nothing but thongs on and gave me incentive to get better faster.

The next day I talked to a few homies and the word got around that I was home. By that evening the apartment was flooded with homeboys and homegirls. Next thing you know there was a party jumping off, a get well party for me and a farewell party for Smooth. They had put in a lot of work since the incident. They didn't know exactly who did it so plenty of enemies caught the blues. I was proud of my Dawgs for that. My injuries wouldn't allow me to enjoy the party so I had to kick everybody out.

Everybody except for Shalleen.

After everything calmed down we got in the bed and I snuggled up on her like her voluptuous ass was a life size teddy bear. We had a lightweight conversation about her moving back in with me. She said she just wanted to be here for me, take care of me. Even though I knew she would nurse me back to health, I suspected it had more to do with being a kept woman. She knew like I knew that she had it good when she was with me.

Sometimes she'd come by and I'd hit her off with something, but things weren't the same. I wasn't feeling her comin' back because me and the homies got to toss bitches up as we pleased up in here. Plus the homies were a big problem for her. And you wanna know the truth about the whole thing? I think I loved her more than she loved me. That's always dangerous, especially if you realize it. Because you're always on edge thinking about what this bitch could be doing out there. I thought she'd go back to her babydaddy Big Will.

But when you know she loves you, like really loves you. That's when life is good, that's when you can kick back. It wasn't a kickback relationship for me and her homegirls like to hit hot spots too. They're always in the mix. But I loved her though so I was in a catch 22.

I told her, "You know this ain't your kinda environment. The homies is still welcome here. Plus it's a lot of shit going on right now. It's wartime."

She didn't protest that. We both knew that she didn't want no parts of that.

I asked her how her daughter Leslie was doing. We conversed a little while the news played on the TV in the background. In between all the drama of killings, fatal accidents, trouble in Iran and weather, there was a report about how much the Spanish ethnic group had passed up the black race economically. I thought for a minute. Mexicans? Those illegal bastards? One thing about 'em though. They will work. They'll take whatever you pay 'em and stack that shit up and buy up your shit right from under you and they do stick together.

I rolled over to my left to face Shalleen.

"Ouch!" Wrong side.

I rolled over to my right. She scooted into a spoon position behind me. I fell asleep thinking about how I used to laugh at the Mexicans selling oranges on the corner.

BIG WILL

I wanted to do this by myself. I wanted to look Keno in the eyes when his life left him. He's been a thorn in my ass for way too long now. I was sitting in my car in a parking stall in a building across the street. I wish I knew how easy it was to get info outta Shalleen a long time ago. I was watching people hanging out and going in and out of Keno's apartment for hours. I didn't know what the fuck was going on. Was it somebody's birthday or was this just how they kicked it everyday?

I wanted to just do all of them at once, stack 'em up. I was amped up enough too. I was playing a song called "Somebody gonna die tonite." I was smoking a blunt with my left hand and tapping my leg to the beat with a Sig Sauer 9mm tipped off with a silencer in my right hand. I was wishing I had a fully automatic with a hundred round drum. I'd burn all them punk ass mutha fuckas right now. For the last week the homies had been gettin' blazed in my hood and I know these is the fools that's been putting it down. These faggots even caught two of my personal homies slipping.

I couldn't take it no more. I was staring a jackpot in the face. I pulled out slow and inconspicuous and went and scooped up my boy Tony and two fully automatic guns with hundred round drums. It all took a little over an hour. On the way back I was bumping some sick killa shit and ready to

58

put in work. But as we pulled up with gloves on and rags around our faces the street was quiet. When we got to the building all the cars were gone and nobody was around. I told my boy to chill in the car while I took the 9mm and crept. When I came up on Keno's window I could hear the TV and people talking inside. I could hear the voices but I couldn't make out what they were saying. I raised my head to peek through the window and Shalleen was laying in the bed with Keno. I started to do both of they asses. But the thought quickly passed. She was Leslies's mother. Maybe she'll go to the bathroom and I could light his ass up from here and be out. I sat on the ground under the window and peeked in every five minutes. The last time I looked they were both asleep all hugged up and shit. I left as quiet as I came.

CHAPTER EIGHT

TANYA

Rush hour traffic on Interstate 55 was ridiculous and it took me almost an hour to get to the beauty salon. The first thing I saw was a couple of flaming homosexuals with bright colors on, one getting his dreds twisted and one doing the twisting.

Live and let live. **My Grandma** would say.

I took a seat in my beautician's chair.

Sometime in the middle of the process, my hairdresser said, "Ooh girl. We got a gray hair."

"Stop playing... I'm only thirty years old and I don't have any stressful kids. Are you serious?"

My stylist said, "Damn girl relax, I was just playing." as she plucked the gray hair and discarded it.

I took a deep breath and said, "Don't be scaring me like that!"

I spent an hour in the chair then stood up fresh and nice. My locks were twisted tightly and looked silky and soft.

After the salon I went home. For the first time I noticed that the neighbor's Dodge had an advertisiment on the side. It was basically a help-wanted sign for internet marketing at home, said he supplied the computers and workspace. It made everything clearer to me. That's why people stayed over so long. The stranger became a little normal. I shut off the engine.

Absolute and Orange juice would be good, It crossed my mind when I stepped through the door of my comfortable home.

I needed something to help me unwind a bit. As I pulled off my business suit I thought about my boyfriend Malcolm.

Malcolm. The object of women's affection.

When he stepped into a room women were drawn to him, like a moth to a flame, ready to get burned by the fire. I couldn't blame them, but sometimes it was annoying. He was more than handsome, more than fine. Malcolm was sinfully gorgeous.

He gave me no reason to believe he was ever unfaithful and I took great pride in it.

Just thinking about him seemed as if it made the phone ring. When I answered, it was him. Malcolm asked if he could come over. I missed him so I said, "Yes". I was a home body and barely did anything outside of work. A visit from Malcolm was always welcome.

I took the stairs to the bedroom and into the shower. When I was done and dried myself, I threw on a yellow oversized t-shirt with green letters on the front that said,

The Smartest Rat in the Sewer.

Malcolm always loved to see me in yellow because he said it went well with my skin complexion. While I waited for him I lit a few yellow aromatherapy candles and cleaned up a little.

Music played in the background. I hummed along as I picked things up.

The doorbell chimed and I smiled. Before opening the door I looked in the mirror that hung in my foyer, checked myself out, ran my hands through my fresh locks then opened the door.

Malcolm licked his lips.

I laughed and we hugged at the door then I stepped aside, allowing him entry. He went to the living room while I went into the kitchen to get him something to drink.

"What's this?" he asked, when he took the drink.

I sat down next to him, "Pomagranate and cranberry juice with a couple shots of Vodka." I replied.

"Okay, something different huh?" he asked.

Innocently, I shrugged my shoulders. "It's good for you too."

Malcolm pulled out a small bag of weed from his pocket. I'm not a weed smoker but I would take a few pulls when sex was eminent. I would need to be in a different state of mind to get into it. Ordinarily, I would have no interest in sex. My feelings toward sex weren't good. "Getting your juices flowing" wasn't something that I could relate to normally. The marijuana altered all that for me.

I watched as he meticulously rolled the weed. When he lit it, he took a few pulls and passed it over to me. After taking a pull I coughed a few times and passed it back. My eyes immediately turned red. He hit it a few more times then placed it in the ashtray. He looked over at me with lust-filled eyes and I knew what was about to go down. I would've gotten apprehensive had I not smoked.

"Go put on some heels for me." he ordered.

I rolled my eyes, he was taking advantage. I got up from the couch and did as he asked. It was okay. It made me feel wanted, attractive and loved. Kimberly King had stressed me out earlier and I was ready to relax. Maybe I would pretend I was a stripper. Not the sleezy side but the glamour part of it. In their own world every stripper thought of herself as a queen of desire like Nefertiti, Cleopatra, or a Playboy Bunny, even if only on a small scale for the time being.

I looked through my closet, found and slid on a pair of yellow stilettos and went back into the living room. Malcolm was sitting back on the couch like he was a King. He was a King, he was my King. He treated me good.

"Now that's more like it, walk for me. Walk to the wall over by the fireplace and back." he said.

I felt kiddish. He knows that i am overweight and he must like it. I walked to the wall and when I came back he kissed me and began to speak. I was all giggles.

"Tanya, I want to talk to you about something."

Darn it, what could he possibly want to talk about at a time like this?

Oddly enough, I was ready to have sex. The weed was coursing through my veins. I was relaxed and ready, but I obliged him and listened. I took a seat next to him and gave him my ear.

"What is it?" I asked coolly.

"Hear me out this time before you fly off the wall and shit okay Baby."

"I'm listening." my giggles fizzled.

"How long have you worked for TSL Investments?"

Now I knew where this was going. The corners of my mouth sagged. Malcolm would get about a thousand dollars out of me every payday. But he wanted more, he wanted it all.

"Several years." I answered, my brows wrinkled.

"Baby, me and you could be the new Bonnie and Clyde. I'm talking about living large, lavishly, not wanting for nothing. We could take trips every year to the finest islands. We could take the world by storm. Like Scarface on some shit. After wiping a few accounts clean you'll never have to work again. Just think about it."

The look on my face said it all but I spoke anyway. "Look, I told you I ain't about to steal no damn money from my job. That would ruin my career."

"Ruin your career? You won't need no career!"

Malcolm had been nagging me about stealing from my job ever since we had been together, maybe the money I was giving him was only peanuts and he wanted the big payday and quite frankly I was getting tired of it. I had worked long and hard not to be the very person he was trying so hard to make me be. It wasn't easy earning my position at my job. Nothing was given to me and I wasn't about to screw up my career and taint my good name because of Malcolm's greed.

"Tanya, we can…"

"Discussion over." I said firmly, cutting him off.

He held up his hands in surrender then rubbed my leg, I immediately stopped him. Suddenly I realized I wasn't high anymore and didn't want to make love anymore either.

"I ain't even in the mood no more. Let yourself out." I said, standing from the couch in the living room.

Leaving the high heels at the base of the staircase I went up the stairs to the bedroom. Dumbfounded, Malcolm watched me walk away.

CHAPTER NINE

KENO

A broken rib and a punctured lung was a whole lot better than having six .357 hot ones in me. I healed up pretty quick I guess. Between Shalleen and the homies, there was always somebody at the apartment.

Everything was cool until one of the homies let the police drive into the apartment complex behind him. He didn't have an I.D. on him so they got him out of his car and found a bag of weed in his pocket. They were sweating him about who he was so he told them that he lived with me. I heard him hollering for me so I opened the door.

That's when it all went bad.

They asked me what his name was so I told them. I mean that's why he hollered for me, to verify his identity right?

This damn fool gave them a fake name. Some shit he just made up.

Who knew?

When they said, "Nah, that ain't it." I gave them another name I knew he used before. "Nah, that ain't it either."

Now I'm on a game show. I got so many seconds to guess the right answer before the buzzer goes off or no prize.

Now I look suspicious. They wanted to search the premises seeing that he said he lived there and he was in possession of drugs.

You gotta expect that.

I told 'em "No!" They violated my rights and went in anyway. They didn't find any drugs but they did find my identification that was in my wallet in my dresser drawer right next to my Smith and Wesson .380, full clip, one in the chamber, off safety.

They made my knuckle head ass homeboy pour his weed on the ground and step on it and made me step into the backseat of the police car instead.

I ended up getting sent to a California State Prison with a sentence of sixteen months. The cement wall said Soledad State Prison. When I stepped off the bus I was greeted with cold stares and mean mugs. I returned them the same, had to let them know I wasn't fresh fish. Maybe my first time in prison but definitely not my first time being locked up. And fucking somebody up wasn't new to me either. I've fucked up some fools in the county jail that was on another trip back to prison.

I saw a few gangstas G-posing on a wall. They had their faces made up like I was the one that answered their girl's cell phone.

One of 'em recognized me.

"Ay yo Keno!" yelled a big cornfed youngsta.

I recognized him too. We called him Country. He was from my neighborhood. I hadn't seen him in a while. So this is where he's been. He introduced me to the other cats, then he showed me where my cell was in my low income housing that wasn't anywhere near low income because the government paid millions a year to run this place. I said, "Damn!" when I found out what these institution's budgets were.

After I threw my stuff on the top bunk and met my celly, Country took me on a grand tour of the prison. I'd engage in a little diplomacy about the bottom bunk with my celly later.

It didn't take long to notice two things. One was that there were more blacks in prison then anything else. I noticed too that there were cliques everywhere. Prisoners grouped up looking like they weren't even tryna fuck with another group about nothing. I know that's how we got down in the street, but in prison? I couldn't understand it. They looked like roaches on the kitchen floor on spilled food when you cut the lights on. When it was time for a bizness transaction you'd catch a smile, handshake, exchange of goods and currency. Wasn't no discriminating on the green or whatever represented it. But then everything went back to normal with the segregation. We walked passed a couple older guys playing chess. One of 'em looked up and gave me a serious look. He looked at me like he wanted something with me.

"How much time they give you for whatever dumb shit you did youngster?" he said.

I snapped, "Off the break old man, lemme tell you something. I don't like the way you tryna carry me!"

"Don't be part of the problem"

"What the fuck is the problem old man?!" I said agitated.

The man ignored me, put his eyes back on the table and continued playing chess.

I was cool for the day. It had already been a long one. I went back to my cell, my celly was gone. He wouldn't be here for the meeting about me getting the bottom bunk. I threw all of his shit up on the top bunk, made up my bed and went to sleep. I didn't think he was a bitch. I just didn't think he wanted to go to the prison hospital.

When breakfast call woke me up in the morning my celly was on the top bunk sleeping like a two hundred pound baby. He didn't go to breakfast. When I came back from breakfast he was sitting up with his feet hanging down.

He said, "You know I ain't tripping about you wanting to be on the bottom." said that like I was his female and he was talking about sex positions.

70

I almost said, *Hold up you bitch ass mutha fucka!*

But he continued. "You coulda hollered at me. Next time…"

I wasn't even listening to the rest. When somebody says 'next time', it's because they gotta give themselves room for why they didn't do nothing about it this time. And the next time they won't do nothing about it either. Unless it happens in front of their boys of course.

I went back to sleep. Fuck Orientation.

I spent the next few days getting my shit together.

Walkman, boombox, cassettes, sneakers, ironing my clothes and t-shirts crispy. Gotta be fly fa life, give a fuck where I'm at.

My celly turned out to be alright. He read a lot. Liked to stay up all night reading but he adjusted his schedule for me. He wasn't a bitch either. I saw him fuck up a man's smile because last time he had told him 'next time.' He had been without a celly for two months and half the time he slept on the top bunk. So he was serious when he said he wasn't tripping, I assume as serious as he was when he said 'next time'.

Two peas in a pod. Two soldiers in a cell. It was all good.

We kicked it, smoked weed and chopped it up about everybody and everything going on.

One night we were so loud the Correctional Officer that works at night, his name was Flint, stopped at the cell door and threatened us on some bullshit that if we didn't be quiet he was gonna put us in the Special Housing Unit, SHU (pronounced Shoe, also known as the Hole)

We conceded.

"Yeah aight Sucka." I said.

He said, "I'ma sucka that go home everyday though."

I had to respond, "Yeah and you bring yo nine to five, one pay check away from committing a crime and being a celly too, ass back up here the next day everytime."

C.O.'s always gotta have something to say. They gotta get the last word so he said, "It's not like I haven't ever done anything wrong. I just never got caught."

I said, "Aight, you right, go ahead where ever you was going. We won't be loud no more."

"That's what I know."

They be thinking speeding or getting into a bar fight is doing crime. The worst thing these type of guys have done is smoke a joint or being a passenger in a g-ride (stolen car).

I didn't even say anything else I just let him keep it moving. We gave that fool about five minutes to make his rounds and we were right back at it. My celly told me that when the female C.O. on the other side works the third

72

shift, he disappears, she disappears, they make funny noises and swap DNA.

We smoked some weed and got indept about something. I forgot what though, then went to sleep.

CHAPTER TEN

SHALLEEN

I had to move into the apartment because Keno got locked up and was gonna do some time. Not like I had to move in but I wanted to. He had a lot of stuff and he wanted me to keep an eye on it. He had more money stashed than he let's on. I know he does. I don't know why he ain't never just bought no house. But true to his nature, he was a thug that loved staying in the hood, keepin' it real. That was where our worlds collided. I say fuck the hood. Can a bitch look out her window at some water or something? Or be all the way up on some shit where the cell phones ain't getting no service.

But anyway I'm down to hold down the fort for a minute. I was happy when I found out Keno only had to do a year on a sixteen month sentence. It didn't seem long especially considering I knew some guys that were doing life and the fact that a lot of guys were getting killed.

He told me to block his lowrider in with an old Camaro he had. Then to have a couple of his boys take the rims off. When I did that I found a paper bag under the seat. It had $30,000 in it. I tucked that.

I had already been thinking about getting a new car too. I wanted to trade my car in for something new. I had a 5 series BMW that was four years old, with damn near 100,000 miles on it. I know you supposed to average about 15,000 miles a year but a bitch gets around on the real. That same night Keno called me.

"Hello"

"What's up?" he said.

"Nothing, missing you. When can I come see you?"

"We'll get to that in a minute. Did you block my car in?"

"Yeah of course."

"So I know your nosey ass found something."

"Huh?"

"If you can huh you can hear. How much was it?"

His ass knew how much it was. He was just testing me.

"Boy, what you talkin' about?" I said but he could hear my little giggle.

"Don't play Shalleen."

"It's thirty large, damn."

"Aight take six stacks and give it to the manager…"

My little come up got light on me just that quick.

"…I'ma be locked up for a year. Tell 'er that's for the rent, and make sure you get a receipt. The rest gonna have to hold you until I get out."

I prayed he was playing with my head. That's only like two thousand a month.

I told him, "You know I was thinking about getting a new car."

He acted like he didn't even hear me. He said, "Ay did you get the visitation form in the mail yet?"

"Umm, no."

"Shalleen, go out to the mailbox and check the mail."

I hadn't checked that shit in the two months he been gone.

"I don't have a key for it."

"It's on the keyring."

I felt like a dumb ass. I walked outside with the phone to my ear and opened the box. All kinds of shit fell on the ground. I was like "Oh shit!" I hoped he didn't hear that. There was a lot of bills and junk mail. Some mail from him was in there too. He made me open the bills and promise to pay them right away. I heard the phone beep, warning that the time was almost up. Fifteen minutes always goes by too fast and doesn't come often enough because he only calls when he feels like it. The phone hung up. I didn't get to tell him I love him or about them bitches that came by.

As I filled out the form I thought about if we would be able to sneak a fuck in on a visit. I was down for it if he wanted to. I sat around and watched cable, counted the twenty-four thousand and arranged all the faces the same way then I recounted it again. I said 'Fuck it' to myself I was gonna trade my car in and put the money with it and get me something new. If he be mad, he just be mad. I did everything else he told me to do. I went and mailed the form back to him, got some money orders from the post office so I could pay the rent up. I didn't pay for no whole damn year though. I paid for six months. Then me and the girls met up at the Cheese Cake Factory in the Marina. That's one of my favorite restaurants. I had steak and lobster. Marijka's bougie ass had prime rib and Cherise's ghetto ass ordered a hamburger. It turned out to be fun because a couple of guys invited themselves to sit at our table. Me and the girls looked at each other with our inside expressions.

Free Meal!

These guys were in the music business, or at least they said they were. One called himself Rich Kid. The other one's name was KB. After dinner we said our goodbyes at the valet. Cherise was in her Cadillac Truck. KB was riding with Rich Kid in his S550 Benz. I rode with Marijka, she had a convertible 645i BMW. I went to sleep that night thinking about what kinda car I was gonna get.

CHAPTER ELEVEN

RICH KID

"Richard!" broke me outta my daydream. I coulda swore I just saw them girls that me and KB met at the restaurant the other night pass by. I was at the Crenshaw carwash on Crenshaw and Stocker. The street had a heavy flow of traffic as usual and three girls in a Cadillac truck is common but I thought it was them. Whether it was them or not it had me reminiscing on the fun we had during dinner.

"Hey Richard!" it was the owner of the carwash calling me. A white haired business minded, Israeli dude. He was trying to get my attention because I was standing in the way of the cars stepping out of the shower.

"Hey Richard. Come here."

After I got out of the way he called me over to him. He called me Richard. That's what he thought I said last year when he asked me my name. He had been calling me that ever since. I tried to correct him a couple times but it didn't work. You know we have always had this language barrier thing going on in L.A. with foreigners. Even if they can speak English, pronunciations are a mutha fucka.

I am known as Rich Kid, formerly known as Poor Boy, and for good reason. But that all changed when I got my lil Mexican senorita pregnant. I met her the first day I checked into Central high school downtown on Sixth and Grand, next to the unemployment office. We felt each other right from the jump. We chilled together everyday at school and before I realized it, we were a couple. I met her parents and they made it evident that they didn't like a nigga. They were praying it was just a phaze she was going through, with her obviously indigent black boyfriend. Hustling wasn't my thing but I would always come up with a few dollars to take her to the movies when something new came out. All that was important to her was that I was always available to give her the attention she needed.

I grew up poor, so as I got older, the need to have a pocket full of money never really did mean much to me one way or the other.

My whole elementary school life I was accustomed to wearing my 'Why pay more when you can Pay Less' shoes until the heels were worn down on the outer corners, giving it the look of a three wheel motion lowriding shoe. Plus my signature hole under my big toe. I had three pair of pants for the week and two of them were identical. My image at school was nonexistent.

Although my wardrobe slightly improved over the years, I pretty much maintained the same image. That was until my Latin mami Gabrielle got pregnant and her father decided it was time to have a sit down with me. That sit down consisted of a one sided conversation. Laced inside it were some threats and offers.

My only input into the conversation was to agree or disagree when he was done talking. It really wasn't a hard decision. It was harder understanding him. He sounded like Tony Montana. His business acumen wasn't much different from Tony's either. He made sure that the choosing would be a simple task. Either I would be able to stay with Gabrielle but I had to provide for her or disappear immediately and she would be forced to have an abortion. If I decided to stay I would be fronted two kilos of cocaine to start off.

That was two years ago. Now I'm moving about five keys a week through a couple other dealers. Gabrielle and my son lived an hour away in the suburb of Valencia.

I get my car for the day washed almost everyday right here on Crenshaw. Most of the time I run across the street to Wings and Things and get me some wings and things while I wait. This day I had some food in my hand from the Jack in The Box next door. I liked them greasy two for ninety-nine cent tacos.

"Hey Richard."

"What's up Jacob?"

"How you doing Richard?"

"I'm just chilling man, you know."

"Chilling? My refrigerator chills."

I chuckled. *No shit huh.* I said more to myself than anything. I guess hood slang wasn't in his language class.

"You funny man. Naw, chilling is doing good. It's relaxing."

"No time for chilling right now. I'll chill when I'm in the morgue. But listen Richard..."

Everytime I heard him say Richard I wanted to yell!, "Rich Kid! Jacob, it's Rich Kid!" but I never did.

He kept talking. "The city is re-doing a lot of things around here. And these buildings..." he said, pointing north in the direction of Coliseum St. "...are going down. That land down there is for sale." he said, pointing towards an empty lot next to Weinnersnitzel. "You should invest in it. The property value around here is going to increase soon enough. ..."

I zoned out. He was still talking. I thought about how long I been coming to this same carwash over the years. I used to bring my mom's car up here. Then I got me a '77 Cadillac. It wasn't pretty but it was mine. I was getting it washed about once every two weeks. Then my uncle gave me a '91 Thunderbird. It had a few dents in it but it was my baby. It wasn't until I pulled up in that brand new paper plated, registration in the window Maserati Quattroporte that Jacob all of a sudden started speaking to me. That type

81

of recognition was new to me and it was addicting. It was powerful. He was still talking. My mind was still floating. I was looking at him thinking

I know who you are. You're the same guy that me and the Mexicans watched out for when I'd slip them an extra dollar to put Armorall on my tires and dashboard. The same guy I had an argument with two years ago because it rained a few hours after I got my car washed but the next day you refused to redeem my raincheck. I'm still that same dude but now I'm driving something that had to get imported and now I haven't paid for a carwash in 6 months.

"… a guy from the bank was telling me about the changes."

"Hold up Jacob, what kinda money we talking about?"

"Oh Richard…"

Rich Kid!

"…not too much. Nothing you can't handle. It'll be good for you. Take your music money…."

I told him I was a producer. That was what we said out here in L.A. But in my case, at least my homeboy was one. My boy KB produces and has his own independent label. I even told Jacob that a lot of the hot singles he heard coming through the carwash all day were my creations.

"…and invest in real estate. Then you will own part of the city Richard."

"Jacob, how much we talking?"

82

"I don't know, I say you spend one, one and a half mil. Then you can relax and do your music."

$1.5 Million! Jacob thinks I have paper like that!

"Maybe you can come by Monday and we'll go see my investment broker at Merrill Lynch."

That seemed like a good idea. An investment broker huh. I didn't have 1.5 but maybe we could see what was up.

"Aight Jacob, we are going to see what's up."

The conversation was interrupted when somebody pulled up behind me with their music bumping something with Lil Wayne's voice coming out of the speakers. I looked around and saw two familiar faces. It was two of the three girls I met at the Cheese Cake Factory and they had another cutie pie with them. So it really was them I saw driving past a little while earlier. I walked up on the passenger side. The one named Cherise was driving. She introduced the passenger. Her name was Vallawn. She was gorgeous and seemed bright like she had a plan for her life and she was being patient. The one I was scoping that night at dinner played the backseat. She was my type. Quiet and fine. She wore a little make up and her hair was pinned up. Her name was Marijka. The J was silent. I reached my hand in the window and shook her hand. I just wanted to touch her. She gave me a casual shake. I couldn't read it. Her timing was too perfect. She gave me full contact but she didn't hold on a second longer than necessary. I was tryna think of something to say but I was lost for words.

Cherise saved me when she said, "You sho' is lookin' cute today."

"As usual." I said stepping back so they call could see my whole body. I stuck a foot out to model myself. My outfit was red and gray from my retro Nikes all the way up to my snapback cap. My body was sporting a red and gray jump suit.

"What yall about to do?" I asked them.

Vallawn answered, "Just a few around the way girls looking for a lollypop to suck on."

Damn she knew how to get a brothas blood pumping.

"That's yo Maserati over there? It looks like they are trying to get your attention." she said motioning over to the Mexican waving my keys in the air. "That's the nice one too." she said. "You must be a big boy."

"Naw, I just been saving my lunch money a long time."

"Yeah I feel you playa. I might have to catch up with you later in the game."

That was an inviting ass comment, sounded like she was giving me some play. That's that recognition I was talking about. I had chosen Marijka but it seems like

Vallawn had chosen me. It's a man's world, a lady's choice but a gentlemen's game. I handed all three of them my card. It wasn't a business card. It was what I call a social card. The background was a real picture of a 24 track recorder faded in light blue. Across the top in the big bold letters it said Rich Kid. Then it had my Beverly Hills mailing address and e-mail address and a couple of phone numbers, and music notes floating around the card gave it the impression that I was in the music business. I told them to holla at me then I started to step off.

I stopped short and told them that my birthday was coming up and whatever I decided to do was gonna be off the hook. I jumped in my car and pulled off with the windows up, air conditioner blowing.

CHAPTER TWELVE

KENO

My counselor had me pissed off, taking his sweet fucking time putting Shalleen on my visiting list. I know he had the form a couple of weeks already. The form had all her information on it and her signature giving him permission to verify it. She didn't have a record so it was just a one, two step.

They like to say shit like, "it's a process." This I know, but if it takes that long then somebody's not doing their job. Paper work is just sitting on somebody's desk for days and days.

In the meantime Country spent the last couple of months pointing out everybody to me that was controlling everything from drugs to gambling and everything in between. None of the groups were black. Some brothas kept something rolling but that was just the individual hustler in them, not a collective effort. They were doing their own thing. Other races had groups and every group pretty much had a monopoly on something. So they all had somebody coming to spend at all times.

No black groups had product or clientele but spent liberally everything they had. That had me mad too.

I fell asleep thinking about and understanding why the Hispanics had passed us up economically.

I never too much been about thinking long and not acting, So I had Country introduce me to this one brotha that was movin' and shakin'. He seemed up on his game. But he was goin' for dolo by himself.

"Ay Mannish." Country said as he poked his head in Mannish's cell doorway. "This my boy Keno from around my way on the street."

I stepped up and extended my hand for a handshake amongst gentlemen and said, "Mannish, you look like you about your business. I like that, I'm about my business too. We should get along fine."

My hand was still out. He left me hanging.

His only response was a plain, "What's up?"

I let my hand down and let out a little giggle. He dissed me. I felt like a dog who just got his nose thumped by his owner's homeboy. I fought the natural urge to show my teeth and growl. Instead I showed my teeth and smiled. I rubbed my hands together and said, "What's up is, I'm tryna get in on the hustle, plug me in. I need to get some dough moving in my direction."

"Well I can't do nothing for you. You gonna have to find your own hustle. Cause what I got coming in, I ain't tryna split. Feel me."

I grimaced, "Feel you! Naw I don't feel you!" then I caught myself and calmed down. I said, "Hold up, maybe you don't understand. I ain't on no freeloading type a shit. I'ma make my own moves. I'm just sayin' put me in the mix."

"I know what you sayin', but what I'm sayin' is ain't no room for you in my pocket homie. Whatever customers you tryna get is money out my pocket. And you want me to just give you that. That's like shooting myself in the foot, feel me."

"Naw, it's more like getting yourself punched in the face!" I said as I punched him in the face.

Country grabbed him and put him in a sleeper hold until he passed out. "and gettin' robbed!" I added as I was going through his pockets. I pulled out a bag out of his jacket. The bag had 200 books of stamps in it. Stamps were the official underground currency in prison. A book had 20 stamps and is worth $5. The next day Country introduced me to a nigga named Halfdead. Word had already gotten around about what happened to Mannish. Halfdead chose to roll with us. I doubt that he was scared of us. He wasn't scared of anything. His name was Halfdead because he'd been to hell and back. Shot, stabbed and should've been dead long time ago. He recognized our gangsta and wanted to be on a team like ours. Smart soldiers find themselves alone a lot. You run into soldiers often in jail but intelligence is hardly one of their finer qualities. And most smart people don't want trouble unless it was for gain. I'm willing to bet that he didn't pay much attention at school but almost getting killed a lot of times teaches you to pick your associates better. That's how I read him.

Later that day at mail call I got some mail from Shalleen and Crystal. In Crystal's letter I found out that she was pregnant. Damn, it gotta be mines. I was putting dick up in her every chance I got and "pull out" to me was a old school car radio.

Shalleen's letter was just about some regular shit. How she misses me and how everything at the apartment is cool. What the real deal was was the fifteen pictures with the letter.

She was posing for me in different lingerie sets. Half of the pictures had her in just thongs. Some were shots from the back. It made my dick hard seeing those big yellow ass cheeks eat that strip of thong up. She bent over and I still couldn't see the thong. Some girls got a big booty but Shalleen gots ass. There was a picture where she peeled' her cheeks open with her hands. I could see the strip running down just barely covering her asshole. She had some shots from the front with a sheer top on. I could see her titty nipples and everything. And she was standing there like, "How do you want it?" My favorite shot is the one where she was sitting on her butt, more like cocked to the side on one ass cheek with her legs wide open. Both her knees are bent, one leg resting on the floor, the other knee up, foot flat on the floor. Her thong is pulled to one side and one of her fat pussy lips is blowing me a kiss.

I taped some of her pictures up in the cell then I went outside with plans of doing a light work out on the bars. Some pull ups, dips and push ups but them photos had me going hard. Working out and reading sex ladened books are the two main things we use to appease our sexual aggression. I worked out hard.

I was drenched in sweat when I was done. Before I went to take a shower I had to sit back and look at Shalleen for a minute.

She was luscious. Beyonce' wasn't ready yet compared to her. I got my shower necessities together then went to the showers. Under my towel I had my baby oil and that ass shot with the thong just covering her brown eye and the one with the pussy lip peeking out at me.

Don't tell nobody.

After I gave myself a good wash up and got that hot shower therapy for about ten minutes I took Shalleen's pictures which were already water proofed in my little plastic ziplock and slapped them up on the wet wall. Then I dried my midsection off. I then squirted a hanfull of baby oil. I think I went overboard. I couldn't imagine no man using that much oil especially in a jailhouse shower. But hey, I was in a stall with a door and this is my world for now.

The hot shower beat on my back. I thoroughly lubricated my dick and balls. I like to rub my balls while I stroked my dick. I looked up at Shalleen with her sexy self while I caressed my little penis into a big dick. I got lost in the picture. The blood pressure in my dick forced the veins and nerves up against the skin enhancing the sensation.

I was inside her warm walls. I was fucking her. It was raw sex. No kissing or rubbing. Just dick in the pussy. I was banging her doggystyle.

I held my dick and jerked it back and forth like I was cocking a well greased shotgun, emptying out the shells.

A lot of shells, about thirty or forty shells.

Then I switched to the double hand pump action for about thirty shells. Baby oil was a good invention. It made me fall in love with myself.

I looked at the picture of Shalleen with the thong pulled to the side and slid in between her legs. One of my hands went down to rub my balls like... like... there isn't anything that I can think of that you rub your balls like. You gotta be gentle then at the same time you gotta handle them with intensity to make you wanna nut a pound of cum. I slid my other hand up to my dick head. Both hands were in a slippery situation. Shalleen's pussy felt so good. I just got my dick tip in, teasing her with shallow pumps. I was sensitive. It was driving me crazy. I was so hard my dick was pointing towards the ceiling. I milked the head. My legs stiffened. I looked at Shalleen's creamy thighs. I remembered how soft they were. I could smell her sweet pussy scent. I didn't even realize when I started long stroking. The sensation got me up on my tippy toes. My eyes rolled into my head. My head tilted back. My feet were dancing trying to keep me balanced like dogs when they stand up on two legs. I stumbled back to the wall. The shower rained down over my head.

Soothing.

Two more pumps and I erupted.

Gush!

I gushed semen all over myself which quickly got washed away by the rain. I came down off my toes. I wanted to lay down. Shalleen was smiling at me.

I let the shower rejuvenate me for a few. I dried myself off and beat my shower slippers against the wall to knock all the water off. Then wrapped the towel around me. I grabbed my soap, pictures, baby oil and clothes and headed to my cell.

Mannish turned the corner and headed my way.

I was slippin'. Ain't no question!

I looked around real quick hoping to see Country or Halfdead, but no such luck. I watched him like a hawk. Mannish seemed like he really didn't notice me. He was walking right past me. Halfway through my exhale he punched me in my fuckin' ear so hard my feet slipped from under me and all my shit flew up in the air.

I'ma keep it real, he knocked the shit outta me. But I hopped back up on my feet with a quickness, and put my dukes up. My towel was on the floor. I was asshole naked but I couldn't do nothing about it right then.

Mannish stepped back and said, "I'ma let you get yourself right." I left all that shit on the floor and stormed off and turned into my cell. I got dressed, put my boots on, then looked out to see where Mannish was at. He was only a few feet away, outside my cell. I slid my door open to let him know to come in.

He stepped in and we rumbled and we rumbled and we rumbled. He left with lumps on his face and a busted lip. I wouldn't say it then but now I'll say he walked out with my respect too. He also grabbed a couple of valuables on his way out. I laid down for a while. My jaw was swollen and my ribs were thoroughly bruised. I was hoping he didn't break 'em again. We shot the fair one. He got some get back. I put knuckles to him too though.

I made sure to keep my eyes on him just in case he wasn't satisfied. Other than that I kept doing what I do best.

Plot.

In another couple weeks I had twelve teammates including Country. We met twice a week to discuss everything that was going on, on the yard. I had already identified all the guys from every race that were holding drugs and stamps. I was about to hit 'em up but I had to think again because there would be a fallout on the blacks. In prison other races don't put blacks in groups like "Fuck these blacks but those other blacks are cool." Only blacks do that. No, when it was on, it was on with all blacks. So I had to consolidate the forces. Wake the brothas up. When I first started plotting I just had the intention of doing what I do. Rob some fools and hustle to have a stream of income coming in. But what was actually about to happen was a transfer of control of the drug trade to the blacks. I postponed the strike and spent some time talking to the brothas on the yard to see where their heads were. I started the conversation with all of them the same. "Ay come take a walk with me right quick… this is just between me and you. Man to man, black man to black man… you know shit is fucked up on the yard right. We ain't making no revenue to help support our families or ourselves... we get charged the most for what we buy and we get the lowest grade... shit is about to change but the only way is that we all gotta ride together. I just need to know if you wanna be on the side of the fence with the power."

I got back all kind of responses but they mostly fell in three categories.

Either they were with it but didn't wanna be a part of something with some other black prisoners that they didn't get along with, or they didn't wanna fuck their time off messing with some unorganized, half assed niggas. And they were really convinced that we couldn't pull off something so big. I was determined to show them fools something and then I was gonna treat them like hoes afterwards. The lowest percentage of the three categories were the ones that were tired of being on the bottom of the power pile, last in the race of races. They were with the move. They looked at it like there was nothing that could happen to make the situation worse. All it could do was stay the same or get better. That was a good thing except that it was only a small percentage of blacks that were thinking like that. I didn't really need them to physically do anything. Just support the idea and know that they peoples was about to make moves. Of the 1200 inmates, 800 were black. The supporters made up 20% of that and that was 160. The other

640 blacks I considered resisters but they weren't the target. 160 supporters was alright with me because the non-black population was just 400, the number that dealt with drugs or benefited from them was way less.

I was ready.

We held our last meeting on a Friday. We would lay low and do our usual routine on Saturday. Then me and my twelve selected soldiers would run up in the stash cells early Sunday morning right after the cells unlocked, having the advantage of the element of surprise.

When Sunday morning came me and my selected soldiers had already been in the SHU=Special Housing Unit for ten hours pending investigation.

CHAPTER THIRTEEN

BIG WILL

It took me forever to sell that fucking Suburban. I didn't just wanna advertise that I was tryna get rid of a black suburban you know with all the whole city looking for one. I was just putting the word out on the low. But either peoples money wasn't right to give me what I wanted, or they money wasn't right to be feeding that monster with these high ass gas prices. I finally took it to the paint shop and sprayed it white. Then I let my cousin use it to drive up to Sacramento to see his dad. He put an ad in the paper up there and some white boy picked it up the first week.

I was having an even harder time talking Shalleen outta her pussy. Ever since I saw her and Keno together that night she had been on some other shit like they married or something, even while he locked up. It had been about two months and she ain't even asked me for no money or nothing.

Plus my connect, Hector was at me tryna give me a fresh load. He was wondering why I wasn't moving them things like regular. I didn't want to tell him about the murders and how I lost some hustlas that were getting a lot of my stuff off, and how I was laying low as a snake's belly. All this stuff had me uptight. That was why I was all for it

97

when my boy Tony suggested we go out to a club. After I got suited and booted and picked him up he directed me to Hollywood. He said we were going to a gay club. I slammed on the brakes and almost caused an accident, I started to turn around.

He stopped me and said. "A gay club for girls, a lesbian club."

I understand what he meant because there was a lesbian club on Pico and 12th ave. name catch 21. A couple of times I posted up out front in the car and smoked weed while I peeped the bitches out. But I didn't like them bitches. They looked too much like men. I like when two broads are together and they both look like bitches. Men too, don't be walking around looking like no bitch. Tony was telling me about how he saw a lot of famous entertainment females there the last time he went. That was when I noticed the crowd outside, we were there. I found a spot to park, tucked my *never leave home without it* in the small of my back and went and got in the mix. The bouncers were turning most of the men away. Only a few were able to get in.

That's when Tony said, "Oh yeah, you gotta be with a female to get in."

Two muscled up goons with tight ass shirts on bumped me coming through the crowd on their way in. I looked back and Tony was mackin' to this girl as she was maneuvering her way to the door. Whatever he was in her ear telling her had her smiling but when she got to the door she flashed the bouncer her I.D. and kept it moving without the smallest hint that Tony was with her. I scanned the crowd to see what I was working with. I saw these three females walking up looking like Destiny's Child. It wasn't them though. I stepped out of all the chaos and walked straight up to them.

I said straight up, "I'm goin' in wit yall. I'ma pay yalls cover charge and drinks on me all night." then I added, "I just gotta get my boy." as we wormed through the crowd. When I got within reach of Tony I grabbed his shirt and pulled him behind me.

Before we got up on the door, while we were still in the mix of the endless busy bodies I pulled my piece out of the small of my back and whispered in one of the girl's ears, "Hold this." and at the same time going up under her jacket and sticking it in the back of her jeans. At first she jumped like I was violating her, tryna feel on her. Then it dawned on her what it was. She inhaled to give me more room to slip it in.

First we showed the big fat security with the tight black t-shirt on our I.D.'s, then we walked in. Another security patted me and Tony down and looked in the girl's purses. They charged us $20 a head and we were in. We all headed over to the bar. The place was dark. Multi-colored laser lights blasted all through the air like a futuristic gang fight. On the way to the bar I eased up behind homegirl and got my weapon back. I was ready to order the first round of drinks and get the party poppin'. I asked them what they wanted. I had to holler over the music. That DMX song was playing. Stop, drop, shut 'em down open up shop, Whoa, whoa. All three of the girls answered back saying they wanted Adios Mutha Fuckas.

I said, "Adios Mutha Fuck! What the fuck is that?"

One of 'em said, "A mixed drink with four kinds of clear liquor. It was blue and after you've had a couple of them you'll know why they call it that. That was if you remember anything the next day."

I told the bartender to hook us up. He sat five of them on the counter. Everyone grabbed their drink and went to go get in the mix of the club. The girls went one way, Tony went another and I went to find a chick to dance with.

This sexy slim goody female walked across my path. I grabbed her hand and said, "Hey Ma." She looked at me like shit was hanging from the tip of my nose. I ain't let it bother me though, cause I know these gay bitches be on some shit like they don't need no man in they life. I ain't gonna lie, I was about to stick my foot out and trip her skinny ass. A couple of minutes later these girls were standing on the edge of the dance floor and bouncing their tities to the beat.

I approached 'em with a big friendly smile.

"They got a spot for all that energy." I said gesturing over to the dance floor. "And I can two-step to any beat."

They looked at each other and started talking like I wasn't even standing there.

"Girl, was that nigga talkin' to you?"

"You know he wasn't talking to me. Shiiit, he betta speed on before he get peed on."

They gave each other high fives.

"Huh, these punk ass men be havin' me fucked up."

I couldn't take it no more. I yelled, "What bitch!" and cocked my arm back to punch one of them bitches in the face, anyone of 'em. My elbow hit somebody's drink and knocked it to the floor. I looked back and it was Tony and one of those big ass goons that bumped me on their way in. I wanted to holla at this big mutha fucka anyway. The bitches got out of dodge. I didn't even look back at them. I looked this swole ass goon in his eyes. He stood taller than me.

"What up Dog!" I challenged.

"What the fucks up witchu!" he barked back, voice deeper than mine.

"Hold up!, Hold up! Big Will!" Tony said stepping in between us. "He cool homie. I'm trying to introduce yall. He moving work out here in Hollywood. Two bricks a week."

Tony knew I needed more outlets. This was a plug. My whole demeanor changed. I stuck my hand out. He relaxed too, his handshake was soft. He said his name was Tracy. I told him mine's was Big Will. We talked a little bit and at first I thought the light was tricking my eyes cause they had all those colors but while we all kept talking I kept looking and after a few more minutes I knew I wasn't tripping. This cock diesel ass goon had on a rainbow belt and a rainbow keychain hanging out of his pocket. I didn't mention it. We took the conversation over to the bar. Me and Tony got a couple more Adios Mutha Fuckas. Tracy ordered a cranberry and Vodka. Destiny's Child came back to the bar for another round. I told them they got all they was gonna get and to speed on before they get peed on. I was mad at every bitch in the club.

Fuck them hoes.

I was hoping one of 'em would've said something slick outta they mouth so I could throw my Adios Mutha Fucka in her face, glass and all. But instead they put their asses high in the air and spun off.

Tony started talking to this chick sitting next to him at the bar. I downed my drink and had to take a piss. Tracy had to take a piss too. When I opened the bathroom door there was a man pissing at a urinal. There were three empty ones left. I went to one, there were two left but Tracy went into a shitter stall and closed the door.

I said, "Oh shit! You finna drop a bomb. Let me hurry up and get outta here."

The other man left fast, didn't even wash his hands.

Tracy yelled, "I'm just taking a piss."

In the shitter? With the door closed?

I didn't hear no piss hitting no water in the stall. When I was done I pushed his stall door open. He was sitting down pissing.

I asked him straight up, "You gay?"

He nodded his head looking up at me just like a girl.

I said, "You suck dick?"

His big ass nodded again. I stepped all the way in the stall, closed the door and pulled out my dick. I told him, "Eat this." while I pushed it through his lips. He gulped it down too. By his neck movements I could tell he been doing this a long time. He was better than any bitch I ever had give me head. He must've had strong muscles in his jaws too cause it felt like he was sucking the life outta me. I leaned back on the door and let him do his thing. When I was ready

103

to cum my legs straightened out and made me stand up straight, my booty cheeks got tight, too tight to squeeze a fart out. And I had to fart too. When he caught the first gush he backed off. I stepped forward and chased his mouth. I grabbed his head and pinned him to the wall behind the toilet. Rammed my dick back in his mouth and gushed and gushed. His eyes watered up as I gushed again. He struggled but I was big too and I had him locked in.

Gush! Gush! Gush!

Cum was leaking out the sides of his mouth.

Gush! Gush! Gush!

I stumbled back against the stall door and let out a long fart. When I gained my strength back I tucked my boy back in my pants and left the restroom, I was good for the night.

I found Tony on the patio smoking a cigarette and told him I was ready to go. He flicked his cigarette and we went back through the club, headed for the exit. Halfway to the door I felt a tap on my shoulder, it was Tracy. He was handing me a card. I almost didn't want to take it. I felt like he was exposing me. He had it up in the air. He looked so bitchy to me just then. They always look like that to me afterwards. I took the card but I didn't want to just slip it in my pocket. I was on some paranoid shit. So I just read it. It said he was a personal trainer and had a cell number on it.

I said, "Aight then."

Gave him a manly pound with the fist and spun off. Me and Tony were on the freeway when he said, "The girl I was talking to at the bar had a friend with her. A sexy ass friend, and they were down for whatever. I went to the restroom looking for you. You sounded like you already had it poppin'. You was in the stall tworkin' something huh?"

"You know how the big dog do it. Bitches be at me." I was tryna play it off.

Then he said, "Then I looked underneath and saw Tracy's big ass feet."

He just let it hang from there. My heart was beating quick. I pretended like I farted and let my window down. But I was really tryna dry up the sweat on my face. I exited the freeway near LAX. I made a few turns and ended up in the air cargo section on a side street a couple of blocks away from the airport. All the businesses were closed. It was dark.

I hopped out the truck and went behind a trash bin to take a piss. I thought Tony would take advantage of the opportunity but he didn't get out. I really had to take a piss but I didn't want to leave any DNA behind. I lingered a few extra minutes. He still didn't get out. I came from behind the dumpster with my cell phone to my ear. I walked away from the car trying to think of something.

Then I came back to the passenger side and said. "I just talked to some bitches in Moreno Valley."

Which was like an hour away.

"They said for us to come thru."

He asked me who they were. I just threw a name out, "Michelle" not even thinking about the Michelle that used to come by the spot sometimes to see me. But that was who he thought of right off.

He said, "Michelle and K.C.?" talking about her even prettier friend.

"Yeah them, we going to Moreno Valley." I repeated.

I acted like I had to take another piss. His door opened. I took one side of the dumpster and he took the other. Since I really wasn't peeing I finished first. I came around behind him and blew his brains out of his face. I scared the shit outta myself when the blast echoed through the air. I hopped back in my car and got the hell outta dodge. By the time the dust from his fall settled I was already back on the freeway. I had to do him, what else was I supposed to do, let him bust me out to the homies? Naw kid, my sexual preferences is my business. It was just something about having my dick on a man's tongue that makes me feel like a king. I like to make my jizz slide down another man's Adam's apple. I'ma homothug. It has a nice ring to it. I call myself that all the time, but if another mutha fucka calls me that I'll bust his head. I got back home and washed Tracy's spit off my dick and balls. I went to sleep hoping Tony didn't tell anybody he was gonna be with me tonite.

Adios Mutha Fucka!

CHAPTER FOURTEEN

TANYA

My grandma's appointment day had arrived and I was excited about seeing her. Memphis' rush hour traffic was sometimes worse than L.A. and today it was just my luck that everybody else with a car had someplace to go at the same exact time. I looked at the clock.

9:45 a.m.

My grandma's appointment was at 10:30 a.m. and unfortunately the doctor's office was across town so again I'd have to get back in the mess called traffic once I picked Ma up. I crossed Lauderdale st. and turned down Mississippi Boulevard. A red light stopped me. I impatiently tapped on my steering wheel while watching a fat man walk across the street and pulling his pants out of the crack of his butt.

The light turned green and I sped off. I pulled up to my grandma's house at exactly 10 a.m. I hoped Ma was ready because the drive to Germantown would undoubtedly take at least twenty minutes and once I got to the hospital I'd still have to find a decent parking space. I blew the horn. My grandma opened the door fussing.

Ma's hands were moving and waving, "Chile I'm comin'. Don't be blowin' no horn fa' me. Come on in." Everything she said was said also with her hands, it was force of habit. Ma had taught sign language to deaf kids most of her life.

I could understand nearly everything in sign language but I didn't practice it. I got out of the car and ran into the house.

"Hi Ma." I said, hugging her. I gave her a big kiss on the cheek and made myself comfortable on the sofa. The décor was dark with paisley patterns on most of the material on the furniture. I noticed that Ma still had the same old walnuts on her table that she had when I was young. Ma also had a habit of sucking the chocolate off of M&M candies and leaving the nuts in the dish. I crinkled my nose like I had a stale nut in my mouth.

"Ma, are you going to the doctor or moving?" I joked when I saw her carrying bags.

Ma sat the bags down on the porch near the front door and said, "Hush Chile. Don't be sassin' me." her hands moved with sterness.

I helped her with her things then we got into the car and secured our seat belts.

I started the engine and made my way to the expressway. I switched lanes and the car behind me blew its horn. I had cut the angry driver off, but I didn't care, I was trying to get my grandma to the doctor's office on time. I was one of them drivers who have accidents all the time but never thought it was my fault. They are usually very minor, small damages here and there. A drop in the bucket of life. My vehicle is nice but too many nicks and bruises to make it in a car show. Ma scolded me about my driving several times. She said her signature phrase with only her hands.

The turtle will always catch the rabbit eventually.

Then verbally Ma said, "Let's hope it's not in the grave."

The clock read 10:20 a.m. as I pulled up to Methodist Healthcare. I dropped her off at the door and went to look for a parking space. My lucky day, a woman in a Black Toyota Prius was moving out, right in front of the door. I smiled and parked.

When I walked into the doctor's office I looked around, found Ma then sat down and pulled out a novel. The nurse called her to the back. I stayed in the waiting area.

I finished the third chapter, then the fourth and fifth.

I would get lost in the book and then thoughts of her would disturb my entertainment.

What's taking Ma so long? I wondered.

I looked at my watch. Forty-five minutes had come and gone.

Patience is a virtue. I reminded myself.

I sat back and read another chapter of the novel. I love this story. When I'd gotten to the tenth chapter in the book I looked at my watch. I was just about to ask the receptionist about my grandma when Ma appeared.

"Mama, is everything alright?" I asked as she made her way out to the waiting room. She'd just seen the doctor and I was a little skeptical about the worried expression Ma wore on her face. Ma was already a light skinned woman but she looked like a ghost at the moment. All the color had drained from her otherwise radiant skin.

"Nuthin' fa' you ta worry 'bout Chile, lets go." she said, giving me a phony smile. I decided to drop the subject. I concluded that she would tell me what the doctor said when she was ready. I held her frail arm and we walked out of the doors of the hospital together.

"Ma you hungry? You want something to eat before I take you home?"

"Naw Chile, Ma is tired. I just want to get home. I'll fix me something after I rest."

Ma always loved 95.7 Hallelujah FM station so I turned the radio on for her and Ma hummed along all the way home. I wanted to go in, but I still had so much work to do so I kissed her goodbye and watched her go into her house.

Something was weighing heavily on Ma's mind, I could tell but I didn't want to push her and worry her more than she already was. For now I would just have to wait and sometimes waiting was the hardest thing. I had never been a patient person and it bothered me to know that Ma may have heard some bad news.

Ma waved through the screen door but there was something missing. Her usual glow wasn't there. The doctors had told her something and she wasn't telling me. It was hard not to worry about her because Ma was all I had. I called her Ma because she was the only real mother I'd ever known.

After all these years, me and my mother still hadn't made peace. Cheryl still hadn't apologized for sending me away and not taking care of me properly, but anyway, that was a long time ago and I wouldn't cry over spilled milk. The only thing to do was to move on. I knew it wasn't my fault and there was nothing I could do about it.

As I drove to work I thought about Ma. The rest of the day at work just kinda floated pass because my mind was consumed with thoughts of Ma's issue.

When I got home my boyfriend Malcolm was waiting on my doorstep.

The neighbor was carrying branch cutters and a shovel from his car to his house. No doubt such an expert garden man would have to keep good tools. It was uncanny how I always seemed to catch him coming and going as I was coming and going.

"What do you want Malcolm?"

"I just want to talk to you. I'm sorry."

Thinking about the previous night's discussion we'd had, made me want to end our relationship because I knew that he wasn't going to stop pestering me about stealing money from my company and that was just something I wasn't about to do.

I didn't want to let him in the house, but his begging and pleading weighed me down so I agreed to let him in.

Like a puppy Malcolm was right on my heels when I entered the house.

Malcolm followed me into the living room and we took our seats. We had a lot to talk about but for the longest time neither of us said anything. The tension in the room was thick.

I decided to start the conversation. "Malcolm, I am so sick of you trying to talk me into stealing. I enjoy my job and I don't want to get fired for doing stupid stuff."

Putting my hands in his, he said, "Baby, I understand where you are coming from but I think you could get away with it. I mean, you deserve so much."

"I am a young black woman and I make plenty money. Look at what I've accomplished. I've always been honest so why should I flip the script now?"

"I understand." he said killing the disagreement.

I smiled up at him. Finally he had gotten the picture, I thought.

"And Malcolm, I need my bank card."

"Okay okay." he said then ran out to his truck and got it for me.

I smiled again.

We embraced and sat back on the couch. We both were fans of basketball so we watched the game together. Malcolm picked up the remote and made himself comfortable. The Lakers were playing against the Hawks and though Malcolm was a huge Hawks fan, I was rooting for my home town team, the Lakers. I went to my closet and changed clothes in front of it. Lakers gear from head to toes. Jersey, socks, scarf, panties and cap.

"Oh. You gonna do it like that huh?"

"Yup!" I said as I plopped down next to him.

During halftime I went into the kitchen and got us a snack but was back in a minute. I didn't want to miss a thing. Kobe had done some phenomenal stuff in the first half.

I looked over at Malcolm and smiled. The Lakers won and I got great joy at rubbing the win in his nose, but more importantly, I was happy to know that we were alright, at least for the time being.

It had gotten late and Malcolm was about to go home.

Before he left he asked me for my bank card again. He'd just given it back but he needed it again. Something small he wanted to order online. I trusted him. I handed it to him and kissed him goodnight and he left, I went to bed alone.

I wasn't alone for long though because the bad dreams invaded my slumber. I tossed and turned, I dreamt the little girl was running.

"You can't run from me lil' girl."

All of a sudden the little girl's pace quickened. She was tired but she wouldn't stop.

She couldn't.

The figure was too close to her. His voice was loud. It resonated throughout the winter night. She didn't have any shoes on and it was cold but getting away was her only focus.

"If you know what's good for you, you better bring yo' lil ass here!" the voice warned. There was just a silhouette in the darkness. She couldn't make out who it was. The voice was loud. Panting, she ran faster and the pace of the figure quickened.

Her breathing was staggered and she was tired.

Suddenly, she felt herself floating into the air. She was lifting from the ground...

I woke up in a cold sweat and panting hard. I was confused and troubled. That dream meant something to me. I believed that everything in life had a meaning to it. I didn't know the meaning of the dream now but I hoped I would soon.

I threw back the comfortor, climbed out of the bed and went to the shower. I thought of California. My old life, the one I loved. The friend I left behind. I thought of visiting my old neighborhood, just to see how things had changed. I thought about talking to a therapist first. I needed someone to help me understand the dreams, the awful dreams. I searched the net and found a therapist in my area named Dr. Golden Hunt. The doctor told me that I could come in that evening.

The drive to the therapist's office was one filled with contemplation. I didn't want any doctor looking at me like I was a psycho but those dreams were scaring me. Dark clouds began rolling in and I hoped I made it to the doctors' office before the rain fell.

Not so lucky, it came down and pelted the top of my car. I parked and sprinted through the door of Dr. Golden Hunt's office. I stepped through the doors half drenched with water from the dark skies. Apprehension set my pace as I walked to the front desk and gave the secretary my name.

"Have a seat. Dr. Hunt will be with you momentarily." The secretary told me.

The waiting area was full. Three rows of connected chairs, only two chairs empty, one in the far back. I took the first available seat. I couldn't believe there were so many "crazy" people in Memphis.

After taking a seat, I looked over to my left. Maybe a little friendly conversation would make me feel better, put me at ease a bit. The lady seating next to me appeared to have her self together so I wondered what she was doing here. The lady was sending text messages on her phone.

I didn't want to disturb her but curiosity got the best of me. Politely, I spoke.

"Hello."

The beautiful young lady gave me that-bitch please-look and went right back to texting. The female was gorgeous and had that-well taken care of, whorish-look. Her skin was deep brown colored and smooth as butter. She had big breasts and full lips, tight eyes and a thick and curvey body. Her face wasn't heavily made up. The only makeup she wore was eyeliner and lip stick. She acted a little stuck up though. As if she was too good to talk to me.

"Excuse me." I spoke again.

The lady took a deep breath, dropped the phone to her lap and looked over at me.

117

Her eyes were a beautiful light brown.

"Yes."

The fake smile she wore was evidence of her exasperation toward me.

I leaned over and asked, "What are you here for?"

"Not that it's any of your damn bizness..." the lady said hotly. "...but I'ma tell you anyway." She leaned closely and whispered, "I have a sex addiction." then she smiled.

Her perfectly aligned teeth were sparkling white.

I smiled.

The lady stuck out her hand for me to shake.

"My name is Katrina." she said.

"My name is Tanya."

"Tanya!" my name sounded in the air.

At the calling of my name, I looked up and saw Dr. Hunt standing in the door way. I stood up and followed her.

Once we were in the privacy and comfort of her office the doctor told me to have a seat on the chaise. I did, I sat down and laid back. The carpet was a light butter cream color. I could see where my wet shoes left marks. The walls were painted an off white color and covered with plaques displaying the doctor's many achievements. Soft jazz filtrated throughout the office.

The first thing I said as I looked through the doctor's window was, "I hope it's not raining like this when I leave." I felt the need to straighten out the blinds.

The doctor said, "Enjoy it. The rain is liquid sunshine." then she said, "Let's get right down to business." while sitting back in her chair, but not before pressing the screen on her phone and pulling out a notepad.

She got comfortable, with her pen in hand. I closed my eyes and re-lived the dream I'd experienced the previous night.

I took a few seconds then began "in... in..." I took a breath. "in the dreams it's always dark and the little girl is being chased. It's... It's cold and..."

"Wait. Who is she running from? Do you see anybody?"

I gritted my teeth and tried hard for it to come to my mind. Unfortunately in my dreams, the person isn't clear. I didn't know who it was or what exactly they were about to do to her.

The dreams only revealed bits and pieces to me.

"Take your time Tanya. How do they make you feel?" Dr. Hunt said soothingly.

"I feel sad. I feel helpless."

"Why do you feel like that? Why do you feel helpless?"

Tears rolled down my cheeks and silent sobs escaped my lips.

"I always have. Since a child when my mother shipped me off from my friends, my school. I was scared of starting over. She didn't understand that. She wasn't there when I needed her."

I told her all about my upbringing and my strung out mama, Dr. Hunt didn't interrupt me. The doctor listened to it all. When I finished my story I asked the therapist if I was crazy. I feared insanity.

"Of course not." The therapist said, assuring me. "You have unresolved issues and I want to see you every week. It's important that you continue these sessions. You need release and recovery."

But was it something possible to recover from?

CHAPTER FIFTEEN

RICH KID

I could tell it was gonna be one of those good Mondays. My car was still gleaming from the carwash the day before. The sky was blue as the blonde haired Devil's eyes. Even the 405 freeway wasn't crowded. When I got into the city around my usual time (between 11-12 midday) and stopped at the first red traffic light, I saw a girl in a jeep.

Walking across the street in front of me smiling was a girl with braids and a stank attitude, with a fake ass Louis Vutton purse on her arm. And will turn her nose up at you if your car doesn't cost fifty plus. I put my car in neutral, stepped on the gas and scared the shit out of her. Haha.

The light changed. Me and the girl in the jeep pulled off. I rode next to her, a natural beauty. Her face was clean and she let her hair fly, at first I thought it was Marijka, the features in her face were a little different but close enough for me to stare at first thinking it was her.

Then I noticed the way this girl swung her head to the music her mannerism sealed it, it wasn't Marijka. That Usher song came to mind, "You remind me" I was gonna let the first two lines of that song be my introduction to her but I dismissed it as corny. I was in my S550 Benz, so I let my whip talk for me. She looked a couple of times and I said to myself, "If she looks again I got her." She looked again. I let my passenger window down.

"What up girl?"

"Hi"

"Where you goin?"

"To meet my friend."

Seventy-five percent of the time "my friend" is a dude. Otherwise she would've said my girlfriend or my homegirl. But twenty-five percent of the time they'll surprise you and it will be a girl.

"What yall getting' ready to do?" I asked her, her next word is the giveaway. She could say something like, "She want me to…" or she could say, "We about to…

"We" means her and him.

But she told me, "I'm going to spend the day with him."

Him. Oh well. I poked out my bottom lip.

Then she continued. "He's seven years old. He's my friend. But his mother was my friend first. I got him for the day while her man takes her out for the day to Catalina Island."

I said, "I can dig that. I wish you had me for the day."

"Maybe next time."

That sounded promising. I snapped a picture of her with my camera phone. I caught her hair blowing wild in the wind. She didn't seem to like that but she let it go. It was already done. She told me her number and I programmed it in with her picture. She said her name was Mary Jay. By this time we were passing up Yum Yum doughnuts coming up on Rodeo and Crenshaw. I told her I'd call her, made a left and pulled into the Ralphs supermarket parking lot. My destination was Cameo cleaners next to it. I'm on that bouigie shit. I like to patronize places that got pictures of famous blacks that patronize the place too, especially, if it's in the hood. Then I stopped at Daddy Dave's on 43rd to get a grilled Turkey sandwich cause Dave got pictures too.

When I walked outside, two gangsters ran down on me hollering, "Break yourself!" It was fuckin' 12:00 middday On a Monday! On Crenshaw Blvd! One of them held his hand in his pants like he had a gun. I'm thinking, *Is this one of them fools that believes that if you pull your burner out, you gotta burn something?*

The other one reached and put his hand on my watch. My $35,000 watch.

"This me." he said.

He tried to unclasp it. I twisted my wrist back underneath.

Bam!

Before I could dodge it he punched me in my jaw and dropped me. I'ma keep it real, between me and you, I ain't no fighter with the fists or the guns. I'll put up a little rah rah front sometimes but I aint tryna kill nothing ain't tryna let nothing die. I could hear the people that were kickin' it next door laughing. The gangster with the gun stood over me with that-any second I'ma pull this thang out-look. The other one pulled my chain over my neck. Good thing I didn't have on my proper piece. This one only cost $2,000. Then they got my watch and my car keys that were in my hand. When they backed off the gunman took his cellphone out to show me he didn't have no gun. If I was a gangsta I would've rushed him. But I ain't so I didn't.

They got in my car which told me they were watching me when I pulled up. At first they-broke ass-ain't never had nothing asses-stared at the laser sensor key like it was broke. About two minutes passed before they put it where it belonged and got the engine started. They pulled off. It still looked beautiful moving into traffic.

People were laughing at me. I ran up the street like I was trying to chase the car. But if they would've pulled over I would've ran right past them. I just needed to get away from all the ridiculing. I pulled my cellphone out of my pocket.

I had a thousand and one people I could call but I called Mary Jay. I don't even know why I called her but when

I did she told me that her girlfriend wasn't gonna go to Catalina Island until the next day. I told her that my car had gotten stolen while I was ordering some food and could she come get me. She said she was on her way. I told her I'd be in the parking lot of the Washington Mutual Bank on the corner of Vernon.

I called Gabrielle and told her to report the car stolen. Then I called Jacob and told him something came up and we would have to reschedule to see his investor.

By the time Mary Jay called me back to ask me where I was, I was at the Ford dealership on 56th. I had just kept walking. I
stopped in front of the Crenshaw wall for a minute and looked at the so called art. I reminisced about back in the day when it was hit up from end to end with graffiti. That was what made the wall history. Now the clean up job they did, the so-called meaningful art was just some bullshit on a wall.

After about ten minutes I kept walking. I saw her pull up in the jeep and park out front. I told the salesman I'd think about it even though I had no intention of buying a Ford. I was just passing the time until Mary Jay showed up. Every since my Thunderbird I could never forget the acronym F.o.r.d. for Found On the Road Dead or Fix Or Repair Daily. I hopped in her car without using the door because there was no top. I landed on the seat first then put my feet on the floorboard and sat down. I would've cursed her ass out for stepping on my butter soft seats but she didn't trip. I smelled the weed before I noticed it between her fingers. Smoking ain't my thing but right then I needed to take my mind off the loss I had just took. She passed it. I puffed, puffed and passed it back. We did that rotation thing until it was gone. And by then my eyes were Asiatic. I was sunk low in the seat and hungry as hell. She was hungry too. She took me to Big Daddy's on Slauson and 7th Ave in the parking lot with the liquor store, while she went and ordered us a couple plates of their special red chicken meals. I stared up the block at the green and red Marcus Garvey afrocentric elementary and middle school, considered to be the best school in the city. And damn well should be for $500 a month. When she came back with the plates I got out the jeep and we ate at some patio tables and chairs they had out there. A couple of Rolling 60 Crips walked by. Not without throwing their hands up with the index and middle fingers separated pointing down with the thumb in close symbolizing an N for neighborhood, as in NHC for Neighborhood Crip. They were just letting me know who's hood I was in, incase I didn't know. After we ate she lit up another blunt. We got in the jeep and puff puff passed until it was gone. Me getting jacked had completely altered my plans for the day. So I let her smoke me out. Now I was laid back in my seat like I was at home in my recliner. I was sleepy. I wanted to go home. I wanted to go lay down. I couldn't think, my brain was shut down or on snail speed. The clock on her radio said 1:57pm. I closed my eyes.

She tapped me on my leg saying, "That looks like your car."

I looked at the clock. It said 2:17pm. I looked at where she was pointing and right in front of us at a light was my car. It had four gangsters in it. I told her that it wasn't mines.

She said, "You sure." as she turned the little knob on the glove compartment. It dropped open. There was a gun in there.

"Naw, that ain't my car." I said pushing the glove compartment back closed. She went down a few back streets in Ladera and came out on Centinela, then drove into the Best Western Hotel on La Cienega.

"Don't think you gonna get some ass. I'm just looking out for you cause I got you high. You need to rest your head."

She paid for the room. I went in and went right to sleep.

I could hear my phone ringing in my sleep but I ignored it and turned over. A little while later I felt fingernails lightly moving down my face like a light scratch. I opened my eyes and Mary Jay was straddled across me. She was saying, "Wake up Mr. Rich Kid, it's 4:00pm and you don't strike me as the type to sleep all day especially on a Monday and somebody named Papi has been trying to get in touch with you."

She had my phone in her hand. I took it and sat up in the bed, slid back and put my back on the headboard. I glanced around the room and before a word came out of my mouth my phone rang. It was Papi, that's Gabrielle's father. I pushed Mary Jay aside and jumped off the bed like he had just opened the door and walked into the room. I put a finger up to my lips like, "Shhh," then pushed the 'Send' button to answer. He told me he was trying to call me for the last two hours and asked what I was doing. I told him that I left my phone in my friend's car for a minute. You would've thought he was my daddy and that I was only twelve years old. He said Gabrielle told him that my car was stolen. He said he told me about being flashy for no reason, to impress people who don't have anything or appreciate anything. I wasn't tryna hear it. It was all about the recognition. But I still listened. He continued on to say that the police already found it because of the GPS scanners. He said that just like Scarface when he was talking about buying the Porsche in the movie. He told me that as far as they could tell nothing was wrong with it and that Gabrielle could pick it up after they lifted any fingerprints but that wasn't the reason why he was calling me. He wanted to talk some business he said he was at the Mexican restaurant in Huntington Park, that's the hangout for a lot of Papi's and high priced senoritas in the game, although an outsider would never be able to tell. He told me to have my friend bring me.

They were good for getting you drunk so they could see who you really are. It worked on me. Papi got me drunk one time and then put this Selena looking chick on me. I ended up banging her in my backseat in the back parking lot. She tried to put me up to rob one of Papi's friends inside. She said he had five kilos in his car and she could get the keys out of his pocket. I turned it down and finished pumping her missionary style.

It was all a test I found out later. So Gabrielle's father found out that I didn't have larceny in my heart. I was in after that. But he also found out that I would cheat on his daughter. He accepted it because he'd fucked Selena too and half the other women in there. But he took care of home.

He wanted to see what kind of man my friend was. That's a problem. My friend wasn't male. I thought about just telling Mary Jay let's go. It was not like were fuckin'. But I'm lookin' at her like "we will be though." I shook the thought of taking her because I knew it would be stupid. Plus I knew she didn't want to be around a bunch of Mexican drug dealers. I decided to call a cab to take me there.

When I hung up the phone from telling the front desk to handle that, Mary Jay said, "I could've taken you." she stopped, then said, "Oh yeah, the way you jumped up maybe that's not a good idea."

I just said, "Yeah."

"Sounds like the police got your car. If they wouldn't have found it so quick you still would've been alright, right? I mean you do have more than one car right?"

It was times like this that let me know I'm doin' it right.

"Yeah I got a 760Li, a Lincoln Mark LT truck and some mo' shit."

I seen a sparkle in her eyes. I let her imagine what else. It could only be better than the truth because what else I had was my Thunderbird and a '77 Caddy.

The sleep had me feeling refreshed. I decided to take a shower before I went to see Papi Scarface. I was in the shower singing some old school Jodeci and she just came in and stepped between me and the showerhead. The water soaked her immediately. Her hair joined in long wavy locks. Looking down at her wet lips made my dick poke her short ass in her soloplex. She put her hand on it. Held it like it was a child's arm in a crowd. She put her mouth on my right chest nipple and held it between her teeth then put her tongue on it like she was tasting me. Then she sucked on it like she was trying to get some milk out of it or something. It felt good. I felt her stroke me a few times. I got harder, then she got out of the shower.

I said, "Ay, where you goin?"

I was now willing to stand Papi up.

She said, "I just felt like doing that, that's all." and walked out.

I got out too and got dressed. While I was getting dressed I heard the phone ring. I knew it was the front desk telling me that the cab was downstairs. I heard her tell them that I'd be down in a minute and hang the phone up.

When I came out of the bathroom she was still naked laying on her back in the bed. She was thick in the thighs. I was fully dressed but I tried to lay on top of her. She raised her feet and blocked me off and said, "You have people waiting on you."

She was right. So I left.

Damn! I thought on the way out. *I could work with that.*

CHAPTER SIXTEEN

KENO

Me and all my boys were separated. I was in a two man cell wondering what the fuck had happened. Wondering how in the hell could I be in the SHU before I even put the move down. I thought about the movie Tom Cruise played in named The Minority Report where people got locked up before they committed the crimes. The law knew they were predestined to do certain crimes.

My celly was under the covers and appeared to be asleep. Personally, I hadn't slept a wink all night. Being in prison and going to the hole was just like being on the street and going to jail. Same emotion. They rushed us last night. Waited until 11:00pm lockdown and plucked us each out of our cells one by one.

I wondered who I was celled up with now. I could see the predawn light seeping into the dark blue skies outside when the Correctional Officer opened the slot in the door to push the breakfast trays through. He sat a tray on the slot and said my name. He was looking at me through the 3 by 12 inch glass in the door.

The C.O. was a white dude, about thirty-five years old, blonde hair and no moustache. I didn't move, just looked at him.

132

"You on some real gun ho stuff huh?" said it not in an intimidatingly but more in a, *I like your spirit kinda way*. He continued, "But let me tell you something, it's good the way it is because niggers are bad for business."

I jumped off of the bed with a quickness, ran to the door and shoved the tray. It fell on the floor and spilled all over his pants and shoes.

He said, "You guys are too emotional. Always ready to kick the shit outta somebody's ass at the drop of a hat. But guess what Rocko? That's only good if you're in the ring."

He put a forearm up to rest on the door. His other hand went up to smooth his moustache. Maybe he used to wear one. He took a deep breath like he was thinking about something.

Then he said, "I used to date this black bitch..." said that like he wasn't talking to somebody who would fuck him up for talking like that. "...Check out what she does. One day I dumped her because I got tired of her arguing about nothing. I mean I'm helping her with the bills and everything else. But she likes to talk shit right. So I says 'Fuck it! I'm outta here."

I wanna know where he's going with this. I wanna spit in his face.

He continues, "She goes to work pissed at the whole world and when the boss complains about her productivity

133

or should I say lack of, she tells him to do X rated things to his mother, quits and walks out with her attitude high on her ass."

I was staring at that fool through the glass wishing I could unlock the door with my will.

He started talking again. "Now your standing there looking at me mad as a bull in a red room, and I have to admit, I've gotten into quite a few riffs because of my frankness, but it's the truth I speak. If I'm lying you tell me I'm lying and I'll unlock this door right now and handcuff my hands behind my back."

He wasn't lying. I wanted to lie and say he was lying but I didn't say nothing.

He looked at his feet and said, "I hope you enjoyed your meal." and closed the slot.

About ten seconds later the slot opened back up.

"It was one of your selected soldiers that told us what was going down. I would even tell you who told, seeing as you guys don't usually deal with your snitches but I think you just might and I don't want to get stuck with the paperwork."

The slot closed again and the C.O. was gone. I went and did to the Plexiglas what I wanted to do to his face. It absorbed my punch. My knuckles were on fire but I ignored it and stared out of the window at the brick wall with the razor wire at the top for a while.

Out of the blue I heard a voice say, "What color do you think the people were that brought down the Black Panters?"

I spun around. "What?" I said and looked dead in the face of the old man that I had walked by playing chess my first day.

He said, "I knew you would run into a wreck. You weren't ready for what you were trying to do."

"There you go with that bullshit again. I'm always ready Pops. I been doin' this since…. hold up. What you mean anyway? How you know what I was tryna do?"

"I'ma let you call me Pops but the name's Mack. Don't you forget it. I can't tell you exactly what you wanted to do but you were going up against the status quo. Anyway this is prison. There's only a few things someone with your energy could get into."

"Hold up a minute. What the fuck is status quo?"

"It's the normal operation of things. And you were going against it. But you weren't going to be successful. So you should thank God you got pinched before you went through with it."

I told him with an attitude, "You one of them niggas that think they know everything!"

He snapped back, "Boy I already forgot more than you'll ever know, and still got more information in my head than you and all of your buddies together but what I don't know, will fill the Universe."

I had to think about that one for a minute.

He continued, "Listen Son, Knowledge is King but if I don't pass it on it's worthless, like a bunch of coal. But if I give it to you it becomes a jewel, and with your energy you need the jewels dropped on you."

Something about this man told me it was time to take the backseat and let somebody else lead for a minute. He spent the day telling me about the dynamics of the struggle, how treacherous the struggle was and how the greatest wars were being fought without guns. When he said "struggle" it meant the problems in the black race. He had a lot of books under his bed, a few stacks. He slid some to the side and pulled out a stack of manila envelopes full of printouts and copies of different things out of books. He shuffled through a few like he was trying to decide what to give me first. What direction he wanted to take me in. He decided and handed me one. I took it and laid back on my bed. I took about ten sheets of paper out of the envelope. They were photo copies stapled together.

The first page said, The Willie Lynch letter.

It was a documented speech that a white man named Willie Lynch, a British slave owner in the West Indies gave for the slave owners on the bank of the James River in the colony of Virginia in 1712. It was a "How To" on maintaining control of the slaves by psychological conditioning and he guaranteed it to last at least three hundred years by being passed down through generations of slaves.

Greetings:

Gentlemen, I greet you here on the bank of the James River in the year of our Lord one thousand seven hundred and twelve. First, I shall thank you, the gentlemen of the Colony of Virginia, for bringing me here. I am here to help you solve some of your problems with slaves. Your invitation reached me on my modest plantation in the West Indies, where I have experimented with some of the newest, and still the oldest, methods for control of slaves. Ancient Rome would envy us if my program is implemented. As our boat sailed south on the James River, named for our illustrious King, whose version of the Bible we cherish, I saw enough to know that your problem is not unique. While Rome used cords of wood as crosses for standing human bodies along its highways in great numbers, you are here using the tree and the rope on occasions. I caught the whiff of a dead slave hanging from a tree, a couple miles back. You are not only losing valuable stock by hangings, you are having uprisings, slaves are running away, your crops are sometimes left in the fields too long for maximum profit, you suffer occasional fires, your animals are killed. Gentlemen, you know what your problems are; I do not need to elaborate. I am not here to enumerate your problems, I am here to introduce you to a method of solving them. In my bag here, I have a full proof method for controlling your black slaves. I guarantee every one of y hundred ou that, if installed correctly, it will control the slaves for at least 300 years. My method is simple. Any member of your family or your overseer can use it. I have outlined a number of differences among the slaves; and I take theses differences and make them bigger. I use fear, distrust and envy for control purposes. These methods have worked on my modest plantation in the West Indies and it will work throughout the South. Take this simple little list of differences and think about them.

On top of my list is "Age," but it's there only because it starts with an "a." The second is "Color" or shade. There is "Intelligence, Size, Sex, Sizes of Plantations, Status on Plantations, Attitude of owners, whether the slaves live in the valley, on a hill, East, West, North, South, have fine hair, course hair, or is tall or short.

Now that you have a list of differences, I shall give you an outline of action, but before that, I shall assure you that Distrust is Stronger than Trust and Envy is Stronger than Adulation, Respect or Admiration. The Black slaves after receiving this indoctrination shall carry on and will become self-refueling and self-generating for hundreds of years, maybe Thousands. Don't forget, you must pitch the Old black male vs. the Young black male, and the Young black male against the Old black male. You must use the Dark skin slaves vs. the Light skin slaves, and the Light skin slaves vs. the Dard skin slaves. You must use the Female vs. the Male, and the Male vs. the Female. You must also have white servants and overseers [who] distrust all Blacks. But it is Necessary that your slaves Trust and Depend on us. They must Love, Respect and Trust only us. Gentlemen, these kits are your keys to control. Use them. Have your wives and children use them, never miss an opportunity. If used intensely for one year, the slaves themselves will remain perpetually distrustful. Thank you gentlemen."

This was the first time blacks were pit against blacks. They were put in every opposing category. One classification would be favored over the other, creating jealousy and dissention among other things superiority and inferiority complexes.

Them few pages stapled together got deep on me. I read them and went to sleep like Whoa! The next day he slid me something about Harriet Tubman and her underground railroad. I used to hear about it growing up and for some reason I thought it was literally underground and was maybe not a train but at least some kinda little contraption that moved on the tracks. But anyway what I was reading was talking about some of the slaves being so psychologically conditioned into thinking they were being taken good care of even though it was nowhere close to the lifestyles of the slave masters. They were so brainwashed that when Harriet Tubman showed up to the plantations to sneak them into freedom in the north she had to pull a gun on many of them and give them ultimatums.

"You coming with me to be free or you dying right here tonite."

I looked at Pops and told him, "This shit is cool to know but on the real, all that stuff is over. Ain't no slave masters or non-a-that shit no more."

He said, "Son the greatest trick the Devil ever pulled was convincing the world he didn't exist."

He let me chew on that for a minute, then he said, "The slave masters don't look the same but they're still there.

Nowadays they look like school teachers and politicians and a lot of them are even black."

"Black! What you mean?!" I wanted to say, *You crazy as fuck!* But I had already figured out this old man wasn't. He said the plantations were still around too but they didn't look the same. He said we were in one as we speak. I was rejecting the shit he was telling me simply because it was my first time hearing it, and some stuff he was telling me was the opposite of what I'd learned already. I gave his ass a hard time but he wasn't tripping. He understood. He understood everything and his mind was on point. Me on the other hand understood nothing and was confused. He was pulling out printouts and showing me pages in books where sections were highlighted. Did I tell you he was on point? He had a Bible and a Koran and knew them both back and forth. He showed me some scriptures but he said religious faith was a dangerous subject to discuss. He said none of it had anything to do with logic and to always remember faith and fear are the most powerful forces that move people.

He wasn't all just about knowledge, knowledge, knowledge either.

He had stories for days about how he used to get down in the street before he got locked up thirty three years ago. He told me how he got caught up on the case that got him here.

It was 1975. A few years after the Lakers won their first championship. A dark brown 1974 Cadillac pulled out the parking lot of one of the few surviving speakeasy clubs left on Central Avenue on the east side of town. It was called the Black Hollywood. Three heads were in the car, they all had liquor on their breath and a plan on their minds. They took Vernon Avenue. It took them from L.A.'s eastside to its west. Mack was in the passenger seat he had a half an ounce of cocaine in his jacket pocket. His Caucasian customers in Baldwin Village requested it. Baldwin Village nicknamed "the jungle" is completely an apartment community at the foot of Baldwin Hills. The streets were no more than a maze full of dead ends that stretched from La Brea to the back of the Baldwin Hills Plaza more commonly known as the Crenshaw Mall (which actually wasn't there at this time) The area was still predominately white at this time which gave the police good enough reason to stop a car carrying three blacks. The officer blinded the occupants of the car with their searchlights and flashlights as they approached the car.

Although the driver produced registration and a valid license they still made him get out of the car. Mack stuck the wallet and the bag of coke deep down in his pocket. The rear passenger Lionel stuck his Saturday night special .38 revolver under the front seat. Mack heard the metal gun clank on the metal under the seat and automatically knew what it was, but he said nothing. He'd deal with Lionel if they got to continue on their journey. They could hear Raymond complaining about being harassed because he was black. They heard an officer holler for the passenger to exit the vehicle. Mack knew they were talking about him but he hadn't figured out what his next move was yet. He told Lionel to get out first. Lionel did as he was told for more reason than any to put distance between him and the gun and the drugs, especially the gun.

Raymond was yelling, calling the cops racist. When Lionel got to the back near the other cop, the officer gestured to the trunk. He wanted them to open it so he could search it.

Raymond swung at the cop's head. The cop ducked but didn't calculate the second half of the combination. The left fist caught the officer in the top of the head followed by a right knee *that raised him backup in line for another right, left set. He was out before he hit the ground.*

Two slugs from the other officer's gun went through Raymond's abdomen and out of his back. Lionel broke into a run down the street but before he could duck behind something three shots rang out and two of them lodged in him, one in his shoulder and one in the back of his neck.

Mack watched from the passenger seat horrified.

The officer turned his attention to Mack. He was already juiced from shooting the other two. One more nigger was even more brownie points. They locked eyes for a second. Mack knew there was at least one more bullet in the gun. Then in a quick move the cop ran and plucked the weapon from the holster of his unconscious partner, he walked up to the car firing into the passenger seat. Mack was already in the back laying on the floor. The cop noticed the seat was empty he quickly perused the proximity to see if Mack had managed to get out of the car while he was reaching for his partner's gun. Then the back window exploded. The bullet that blew out the window went wild. The cop jumped almost out of his skin from the fright, then he looked in the back to see where to plant his bullets. All he saw was one of the four flashes that preceded the bullets that entered his face.

Mack had me hanging from his every word. He said there must've been another police car real close by because before he could get out the car they were on him. He said rumors circulated that he was killed in the incident.

He knew he could never beat the case and once he lost the case he would never get out of prison. So he never communicated with anybody on the outside to clarify the rumors. To the streets he was dead, but I was looking at a man who was very much alive.

After seven years he'd gotten an appeal, and was somehow able to bail out during the process. He'd spent one year on the street before he was remanded for so far the next twenty five years.

He told me that he wasn't in the SHU for fucking up. He'd been around too long to be a fuck up. He said he checks himself in from time to time to get away from the people and the system that he was stuck with. He said sometimes a man needs to be alone to think straight sometimes fifteen minutes a day or before you make a move is sufficient he said sometimes you need a whole day, days, weeks, months depending how deep you need to think and how many things you need to think about. He said unfortunately the average man doesn't have that kind of time. But Mack did. Then eventually he'd miss the same things he was once trying to escape from and that's when he would return to the general population, always with a better understanding. He reached under his bed, got a book and handed it to me.

"Read this Son." he said.

The title of it was the Isis Paper written by a woman named Dr. Francis Cres Welsing. I fluffed up my pillow and got comfortable, then turned to the first page.

RICH KID

A couple of miles up the cab driver asked me again what the name of the Mexican restaurant was. I told him. He had snapped me out of my daydream. Mary Jay was looking so damn good on that bed, I wished I coulda just hit that for the rest of the evening, with her thick ass. She seems like a freak too for the fact of all the shit she did, I know I could fuck and it ain't gonna take long either.

MARY JAY

I called the front desk and asked them if the cab my husband got into was still outside. They didn't know Rich Kid wasn't my husband and I knew the cab had been gone already ten minutes. When they told me it was already gone I told them that I couldn't call him because he forgot his cell phone and I was to meet him in a little while but I couldn't remember the name of the restaurant and for them to call the dispatcher and have them call the unit to find out for me. I used my phone sex voice and told the guy I would appreciate it. He called me back in less than five minutes.

I wrote the name of the restaurant down on the same paper with the name Papi and the number that came up on Rich Kid's cell phone or should I say Dion Davis like it says on his California driver's license. I went down to my car first and I threw out the weed and ashes. That stuff makes you lazy. That's why I don't smoke it for real. Then I got my make-up kit out of the trunk. My make-up kit is the size of a large suitcase. I have enough make up and wigs to make me look like any nationality on earth. Some just take longer and more preparation but I can do it. I was going for the Maria Jimenez look this evening. In an hour I was ready.

145

CHAPTER SEVENTEEN

TANYA

When I walked through the doors of TSL Investments, I smiled and was greeted by Stephen. Stephen Hill was a brotha who had caramel colored skin and a great smile. Stephen was the only black male at the company. He stood at around six feet tall and his muscular build always looked good. The way he filled out an Armani suit often left women fantasizing about what was beneath. His dreds were pulled back into a neat ponytail.

"Hi." I said, giggling nervously.

"Hello." he replied.

Talking to Dr. Hunt had helped me, if only a little. I felt lighter, at least now I knew that I had help to figure it out. I told Stephen I'd talk to him later.

Once in the privacy of my office I began working on the resort account. The end of the day came quickly and I headed home.

I took a few shortcuts and got home a little quicker than usual. A smile pierced my lips when I saw Malcolm's truck. I pulled up and looked inside the truck.

Where is he? I thought to myself. Then I remembered he had a key, he must be in the house. I'd forgotton because he barely used it.

146

Soft music was playing when I stepped through the door. Candles were lit and rose petals covered the hard wood floor. I followed the trails of the rose petals which led me to the bathroom.

The Jacuzzi tub was filled with an inviting bubble bath. There was a tray filled with chocolate covered strawberries and wine nestled on the floor right next to the tub. Just as I was turning around I felt strong, muscular arms enveloped me. I smiled as I got comfortable in Malcolm's arms. He lit a blunt of nice weed and we rotated it back and forth for a minute. When he could tell I was high, he nibbled on my ear and a guttural moan escaped me. The pheromones I released where turning him on but this night was about me, and Malcolm would take his time in pleasing me. The direct contact was making me want him. No, at that moment I needed him.

Slowly he began taking my clothes off. I stood before him in the nude, self conscious about my body. I stepped into his arms and wrapped mines around his muscular build. I put a few tender kisses on his neck and made his manhood as hard as a rock. He reached down and rubbed my vagina, I almost pushed him back but I caught myself and relaxed. He didn't notice my apprehension. He began massaging my vagina lips gently. I moaned, he went in close and kissed my clit but I was quick to stop him.

147

He said, "Tonight is all about you, and I am going to take good care of you. Now enjoy your bath while I finish cooking."

I walked away to catch my breath and went to get a hairpin off of the sink. I lifted the bathroom window and took a look out of it. There were three young white boys arguing in the backyard over the fence. They were getting louder and louder. I could hear that the argument was about methamphetamine and oxycodone. They were very loud like they were coming through the window.

Suddenly, Malcolm appeared behind me with a small pistol in his hand. He moved me out of the way and looked out the window. Straight up, by any means necessary, Malcolm X pose. When he realized that there was no threat to me he closed the window.

I looked at him in awe then said, "What the hell are you doing with a gun?! Not only do you have a gun but you have a gun in my house!"

"Relax baby, I'm here for you."

I couldn't take my eyes off of the gun.

"Malcolm, I don't feel comfortable with that thing in your hand."

"Okay, no problem, I'll put it up."

"Thank you. Where are you going to put it?"

Without a word he stuck it in his pants.

148

I kept staring at him.

"What?" he asked.

"That aint gonna get it!"

"Alright, when we finish eating I'll put it in my truck."

I walked into my bedroom and said, "Why don't you put it somewhere out of the way right now, like in a drawer or something."

I looked around the room quickly then walked over to my armoire and pulled out my underwear drawer.

"Put that thing in here."

He did as I asked and headed back to the kitchen looking like a kid who was just reprimanded for being bad.

Although I was apprehensive, I consciously knew that Malcolm was just trying to be there for me.

I went back into the bathroom, and got into the tub, I rested my head on the back of the Jacuzzi. I could smell the food in the air. Finally I could unwind from the day's hectic work schedule.

The water was steaming hot, just like I liked it. As I washed my body I visualized Malcolm doing it for me. I washed up then laid back, just relaxing for a minute.

A woman could get used to coming home to this, I thought.

A light tap resonated throughout the bathroom.

"Come in." I said through the door.

He cracked the door open.

"Dinner will be ready in about ten minutes."

I thanked him and as soon as he closed the door I climbed out.

When I stepped through the door of the kitchen my senses picked up a good wiff of dinner, I took a seat at the table.

"Smells good."

Malcolm wore a pair of basketball shorts and no shirt. I couldn't help but to admire his biceps and triceps. His gym regiment kept him in tip top shape.

I looked around my kitchen. The stainless steel appliances, granite countertops, cherry wood cabinets and hardwood floor had been personally picked and remodeled to my liking. The kitchen was the only room in the house I didn't like when I purchased it, so I totally gutted it out and made it into something that showed my personality and would be more suitable for me. My kitchen looked like something out of Architectual Digest magazine. The only thing I was missing was a chef.

I watched Malcolm prepare the plates in awe. When I saw what Malcolm had done I was speechless.

Baked chicken, rice, red beans and corn with garnishments on the side.

I said he missed his true calling. He should have been a chef because he could really throw down in the kitchen. He didn't miss a beat. Once he finished making the meal, he made two hefty plates and walked over to the table.

"You like?" he asked.

"Very much." I replied.

He'd gone through all the trouble and I wanted to show him how much I appreciated him.

"Thank you." I replied subtly after he poured me a glass of Merlot and placed my plate in front of me.

The moment was perfect. As we ate, he couldn't stop looking at me. The lust in his eyes made me shiver. Malcolm reached under the table and rubbed my thigh. The weed had me ready.

Malcolm leaned back in the chair, slipped his middle finger in and out of me and was turned on by the squishy sounds he heard. He stood from the chair and he led me to the bedroom.

Once we made it to the bedroom he pushed me back onto the king sized bed, looked in my eyes and said, "I just want to please you."

With a timid look on my face I leaned back and Malcolm was in charge. Malcolm pulled at his shorts and his nine inch dick instantly popped out. He was as hard as a rock. I groaned. He licked his lips and dropped to his knees.

He wrapped his lips around my little pink bud. He suckled on it a few times. Inconspicuously, I peeped down and saw him going to town on me. I should have gotten great pleasure but something inhibited me. He should have been turning me on but he didn't and I was almost embarrassed about it. He gave his dick a few strokes before he told me to scoot over on the bed. I did as I was told and laid flat on my back. When he thought I was ready he positioned himself on top of me to sink deep inside of my wet and tight center. Just before he stuck his dick inside of me, the phone rang.

"Let the machine get it." he said.

He slipped inside of me then pumped once and the phone rang again. The machine picked up and we heard a nurse's voice. She was calling from Memphis Hospital and the first person I thought about was my grandmother.

I pushed Malcolm off of me and eagerly reached for the phone and answered.

"Hello?" I said.

"I'm looking for Tanya Glass?"

"This is she." I said, a little impatient.

"You need to get to the hospital as soon as possible!" the nurse said urgently.

"What's wr-wrong?" I stammered. I had already gotten up and now I was fumbling through my dresser, trying to find something, anything to throw on.

My heart was beating so fast I thought it was going to jump out of my chest. I could hear my heart beat. Big beads of sweat rolled down my forehead and hit my top lip. I could taste the salty residue. My breathing became staggered and it felt as if the room was closing in on me. Was I having a panic attack?

"I can't talk to you over the phone. Just get here as soon as possible." The nurse said then ended the call. Malcolm sat straight up in bed.

"What's wrong Baby?" he asked.

"I need to get to the hospital right now!"

CHAPTER EIGHTEEN

RICH KID

When I got out of the cab in front of the restaurant the first thing I saw was that girl I fucked the first time I was here. She still looked like Selena. Some dude was arguing at her. I can't speak Spanish but I could tell by the body language that he was on some jealous shit.

I thought, *All races have the-tryna turn a hoe into a housewife-situations.*

Another dude walked out of the club and pinched her ass on the way to his car. The first dude tackled him.

I went in the restaurant laughing. Papi was sitting at a table with a younger Mexican guy. I saw a female come up from under the table by Papi wiping her mouth and headed to the back toward the bathroom. I watched her little cute butt cheeks peeking from the bottom of her tiny shorts. But before she could make it two guys that came in the back door stopped her. One introduced her to the other as he put his arm around her like she was his girlfriend then he French kissed her for about a full minute savoring the juices of her mouth.

Yuck!

I sat down at the table with Papi and the young guy. He was about my age. There was an empty bottle of Patron

Tequila on the table and another one they had worked halfway down. Papi introduced us. The young man's name was Hector, he was Papi's nephew, so I guess that made him Gabrielle's cousin. The first thing Hector told me was that he liked to do business professionally. That was cool with me because so do I. He said he was waiting on someone named Big Will that he deals with but wouldn't be any more after today. He was pissed because Big Will was already an hour late. He was supposed to have gotten here before me. He said that Big Will's turn around time had slowed down so he was passing me his unprofessional lightweight, and evidently Papi thought it was a good idea. Hector said Big Will was good for five bricks a week at first but his last pick up had been three weeks ago. I didn't say anything, I just listened. When Papi began talking he said that the main reason for the meeting was to introduce me to Hector because he was stepping back from the game. He had a feeling he was hot, like the feds were trying to get close to him. From now on I was to deal with Hector. Just like that I picked up a new source and a new outlet. Two mutha fuckas I didn't know. I didn't like that but what was I supposed to do, tell Papi 'fuck that'? I don't really think so.

About the time my tongue was getting a little loose from the third bottle of Patron, warm enough to tell Papi I didn't like the new arrangements, Big Will came in and sat down. His demeanor was shady which confirmed my apprehension. He looked like he hustled no doubt, but the grimey type, not even really in his appearance though, his appearance was up to par. He had about ten neat cornrolls to the back and a stocky build, crisp jeans, fresh all white sneakers, the shadiness was in his eyes. Maybe even a couple tattooed tear drops under his eyes (murders) but I said nothing, just extended my hand for a handshake. His mask had a smile on. Hector got right to the business of letting him know what everybody else already knew, I was his new go-to man. I read the look on his face, at first I was trippin' because I thought it would look similar to mine when I found out about the arrangements but it was the opposite. Then I figured out that it was more of a relief because he thought he was getting cut completely off, the professional way, over dinner.

I got the feeling I was breathing the same air with people like that. People that would have dinner with you knowing that they weren't going to let you make it home alive, maybe not the people at my table, hopefully not the people at my table.

Big Will was content to know he was still in the mix. I already made plans to deal with him on my terms. No consignment and no business after six in the evening.

Hector never introduced Papi as the Man. He didn't introduce him at all, and Papi just sat back, ate and drank like he was just a freeloading tag along. Me and Big Will exchanged phone numbers and watched a few bitches work the room with such finesse that if you didn't know then you wouldn't have known. Selena was one of them.

Big Will downed a couple of glasses then got up to leave. He said he had business to take care of and he probably would be getting with me soon. Then he was gone. Gone before the alcohol could open him up. That was what I wanted to see and hear.

Thirty minutes later me, Papi and Hector walked out together. They were parked in the back, they both had Dodge Ram trucks but nothing indicated that they had the Hemi motor in them. Papi's was black and stock. Hector's was candy green flake with twenty-six inch rims on it. I was riding with Papi. Before the engines started, one of the Mexican girls from inside came out and walked in between the trucks. She was saying some sexy shit in Spanish. She was pretty, looked mixed, had green eyes and a mole on the top of her lip.

Papi told me she was talking about fucking one, two or even all three of us if the money was right. That's one thing I liked about the girls at this place, they kept it all the way real. They wasted no time playing games like the bitches in the hood, when it still boiled down to the same thing, if you paying you can fuck.

Papi looked at his watch to see if he had enough time to spare. She dug into her purse for something and it fell to the ground, stuff spilled out everywhere. She bent down and started retrieving things. She had on a form fitting red silky dress. No skin was showing but her curves were plain to see. She actually had a body that most black girls died in and most Mexicans would die for. We didn't even think to help her. We all preferred hanging out of the windows gawking. Papi was hanging all over my shoulder and shit. He almost fell out when she reached to get something from beneath the truck and then again when she reached under Hector's. She got all her stuff and came back up she started smiling and talking again.

I wondered what she was going in her purse for when it fell, she seemed to have changed her mind. She was smiling but now Hector and Papi were not.

I asked Papi, "What's up?"

He said, "She's crazy." as he put the gear shifter in reverse and burned a little rubber backing out of the space.

"She's crazy?" I said puzzled.

He said, "She wants to see two men…you know…"

He didn't want to say it. I assumed she was pro-homosexual. He put the truck in drive, Hector did the same. I stared at her as we left.

Damn! I thought on the way up the block. *I could work with that.*

MARY JAY

It took about forty-five minutes to get all dolled up mamacita style. I practiced my Spanish all the while. The make-up took the longest. Men have no idea. They think we wear make-up just to hide bad skin but they don't know that if applied with expertise it can make your features look different. I even added an ole Marilyn Monroe mole on my lip, shit like that takes attention away from other areas.

As an afterthought I picked out a pair of contacts to top off the look. I could look my best friend in the face and she wouldn't recognize me. I slid myself into a dress that was too tight on me five pounds ago. I went to the mirror and fastened on a long black straight wig with a slight wave to it. On the way out the door I stepped into some flat uppers. I'm already 5'7", some heels would not be conducive to my disguise. Most Mexican women are 5'7" in 6" heels.

I swung by a Starbucks for my drug of choice and went to the restaurant. It was more of a social place than I thought. There was a dance floor. I had already been there thirty minutes when a big black braided dopeboy came in and sat with Dion... I mean Rich Kid, another older man I assumed was Papi and another fella.

I was getting a lot of cold looks from a lot of the other girls although they were trying to remain cordial in front of the men. I guess in every race women feel threatened by the presence of a new pretty face.

I went outside to try to pick out the new arrival's vehicle. Call me psychic but the blue 300c Chrysler with the blue bandana hanging from the rearview and XXL hip hop magazine on the backseat was his. I memorized the license plate number and went back inside. They were eating hearty and opening another bottle of Patron.

I played the background as much as I could. I dipped into the restroom a couple of times to waste some time. I had surveyed the back parking lot and couldn't figure out what the other two were driving so I had to wait until they showed me.

On my third dip into the ladies room I was followed by a very healthy young thing that took off her heels as soon as she walked in. She glanced around to make sure we were alone and locked the door. She took two steps toward me with a finger pointing at me like she was going to tell me a thing or three. She had taken her shoes off in case she had to kick my ass. I didn't want to hear it so I took two steps toward her and doubled her speed to get to me in half the time.

I put hands and elbows on her, once each clockwise. She was out on her feet. She fell stiff like somebody pushed over a life size statue. I drug her into a stall then looked in the mirror to check myself, not a hair was out of place. I did chip a nail on my pinky though but I ain't gonna complain, babygirl in the stall had bigger problems.

When I walked out of the restroom and headed back into the dining area I passed up my three boys on their way out. I didn't want to seem obvious so I made a round through the restaurant and then out the back. Men are predictable. Pussy has taken down more men than all drugs combined. I did the same thing to them that magicians do to their audiences, misdirection. I gave them my ass to watch while I planted magnetic GPS tracking under their trucks then I made them feel like they dismissed me.

CHAPTER NINETEEN

TANYA

My grandma was in the hospital. I was frozen with shock and fear. I was at a loss for words. Tears formed in my eyes. I had to get to the hospital.

I finally jumped up and threw on a pair of worn blue jeans and a tank top. Quickly I pulled my long black locks back into a ponytail and slid my feet into a pair of thongs. When I was done, Malcolm was waiting for me in the living room.

"You ready?" he asked, standing from the leather couch.

Solemnly, I shook my head. I tried to speak but no words escaped my lips. Thinking about my poor grandma brought tears to my eyes. I loved her so much. She took me in, raised me and showed me true and unconditional love. My mother certainly wasn't able to do the job but my grandma had filled a much needed void when I needed it the most.

Malcolm made his way toward me and rubbed my arms.

"Everything's going to be alright." he said soothingly.

I closed my eyes, trying not to cry. I squeezed them shut, trying to keep the tears from falling. I wanted to believe him but something deep within me told me everything wasn't going to be alright.

Frantically, I ran through the emergency room doors of Memphis Hospital. My breathing was staggered. I could hardly catch my breath. If anything happened to my grandma I would probably loose my mind. Stopping at the nurse's station, I asked for Helena Glass' room number.

"Ma'am, are you alright?" the younger nurse asked.

Just then some paramedics rushed through the door with a trauma patient. The patient was transported in a helicopter from Atlanta, GA. which was a state over. Memphis Hospital had a new young brain surgeon. If the patient was able to be stabilized long enough to make the trip then there was an 80% chance that the young doctor could save them and a 50% chance that they would recover fully.

The paramedics almost knocked me down in their haste to save the man. One of them looked my body up and down. Usually looking neat, I felt I looked terrible at the moment because I left the house so quickly.

I looked back at the nurse and said, "I'm looking for my grandma."

"Ma'am, take a seat and the doctor will come out to talk to you."

I noticed the uneasy looks being shared between the nurses and I was growing even more nervous. I felt like I was about to throw up. Bile rose from the pit of my stomach to my throat.

"Oh, my God, what's wrong?" I asked.

I was growing hysterical so the younger nurse gave me a bottled water and led me to the waiting room. Malcolm soon appeared and took a seat next to me.

Shortly after, a fairly young Caucasian doctor with curly hair stepped into the waiting room. He was tall, at least six feet. I couldn't read his expression.

"Tanya Glass." he said crisply into the air of the waiting room.

I stood immediately and went to the doctor. He looked down at his papers and began shuffling through them.

"Helena Glass is your grandmother?" he asked, before looking up at me.

"Yeah, she's my grandma."

"Okay, Mrs. Glass has a serious case of breast cancer and it's gotten into her lymph nodes and mastastisized and has spread throughout her body."

My knees turned into jelly. I felt like I was about to fall but I had to be strong, at least for my grandma. I knew Ma was hiding something that day I took her to the doctor but never did I think it was so bad.

"We're trying to get her to take chemotherapy but your grandma's a feisty one. She won't hear of it and I'll be straight with you so you'll know, if she doesn't begin chemotherapy there's little chance for her to live much longer."

My voice was caught in my throat. I stumbled a little and my hands went up to my heart. Death was so final and I didn't know what I'd do if I lost my grandma.

Lord, how would I convince Ma to change her mind? Ma was as stubborn as a mule.

The doctor looked at me expectantly.

"Wh-where is she?" I stammered. "I just want to see her and maybe I can talk to her about it."

"Room 321, good luck Miss Glass." he said before I hurried off. The elevator ride was the longest one I'd ever taken. I had so much on my mind. I had to sort some things out and I had to convince my grandma to take the treatments.

I couldn't fathom losing her. When I exited the elevator I was right in front of the room. My legs felt like weights and I was scared to step in. I was used to seeing Ma strong and I could barely stomach seeing her fragile.

Silently, I said a little prayer before stepping into the room. Ma was pale. She was hooked up to several tubes.

"Ma." I called softly.

I sat on the edge of the bed and grabbed Ma's small and wrinkled hand.

"Everything's going to be alright." I said, trying to convince myself as much as I was trying to convince Ma.

Ma looked at me and gave me a weak smile that didn't quite reach her eyes.

I'm sorry for not telling you Ladybug. Ma signed with her hands.

I smiled at the mention of the childhood name Ma had given to me.

"You got your own life ta live an' I dont want ta cause any strife in yo life so I didn't tell you." Ma said, weakly.

"Ma, you are my life!" I said, looking into her pretty brown eyes.

Ma meant everything to me and I wasn't about to lose her without a fight. All my life she'd raised me to try, it wasn't in her to give up.

"Ma, the doctors said chemo is your lifeline. Why not take a chance and get treated? Without you I don't know what I would do." I begged.

I was helpless and really didn't know what to do.

Ma said, "Always just put God in as your first ingredient Chile. The good Lord has given me seventy-five years an' in dat time I've been very blessed an' if it's my time den it's my time. I will not run from death." she said with finality.

"Ma, I just don't want to lose you." I whispered.

"You leave all things sooner or later as well as life as we know it Chile."

A tear rolled down my face and Ma looked away. Tears clouded her eyes too.

"I don't want you to leave me. What about your great grandkids? They'll need you."

Incredulously, Ma looked at me. I had never talked about kids before and really I didn't want any, but I'd do anything to get Ma to take chemotherapy.

"Please don't have no babies with that damn Malcolm. He ain't nothing but trouble." Ma warned.

I knew Ma was serious because Ma never liked him.

"Ma, would you consider doing the therapy for me?" I begged some more.

I looked at Ma, hope brimming from my teary eyes.

"My baby." she whispered, patting my hand.

For now, I dropped the subject and we talked for another thirty minutes before Ma started yawning.

Like a baby, I cradled Ma in my arms until she fell asleep and just before leaving the room I kissed Ma on the cheek.

Ma mumbled something that was incoherent. But with her weak hands she signed, *I will always watch over you Ladybug.* I smiled and walked to the door. Just before leaving the room I turned back around and smiled.

Malcolm met me by the exit doors.

"How is she?" he asked.

Before I could answer I broke down.

Malcolm held me for a while then got me back home. I went straight upstairs to my bedroom, undressed and took a glance out of the window. The neighbor was dragging a big black plastic bag across his backyard to his garden.

Fertilizer. I thought to myself.

I climbed under my sheets and thought about life. The meaning of it all and the decision my grandma would ultimately make.

The sound of Three Six Mafia's first CD started blasting throughout my house. Juicy J and DJ Paul were cool but I wasn't in the mood for that. My blood began boiling. I threw back the covers and went down into the living room. Not bothering to tell Malcolm to cut the radio down I stormed over to the stereo myself and shut the power off.

Malcolm was lying back on the couch with his eyes closed and a blunt in his hand but as soon as I cut that radio off he jumped up.

"What you doing?" he asked.

"I don't want to hear that shit! My grandma is on her death bed and there's nothing I can do to help her."

My voice began trembling and I was about to cry, but not before asking Malcolm to leave. He stood up and made his way over to me. Rubbing my arms tenderly he apologized but the sentiment came just a little too late. He'd been inconsiderate and I just wanted to be alone. He tried to protest but he knew I was serious just by the way I looked at him.

As soon as he left I secured my lock and went back to bed. I just wanted to sleep. Maybe, just maybe, this would all just be a bad dream...

The little girl was tired of her mother's many boyfriends, or Uncles as she was made to call them, flirting with her. As usual her mother had passed out from being so high.

Suddenly, her stomach started doing somersaults and she felt sick as a dog. She was backed up and she thought about running.

"Don't be difficult." the voice echoed, reaching out for her.

The room felt smaller than it already was. She felt like she was about to suffocate, like she couldn't breathe. The little girl wanted her mother, yearned for her mother's love and protection.

Here she was, ten years old trying to fight for her virginity. Finally she'd backed up as far as she could go. Her back was against the dingy yellow wall. Two huge grimy hands reached for her, she turned her head in great disdain. After pulling down her shorts, the hands ripped her small Dora panties off in one swift motion.

"No!" she screamed.

I jumped up before the alarm clock sounded. I was nearly hyperventilating. I looked around in the darkness and quickly reached over and cut on the lamp that sat on my cherry colored nightstand.

"Not another dream." I muttered.

My t-shirt was drenched with sweat, so were my sheets and my hair. Sweat poured down my forehead, I looked over at the clock.

Three a.m.

It was too early for me to get up. I still had three more hours of sleep to try and get. I closed my eyes, tried going back to sleep, but I couldn't.

The dreams were taking a toll on me and something had to give.

CHAPTER TWENTY

BIG WILL

"Uh, oh yeah, oh yeah…" When I started cumming my foot had the gas pedal to the floor. Good thing the engine wasn't on. I was sitting in my car in front of Tracy's house in Hollywood. His boyfriend was in the house so he polished me off in the car.

"Oh shit, oh yeah, ahh, oh yeah, uh huh, uh huh, oh yeah…"

Tracy sucks like a machine. I had my arms cupped around his head like a football so he couldn't run from my gush when I erupted.

"Whoa!"

It felt Magnificent!

Gush! Gush! Gush!

Another job well done. He took a swig of his diet Pepsi and swished it around in his mouth before he swallowed.

After I tucked my jimmy back in my pants, I reached in the backseat and patted the bag he'd brung me with the $25,000 in it. I gave him a deal to make sure he'd get them quick. I grabbed the bag with two kilos in it and handed it to him. He started for his house, I started my car.

I took Hollywood Blvd. to La Brea Blvd. made a right then cruised down La Brea feeling relieved, relieved cause I got some good head and busted a good nut, relieved cause I finally got off them last two keys and relieved that Hector didn't cut me off.

I been getting them thangs from Hector for $10,000 for about six months and my money been looking right ever since, that is until some of my main players got killed. I was gonna get the ball back rolling though. I just hoped this nigga Rich Kid didn't start acting funny.

When I walked into the restaurant he was looking at me funny. At first I thought maybe he was back up for Hector, him and the other dude who was acting like he really wasn't paying attention. Sometimes when shit starts moving slow your connect starts acting funny, they act like they don't understand that it be like that sometimes.

I had my .357 in my pocket, cocked and off safety. Same one I shot Keno and Tony with.

If this fake reggaeton ass mutha fucka Hector woulda tried to cut off my supply, I woulda deaded all three of 'em. But it's all good though, I was still in, matter-a-fact I called Rich Kid right then and set something up for five of them thangs. I got out my phone and sent an alert on his chirp. He hit me right back.

"What's up. Who is this?"

"This is Big Will. What's good Baby?"

"Oh alright. I gotta program your name in my phone. what's up?"

"Let's break the ice with five of them joints."

He didn't reply to that.

He just said, "I'ma talk to you tomorrow morning."

I thought maybe he was one of them hustlers that didn't like to do nothing in the evening. But what if I wasn't one of them kinda hustlers? Why hold me up?

But I just said, "Aight Kid. It's your world." and hung up.

I had nothing planned for the rest of the night so I just cruised, I made a left on Santa Monica and was disgusted by the sight. Santa Monica Blvd. is famous or maybe I should say infamous for prostituting transvestites. Remember Eddie Murphy and his chick with a dick? Guess what street he picked him up on. They were everywhere. If you see a hoe walking down the street, believe me it ain't your traditional hoe. These Mutha Fuckas make my stomach turn. I couldn't stand it. I started cursing at them. I even pulled out my gun on a lot of 'em and made 'em run then I turned off on another main street. I hate when dudes try to look like women.

CHAPTER TWENTY-ONE

KENO

I came back from the little gated off 10' by 10' yard they let us go to once a week then I finished reading. It took me three days to digest the book Mack gave me named The Isis Papers. I told 'im that it was deep but that he had told me about some modern day slave masters and that's what I was looking for the whole time but didn't find.

He said, "I gotta show you some things first so you can understand why people do what they do. Did you get what she was telling you?"

"Yeah, she was talking about the problems white people face with extinction. Number one, because they have zero population growth which meant that as fast as newborns were coming into the world (they are not natural breeders, there's usually 1-3 children born to a couple.) they were losing an equal number or more to death by old age, accidents, illness, etc.

"The book also talked about the fact that every time a baby is mixed with black genes that baby is considered black, so the blackman's dick... I mean his male genitalia is considered a weapon with the potential of offing... I mean, decimating the white race. Talk bout weapons of mass destruction, then she says in retaliation they created the gun,

175

in desperation they promote racism, promote it to avoid mix breeding."

He looked satisfied with my little summary. He was smiling. I gotta keep it real, he was teaching me shit that I never knew, and the cold part about it was none of the books he had were new. Some were older than me. I told him that just the amount of books in one of his stacks I never read in my life.

"Why do you think that is?"

"Because it's always something better I could be doing."

"Like what?"

"I don't know, playin' ball or video games, choppin' up game with the homies, bumpin' some music, getting' pussy, most of all gettin' paid."

"Which one of those is gonna make you become a better man?"

"That pussy." I said immediately, laughing.

He gave me a half a smile.

"Come on Pops, you been down a cool minute. That pussy is a major part of life, matter-a-fact, I'm tryna hit something in the visiting room first chance I get. But the C.O.'s be paying attention to you too tough when you visiting from the SHU."

"Tell me something Son, when you were on the street, how did you treat black women before and after getting pussy? Did you throw money at them? Did you flash materialistic things at them to get them in the bed and how about afterwards? Do you leave them with empty promises and move on to the next like you're trying to hump them all?

"Hold up Mack, I hear what you sayin' but they be on some bullshit too. If you ain't shining or paying they look at you like you less of a man."

"You're right. It was just a question I asked. I'm not condemning you because I was guilty of it myself, well not the way you guys are acting now-a-days, which I'm going to tell you is totally wrong. You guys are acting like the savage white slave masters. You guys disrespect the black women worse than any other human. Your dogs get treated better, then yall leave 'em to raise your children with the misrepresented view of you and herself. The child or children she raises are going to be little yous and little hers. The women are messed up too and we men are to blame for that. Since the beginning of time women have flocked to the man that was shining but they came to be protected, taken care of, to bear children for a strong man but now when they flock, you guys fuck 'em and feed 'em fish as we used to say. Then she finds another man and he fucks her and shits on her too. After a few years of that, she's kicking herself out directly or indirectly even if she has a good man, but like I said I'm not condemning you because I'm guilty of being flashy to catch women's attention too but I was a lover man. I bedded many women, made 'em feel like Queens when I did but I just never settled down.

I got a daughter out of the deal though, she is the only person I communicate with in the outside world. Her mom is just a woman that I got it on with a few times while I was out on appeal. I saw my daughter one time after she was born and not long after that I came inside for the last time. Her mother died when my daughter was young but old enough to stay in touch with me on her own. She's about twenty five now."

He seemed like he was reminiscing on his former life for a minute, then he snapped out of it and started talking about how the modern slave masters were black, then he reached down under his bed and grabbed a book and handed it to me. The name of it was The Miseducation of the Negro by a man named Carter G. Woodson.

I really didn't feel like reading this shit. I wanted to talk about females more but I said. "Fuck it." I realized I was in school so I laid back and opened the book. Before I got passed the acknowledgements a C.O. screamed my name from down the hall and said I had a visit. Wasn't no question who it was, Shalleen was the only person on my visiting list, well besides Crystal. Crystal had just had a baby though, so she wasn't coming around here no time soon I guess. It has to be my baby. I was fucking her a lot back then. But right now I just fell back from everybody but Shalleen for a while.

Shalleen had came a few days earlier and since we only get phone calls once a week in the SHU, I hadn't talk to her. She just popped up to visit today. When I walked into the visiting room she was sitting on the side in the section for inmates in disciplinary housing. We stand out like tomatoes on a banana tree. We wear red jumpsuits and the other inmates look more regular with jean outfits on. When she stood up to give me a hug all them other prisoners looked. She be doing that shit on purpose. She had on some white Dolce & Gabana pants with no pockets on the back and you could see the t-strips of her pink thongs on the top. When them prisoners saw me looking over her shoulder they turned their heads, their girls were slappin' them and shit.

Shalleen was a hot tamale and she was with the kid. My trophy, even though she was always asking for money. Her stupid ass had went and bought a car with the first money I gave her so I was gonna make her stress for a while. Leave it up to her I would be broke when I get back. The one face that I noticed that didn't turn was Mannish. I ain't mad at him though, that boy got heart. I didn't tell them other prisonerscats to turn their heads. I grabbed two extra large handfuls of Shelleen's ass before I sat down, Mannish smiled. We sat at a little table against the back wall made for two people. She sat with her back to the room, I faced everybody so I could see everything moving.

I asked her, "What you doin' here today. Didn't I see you a few days ago?"

She leaned over the table and kissed me. Her ass was in the air. I heard about five prisoners get slapped.

The C.O. yelled, "Everybody must stay seated unless going to the restroom or vending machines."

See that bitch ass shit is how I know them C.O.s is gay. Anyway I told her, "You kissin' me and shit, you must want some money but I already told your ass 'no' the other day. You spent what you had on that car, let's see if you can get it to give you some money."

"Did I just say that I wanted some money?"

"Then what you here for?"

"Damn, you act like I don't care for you. Like I just fuck witchu for money! It's plenty of guys out there wanna sneak a high priced cookie or two out of this jar. Don't get it fucked up. Anyway my homegirl Cherise came to see her babydaddy and I took the opportunity to see you."

When she looked over at Cherise I was shocked because she was sitting right across from Mannish and I didn't even notice her. She was Shalleen's friend, on again, off again. I guess right now they are on. I was bugging off of the fact that she was Mannish's babymomma.

Me and Shalleen settled into a good conversation. She was bright. It always makes me think about how crazy life is. She just got caught in the relationship between her beauty and a hustler's money. But no matter what we talked about, my mind just kept on going back to Mannish.

"She is his babymomma?" I said apparently still surprised.

"Yeah what, you know him or something?"

"Yeah or something."

And before I could even get my thoughts together good on that note, I saw her hand him a fat package under the table. I was shocked, surprised and everything in between.

Usually we would have our girls stuff some little balloons with the drugs and package them the size of peanut M&M's then she would either hold them in her mouth and she would come in and give you a five to ten balloon kiss or she would put them in a condom and put it in her pussy, then sometime in the middle of the visit she would go to the restroom, bust the condom open and put them in her mouth. As we conversed she would pretend to drink while spitting them into the cup. A couple minutes go by, then we would pick up the cup and wash them down. Depending on how good you are with your digestive system, you could either throw them back up when you got to your cell or take a laxative. That was the extent of the average hustla. But I just saw Mannish stick a few ounces in his pants. It was smooth but I saw it. I instinctively looked over at the C.O. and I could almost swear he saw it too but instead he hollered at another prisoner who was about to walk in the men's restroom. The C.O. told him that it was for visitor's only, and that prisoners pissed before or after the visit in the back.

Homeboy's girl was already in the restroom waiting on him. A few minutes later she snuck out unnoticed. She was ready to fuck him with her flower dress on and some high heels. She had her hair in a ponytail. I imagined homeboy in there riding that pony. When I get out of the SHU me and Shalleen would try that before the visit was over.

Before she left she asked me for some money. I knew she would and she knew if she kept asking I would give her some, but look how she did it. She walked over to the vending machine and hypnotized me with that back shot, letting me know what she was holding for me and only me, let her tell it.

I told her, "Remember that movie Next Friday? Remember where the Mexicans had the money hidden. Okay there's four of them in the trunk of my black low rider. The third one has no hydraulic fluid in it. There's fifteen grand in there, put five on my books and make the rest last you. You can't be all up in the mall buying thousand dollar purses and shit."

I knew that went right out her other ear. After the C.O. caught a female giving her man a hand job I was ready to go. I kissed Shalleen, slapped her on her ass and went back to jail inside the prison.

Mack was reading a book as usual. I told him about my visit, you know, bring a little of outside into the cell. I told him about the one trying to slide up in the restroom to slide up in his girl and about the one getting jacked off. I told him about Mannish's move with the package, not like I was tryna tell his business but I was still fucked up by it. Either he had the balls of an elephant and the heart of a lion or he was working with the police. Mack said he'd been watching Mannish for a year and a half and he couldn't put his finger on it but it was something about Mannish. He definitely liked him and he knew Mannish definitely didn't fuck with the police. They'd never spoken but Mainnish reminded Mack of himself. I have to admit I liked Mannish too and I knew why. He was about gettin' that money. I can imagine the moves he makes in the streets. Anyway, I laid back and picked up the book I had started to read before they called me for visit. I really didn't feel like reading it so I put it back down and just kicked back and thought about those white pants and pink thongs Shalleen had on.

SHALLEEN

I wasn't tripping off the guys out here or Will's ass either. I just stopped fucking for a while. I'm cool. Keno knows how to take care of me, plus he ain't gonna be gone long. I got my new car. He was mad but men that's locked up don't get mad as they do when they ain't locked up. I'm still his bitch because he knows if he needs something done I'm here for him, although he hasn't asked me to do anything other than things around the apartment. I guess he's got other stuff on his mind. I'm glad as shit Cherise went to see Mannish and take him something. I took her to Will to get a few ounces from him. We just cut out the guy Mannish had told Cherise to get it from and we went to Will. For me he cut 25% off the price. He knew it was for someone else so I couldn't get it free but that gave us some extra money to blow on pampering ourselves. It was a win win for me and I didn't even have to touch the stuff. Even still I know Keno would try to leave his foot in my ass for that. I already know how he felt about Will and either I'm trippin' or Mannish is bleeping on his radar screen too. I just hope that it's in a good way because I would hate for my man and my friend's man to bump heads because them two don't know how to act. Both of them is real with this gangsta shit.

It's a small world especially in our small world. It's funny because you can stand up on a main street like

185

Crenshaw Blvd. all day everyday and see a thousand unfamiliar faces of around the way people and wonder where they all keep coming from, then you pull into a carwash with your homegirl and see your babydaddy talking to a guy yall kicked it with at a restaurant not long ago.

I told Cherise to look at Will over by the carwash entrance talking to Rich Kid. They saw us pull up so we walked over to them and spoke. It was an awkward moment everybody knew each other, I thought back to Keno and Mannish being in the same prison. I thought about how things probably would've never connected if me and Cherise didn't go to the prison together and if we wouldn't't've pulled up to the carwash at the time we did, but it was all god though because me and Cherise were in the clear.

Rich Kid asked where Marijka was. I told him I could call her if he wanted. He said to just tell her to use the number on the card when I talked to her. I know Will was wondering how the hell Rich Kid knew us all but he didn't ask. Instead he told us to keep it moving and doing what we were doing because him and Rich Kid had something they were doing. Rich Kid didn't know I was Will's babymomma, I started to tell Will to give me some money and make him look like a big trick for shooing us off like that but I didn't.

We got our ticket receipt from the carwash and went across the street to the little Jamaican store next to the

186

cleaners and bought some meat patties. Then we went to The Liquor Bank on the corner, where they filmed the part on Baby Boy where Tyreese... I mean Jodi got his bike stolen and his ass kicked by some little gangbangers in training. Same spot where he told his homeboy that line about commerce and how everybody was making moves but them. See I don't fuck with broke mutha fuckas like that. We bought a bottle of Moet Champagne out of the store and some strawberries from a Mexican who was in the street making moves. By the time me and Cherise picked out a couple of bootleg DVD's and talked the young brother into giving us each seven for $20 and looked across the street, my elegant all black 645i was gleaming and ready. When I saw Marijka's I knew I had to get one. I hardly see her drive hers though and mines is a hard top. When we got back to the car Will was gone.

Rich Kid was still around but was in a conversation with the owner of the establishment. Me and Cherise just got in the car and selected Sean Paul and Beenie Man on the iPod to put us in the mood while we ate our Jamaican pies and sipped on Champagne and strawberries. Life in L.A. ain't easy but somebody gotta do it.

BIG WILL

I had given Rich Kid the money I owed Hector for the last load, but this punk ass nigga didn't give me nothing else up front. What the fuck is up with that? I don't believe in paying for dope. Only little niggas and user's pay for dope, everybody else up the ladder should just make money off of it. I'm sure he was getting it fronted. I know Hector wasn't paying for it. Was he trying to tell me that I was a little nigga? Fuck that! I told him to give me the money back if I couldn't get another load I could flip that shit somewhere else.

That nigga told me "No."

No!

That was $50,000! I've killed people for less. I called Hector right on the spot. Maybe he didn't understand how we get down.

I had Hector on the speakerphone. Hector said it was Rich Kid's show, however he wanted to do it. He spoke to Hector. He told 'im I tried to get the money back. That's when I knew shit wasn't gonna work out between us on the business tip. I said I was just playin' with him and disconnected the line. I had some money at home but like I said I should'nt have to pay for it. I knew the five kilos were in his car too. That's what burned me up the most. I wanted to burn his ass and take the dope but too many people were around.

I shouted, "How you know my bitch anyway?!"

I could tell I scared him. "Who is your bitch... I mean woman?"

"Shalleen!"

"I met them at a restaurant. I was talking to her friend."

I noticed how scary he was, so I pushed.

"Just give me them pies since we here. I'ma bring your money back."

I started walking to his car before I was even finished talking. He hesitated a second, then fell in step.

I said. "I got you O.G." to make 'im feel better.

I took them thangs and went straight to my new hide out off of Hyde Park and Centinela. I knew Tracy would be good for two kilos in another couple days, and the other three I was gonna try and get off in the next week. If not I knew Tracy would probably be back the next week. I was definitely thinking about not payin' Rich Kid shit but I don't know, maybe I will. I pulled up in the apartment complex I used to keep all my shit. Some little bangers were hanging out in front of the building as usual, flamed up in red from head to toe and as usual I hollered out the car window for them to take that shit down the street. They made the spot hot.

I heard one of 'em yell, "Fuck you, you crab ass nigga!"

I acted like I didn't hear it. I parked and grabbed the backpack with the five kilos out of the trunk. I had to walk past them on the way to my apartment. It's about five of them between 14-18 years old. Gangbangers in training like the little ones on that Baby Boy movie. I wanted to punch them out like Omar Gooding and Tyreese did them fools in the movie but instead I pulled my gun and pistol whipped the closest one to me. Slapped him across his head with the steel a couple of times. His punk ass homeboys ran. I went inside and got on my job like it was a job. I dumped the five bricks out on the kitchen table. I got my box cutter and slit the side of two of 'em open and emptied each one out in its own bowl. I pulled out the big package weighing digital scale like the ones they got at the post office, never mind how I got mines I'm just wondering if I could get a charge for possession of stolen federal property, anyway I weighed them both and they both were short, one by one ounce and one by an ounce and a half.

What-the fuck-ever.

I weighed out a eighth out of each one and put that to the side then mixed back in some cut to bring the weight back to 36 ounces, (1,000 grams) each, then I put it back in the wrap. Tracy would get those. I opened another one and dry cooked it. I put it in a glass pot and added eighteen ounces of cut and eighteen ounces of baking soda. I kept stirring while I poured in a quarter cup at a time of hot water until it was all wet and looked like cake mix when I let it dry. I had 72 ounces of hard crack ready for distribution. Drugs only purpose was to make money off of. You'd be surprised at the things some people did to stretch the money. I looked at the other two keys on the table and decided Fuck Rich Kid! I ain't paying him shit, then I heard,

Pop! Pop! Pop!

I dropped down to the floor, glass from the living room window burst from the impact from the shots. Somebody was shooting up into my window. The gunfire stopped just as fast as it started.

Just three bullshit shots.

They shot into my living room. I wasn't even in the living room. I ran to look out the window. I saw them little wanna be niggas running.

CHAPTER TWENTY-TWO

KENO

Mis-education of the Negro was the name of the book. It took me a few days but I finally got through it.

Now that I had read it Mack broke it down in the simplest terms.

He said, "The main thing to understand is that what the black man in America in general is a result of the white man's teaching. A special self destructive teaching, going back to slavery times. The black man was taught the disrespect of any black person of authority. Taught not to put another black person above himself. They taught him that whether he was qualified or not that he was the top dawg amongst his peers. Can you imagine a whole group of people thinking like this? You see it everyday, too many chiefs and not enough Indians, taught not to put anyone above themselves. Gonna look to anyone for guidance or leadership make it a white person. Carter said the most influential institutions in the hood for blacks was the church but even in that forum you have opposing groups tearing down what the other tries to build. He touched very lightly on my proposed solving method do you know where?"

"No where?" I said.

"When he said 'when a qualified sister was put in a supervision position, the subordinate black women would respond negatively and work performances would decrease. The company president will replace her with a white woman with the same qualification if not less and the women would shape up and performance would rise, instead of firing them all and hiring black women willing to work with a qualified supervisor and get the job done. The mentality of most black people is what part of the problem is. Do you remember what the first thing was that I asked you when you came in here?"

"Yeah, you said 'what color did I think the people were that brought down the Black Panthers."

"And?"

"I don't know for sure but I'm guessing they were black.

"Yeah black undercover CIA agents. You gotta ask why would black people destroy the mission of black people to get the white foot off of black people's necks. You might say, well they were doing their job but what is the black man or woman doing being part of something that targets black men to fill up their prisons, and it didn't just start there. The first black police were in the south. Their job was to police the slaves to keep them from running away and find them when they did, and things like that. They couldn't arrest white people or much else. The brainwashing started a long time ago and it's just been evolving every since. Look at Condoleezza Rice, her skin is just black but she thinks just like Bush, that's why she had such a high position in a completely racist cabinet.

"There's no other ethnic group on the planet that would have one of their own in such a position and the world not see the support and changes visibly for their people, because when they no longer have that position they're still gonna be who they are, in her case, black.

"Don't ever forget hurricane Katrina. It was the seventh hurricane in thirteen months. Then there was another one two months later in Florida.

In New Orleans it took the government a week to get in the reinforcements, while people were dead and floating, while others were trapped in their houses with no food and no way to run. Water levels were above the doors and windows. Over eighty percent of the New Orleans area affected was black, did Condoleezza get mad? Check the response time of the other hurricane's. It's just some things to dwell on. The mind state of the people with positions, yuh know."

He also said that the book said that when people make it and don't use it to fix the problems, is the true understanding of Miseducation. It works hand in hand with another system that limits the options to just a few degrading jobs outside of crime. They like to say that everyone has the same opportunities and it's true to an extent. Everybody wouldn't make it, but more would make it than those that do if the playing field was even. That's why they start off while you're young at school, limiting your options. Everybody can remember the day when everybody in class hollered out their dream, "I wanna be a fireman." "I wanna be a doctor." and so on. Isn't it the teacher's job to nurture those dreams? If not, then who? But it dies right there and nobody even realizes it. Once you grow up and you really understand your full potential and what you were capable of doing had you been nurtured with the right information and gone down the right avenue, but by then your on a one way street. Sure you can cut off at one of the many forks in the road and do better but you cannot turn around go back and get on the best route.

Then guess what?

Since you never actually went the best route you don't know the best route. You don't know the best route so you can't show your children the best route. And if by chance you get blessed enough to learn the best route, chances are, your kids have already passed a major intersection. What I mean is, the things they've picked up, things they've seen, they've been partially developed with the bullshit. So mostly, the cycle continues.

I've been around long enough to see it. I've seen three generations of men from all over turn into broken men since the time when I first came in. I watched guys older than me watch their sons my age come in.

Maybe not in the same prison but prison's prison. The only difference is the part of the map it sits on. County jails are prisons too, you just don't stay as long and you can't move around as much.

Then I've seen those sons watch their sons come inside which is your generation. My personal philosophy is that if your generation gets fed the information then we'll have hope for your kid's grandkids. Yeah I know it sounds far but that's how long it's going to take to sink in and undo what took many, many years to do."

I was still digesting everything he told me when he just switched lanes on me and took me on one of his memory lane rides.

The lights in the club were dim, the walls had booth tables lined along two of the sides. In the center were round tables with wooden chairs half filled with the remnants of the regulars. The group on stage was singing their last ballad for the night. The group consisted of four local brothers who were on their way to stardom if only the right person took notice of their undeniable talent. They swayed in unison to their choreographed dance steps. Mack laid back in a booth with two of his buddies Raymond and Lionel. Mack had just sat back down from using the payphone. He had just gotten an order for an ounce of cocaine. He told them that he only had a half an ounce left and that he would be there in about thirty minutes. This place he was relaxing in was black owned, run by blacks and catered to blacks. That's why the white man in the tan slacks and sweater stood out. He was walking in Mack's direction. He slid in amongst the three blacks comfortably.

"What's up Mack?" then as an afterthought he said. "you guys doing good?" to the other two men.

Mack was his business associate. Mack's buddies, the white man considered flunkies.

The two didn't answer him.

"Raymond, Lionel." Mack said.

The two got up went to the bar and gave them some privacy.

"How's life treating you Mack?"

"I ain't gonna complain."

"Complain? No, you can't complain, and who treats you the best huh? Who makes sure you are supplied with the cream of the crop eh? That good stuff the average nigger can't get his hands on. No offense to you Mack because you're different."

"I know what you tryna say." Mack said with a smile on his face. "But if you don't watch it I'ma haveta kill yuh."

"Anyhow, listen Mack, a shipment came in. Some A-plus stuff. I got about twenty kilos of it but I'm going to have to charge you more for it, about three large a kilo more, but..."

"Are you crazy? Last shipment you went up a grand on me. What do I look like to you, a bank? You know what the problem is with you Crackers? You don't just want your piece of the pie. You want the whole pie. Everybody's piece."

"Am I crazy?! Am I crazy?! You're asking me if I'm crazy? You should ask yourself, are you crazy, I make it possible for you to have a piece of the pie. Without me you would be waiting on your government check like the rest of the fucking niggers!" Mack restrained himself while White Man continued. "I even turned you on to a few white customers, otherwise you would only be moving two's and fews with these nickel and dime monkeys."

When White Man finished his tirade Mack seemed strangely calm.

197

"You're right, I apologize, let me see a sample."

White man wiped the sweat from his forehead. "I didn't bring any samples. Take my word for it. It's good stuff."

"Well let me have two."

"They're at home. I can hook up with you in the morning."

"That's fine." Mack said, standing up. "Let me give you the money now."

Mack walked toward the rear exit, White Man followed, Raymond and Lionel followed. When Mack got to his Cadillac he reached into his glove box and pushed the button to pop open the trunk. White Man got confused, he expected to see a bag or maybe a suitcase but there was nothing but a spare tire and bumper jack. Mack picked up the bumper jack and swung it wide at White Man's head.

White Man raised his arm and blocked it, snapping his femur bone. He let out a scream but there was no one around to help. The short Mexican parking lot security stepped inside the club to mind his own business. White Man was on the ground whimpering. Mack reached into Lionel's waistband and took out his .38 and pumped two shots into White Man and handed the gun back to Lionel. The three men picked him up and threw him in the trunk. Mack went through his pockets and retrieved White Man's house keys and wallet. He flipped through it quickly to make sure the ID with his home address was in it then slammed the trunk closed.

"Raymond you drive."

"You know Son, there are always times in your life when you have to ask yourself why did you do things in a certain order which was ass backwards or back asswards, but no matter what answer you give yourself, it's too late. It's done."

He didn't say anything else for the rest of the day I didn't either. He didn't give me anything to read for a change. That was cool with me because I had enough to think about.

CHAPTER TWENTY-THREE

RICH KID

"Yeah mutha fucka you fuckin' wit my money, what you think, shit sweet? You betta call your agent and get your life insurance right cause I'ma kill yo ass when I catch up witchu, that's fifty thousand you owe me! I'm take your life for payment but I'm still gonna take a loss cause your life ain't even worth that much you low life mutha fucka!"

Beep.

His answering machine cut me off. I was on a roll too. Damn! I wanted to tell him I was gonna rip off his head and piss down his neck too. I been calling Big Will for over two weeks and getting no response.

That's almost a hundred thousand dollars worth of losses I've taken this month, and my birthday is right around the corner.

Shit!

That's more money I gotta spend, but I can't let nobody see me sweat. My image is on the line. I gotta do it up Big no matta what. I told KB about the idea that I had cooking up in my head for the last few months. He thought it was so good that he said he would go half with me and shoot a video while the party was going on. It got even better when we went down to the boat rental agency to reserve a

200

double decker platform style party boat. The man told us about a new vehicle that was way more expensive but guaranteed to be the talk of the town for years. He showed us a brochure. The name of it was the Terra Wind. The price tag was $1.6 million!

Whoa!

I was grateful to whoever came up with the concept of renting. There was no doubt in my mind that we had to get that one. We told him we were still gonna need the double decker platform though. We made all the arrangements and left.

On the way back to the city, I brought up the idea of going all out and having the party in Las Vegas at Lake Mead.

I told him, "You know that's a cool ass lake."

He said, "Yeah I know but where's everybody gonna stay?"

"Fuck it, we'll rent out a couple of floors at a hotel."

"I don't stay nowhere but the best when I'm in Vegas, and I aint' paying for two floors just because I wanna shoot a video, the party already about to cost up the ass."

"Man stop trippin'. I'd pay for the rooms, cause I'm thinking about that lake. You know you can run your boat at full speed for an hour straight and still not be able to see the other side."

"Damn! I didn't know that." he was smiling.

I said, "You feel me now?"

"Yeah but listen I can't be taking the equipment and camera crew to another state. I'm just independent, I ain't Interscope, plus you know how it is, you gonna get out there and mutha fuckas ain't gonna be showin' up, talkin' bout it was too far or they had to do this and do that."

"Yeah you right."

"Look after this album hits gold status me you and my artist will grab a few bitches and take a sixty footer out there for the weekend."

"Aight bet, but I'll wait till the album goes platinum."

"Don't get caught up in the hype. Platinum's great but an album doesn't have to go platinum to be a success. If you can get a half a million people to buy your album you're no small fry. It's because big companies spend millions on an album's production they need it to go platinum.

I haven't ever sold a million albums for any one of my artists, but I could quit all this shit today. I'll still have my mansion down the street from Madonna, this customized Hummer we in. While you over there farting in those red softer than your bitch's ass seats of mine, that blue S600, mine, that Harley, mine and some mo' shit and won't none of it get re-poed. But speaking of a budget, not to change the subject but I saw Doctor Dre and I asked him how much I could get a track for. You know what he told me? Some astronomical shit, the number was so high it went right out my other ear. I swear to God I can't even remember what he said, but I remember I was like, "For one track!? Yo suck my dick!"

"You shoulda Suge Knighted 'im."

"What you think he sold 'em all?"

"I woulda rushed that fool!"

I was just talking. Me and you know that I ain't got no Pac in me KB knows it too.

CHAPTER TWENTY-FOUR

SHALLEEN

Me and the girls were at the mall shopping because Cherise had found out that Rich Kid's birthday party was today on the water in the Marina and he wanted all the girls to wear red silk or satin dresses or skirts and white formal attire for the men.

It was scheduled to start at twelve noon but at twelve we were just getting to the mall. I found this red dress that had my shoulders out it flowed off of my hips and hid my ass a little.

Both Vallawn and Marijka wore form fitting dresses that accentuated their curves. At first Marijka didn't want to come but I persisted. Cherise the hoochie momma of the bunch wore a red top that left her shoulders and her belly out. Her skirt was the size of a playboy magazine.

On the way we were scared that we had missed it, that the boat had probably already taken off and left our forever late asses but when we came around the bend we could hear the music jamming. There were cameras and lights posted up in position like a video shoot to catch people pulling up and getting attended to by valet. The cars were being parked around the perimeter of the parking lot. We were looking a bit confused because apparently the parking lot was the party. Valet had left us standing in the middle of an outside club. People who had already got a good buzz going on by the chronic being passed around or the alcohol were breaking down their dance moves to the beat. Red and white fabric was everywhere. The sky was blue and cloudless. You could smell the sun in the air. It was that good picnic bar-b-que weather, a song by Lil Kim came on and Cherise started poppin' her ass.

I walked around for a minute. On the right side of the parking lot there were a few tables with every kind of fruit you can find in a supermarket. They were cut up in slices, cubes, triangles and balls.

On the left there were freestanding human sized blocks of ice. You could see bottles and cans trapped inside. It held beers, sodas, juices and bottles of champagne. As the sun slowly erode the layers of frozen bondage, someone would swing by and pluck out an ice cold beverage and that's just what I did.

About another thirty minutes went by then the DJ mixed in the rap artist's single. On que, the artist pulled up and hopped out of a fat ass red Hummer that looked like a Cadillac Escalade in the front. He was wearing a white two piece suit. He went through the motions of lip-syncing his lyrics to the record.

Three light skinned girls in red satin mini skirts got out of the truck and went into a choreographed dance routine, then one of the girls removed the artist's jacket. Underneath he had on a wife beater and a thick half gold half platinum chain. Either he was a natural or he practiced at home for days on end because he got the first verse done in one take and I heard someone say it was his first video.

The Dj mixed in some T-Pain and everybody kept boogie-ing. Now the artist was mingling with the crowd, experiencing the beginning of stardom. Me and Rich Kid lounged in some director's type chairs over by the camera crew. KB and some other guys were discussing the next scene of the video. Cherise was on the floor cutting it up. Marijka and Vallawn played low key. After a couple of songs the music went off and the DJ looked like he was packing up. Then we noticed about a hundred yards out in the water music was coming from a red and white party boat.

Aight! Now that's what everybody was expecting to see from the jump. It took a while but we weren't mad at that. The parking lot party was jumping but after a few minutes we noticed that the boat wasn't coming any closer.

Somebody yelled, "What the fuck we gotta do, swim to the mutha fucka?!"

"I guess so." Rich Kid said, while behind him three RV's were pulling up.

206

"Come on everybody." he said stepping up on the first one. "Pile in."

"What we gonna do, drive to the boat?" somebody said sarcastically on the way up the steps of the RV. Everybody piled in all three of them with standing room only. Immediately, I got a whiff of the all leather upholstery with Terra Wind stitched into it. There were two sixty inch flat screen TVs linked to satellite. It had Marble floor and a large Whirlpool Jacuzzi in the back. The speakers were jamming R Kelly's "Whine for me", turning the situation into a dance floor on wheels. I smelled chronic smoke in the air again. I was sure the same thing was going on, on the other RV's.

Me and Rich Kid were in the same one. Cherise and Vallawn were together and Marijka was on the other one. When they started moving no one even noticed, until the music went low and someone's voice came through the speakers saying, "You beautiful party people are on board the world's only luxury amphibious RV, created by Cool Amphibious Manufactures International." then he said he was putting the road transmission into neutral and the marine transmission into gear. He said a pontoon projected from each side to keep us from tipping over. The RV rocked as everybody including me rushed to the side windows and flooded to the front windshield to see it take on the water.

Three quarters of it sat high above the water with the pontoons connected so low that the water only came up to slightly over the wheel wells. We were afloat and headed out to the open water. When we got closer we noticed the party boat was headed deeper out too. We had a caravan goin', a party boat and three RVs in one line. A camera man stayed back on land and recorded the whole thing. After a thirty minute cruise which we were partying the whole time mind you, the RVs maneuvered into position at three sides of the party boat about thirty feet away. When the doors opened somebody from the party boat threw out a bridge made of wood and rope. Once it was secured to the steps of the RV a red carpet was rolled out along the length. Most people went over to the bigger boat. It had red and white material hanging from the ceiling almost in cubicles. A few people hung back and enjoyed the RV lounge area since they finally had room to. Some girls were naked in the Whirlpool. Cherise's ass was one of them. She was chilling with a glass of champagne in her hand. I told her to get her ass out and put her clothes on but she didn't pay me no attention.

The music in all four boats was different. There was popular hip hop and R&B on the big boat. One Terra Wind played Reggae and Dancehall. One played Oldies but Goodies, and the other one played the new craze Regggaeton. Once the party was poppin' full fledge, the crowd noticed the music in all four areas was playing the same single from the video shoot earlier on shore then we noticed the artist coming up from behind on a Sea Doo jet boat. There were camera men on other small boats video recording his performance for his second verse. I found out later that back on land they did a few scenes where he missed the departure of the party because he was in the van freaking with a Mariah Carey looking groupie. Then he stole somebody's boat and chased after us. He got on board and ripped the third verse in the middle of the crowd. Everything was good. He did it all effortlessly in one take. He went and got in one of the Whirlpools in one of the Terra Winds with Cherise and a couple other girls and did the song again. The director told the girls to step in and out of the water a lot. He said he was going to make a version for B.E.T. uncut or Worldstarhiphop.com videos.

After that we just partied with Rich Kid for his birthday. For the rest of the evening the camera men just hung around getting footage to add in.

CHAPTER TWENTY-FIVE

KENO

"Let me ask you a question." Mack said but I knew he was setting me up so he could drop another bomb on me like he been doing for weeks.

He said, "If there's any drug that you know for sure that black people deal with more than any other race what would it be? And don't say weed because all races mess with that."

"Ain't no question, rocks, crack." I said.

"Why is it that's the worst drug to get caught with? The federal guideline says you get a mandatory minimum of ten years for fifty grams. That's not even two ounces. Any young black kid can get his hands on two ounces but for powder cocaine the ratio is 100 to 1, which means a mandatory minimum of 10 years for 5000 grams that's 5 kilos. Do you know why?" He didn't wait for me to answer, "Because that's white folks drugs of choice and you gotta be a very heavy hitter to get caught with 5 kilos, you understanding what I'm saying Son?

The black men are under attack and then we got you guys killing each other on the street. One gets dead and the other gets locked up for life, there getting two for one. You guys are the soldiers. You're not afraid to kill or take big

210

risks to get the job done but the black race is losing its soldiers more and more. We're losing soldiers everyday and in the middle of a war. Can you imagine the U.S. soldiers killing each other in Vietnam or Iraq? You can't fight the enemy along side the enemy."

"But how do you know who the enemy is?" I asked.

"That's part of the problem. You can't tell by appearance because all white folks aren't your enemy, but they all do benefit in some ways from our enslavement. First you have to concentrate on your own because everything starts from within.

You can't have a movement without a united people, people who are counterproductive to the movement are a disease. Disease spreads and destroys and so it must be purged from the system. Do what you do but stop doing random things."

I never responded, just laid there.

About two hours passed then Mack said, "Make sure you find a wife son, and not just any wife. One that's gonna make you come home at night. One that you wanna go home at night to."

"Why you say that Pops?"

"That's a survival tactic men like us need to keep us grounded, alive and on the street. There was this one woman I will never forget. Her name was Gladys, Gladys

Johnson. I think I would've married that woman. She used to pass my house everyday going to work while I was on my appeal and I used to try my luck every time but she was married and a faithful woman, until one day I don't know why but she showed up in front of my house in a taxi. She spent a day and a half with me and let me tell you something. I made love to her until I had no more cum left in me and then just like she appeared she disappeared and she never even spoke to me after that again. Well it wasn't long after that, that I left the streets forever but she's the one that might have slowed ole Mack down. I guess I found another way to slow down huh."

"Let me find out Ole Macaroni Toni got sprung off a shot of pussy."

"Naw son, I'ma Mack from way back, it was her aura."

"Macaroni, let me find out."

He threw a book at me, a big orange and blue book.

The 48 Laws of Power by Robert Green.

CHAPTER TWENTY-SIX

TANYA

At 3:30am I climbed out of the bed and walked into the kitchen.

Maybe a warm cup of milk would do the trick.

It had worked a few times in the past when I was unable to sleep.

As I warmed my milk I sat at the table. My mind was filled with thoughts, thoughts of my grandma, thoughts of her future and I wasn't afraid to admit that I was scared.

Scared of change. Scared of the unknown.

I looked out of the window and the neighbor was dragging another big black bag out into his yard. I lost sight of him when he went back into his back door.

The neighbor's house held a stench that could only come from multiple decomposing bodies. He opened his fridge to get a cold drink. Next to a glass of milk was the head of an African college student. In front of a box of baking soda and on a plate with a slice of watermelon was an arm of a black male skateboarder. Blood dripped from both severed parts into a dark red puddle beneath.

He drank down the glass of milk.

Dragging 200 lbs. of body parts can make a man thirsty.

The neighbor was a hunter who usually lived in the woods and hunted wild game with bow and arrows. There was an innate desire in him to kill and moving to the city didn't quell that desire.

He returned to the back yard to continue to bury the body parts in his garden. It always worked for his vegatables better than anything else. Tanya was clueless.

I poured my warm milk into a coffee mug and returned to the table. I took small sips.

What was I going to do?

I knew I had OCD (obsessive compulsive disorder) because nothing could be out of place in my house. When I was done I washed the mug and placed it back into the cabinet.

I thought for a while longer before my eye lids grew heavy. My head hit the pillow and before I knew it I was counting my last sheep.

I didn't get much sleep before the dream had occurred again. I lay restless until morning.

I called Dr. Hunt's office and luckily she told me to come on in as soon as possible. I showered and dressed in a pair of jeans and a t-shirt. I pulled my hair back into a ponytail and grabbed my bag and headed out.

Traffic was jam packed, so to occupy my thoughts I turned on the radio to tune in to Mike Evans' early morning show. Mike, Prescott and Big Sue knew how to start my day. I turned on Elsey Avenue and Raines Road and took Austin Peay Blvd. all the way down to the therapist's office.

The office was empty with it being so early. I was immediately called to the back. We exchanged pleasantries

214

and I laid back on the chaise. Dr. Hunt took a seat in her chair, pressed record on the computer, poised her pen to write and asked me about my day.

I told her about my grandma and the cancer situation.

"I'm sorry to hear that. Everything will be okay." Dr. Hunt said sincerely.

I wanted to believe her. Wanted to rest assure in that fact, but my mind wouldn't let me. I wanted so badly not to worry about Ma, but I couldn't relax. Dr. Hunt took a deep breath and asked me what was going on in my love life. I didn't have an answer for that.

"Dr. Hunt, I might need to come back another time. I really don't feel up to it today."

Thankfully the therapist understood and I left the office. I just needed to be alone for a while. Sort out my feelings, although, I really didn't need to miss my appointment with Dr. Hunt, I had to be willing and able to divulge my innermost thoughts and this day wasn't the day.

As I drove down Mt. Mariah Street and turned on Knight Arnold Street, I thought about life.

I needed to get away.

The West Coast.

I needed to go back to my old neighborhood.

I drove up to my house. The neighbor's music was blasting but after a couple of minutes it went down.

Thankfully Malcolm wasn't here so I would really be in peace. I grabbed my purse and went inside the house. As soon as I stepped through the door I lit my aromatherapy candles and put in one of my CD's from Mary Mary's collection. I walked into the bathroom, stripped naked and gathered the toiletries I needed for my relaxing shower. I stepped into the hot shower. The whole bathroom was steamy, just like I liked it.

My eyes were heavy and the sandman was whispering in my ear. It was barely noon, maybe a little nap would do me some good. I dressed in one of Malcolm's t-shirts and climbed in bed. The dreams continued…

She could hear him lick his lips hungrily. No where to run. No where to hide. She knew what was about to happen.

Gulp!

She felt arms on her. She was grabbed and thrown to the floor. Her shirt was ripped off, her back touched the filthy floor. Her mother never cleaned up and roaches and mice ran like crazy in the apartment. She hated being on the floor, but she was helpless. He was much bigger than her and his strength was undeniable. A body laid on top of hers and she cried out in pain. In her mind she drifted off into a fantasy world but her body was still in that cold, funky room with him. Her vagina was extremely tight but he didn't care about that at all. He only worried about himself, not taking it easy on her at all. Being that she was so young, her vagina was so dry that when she felt his dick forced inside her she screamed out in pain and stiffened.

"Oh my God!" I screamed, as I jumped up out of my sleep. I was wet and the t-shirt I wore was stuck to my skin. I jumped out of the bed, panting hard and breathing heavily. I paced the floor a bit and tried to calm myself but it was nearly impossible.

I was quite sure the little girl was close to death that time. My stomach flipped and I ran to the bathroom. I made it to the toilet just in time.

I dropped to my knees and threw up. I was so tired. Soaked with sweat and exhausted I collapsed near the wall, brought my knees up to my chest and cried. At that moment I felt very much like that helpless child. Vulnerability overtook me. That man was taking much more than the little girl's innocence, my peace and sanity was being taken also. I looked at the clock that rested on the bathroom cabinet. It said it was three a.m.

I had to see the therapist first thing in the morning. That dream was even more frightening than the others. My head fell back on the wall and I exhaled. My stomach was sore from all the vomiting but I pulled myself together and got up from the floor. I walked into the bedroom and climbed back in bed and closed my eyes, but no sheep appeared for me to count, so for the next few hours I tossed and turned and couldn't wait for seven a.m. When the alarm clock sounded I was restless. I had already been sitting on the toilet for an hour, just sitting there.

I dressed in a white pantsuit and looked into the mirror. I leaked a smile. Right after sliding my feet into a pair of white heels I grabbed a white oversized purse and went to work.

When I was behind the wheel of my car, I put on some Neo Soul music. I heard one of my favorite male crooners, I needed something to relax my mind and lift my spirits. My grandma still weighed heavily on my mind. I hoped Ma knew that I loved her to death.

CHAPTER TWENTY-SEVEN

KENO

Me and Mack got cool over the couple of months we were locked in together. His new name was Macaroni. That was my code word for sucka for love, ever since he told me about his sweet thang and his day and a half fling with Gladys. But in the meantime my knowledge and understanding grew like muscles on steroids. That book the 48 Laws of Power was on some shit, mind games, heartless shit, but nonetheless real shit. Anybody looking to win on any level in this game of life would want to take some notes from that book, it became my Bible. My Basic Instructions Before Leaving Earth.

In between trying to commit as many laws as possible to memory and sponging off of Macaroni, time went by kinda quick until I was released from the SHU.

They finally ended the investigation, the authorities had heard about the alleged plans but since number one, it was plans of taking illegal drugs from other prisoners, they couldn't sanction me. It could be conscrued as they were protecting illegal activity. Number two I didn't act on the alleged plans. And Number three I still got punished and locked down anyway.

They let me out the hole. School was over. I don't know about all that shit that Mack was talking. If that's his mission, that's cool but me, if I'm part of the problem then so be it, cause I gets mines in.

I touched back down on the compound. Everybody else, like all my selected soldiers had been back on the yard for a few weeks already. Since I didn't get a write up or anything they put me back in the same cell with the same celly. The first thing I did was find Country. We walked the track and talked more about how the C.O.'s got the word than anything else. I had my suspicions though Country was clueless. I was reading him trying to figure out if he was an asset or a liability for the moves I had on my mind. I came to the same conclusion of what I already knew. Country was the type that needed a good leader like my homie Smooth was. Then it dawned on me that I had eyes on me every second from every angle. All the stares were accompanied by whispers. I had become a celebrity overnight. It just took me a couple of months to find out.

Over the next few days I realized that, like in most celebrity situations I had the dick riders and the haters. It's hard to tell the difference from a hater and a dick rider because they all come with smiles, disarming smiles. I couldn't help but evaluate them in terms of whether they were to be spared, used or slaughtered. It was cool to be The Man though.

Unfortunately, anything that happened on the inside of these walls didn't count in the real world.

I called a meeting of my twelve selected soldiers. Country was the cook of the group. He grew up around a lot of food. He collected pounds of tuna, mackerel, tomatoes, onions, bell peppers and noodles. He mixed it all together. It's called a spread in prison. We slid two tables together inside the gym and feasted. I felt like Jesus at the last supper with his disciples and just like him, I had a Judas among the group. I watched everybody eat as I tried to figure out who Judas was, but like I said I had my suspicions. I had two months to dwell on everybody's characteristics.

Then suddenly I said. "You know the C.O.'s told me who the rat is!"

They all stopped eating midchew. One of them almost choked on his food. He just so happened to be sitting next to me. I threw a swift hard elbow to his throat and crushed his Adam's apple. I felt the bones crunch. He fell back on the ground holding his throat and gasping for air. His attempts to scream for help were in vain. He shook violently for about two minutes then all movement stopped. I was calm as a mutha fucka, looking at everybody's expressions.

I said clearly and slowly, "My guess is, he's the rat. But... I could be wrong. We gonna say he choked on his food. If that story doesn't change, I'll assume I was right. Now somebody go grab a C.O. and tell him to come quick but wait another couple a minutes to make sure his ass is dead." Then I finished my food.

When the staff came they scooped him up off the ground and interviewed everybody. We were all sent to our cells right before 10 o'clock count. For the fact that I made it back to my cell told me that I had done something right. I thought about one of the laws in the 48 Laws of Power. It said "Always keep your hands clean" so I went over to the sink and washed my hands. I knew it wasn't meant to be taken literally, it was a metaphor for getting other people to do your dirty work for you. But keeping my hands clean literally in the sink was the best I could do at this stage. I liked to do the dirty work.

CHAPTER TWENTY-EIGHT

BIG WILL

"Naw, it wasn't even like that, I wasn't tryna fuck you over I had just went outta town to set up shop, get some new avenues to dump shit at. I'm back now and I got your money, please except my apology for the misunderstanding. I got your money and I got the money for five more. Whenever you wanna hook up I can get that to you. You can give me the five thangs and we can let by gones be by gones. I'm even gonna forget all that rah rah shit you was talking on my answering machine."

"Yeah aight, so you sayin' you got a hundred thousand for me?"

"That's what I'm sayin' Rich Kid my nigga."

"Aight meet me at M&M's Soul Food Restaurant in Ladera in two hours."

"Aight fa' sho'. No problem. I'ma go get that for you right now."

I knew he would fall for it, who wouldn't? That's a hundred grand. That kinda money calls people with a loud voice to come get it and calls 'em to their death too. One mo' body on my 9mm and it's in the river. I'll take a trip up by Magic Mountain and throw it in Castaic Lake. This will make four bodies, counting that little wannabe banger I caught slippin' by my spot the other night.

I only had one kilo left so it was time to re-up and after the five I get today runs out then I'll figure out who I'll get the next batch from. Ten kilos for free is worth going through the hassle of finding a new connect. I might even be able to go back to Hector and get fronted again since I'm gonna eliminate the middle man.

I was ready whenever Rich Kid was ready. He said two hours so I had a little time to kill. I went to Blockbuster down the street from where he wanted to meet and bought the Belly DVD. I had been meaning to buy another one long time ago. Somebody stole my last one.

I smoked a blunt, reclined my seat and watched it right there in the parking lot in front of Blockbuster.

I must've fucked around and fell asleep because the screen on the monitor was blue and the last thing I remember was when Lennnox checked Tommy Buns for calling him scared. Ay Lennox's remote control was crazy big right?

When I woke up I was a half an hour late for my meeting with Rich Kid. I hurried up and drove down the street. When I got in the parking lot I was shocked as a mutha fucka to see Shalleen out there leaning up on the window of somebody's truck. A black Lincoln Mark LT. I slowed my roll and parked. Good thing I wasn't in my 300C. I was in my new sandy brown Lexus truck a 470 LX. When she moved to the side a little bit I saw that the fool in the truck was Rich Kid

What the fuck is Shalleen doing with this nigga right now?

Fuck!

This is getting ridiculous. This is the second time her ass been all up in the face of who's head I'm tryna blow off. She must be fucking him too. Bitches ain't shit! She crept on me with that punk Keno now she creeping on Keno with Rich Kid. Rich Kid is paid, that's why she ain't been sweating me for no bread. I should just bust caps in both they ass right now.

Damn you! You bitch! If you didn't have my daughter I'd split yo soul from your body!

I had to lay in the cut and see if I would get a chance to get him. This bitch had me heated. I was already late, now I had to wait some more because I couldn't let her see me approach this clown. I ain't got no money for him so once I step to him I gotta make my move. I know he got them thangs on him and I can't let them go unless she gets in the truck with him. And I damn sure don't see her car nowhere in the parking lot.

Why the fuck is she leaning on his door talking to him? Is she riding with him or what?

Maybe she went in and ordered something to go and she's just waiting for it before she gets back in the truck.

I couldn't do nothing but wait, I started watching the rest of Belly. I had barely found the scene where I left off when she went inside. I made my move. I walked up to the passenger side of the truck, the door was unlocked. I just opened it, got in and sat down. I startled the shit out of him. He didn't even see me coming, this nigga ain't from the street. It amazes me how lames get plugged with the connection. I whipped the pistol out and told him to hand over the goods. He reached in the back seat and got a bag. I realized I didn't have a silencer on my gun and I was really about to blast him. I told him to roll up the windows. While the windows were going up I told him that I hope he called his life insurance agent then I squeezed the trigger three times. One hit him in the forehead and jerked his head to the side. The next one caught him in the temple, it must've ricocheted inside his skull because it came out the bottom of the back of his head. The bullet's exit sprayed all kinds of juice on the headrest of the seat. Noodles were hanging out of the opening.

The third bullet missed him completely and busted the driver's window. That shit was loud! I had to go. I grabbed the bag. His mouth was making funny noises. I don't know if he was tryna talk but whatever it was, he wasn't thinking straight. I didn't have time to get the platinum chain he had around his neck or that nice watch. I really shoulda peeled him for it before I shot 'im. It was too late now, I had to go. I got in my truck and got on. I didn't even look back. I made that left by 7-11 and came out on La Tijera Blvd. made a right and jumped on the 405 freeway north. Five kilos to the good.

CHAPTER TWENTY-NINE

SHALLEEN

Rich Kid's birthday party was nice. I'm sure people will be talking about that for a long time. I had been keeping in touch with him because he's cool and knows how to kick it plus he's paid too. I'm not looking into upgrading or nothing but you gotta keep your plan B, C's and D's in perspective. Me and Cherise were on our way to M&M's Soul Food Restaurant on the Westside because we had just talked to him and he said that if we weren't doing anything he would treat us to something to eat and you know how we get down.

Free food! Oh we there!

So we got in Cherise's Cadillac truck and was on our way over there. I called Marijka and told her we were meeting with Rich Kid but I couldn't convince her to join us. She always seems to be kinda standoffish when it comes to being around him. I guess she just ain't feeling him.

When me and Cherise got to M&M's Rich Kid wasn't there yet so we parked and waited in the truck for a few minutes. After a little while of watching people coming out of the restaurant with their bellies poking out we got impatient and went in to make our bellies poke out too.

We were only in there a couple of minutes when he called my cell phone telling me that he was outside. He said to give him a minute and he'd be in. He asked me if Marijka was with me. I told him "no" that it was just me and Cherise. He sounded disappointed. I felt a little sorry for him. It was obvious Marijka had caught his attention but she wouldn't care if he died today. Usually she would let somebody like Rich Kid tear that money off tryna please her.

He said that his boy Hector was with him. When I saw Hector at his birthday party I recognized him immediately because I'd been with Will when they met a couple of times a few months back but I wasn't sure if Hector knew Rich Kid or if maybe he came to the party with somebody who knew Rich Kid. Them being together right now clears that up and confirms what I thought when I saw Rich Kid and Will talking at the carwash. He sells drugs, talking about some producer shit when we first met him but then they did shoot a video at the birthday party. I ain't mad at him. Get yo money boy. He might wanna stay away from Will's scanless ass though.

While the waitress was taking our orders Hector walked in. We exchanged pleasantries then he told the waitress what him and Rich Kid wanted. Then he started macking to Cherise. She had already put 2 and 2 together too. She knew he was the dopeman and he had a touch of jungle fever too. I knew she was gonna give him some play for so many reasons. It's easier to get money out of any non black man plus the next time Mannish sent her to go pick up some ounces, she could probably get them from Hector for free. We be thinking that way in advance. Yeah well that's why our pockets be fat. I wish I would be stupid enough to be getting my ass up at six in the morning and be gone to work all day til the sun be done gone down to bring home a few G's a month, please. The three of us talked for a few minutes. When the waitress brung our food to the table we realized that Rich Kid still hadn't come in yet. I got up and went outside to tell Rich Kid to come on before his food got cold. When I stepped out I didn't see his S500 or 745 LI. I thought maybe Hector drove. I was about to go back inside and ask Hector what they were driving when I heard the tap of a horn and a arm waiving out of a black Lincoln pick up truck right in front of me. I walked up to his door and asked him what he was waiting on. He didn't answer me, just asked me what happened to Marijka. Rich Kid was cool so I just told him the truth, that she wasn't feeling him for whatever reason.

He said, "Damn, I picked the wrong one huh?"

"I guess so."

"What's up with Vallawn?" he asked me.

That kinda caught me off guard. She wasn't even at The Cheese Cake Factory that night we met. They didn't even speak at the birthday party.

I leaned on the door and asked him, "How you know Vallawn?"

He told me that they met at the carwash. She was with Cherise and Marijka a few days after the night we all met.

I told him straight up that I didn't know the bitch for real and had no desire to. She was Cherise's friend. She had just popped up outta nowhere. Whenever I said anything about her Cherise would act like I was being jealous but that bitch Vallawn is phoney, I just know she is.

He detected the indignation in my voice. I tried to put some humor into the conversation by saying, "Why is Hector in there tryna put some chocolate in his diet?"

We both laughed.

I said, "I'm hungry, you can let your food get cold if you want but I like my food hot. I gotta go feed this ass."

"I'll be in there in a minute."

"Alright." I told him and went back in.

I sat back down with Hector and Cherise, they were getting along fine. When he realized Rich Kid wasn't behind me he wiped his mouth and stood up. He bumped the waitress walking behind him and spilled a little soup on his shirt. She apologized and tried to help him clean it off with a cloth and a glass of water. Which was a lot better than what he would've gotten from me. He should've been watching what he was doing. He told her it was alright and went into the restroom to clean it up himself. While he was in there we all heard a,

Boom!

First we all ducked down then when we didn't hear anymore booms we went to look. The first place I looked was in Rich Kid's direction. I could see the driver window was busted and glass was everywhere. Before I could move, Hector ran past me.

Me and Cherise ran behind him. Somebody was pointing at a Lexus truck making a left.

When we looked in on Rich Kid he was fucked up. A bullet hole in his forehead was draining blood. One in the side of his head was draining blood. The back of his head was wide open with his brains hanging out of it. His back was soaked with fluids. His eyes were open and his tongue was hanging out of his mouth and his jaw was moving up and down like he was stuttering. Then right while I was looking, the blood stopped pumping out of his holes. I was astonished. He died. I just stared at him. I couldn't believe it. I was just talking to him.

It doesn't matter how many times you've heard about death. When you see it up close and personal, it's scary! Especially if the person's brains are blown out.

A lot of shit was going on around me, a lot of noise, a lot of people talking but I was somewhere else. My mind was gone, staring at Rich Kid. That's until I heard Hector say Big Will's name a few times in between a lot of curse words. That snapped me out of my trance.

"Big Will? What about Big Will?"

"That Mother Fucker did this shit holmes. I shoulda been out here, that Puto Mother Fucker!"

He was looking in the backseat. It was obvious what he was looking for wasn't there and it was obvious who he thought took it. I thought I knew which Big Will he was talking about but I didn't want to come to that devastating conclusion.

Hoping I was wrong I asked, "Who is Big Will?"

The Big Will I knew was considered a piece of shit to a lot of people. So I asked the identifying question, that one question that identifies everybody in L.A. better than your name.

"What kinda car he got?"

"A blue Chrysler that 300c bullshit."

Oh Lord! That's my daughter's father.

"You know what, we have to go before the cops come." he said.

Somebody was saying, "A big black dude with braids did it and left in a tannish Lexus."

I didn't want to leave Rich Kid like that but there was really nothing I could do. I didn't know anything about him to help get in touch with his family or nothing and I sure wasn't going to tell anybody I knew Big Will. The two people I was with, was moving towards Cherise's truck so I was outta there too.

Hector had us take him to a Mexican restaurant in Huntington Park and drop him off. On the way there he was saying that Big Will stole a lot of stuff and would be dead by the morning. He said that Big Will was worse than dog shit because he didn't respect professional business.

I couldn't hold it in, I blurted out, "Big Will is my babydaddy."

Hector looked at me for about thirty seconds without saying nothing.

Uh Oh! I thought he was gonna choke me to death.

Sometimes I say the dumbest shit.

After the thirty seconds he said, "You serious?"

"Yeah." came out like a sigh.

"How can you have a kid with that piece of shit?"

"I often ask myself that same thing."

"I don't think you had nothing to do with this."

"You mutha fuckin' right I didn't have shit to do with it!"

He was quiet for the rest of the ride. When we got to the place he got out, walked around to my window, looked at me and said, "I'll wait three months because of you."

That would be the hardest ninety days of my life, knowing Will's days were numbered. I almost just wanted to say just kill him now.

CHAPTER THIRTY

KENO

I don't know what time it was when my celly woke me up.

"Ay celly."

I heard that shit but I didn't respond. After a few seconds he tapped on the bunk. I grunted like he was disturbing me, which he was.

"Celly!" he said a little louder this time.

"What?!"

"You sleep?"

"What you think? Yeah."

"Can I ask you something?'

"Naw, in the morning."

"Say you went to jail for something you didn't do right. Say they gave you a lot of time but while you was waiting on your appeal you escaped right. Then you get caught up and they give you some more time for the escape then Bam! You beat your case on appeal. Should you still have to do time for the escape?"

"Go to sleep Foolio."

"I'm serious cause my case is on appeal right now but I'm still thinking about climbing over the mutha fuckin' wall. Cause I want some pussy bad."

236

"It's pussy up in here you got atleast ten C.O. bitches walking around here with they pants up they asses."

"I know huh and please believe if I had the chance I'd punish some pussy up in here."

"Mutha Fucka, you ain't punishing nothing. You ain't had no pussy in how long? It don't even matter. I know it been long enough. If you drop your little dick in something hot you skeeting all over everything immediately."

We both laughed.

"Yeah you right." he said. "Ay you wanna smoke some green?"

He was already up out of his bed before I could reply so I didn't say nothing.

He dug his hand in the toilet water and grabbed a string that was tied to a bag that he flushed. He pulled out a bag that was concealed in a rubber glove that had about a quarter ounce of regular weed in it. He rolled a cigarette sized joint and took two puffs then he tried to pass it.

I told him, "I'm cool right now. I don't feel like smoking. I got some shit on my mind now that you woke me up."

"More for me then."

He got back in his bed and laid back with his weed like he was at home.

I said, "You trippin'! You betta blow that shit in the vent before you get us raided."

"Stop buggin'. You know trick daddy Flint is working tonight. And you know Miss Big Booty Ponce' is working on the other side. So you already know the bizness."

"Oh alright. I know she got that good stuff too. I'd hit that but she need to do something about that wig."

He busted out laughing.

"I know huh that shit look like a beard."

Then we settled down and the room was silent for a while.

Out the blue he said, "Is there just no more morality in the consciousness of humanity."

Oh shit! He was feeling the effects of the weed.

I craned my head over to look at him. His eyes were red and he was high as gas prices. "I had to see who the fuck that was talking. Where'd you get that shit from?"

"I saw that in this book I was reading."

"See when you get high you start talking like a Harvard student and shit."

"It was a book by this conscious broad. It was talking about technology and stuff too. It said technology makes everything faster, vehicles and information and shit and making shit smaller too but it's fucking up the ozone layer. The more they create shit the more chemicals they spitting into the air. All the shit rises up and deteriorates our protective shield from shit like the sun's rays."

"Ay." I said.

"What's up?"

"Shut up."

"Fuck you Keno I was just puttin' yo ass up on some shit. When I get high I just go flipping through my mental files and shit."

"Well what you got in the pussy file?"

"You know what I just thought about since you said that?"

"What?"

"The first time I got some pussy, guess who it was?"

"Your sister."

"Fuck you."

"How the fuck am I supposed to know who it was?"

"Aight guess what it was?"

"Damn, let me find out it wasn't even human."

"Lemme just tell you cause you trippin'. It was a crackhead."

I almost fell out of my bed laughing.

He said, "And I'ma keep it real, it was a crackhead, crackhead. A smoked out crackhead. I fucked her in a closet, on some dirty clothes in another crackhead's house."

I was still laughing.

"I was fuckin' her like she was my bitch too. I think I got that shit off of watching movies or something cause it was like I knew what I was doin'. I didn't know you fuck different bitches different.

After that I fucked so many crackheads I can't even remember the first real bitch I fucked. And I kept that shit a secret, wouldn't let none of the homies know I was fuckin' them crack heads either. But then they'd try to come on the block and get some crack on credit from me. Then I'd have to front them bitches off in front of the homies and probably kick 'em in they ass too. Then that night I'd be in a motel with 'em and shit. Them bitches would suck a nigga's nutsack stainless. Oh I remember this little dusty bitch up the block. She might've been my first non crackhead shot of pussy, even though it wasn't no better. I fucked her in my driveway up against my mom's old Ford, standing up, from the front.

Oh yeah then there was these two bitches that just popped up in the hood all of a sudden. We didn't know where them bitches came from, they just hung around for about six months staying with whoever.

I had one of 'em for about a week while my momma was away on a trip and there was this other girl…"

I fazed out on him into a deep sleep.

The next day I walked the yard alone. On my second lap Mannish approached me. I put my guard way up but not my fists. I was ready though. He fell in step and walked with me. He said he had to tell me something about Shalleen. Cherise had filled him on an unfortunate incident. I was all ears.

The Street was dark and very quiet. No doubt everyone in the neighborhood was sleeping, except the dark gray cat standing in the middle of the street declaring ownership of the block with a "Meow" also awake were the moths bouncing off of the street lights. Headlights approached and pulled to a park near the corner. The cat ran. The two female occupants in the car never saw him.

The driver said, "You ready?" as she pulled a gun out of her purse and ejected the magazine and inspected it. She tried to compress the top bullet to make sure the clip was full, it was. She slid it back into the asshole of the pistol and jacked it off one time to release a round into the chamber. The passenger's eyes almost popped out of the socket.

"I didn't know you had that!" the passenger said.

"Bitch don't play with me, you know me."

"Bitch", was a word used very loosely among these long time friends.

"I didn't know you were bringing it."

"Why wouldn't I? I wouldn't let you walk into some shit empty handed, eventhough, you know Edward is a goof ball and number two, they sleep."

"I got two for you, one, Edward might be a goofball but Johnathan ain't and two, we don't know if they are alone or sleep."

"They gotta be asleep because that potent weed I gave them was that same stuff we had yesterday that put us to sleep at six in the evening and what time did we wake up?"

"Not until the next morning."

"Okay then you ready?"

"How we doing this?"

241

"The bathroom window is never locked." she said as she pushed the driver door open. She handed the pistol to the passenger and told her to stuff it in her jeans and exited her side of the car, the house was ¾ down the block. It took them about 45 seconds to make the short trek. They walked quietly up the driveway and around to the back of the house. The driver, who's name was Cantrell pointed to the back door she would open for Shalleen, the passenger, once she was in. They crept up to the bathroom window and,

Uh-Oh!

It was open, the light was off but someone was grunting. The foul smell of someone taking a crap escaped out the window. Oh My God! They both jerked back about a foot.

Cantrell held her breath and peeked in, she peered through the dark and saw that it was Edward, probably the Mexican food they'd eaten on the way home earlier.

"Come on." she gestured to Shalleen.

They went back to the car.

"See, I told you." Shalleen said.

"What the-fuck ever, we gonna wait it out. This is a one chance thing. We won't have the opportunity again. One shot Ershkin."

"Tell me the story again."

"I told you the story already."

"You got me out here at damn near 3 O'clock in the morning probably, risking my life tryna steal something I never heard of and the mutha fucka in the house is awake. I wanna hear why again!"

"Okay damn. Edward called me to pick him up early from work today, he got this new job at this auction house, only been there a month. When I get there he gets in the car with a nice size white card board box. He puts it in the back seat and we leave. He seems all nervous and shit but he never speaks on what's in the box. I never asked. I was hungry so we stopped at Campos on Robertson Blvd. and got some Mexican food, chicken enchiladas for me, beef burrito for him. We ate and I brung him home."

She paused, leaned over toward Shalleen, lifting her left butt cheek off of the seat. An audible fart came rolling out, stinking up the car instantly.

"What the fuck!" Shalleen said reaching over turning the key and letting her window down while she held her breath.

"Sorry." came from Cantrell, embarrassed.

After Shalleen had her head stuck out of the window for a minute of ventilation, she said, "Finish?"

"Pooting or the story?"

"The fucking story!"

Shalleen almost wanted to laugh, although it may stink you would think that a fart was laughing gas because whenever it's heard 90% of the time someone's gonna smile, giggle or laugh.

"Okay, okay." Cantrell thought back a few hours prior.

Cantrell and Edward had been there alone all evening just chilling. He obviously had no important or pressing engagement, so Cantrell was somewhat puzzled as to why he had needed to leave work early. The box sat in the middle of the living room on the floor just as simply as the smile that sat on Edward's face, something like the dog that caught the cat or the cat that caught the rat.

Johnathan finally came home around eleven, saw the box and everything exploded. He already knew where it came from and what it was. Johnathan was the reason Edward had gotten the job. Johnathan had friends there and guess who was the second person called when Edward didn't answer his cell phone?

Some wealthy Russians lucked up and won a 3 million dollar bid on something that was easily well worth 4 times as much. A sculpture Michael Angelo had created the year prior to his departure from earth. It was confiscated in a raid of a Russian mafia bosses Scarface styled house. They had kept track of it and bought it back.

Edward's job was to package sold items and have them ready in the pick-up department. One more guess at who grew a brain at the wrong time and who's fingers got sticky?

Not only were the police and the feds involved but the Russians had obtained Edward's name, number and address also.

Johnnathan was enraged at how Edward could be so fuckin stooopid! Edward fired back with the fact that this could be the smartest thing he'd ever done. Cantrell sat pressed into the corner of the couch and took in everything like a fly on a wall. Extreme fright and paranoia mixed with extreme excitement and impending luxurious adventure made her stomach bubble. She leaned over and released gas. Johnathan and Edward both looked at her.

"Excuse me." she whispered, ashamed.

With nothing else to say Johnathan stormed into his room and slammed the door shut. Edward stomped outside and sat on Cantrell's car in the driveway. Cantrell's nerves were crawling up one side of her neck and down the other. Her best idea was to roll a fat blunt of some really sticky medicinal marijuana. She tore it in half and knocked on Johnathan's door, no answer, she knocked again. Johnathan snatched the door open with a mean mug on his face. He didn't know it would be Cantrell. He tried to relax his features but his temperature wouldn't let him, she could tell. She extended the half of blunt to him and said, "That's all you."

"Thanks." he took it and closed his door. She went outside and smoked the other half with Edward. Actually, she took two puffs and watched him smoke the other half. Shortly after, they retired to Edward's room. A compulsory session of sex jumped off as usual and as usual, drowsiness kicked in. He fell asleep. She couldn't. The nervousness from the situation ran down her back and did flips in her stomach. She let go of a silent one, it stunk. Unconsciously, Edward rolled over and dug his face into the pillow. His alarm on his cellphone sounded off like the gunfire in a video game. He raised his head and looked at it. It went off too early. It needed to be reset. It was urgent that he didn't miss his phone call. He reset it and fell back asleep.

Cantrell couldn't sit still. She left, force of habit made her lock the door on her way out.

It was passed midnight.

Cantrell never saw the man hidden amongst the trees dressed in all black because he blended in like a drop of ink in a bucket of tar. He didn't move, he was sent by the Russians only to observe and report.

244

Cantrell was finishing up telling Shalleen the details for the second time.

"…and when I got home I was talking to you and that's when I decided, fuck it, why don't we take the damn thing."

Shalleen's only response was, "Fuck it twice! I'm in. How long you wanna wait before we go back?

It was 2:45 a.m.

The two girls exited the vehicle once again this time it was all or nothing. They walked quietly side by side.

Cantrell was the shortest of the two with darker skin, something more along the lines of a coco caribbean color. Her butt was shapely with a rhythmic bounce as she sidled down the street. She wore jeans, pink ballet type shoes with a pink blouse, no jacket. The night was warm, her hair pulled back in a neat ponytail.

Shalleen wore a lighter complexion, her attire was dark and ready for action with black Nike sneakers on her feet. Her hair also in a ponytail but covered with a black cap.

They made it down the street and turned up the driveway and around the back of the house. The window was still open and the toilet was unoccupied. The house was dark and still.

Cantrell climbed into the window head first like a four legged feline. She went in, one hand on the back of the toilet then the other. One hand went down a little further, on the side of the tub then the other as Shalleen held Cantrell's hips for support. One foot then the next on the back of the toilet. Her hands made it to the floor, then one foot. The follow up foot hit the toilet seat and it fell.

Uh-Oh!

Just before it slammed down that same foot caught it softly. She slowly let it down. She lowered her foot to the floor. She was in.

She stayed low, stayed on the floor and crawled out of the bathroom. She crawled through the living room and was headed for the back door. It felt way too awkward to be crawling through a house that she practically lived in. She had spent many a day and many a nights here. She thought about why she was even there stealing and it didn't take long to conclude the facts which were that there was no real relationship and no real prospect of a future with Edward. She had just been a convenience for him and place to deposit his semen rather than into a towel or a wad of toilet paper and he was just something for her to do while her life was stagnant.

She continued to crawl through the darkness of the house. The box wasn't where it was left on the floor earlier.

Damn! She didn't like that, they would have to tip toe into the room and search for it.

She was now at the back door. She stood and unlocked it with a click! Cantrell pulled slowly on the door. Shalleen stepped in, she was two steps in when Bam! Cantrell was snatched backwards with great force! Two hands grabbed Shalleen's shirt. She fired 3 shots!

Boom! Boom! Boom!

Johnathan was hit in the left shoulder. It twisted him 90 degrees. He squeezed the trigger in his right hand twice.

Boom! Boom!

Shalleen hurled her body at the closest person, Edward. They tumbled. Johnathan burst two more shots from his gun. Every shot electrified the darkness with a split second of light. Still he couldn't decipher who the intruders were. Three more shots rang out towards Johnathan from Shalleen's gun as she grabbed Edward in a chokehold from behind. A bullet lodged into Johnathan's thigh. He fell on top of Cantrell. He grabbed her and shuffled backwards in the dark. He backed into a coat closet. He haphazardly reached for the door handle and shut himself and Cantrell inside. Blood poured from his shoulder and sweat poured from his face. Cantrell's body shook terribly. Shalleen had backtracked with Edward to the far wall near the front door under a window. No one moved. The silence matched the darkness.

It was 2:55 a.m.

After several seconds passed inside the closet, Cantrell struggled and said, "Let me go!"

Recognition slapped Johnathan's mind. It was Cantrell's voice.

"Cantrell?"

"Yeah, would you fucking let me go!"

"What the fuck are you doing sneaking around in the dark?"

"Wasn't nobody sneaking around! I just hadn't turned the light on yet." she said, lying.

"So that's your friend Shalleen out there?" he said ignoring her comment. "What is she doing with a gun?" before she could answer, he yelled through the door. "Yo Edward you alright?"

Shalleen had a tight grip on Edward though he couldn't see her.

"Yeah I'm okay. You?" Edward answered.

Jonathan said, "I'm hit in the shoulder."

The blood was all over Cantrell by now.

"I'm shot in the leg!" Shalleen yelled to Cantrell.

"Oh no." Cantrell said to herself. She felt horrible. "Is it bad?" she yelled.

"I don't know. It hurts like hell."

"We're coming out!" Johnathan hollered, then swung the door open. They scooted out and away from the closet.

"My shoulder burns like a son of a bitch!" came Johnathann's voice in the dark.

Edward said, "Cantrell what are you doing here?" he was feeling betrayed.

It was 2:58 a.m.

Suddenly, the light flicked on, illuminating the room. Two tall men dressed in long coats came through the still open backdoor.

"She's no doubt here for the same thing we're here for. You must be Edward." one man said, pointing at him.

Edward didn't answer.

"You, we are going to kill but first, where is the box?" the other man said as he looked into Johnathan's room quickly. He then stepped into Edward's room, found and grabbed the box.

It was 2:59 a.m.

Boom!

The front door crashed open under the force of the hand held battering ram. Four officers quickly filed into the living room with weapons drawn and ready! Two local officers responding to the report of shots fired and two Federal Agents who had been parked outside all night. Everyone was caught by surprise, they all

247

pointed their guns at the cops as the cops maneuvered strategically into the room. No one really wanted to shoot an officer. No one spoke. Tension was thick, intensity was high.

Gunshots rang out!

Everyone cringed, nobody knew who shot but everyone responded with a flurry at the opposition.

"Noooo!" Edward screamed "It's my alarm!"

Nobody heard him over the guns blazing.

Edward had set his cell phone alarm for 3 a.m. He had to make a call at 6 a.m. East Coast time. He had a buyer for the sculptor in Philadelphia. This person had also kept track of the sculptur and had informed Edward before it even reached the auction house.

Blood, clothing and plaster kicked up all over the room. Bodies fell, bodies got pinned up against the wall with a magnitude of holes. Between all the weaponry, over 200 bullets flew and pierced flesh.

Everyone expired. All fell quiet, smoke floated around the room. The box sat on its side in the small hallway near Edward's bedroom door. It all ended it seemed as fast as it had started.

Call Edward a dumbass for getting himself along with 9 other people killed or call him Lucky with a capital L, for being the only survivor. His heart beat uncontrollably though his body lay absolutely still. Shalleen's body covered his somehow. Her eyes frozen open, locked into his. He moved his arm, surprised that he could. The smell of gun powder soaked the air. He pushed Shalleen over and he stood. He inspected himself, no holes he wasn't born with. His phone beeped, alarm reminder. The carnage across the floor caused undigested Mexican food to come up. He couldn't contain it. Maybe he would get over it and live a normal life and maybe not. What he did know though was that Cantrell's car had to be outside. He got her keys, his cell phone and the box and made way out of the front door. The last thing he left behind was a glance back at the price paid for his future.

I was in tears for a minute when I found out that Shalleen had gotten killed. I think that's really messed up. And who knew where this fool Edward was.

The Grapevine had told me that two of Big Will's homeboys was here. One of them was Mannish. Mannish didn't hang with his other homeboy or Big Will. He was a man to himself. I let Mannish be.

As for the other homeboy, well, they found him sitting on the toilet with his pants around his ankles and a turd halfway out of his ass. He was leaving this place with more holes in him than he came in with. The knife was still sticking out of his eye socket. His eyeball was split in half and hanging near his jaw.

Before I knew it my release date had crept up on me. I was 24 hrs from being back on the street. It's fucked up that Shalleen got killed and all my stuff got trashed but at least I'll be free. Wow! Shalleen is gone. I had Crystal on my team now. I can come up again. Another Wow! Me and Crystal made a baby.

CHAPTER THIRTY-ONE

Crystal had picked up Keno and they were in the car headed north, crossing Imperial, the higher end of one of the most popular streets that ran through Los Angeles, the Crenshaw Strip.

Crystal hit a pothole and something underneath the car rattled. No doubt it was time for a new one. It was a dark blue Ford Thunderbird with a bullet hole in the driver's side fender.

Keno and Crystal were on their way to Superior Supermarket on Manchester and Western in Los Angeles. This was the day her government assisted EBT card redeemed with $350 to shop with.

Keno must've been in a daze because Crystal kinda startled him when she said, "Damn! You sure are staring hard at that thing."

At first he didn't know what she was talking about but he snapped out of it and realized that he was staring at the Wells Fargo Bank that they were passing. A beautiful young light skinned lady with curly hair was exiting the door with an oversized black bag that Keno imagined was full of cash.

Keno wondered to himself if what Crystal was saying was at all true. Was he staring at it that hard?

He shrugged her off but to himself he thought, *Well that's where the money is. If there's anything I should stare at, that's it! Damn, was I staring?* he wondered.

Crystal was driving. She has light skin and beautiful eyes. She is short in height, fat booty and a short cute hair style to match. She let the window down and the nice breeze freshened her face on this God awfully hot summer day. Of coarse the air conditioner didn't work but still Keno was happy she even had a car.

They hadn't spent a lot of time together but irresponsibly just about enough to have a one year old child sitting behind Keno in the baby carseat.

On the iPod was a Jamaican artist, it was plugged into the car radio and blasting through the system, probably ruining the baby's hearing for life. But they still enjoyed the cool sound coming through the speakers.

Crystal's rent was due in three days. Keno had about $200 but not much more. Presently, they were both unemployed.

CHAPTER THIRTY-TWO

KENO

Crystal's phone rang, she answered it and handed it to me.

I looked at the phone then said, "Hello?" with a puzzled look on my face.

"Whutz up Homie, whut you got going?" my boy Jo-Jo said.

He always asks that. He's from the other side but we're cool. Jo-Jo is a guy that I used to do dirt with but we hadn't done anything together for a long time. Jo-Jo's luck was too good and my luck was too bad. Jo-Jo would never go to jail when he did a lick with someone, but they would. If they ever did a lick on something or someone and somebody got caught, you can believe that it wasn't Jo-Jo.

His road dawg Andre' was usually with him. He was good with his hands. Karate was Andre's thing. He could hit someone in the temple with his finger and dead them right on the spot. If you saw Andre' you saw Jo-Jo. As a matter of fact, they're both from Mannish's neighborhood also, but these niggas is alright. They gave Jo-Jo the nick name Crimey because all of his crime partners were in jail together.

"Ain't shit up, just grinding. Whutz up wit you?" I answered.

"Ah man, I just got outta jail, check." Jo-Jo said.

Wow!

I couldn't believe it.

"You did?"

Jo-Jo continued, "Yeah, me and my girl got into a squabble last night, check…"

Jo-Jo says check after most of his sentences. No one knows why, he doesn't even know why. He's been saying it automatically for so long that he doesn't even hear himself say it.

"…She was bumping her gums about some ole shit, bills overdue and shit, she found some pictures of some freak bitches on my Facebook and shit and lost her mind so I ended up poppin' her one in her mouth, check. Oh why did I do that? Boy, an hour later I was at the 77th division getting my dumb ass booked in. So anyway, the bitch came and got me out, check! You know I wouldn't even be fucking with that bitch if she didn't have all that ass, check. I just wanted to hit that shit a couple times and got caught up. Now I'm living with the bitch and the bills is due so fool, let's do something, check! So I'ma ask you again, whut you got going?"

"Wanna hit a bank?" I said, jokingly, looking over my shoulder at the bank.

Crystal looked at me out of the corner of her eye and sucked her teeth with a look that said, *I knew you were thinking about doing that shit.*

"Hit a bank? Hell naw! I'm broke, not insane, check!" Jo-Jo said in a crazy voice.

"Broke people are insane, Jo-Jo."

"I don't know many bank robbers who ain't locked up, check."

"But you would agree that all of them ain't locked up, right?" I had to ask.

There was silence for a few seconds.

There was a beep in my ear. I looked at the phone. It was a text message.

Thatz whatz up Babygirl? the text said.

It didn't have a name with it, just the number.

I read it to her and asked, "Who is this?"

Crystal asked me to hand it to her. She looked at the text message then the number.

"Oh. That's my daddy."

She deleted it.

She passed the phone back.

I continued my conversation with Jo-Jo.

"I'm cool on the bank shit, check." Jo-Jo said, "What else is up?"

"Well, like I said in the beginnin', ain't shit up. I'm just gonna be a regular guy. Just a fucking Joe Smow with money problems like everybody else." I told him.

Jo-Jo said, "You saying a mutha fucka named Jo ain't shit? or do his last name gotta be Smow?"

I laughed.

Jo-Jo said, "Listen, you wanna do some daring shit?"

"Nah." I said.

Jo-Jo continued as if he didn't hear me.

"I got a buddy who's been talking about doing something, you just reminded me, check. It could be more dangerous than that bank shit but not the same kind of time if you get caught, check. And probably more money, check. I can take you to him and you can see what he's talking about and decide if you got the nuts, check."

Mutha fuckas always talking about doing something and then never do it, so for entertainment purposes only I just said, "Whatever."

"Aight that's a go then, but it's gonna be a lil time before that jump off but if you wanna get some money today I got something we can do right right now, check."

"Nah, I'm on my way to go grocery shopping with Crystal, plus man, can I get a couple of minutes to myself? I just got out, I'm just saying though."

"Aye homie can I tell you something?" Jo-Jo asked.

"What?"

"Your future is created by what you do today, not tomorrow."

"Cut it out! You know me, at the end of the day, it's all about getting bread, yuh know."

"I'll see you tonight, check."

I agreed to meet up with Jo-Jo later on in the evening at 6 o'clock.

CHAPTER THIRTY-THREE

CRYSTAL

Me and Keno were pulling into the supermarket parking lot by now. It sat on Western down on a desolate strip where undesirables frequented liquor stores, pawn shops and supermarkets with less than quality food. Keno decided to stay in the car. He thought it would be cool if he and the baby hung out in the car together while I shopped.

As soon as I got out of the car the baby started to cry. Keno turned around in his seat and tried to play with him to cheer him up and quiet him. "It's okay, it's okay." he said over and over to the baby but babies can be relentless. The baby only screamed louder.

I looked on. It wasn't going to work so Keno gave that idea up, got out, found a shopping basket in the next lane, snapped the baby's carrier onto the top, gave me the cart and got back into the car solo. He didn't want to go in, thought he'd see what was going on around the outside.

I took the iPod not knowing if Keno would want to listen to it or not while he waited for me but I liked to listen to music while I shopped. I walked through the double doors and passed two healthy security guards stationed at one door.

Damn! I thought.

Just as I guessed, they looked at my ass when I passed. I smiled at them and continued on. The first department I came to was the produce. I loaded up on fruits and vegetables then moved on. I got a few pounds of rice and beans. I was the type to go up and down every isle and pick from what I saw rather than to have a grocery list. This is going to take a little while.

KENO

I just sat in the car and thought about things for a while. I laid back my seat and looked at the headliner above as it hung like it was tired of sticking around.

A dusty man I recognized as someone they called Legit, walked up to the car trying to sell me incense. I hadn't seen this cat in quite some time and couldn't believe he was still selling incense! I wanted to respect his grind but he looked bad and he hadn't grown structurally at all. The first time I saw him with his incense was 15 years ago! No lie! A loser is all I saw now. I told him to get the fuck away from the car!

How far can you get by selling something for a dollar on the street corner? How many sales can you make an hour, especially when nobody even burns incense anymore? It clouds up the house like a ganja smoke out. Everybody burns oils in their oil burners now.

I laid back in the cut and watched the people come and go. I saw a few people I'd known for years, some I hadn't seen in a while. Some looked great, like time had been good to them. They were driving new cars and wearing new clothes. Some women were fat as hell, like burgers and fries were the only things on the menu. I laughed at that. I closed my eyes for a while and tried to imagine what Jo-Jo's friend could possibly have to talk about at six o'clock.

CRYSTAL

I bobbed my head to the beat on the iPod as I passed near the guards again. They were watching me walk and when I stopped, one walked over to me and tried to get my name and number. I told him that I needed him to help put a big bag of sugar under the basket for me. We went to the back of the market to get the sugar. Then I asked him to go into the back of the store to find the manager so he could get me some fresh meat out of the back. He did and after I picked and weighed it out he began to put packages of meat into the basket.

They had no clue what was going on in the front.

Four armed men had stormed through the two front doors tackling the posted security guards at each door and stripping them of their guns on the way.

"Yall know what it is! We want it all or somebody gonna catch fire on they ass!" the spokesperson of the robbers yelled as he cocked his shotgun.

The cashiers cringed in fear and punched the necessary buttons to open their registers. Two of the robbers went by and unloaded the cash into big Louie Vutton backpacks. One cashier hadn't opened his drawer and didn't plan on it.

When the spokesman of the robbers reached his station and noticed that the drawer wasn't open he immediately smashed the cashier's mouth open with his gun barrel.

KAPOOYA!!!

Three of the cashier's teeth cut through his top lip and stuck there. The robber gave him a knee to the groin and an uppercut with the butt of the gun. The cashier fell on his back hard, would've thought he got hit with a tree. The robber flipped the register onto the floor and it busted open. A tattoo on his hand showed an aggrevated Cobra with its body wrapped around a dagger.

They were in and out in less than three minutes.

Keno didn't see them go in but he saw them running out. Two of the robbers went left and two went right. One of the two on the left had a backpack full of money and one of the two on the right had a backpack full of money. Keno watched in amazement as two police cars swerved into the parking lot at top speeds and screeched to a halt. They jumped out and pulled their weapons. The two robbers on the left surrendered without any problems. The two on the right ducked behind some parked cars and continued to work their way closer to the gate on the far right.

"Step out with your hands up!" the police shouted.

The two robbers weren't even where the police still thought they were. They were awfully close to the gate. A cop saw one of them through the window of a car.

"They're over there!" he yelled. "Freeze Scum Bags!" then he whispered to his partner, "I always wanted to say that."

The officer popped a shot from his pistol and it struck one of the robbers in the shoulder. They both broke fast and gave it all they had to hurl themselves over the gate. The one with the bullet in the shoulder nearly fell on his head in the yard next door to the supermarket. He landed hard on his back but made it to the car. The other robber twisted his body to avoid falling on his head and fell on his shoulder and almost broke it. He picked up the backpack and limped to the beige Buick Century waiting in the cut. His ankle was sprained.

He got into the passenger's side of the car. The driver turned the wheel and smashed on the gas. The car burned rubber making the tires scream into the air. The driver swung the front end of the car around and into the alley, kicking up dirt and gravel as he went.

The police couldn't give chase because they had to detain the two robbers they had apprehended in the parking lot.

By the time Crystal got to the front of the store with her groceries the police were everywhere. She was stuck in the store for an hour as the police took statements.

261

The two robbers that were captured were taken into custody. One was put into an office in the back of the store. The other robber was put into a mobile unit police van that had pulled up shortly after.

One robber was questioned right away and it was discovered that he was a minor. He was only seventeen and had a nine millimeter hand gun on him. They questioned him but he was hard, hard as nails. He'd never been in real trouble so he didn't know what he really faced. Those types are the most dangerous ever. Consequence means nothing. They haven't lived long enough to comprehend critically suffering later for something you did now. The officers couldn't get anything outta of him.

Hard as nails.

He wouldn't cooperate.

One black detective named Benson reached the crime scene halfway through that interrogation. He halted the interrogation and had someone fill him in on what had transpired. Then he immediately summoned all the possible video. They took some time to review video. He saw the robbers walking to the parking lot. They had parked up the street. A camera up the block caught them pulling up before the robbery. The store had multiple cameras and had recorded the robbery from many angles. When the robbers burned rubber the cameras on the traffic lights on Manchester and Western caught them coming out of the alley at a high speed and turn left. A mile up another camera caught them passing through the intersection of Van Ness. No more cameras ever saw the car again.

"DAMNIT!" Benson hollered.

He'd heard about the tattoo on one of the robber's hands and he needed a snitch, there were no lines he wouldn't cross. He stormed into the back of the van where the second robber was being kept. He immediately got irate. "You piece of shit you threatened that seventeen year old kid to rob this store with you guys!"

"What the fuck are you talking about?" the robber looked confused.

Smack!

Benson's back hand swept the skin off of the side of the robber's face.

Benson shouted, "Don't play with me, he told us everything. He's still talking now. You piece of shit! I'm gonna beat the shit outta you and then I'ma make sure that you spend the rest of your life picking up soap! We found a nine millimeter on him that has a couple murders on it..." Benson said, hoping the robber was too dumb to know it takes much longer to find something like that out. The gun hadn't even left the scene yet for ballistics or anything.

"...The cases in question both have you as a suspect. And now we have the weapon and someone who says you are the one we're looking for."

It was all bullshit Benson was saying but let's see if it will work.

"Man I didn't do none of that shit and he aint telling yall that I did neither."

"Let me ask you something tough guy, if you came home one night and found another man in your house, fucking raping your daughter, what would you do?

"I'll kill that mutha fucka and his whole fuckin family!"

"Okay, what if I told you that you autta pick your buddies better because he's telling on you."

"You got me fucked up, I don't rock with niggas like that."

"Is that right?" Benson said as he headed out of the mobile unit. He got into a car and spoke with someone then went into the back of the store to the 17 year old.

He stepped in, looked at the youngster and said, "So you don't want to talk huh?"

"Naw! Fuck yall. Take me to jail."

"Well, we found a gun on your O.G. that has some homicides on it. He says you are the one that did them. What if I told you that your buddy put it all on you and denied that he hangs with you and he would kill you and your family. He said you'd better take the rap. He said if he wasn't outta here tonite that someone would get busy with your family. I like to think I'm kinda

263

hip but I gotta be honest. I don't really know what 'get busy with your family means."

"Man I don't believe that shit! Fuck outta here! That's my big homie. He's a G! He wouldn't say no shit like that."

"Oh he wouldn't huh?" Benson looked into the two-way glass and said, "Jim play the track."

There was a silence for a second. You could here a voice faintly. It sounded like it was rewinding, then Benson said, "This is when I told your O.G. that the gun we found on him had murders on it. He immediately blamed you and said he'd kill your family if you didn't take the rap." then the other robber's voice played on the recording, "I'll kill that mutha fucka and his fuckin family."

Then Benson's voice said, "I asked him, 'is this kid your buddy?' and he said." the recording played more. "You got me fucked up, I don't rock with niggas like that."

"Like that?" the seventeen year old said to himself. "Well if it's like that I'll tell you anything you wanna know. But what's in it for me?"

Benson smiled, "What's in it for you? You don't spent your life in prison you fuckin' fuck." Then Benson calmed down. "You can save your family.

Now, the guy with the tattoo of the snake on his hand, who is he?"

KENO

When it was discovered that Crystal and one of the security gaurds were in the back and didn't see anything, they let her go.

She finally came out with the shopping cart filled to the brim with everything. I noticed her having trouble with the wheels, like they didn't want to move correctly. I wondered if the weight of the groceries were too much for them. I got out and helped her. I had the same troubles until I discovered a stone under one of the wheels. I backed the cart up, kicked the stone out of the way then loaded the trunk and back seat.

We went to start the car, it clicked twice telling us that the battery was dead.

I cursed.

Luckily, there were jumper cables in the trunk. It took a few minutes but I found someone to use their car to help jumpstart the Thunderbird. The man didn't use my cables. He had some jumper cables that only needed to connect through the cigarette lighters. The man plugged in the cables into his lighter then did the same in the Thunderbird lighter.

I wanted to tell the man to just hook the cables up to the battery because "that cigarette lighter shit" wasn't going to work.

The man told me to start the car and surprising the hell out of me, it started!

I unhooked the cables from the lighters, got in the passenger seat and Crystal drove us home. We pulled into the back of a little white apartment building on the corner of Market Street and Hyde Park in Inglewood. When we got to the unit Crystal went in with the baby and I took the groceries inside. The apartment was badly managed but I still felt fortunate to have a place I could come and go from when I chose.

Being in jail sucks.

After the food was put up Crystal walked me into the bedroom and pointed to a big white plastic bag that was sitting on the bed. I looked at her with a grin, went over and opened the bag. It had in it about four pairs of pants and four shirts. The name brand was Biz-e-Bee Apparel, Just B edition. If you could say that clothes alone had swag, could have swag without being on a swagga tight man then these were them. As I held them up to get a good look I could almost hear the commercial.

The clothes that gives a man swag. Just B.

Lol.

I smiled at Crystal. She had done good. I really liked the apparel. I picked up some brown Biz-e-Bee Apparel pants and knew I could pull it off. Brown is a color that has to be co-ordinated and worn right. I found a brown thermal sweater to match. It had Biz-e-Bee Apparel in white words across the chest and on the wrists. I couldn't wait to wear it.

"I got me some Biz-e-Bee panties and something they make called House Clothes for when you just hangin in the house. I got you a blue and red pair." Crystal said.

I took a load off by flopping down onto the couch. I noticed that the baby was laying in the playpen looking adorable and content.

"Bring me the baby Crystal."

She did as I asked. Seemed as if as soon as the baby realized that it was in my arms he started crying loud. I tried to tickle the baby but no go. I got up, handed the baby back to Crystal and went to the fridge.

I drank a beer while Crystal put the baby to sleep. She took a bath and came out with only some black and pink Biz-e-Bee panties on. Her body looked as if a baby never grew inside it. Her stomach was flat with not a stretch mark. She didn't workout but looked like an athlete. You know that slim/thick look?

The baby was fast asleep on the couch. Crystal pushed me down onto the bed and pulled my pants down to my ankles. On the way back up, she went straight for my dick, moaning all the way. Her titties rubbed up my thighs and knees as she slid up. Her right hand cupped my nutsack.

Her lips covered the head of my dick like a beenie cap on a bald head on a windy evening.

She spoke to me as she sucked, "I love your balls and silky dick."

She rubbed my biceps and pecks as her hands slowly went up across every curve of my chest. When my manhood was fully erect, she stood me up and let me watch her climb onto the bed on her knees. She extended her legs and put her butt into the air then looked at me under and between her legs. I didn't hesitate to mount her. I put my big ego inside her. I slid into her warm wet pussy from the back.

I began pumping like crazy. She moaned in ecstasy with each stroke as she looked on, admiring my work. I was so excited I came in only about ten minutes. I pulled out and went into the kitchen to get a beer. I popped the cap and gulped half of it down. Beer dripped down my cheek. I wiped it with the back of my wrist and set the can down. By the time I made it back to the bedroom I was hard again. I fucked Crystal strong for another twenty minutes and busted another nut. I laid on my back, breathing hard and staring at the ceiling.

Crystal laid on her stomach and rested her head on my chest and gently rubbed my abs just like Shalleen used to. She could feel wetness drip down over her clit and it made her cum again. She came again as I held her with a strong hug. She fell asleep. I stared at the ceiling and like I did so many nights in jail, I contemplated.

Thirty minutes later, I took a couple of cans of beer and went out the door to sit in the car and continued to think about things.

"Take it easy on them beers!" I heard Crystal holler from the room as I stepped outside.

The apartment complex looked like it was in Mexico. Toys and balls lay scattered around the courtyard. Plants and vegetables were growing in cooking pots. Car parts scattered about looked like they were being used for toys. I kicked a ball onto the roof as I walked through. I sat in the car and my mind drifted on the chaos at the supermarket.

Whoa! That was big!

I wondered how much money was involved.

CHAPTER THIRTY-FOUR

MARY JAY

I laid low with my top up two blocks down the street watching the Feds raid Magic's spot. He had it coming. Nobody who knew him would be surprised. Nothing was a secret for him. He was connected to a major supplier and everybody knew it. You would've thought every minute of his day was a rap video. He was too sloppy. I had gotten next to him easier than usual. I put my binoculars down on the passenger seat. It was just his time. I made a U-turn and headed over to the Westside got on the 90 fwy and went to have lunch at Aunt Kizzy's in the Marina. After I ordered a nice garden salad covered in blue cheese dressing with broiled chicken strips on the side and some coffee. I called this baller baller who it had taken me two months to "coincidentally" be at the same place at the same time with. It was one of those situation like Jay Z and the girl in the elevator on the "Excuse me miss" video he didn't even realize that I had on the same outfit as the girl in the video and my make up magic to look just like her. One things for sure and two things for certain, all the guys out there getting money love to re-live scenarios from stars on T.V.

He called himself Milky and he was a milk chocolate fine thang too, too bad he was gonna have to go down. A girl picked up his phone on the first ring. As soon as she said hello the phone hung up. I dialed again, I didn't give a fuck if he had a girl. He answered on the first ring,

"What's up."

I asked, "Is everything alright?"

"Yeah, everything's aight dawg. What's up though?"

I didn't know if he recognized my voice but I doubted it. We never talked on the phone. It was clear that whether he knew who I was or not he was pretending like I was one of his homeboys. I acted like I didn't notice. I asked him if he wanted to join me for lunch. I really didn't. I just wanted to see what he was going to say, "Naw, naw I'm cool but what's up though?"

I knew he was under pressure. His girl must've been right in his face. I knew after I responded his next move was to try to get off the phone. I decided to fuck with him.

"I was wondering if you knew how to give deep tissue massages, I'm sooo tense."

"Ummm…yeah, yeah, ummm."

I almost laughed right into the phone.

He said, "Yeah,… I could do that, when you need that?"

He tried to make it seem like a drug transaction. Yeah he sold drugs but he didn't strike me as the type to talk about it over the phone. His girl should've recognized that.

271

I told him, "Just call back whenever you're free… to put in some work."

Click.

I hung up. The waitress was sitting my lunch down on the table. I took my time and ate while my mind drifted on what I did in life. My lifestyle was crazy, dangerous, and deceptive, but it was for a good cause.

A convertible four door Bentley pulled up in front of the place. That was the thing about good black food and being in the same place forever, rich or poor they're coming to get it.

A tall average looking man with his platinum pieces on stepped out of the car. He looked like he was a basketball player but he wasn't, at least not Pro, because I would've known his face. I'm a basketball fanatic. I started watching the men running around in their shorts but then I ended up really getting into the sport. I even sit around all day and watch the draft picks, if he played another sport I wouldn't know him for sure.

He was about 6' 9" not likely into football maybe baseball. I became curious I made sure I crossed his path on the way to the restroom. I didn't have to turn around to see if he was looking because I had on a short skirt with the right kind of ass and the heels make that ass look even more right.

When I came back out I made sure I walked past his table on my way to mines. He was sitting with a couple of other guys.

One of them was tall and slim with pencil sized dreds pulled back in a ponytail and wore a jogging suit. The other one was big like a football player, a wide receiver. His hair was short cropped in a ceaser.

After I finished the rest of my salad, I ordered apple pie ala mode with vanilla ice cream, just to nibble on and waste some time because me and Mr. Man were gonna talk. Before my desert came he came over and introduced himself. He said his name was Sidney. I asked what he did for a living he said he was a basketball player. When I still had a blank expression on my face like, *For who do you play for?*

He said, "Not for L.A...um...ummm...I play for Texas."

Most girls only know who the players that play for their city and the standouts of others, that's why he said that. I noticed he didn't say what city, he just said Texas. What professional team player would be that vague. I showed interest in my eyes, just cause.

"Oh a basketball player. You must be good, playing for the pro's huh?"

This fool was a drug dealer, which probably meant his friends were drug dealers too. We talked briefly. His buddies or more than likely, his business associates were

273

ready to go. We exchanged numbers and they left. I watched the other guys get into a GMC Denali and pull up next to his car and hand him a duffle bag through the window. The stakes were just raised. Raised him almost to the top of my list right next to Rich Kid.

CHAPTER THIRTY-FIVE

TANYA

Before going home I went to the hospital to check on Ma. Ma lay in the bed motionless. There still wasn't much improvement, I thought about Ma not agreeing to chemotherapy and said, "Ma, are you just giving up on life?"

My hands were on my hips and I was very upset because it seemed to me as if Ma wanted to die.

"Whatcha talkin' bout Chile?" she asked, her eyebrows furrowed.

"I'm talking about you not agreeing to chemotherapy."

Ma folded her arms across her breasts and looked out the window.

"But you promised!" I whined.

"Tanya I aint promise you nuthin'. I said I'd thank about it an' I'm still thankin'."

Time was running out and even though Ma was talking she still was very pale and couldn't get out of the bed on her own. I didn't want to push her so I once again dropped the subject and we talked about my job and the things I liked and didn't like about it. Ma reminded me that there were disadvantages and advantages to every situation.

Ma told me, "Success is rooted in simplicity Chile."

So much wisdom.

I loved being around her. She was my lifeline and without her I felt I couldn't manage. The nurses continued to monitor Ma's breathing and vital signs as I looked on helplessly. Whenever I was sick as a little girl Ma always had a way of making me feel better and I hated myself for not being able to return the favor. Cancer was something I couldn't beat for her, Ma had to do it on her own or succumb to it.

I stayed with her for hours before I realized the time. It was already past nine p.m. and I had to get to work early in the morning. After kissing Ma good bye, I promised I'd come and see her the following day after work.

When Tanya made it home the neighbor was just pulling into his driveway with a female passenger. He waved at Tanya and rushed into his house. He and the girl stepped inside. The stench upset the girl's stomach immediately. It didn't smell right. Didn't feel right.

She said, "I-I think I should go."

He told her, "No Sweetheart relax, everything's okay."

There it is. There's that thing in their voice that tells you that everything is not okay even though they say it is.

Halfway through the living room she about faced, ready to exit the way she came. The neighbor smacked her on the side of her head. She stumbled into the coffee table. He picked up the remote and hiested the volume up on the radio. The speakers boomed an old rock song. Tanya could hear the music next door. The neighbor grabbed the female by her hair and slung her across the living room. The back of her head slammed into the wall, her eyes rolled, she slumped down in great agony. He came down with mighty force into the top of her head with his fist, crushing her neck. Her head fell. He dragged her lifeless body into the kitchen.

My voicemail was blinking. Malcolm had left three messages. After pulling off my clothes I grabbed a container of yogurt and listened to the rest of the messages. Malcolm was worried and he wanted me to call him as soon as possible.

I would call him right after showering and dressing for bed. As I climbed the stairs I thought of ways to break it off with Malcolm. I was just so tired of him and lately he hadn't been a good and supportive boyfriend. In the beginning he was so attentive and supportive, and he understood how I felt towards sex and he stuck in there and comforted me and I did appreciate his patience but now it seemed that he was looking for something in return. It just wasn't worth it.

After slipping on my old favorite t-shirt I slipped under the satin sheets and before I could call Malcolm I was out.

My night of resting was peaceful and exuberant. I felt much better about everything. I had faith that Ma would get better and that was the only person or situation I was concerned about.

Since it was the first day of spring I dressed in a pretty yellow wrap dress and pinned my long hair up with my favorite yellow butterfly clip. I slid my feet into a pair of yellow thong sandals, grabbed my yellow handbag and was out the door. The drive to work wasn't bad. The roadwork on I-55 had been completed. After I parked I saw Kimberly King smoking a cigarette by the door. As I climbed out and went into the building Kimberly gave me a tight smile.

"I'm sorry to hear about your grandmother." she said sarcastically.

It took everything in me not to turn around and slap the shit out of her but silly whores should be ignored.

How does she even know about my Ma?

I walked into the building and took the elevator up to my office. Kimberly had worked my nerve but I wouldn't let it ruin my day. I got off the elevator and bumped right into Stephan Hill.

"Hello." I said.

"Hi." he replied. He was always courteous and spoke and sometimes would chat for a minute.

We talked for a while then I went to my office. I told him I'd talk to him later and he simply nodded his head.

I shut the door to my office and plopped down at my desk. I had a lot of work to do and dwelling on my current dilemmas wouldn't help my work. For the moment I pushed Malcolm and even my grandma out of my mind. I had work to get done. The timeshare investments were going great and looked to be opening on schedule.

I'd been working for a few hours before Kimberly stormed into my office.

"Can't you knock?" I asked hotly.

I stood up and placed my hands on my hips. Our gazes met. Both of us were mad as hell. Me, for being disturbed, but I didn't know why Kimberly was angry. I didn't know why Kimberly even had a problem with me. I had a lot of reasons to hate Kimberly, especially because she was always so rude and obstinate.

"What the hell were you and Stephen talking about?" Kimberly snarled. I took a step toward Kimberly and Kimberly took a step back.

A mischievous smile pierced my lips. I knew Kimberly liked Stephen so I had a chance to mess with her mind a little bit.

"Don't worry about what Mr. Casanova and I were talking about." I said with a hint of sensuality in my voice and laughed. Having the ability to laugh at a lot of things is a great quality.

"Bitch, if you think he wants you, think again." Kimberly said.

Her arms crossed her full breasts, I smiled at her. I really didn't have time to play with Kimberly because I had a lot of work to get done and I wanted to see Ma later on.

"Kimberly get yo ass out of here." I said nonchalantly, like the cat that was tired of playing with the half dead mouse.

"Okay, but know that if you fuck with him you will be sorry."

She stared at me with those cold eyes before walking out the door. This time I locked my office door before heading to my desk. I continued working. I shook my head as I thought about Kimberly.

Lunch rolled around and my friend Fatima met me at the entrance. We were having lunch together. I saw Kimberly and Stephen talking and as soon as Kimberly saw me she began overly flirting with him. I had to stifle a giggle before climbing into Fatima's black Camaro.

"What do you want to eat for lunch?" Fatima asked.

We agreed on Sammie's Bar and Grill and in less than five minutes we were parking in front of the restaurant. Quickly we were seated and handed menus. The nice waitress took our drink orders before leaving the table. As we looked over the menu I told Fatima about Kimberly. We laughed a minute and soon the waitress reappeared. I ordered a grilled chicken salad and Fatima ordered breakfast with pancakes and bacon.

"Be right back." the waitress said.

She sat our lemonades down before leaving once more.

Fatima worked as an investment broker also but she worked for a different company. Me and her met at a workshop in downtown Memphis that our companies had sent us to. We'd been friends for at least ten years. Fatima was considered a close friend.

"What you got planned for the rest of the day?" Fatima asked.

"I'll probably work until about seven or eight o'clock then go home." I replied.

"Well me, I plan on doing plenty fucking."

We laughed.

The meals arrived and we ate.

"I could use this." Fatima said, smiling devilishly as she wrapped the syrup in a napkin and stashed it in her purse.

After lunch Fatima dropped me off in front of my job and my co-worker Jalisa was waiting for me.

"Uh oh, I forgot that Jalisa and I were supposed to have lunch." I said to Fatima then told her goodbye and that

I'd call her. Jalisa was upset but I apologized and told her that I'd make it up to her. Jalisa seemed to get over it.

Once in my office I worked for another couple hours then decided to call it quits for the day. My watch said it was only three o'clock.

"Damn." I swore to no one inparticular, thinking about Malcolm.

I gathered my things and left. I couldn't wait anymore to talk to Malcolm. I had to get some things off of my chest. He lived in Highland Park so I had a forty-five minute drive ahead of me. I played gospel-soul as I drove the length of the way.

I took the expressway to my exit. Once I arrived in Tipton County I stopped to get some gas and a little snack. I hadn't eaten since lunch so I stopped at Mc Donald's for a Big Mac combo. I'd loved Mc Donald's fries since I was a kid. You could see Mc Donald's all around my waist.

I was just finishing up my orange drink when I pulled up to Malcolm's house. I pulled out his house key and walked up to the door and I let myself in.

I wanted to surprise him and the expression on his face would influence my decision on whether I broke it off or not. Ashanti's music was playing through the speakers and the table held two glasses with wine leftovers puddled on the bottom. The television in the living room was on. There were greasy plates on the coffee table. On the way through the house I glanced at the kitchen and saw that Malcolm had cheffed up a meal. I walked down the hall and heard a giggle. A female giggled and the voice sounded sooo familiar.

Oh, Hell Naw!

CHAPTER THIRTY-SIX

<u>KENO</u>

Six o'clock had come fast and it was time for my meeting with Jo-Jo. My mind was wild with anticipation.

Crystal made me feel better about most things like a good girl should and she was good to me, kind hearted, made me feel like I could conquer the world. It was her who without saying it, made me confident, willing and ready to go and get some big money so I could raise our baby without any financial pressure.

I showered and dressed. I stopped by a mirror and just stared at myself for a bit.

Engraved in the top of the mirror it said, *What's the first thing people notice about you?*

I looked good, my skin looked good, my clothes looked good. I was ready.

The bottom of the mirror said, *Dream as if you'll live forever, live as if you'll die tomorrow.*

I could hear Ice Cube in my head saying, "Once again it's on."

If this were a movie as I looked in the mirror the narrative voice would be saying. *You never know how something is going to turn out. All you can do is just go for it* I had been on a lot of licks in my life and most turned out better than others but some landed me in the big house staring at a hell of a prison sentence. Those were the times when I wished I'd done the right thing and finished school, got the degree and good secure job. But hey! Who was I kidding? I never had a chance from the beginning. Sometimes it just is what it is and I'd been doing the best that I could with the brains I was given by the Lord. I looked up into the sky, kissed my two fingers (index and middle) and threw them up to God. I grabbed the Biz-e-Bee Apparel lettermans jacket Crystal had gotten me and was out.

The car overheated as I was passing the cemetery southbound on Prairie on my way to meet Jo-Jo. Same street I drove down trying to get away when Big Will shot me. I pulled to the right just before Manchester.

When I got out to check the car, I noticed a pretty young Asian girl in the street in the midst of two crafty, gutter looking gangsters. It looked like she had run into the back of their car. Me, being the opportunist I am, I dashed to be a part of the come up by saying I was a witness. But when I got closer and within ear reach I learned that they were trying to pressure her for money with intimidation. She hadn't even hit their car, just came close to it.

I intervened and reminded the two gangsters that they were in the middle of the street committing a stupid felony, which she is sure to tell if the police pull up. "...and yall know Inglewood be hot with police." Their scheme was foiled and what I told them held weight. The gangsters just turned around, got in their car and left.

The girl's eyes screamed Thank you. She asked her savior what my name was. I don't know why but I told her my real name.

"Keno Brown."

She was very appreciative but I turned my back to her and began walking. I wasn't doing it for her. I just didn't want to see two brothers going down behind a woman of another race. I didn't want her "thank you" unless it was monetary. I went back to the car and shockingly, it started.

It was okay that I helped the girl. Maybe it could possibly balance the wrong I had done and was about to do. Maybe the good deeds added up.

I remembered a time when I was a young boy going to Emerson Elementary School,

It was the first day of school. Keno was in the 5th grade. The teacher was calling everybody by their first and last name.

"Keno Brown." The teacher called out.

"Here." he answered.

She checked him in. A few names down the line she said a name that tickled everyone especially Keno.

"Solomon Alexander Sweetwater!"

Keno burst out laughing, almost spit out the candy he had in his mouth. Solomon looked at him with an attitude. Keno knew

he was soft by the look on his face. His eyes said he wished he had the balls to teach Keno a lesson.

He looked back at the teacher and said, "Solomon Alexander Sweetwater here."

Keno giggled again. Solomon looked back at him. Keno pursed his lips and said, "My bad." still giggling. He couldn't help it. He wasn't trying to diss the boy. But a black dude with that name, it killed Keno!

After that Keno was extra nice to him because he was cool, his name wasn't his fault. They didn't hang out but Keno would be a friend when needed.

For example: like the time when some young Crips were messing with Solomon because he had on a red shirt. It was just him against four of them. Three were in his grade and one was in the grade under him. Solomon was spooked as hell, he didn't know what to do.

At a young age the three young boys were already the type to prey on the weak. Keno stepped up just as the youngest one pulled a gun. Keno froze for a second, never actually seeing a gun up close, let alone in someone's hands smaller than he was. Keno stepped in like a super hero and told the young boy he'd have to shoot him first. The youngster closed his eyes and squeezed.

Click!

Oh Boy!

Keno almost shyt like he had on a diaper.

Nothing happened.

The young boy was really too young to know how to use a gun.

Thank God!

Then one of the older boys said, "Put that shit up! I think the school security is coming this way."

Lil man stashed it in his pants and they strolled off.

"You okay Solomon Alexander Sweetwater?" Keno asked mockingly.

He was okay now that it was over.

A lot of things happened that day. Lil man became destined to pull the trigger on someone. Keno became fearless in the face of danger and Solomon became eternally indebted to him.

287

The light for the transmission was beginning to shine on the Thunderbird's dashboard. Now I was worried about when that would fail on me or Crystal. I continued on and met up with Jo-Jo on Imperial Hwy and Crenshaw Blvd, the same area I was passing when we talked earlier. I drove into a shopping center parking lot where there was a nail shop that all the girls were magnetically attracted to for some reason.

I noticed Jo-Jo driving down the aisle. I made a quick park and got into Jo-Jo's Buick as Jo-Jo made a phone call. After a little back and forth he said,

"Aight we on the way to the house, check?"

Jo-Jo hung up the phone and drove out of the parking lot. I wondered who the guy Jo-Jo talked to was and how serious he was about getting money.

Jo-Jo had got to keep $3,500 of the $9,100 in the bag from the supermarket lick. $1,500 went on overdue bills. He spent $200 at the Slauson Swapmeet on a pair of sneakers, a couple jeans and a grey knock off YSL t-shirt and kept the rest in his pocket to accommodate his habits until more money came in.

About ten minutes after Jo-Jo and me got together we were pulling into a driveway on 121st street and Van Ness. It was an unincorporated area. It didn't fit into any city limits. When the city lines were drawn, every piece of land wasn't included between Los Angeles and Gardena. It was one of those quiet streets surrounded by bad neighborhoods on all four sides. Most of the houses were mid-size stucco with bars on the doors and windows.

We slowed in front of a house and pulled down the driveway to the back and into the garage.

As soon as the car was in Park, a man came out of the back door of the house and got into the back seat of the car. He was about 30 years old, medium everything. He was a medium size guy with a medium length of hair on his head, it wasn't long hair but you couldn't call it short either. His skin color was like a medium brown. The kinda guy who wants a medium soda and medium fries with his combo. He smelled like he had been smoking a Black and Mild cigar, do they come in medium?

"Whut up Jo-Jo?" he said.

"I'm good, check. What's up wit you homie?" Jo-Jo said.

"Nothin', chillin'." he said.

"Whut up, I'm Sonny." he said to me and offered his hand over the seat.

"I'm just tryna get paid. What you got that's gonna get us paid?" I said while shaking Sonny's hand slowly.

"You don't waste no time huh?" Sonny said, looking me in the eye.

"Nah." I responded, returning the look, eyes locked then unlocked.

Sonny smiled and said, "I like that. Aight this is the deal. I'm talking about robbing a club. Right now I ain't gonna tell you which club but best believe it's a lot of money up in this joint. We gonna take everything them mutha fuckas inside got and when I say everything, I mean everything, from the money in they pockets and purses to they jewelry. I might decide to take the mutha fucking DJ booth." Sonny was real animated like he couldn't wait to do it. "I'ma tell you one mo' thing. This is one of the poppinest clubs in Hollywood. Oh and the #1 artist on the pop charts is performing on the night of the come up."

After saying that, Sonny was quiet. He sat back and controlled his breathing.

It was my turn to talk. I said, "I don't know about all that, I can't see how that shit is even possible."

"What you mean possible?" Sonny sprung up! "Not only is it possible but its probable. And not only is it probable but muthafucka, its inevitable!"

"Inevitable? What does that mean?"

"That means it is what it is. Ain't nothing or nobody gonna stop me from doing it!"

I said, "I could see if it was something where you only had to worry about one or two security guards even if they did have guns, but a whole packed out nightclub full of security, I don't see it?"

"So you saying you would hit something with only two guards even if they had guns?"

"Yeah."

"Like what?"

"Like a bank or something. But I aint saying that's what I want to do. I'm just saying this club shit is extra-ed out!"

"Aight, I see where you coming from. I'ma make you a believer. I got something we can do. I'ma put it to you like this, there's a place, got plenty money, only two guards, regular guys. If you with it, come over here Saturday evening and we gonna put a move down."

I started to ask for more information like what kind of place he was talking about but instead I just said, "I'll be here." I had to admit to myself that I was a bit intrigued.

With that, Sonny got out of the car and we backed out the driveway. Jo-Jo never said a word. The whole time he was just smiling.

On the way back to my car we didn't even speak, I just stared out of the window. This was a day that my mind was anxious. On the inside I was smiling. Sonny sounded like he was about business but time would be the decision maker.

We pulled up next to a Range Rover at a red light. It's hard to not have what you think you deserve then see people pass by you who you don't think deserve what they have.

My lips curled up at the thought of finally having a Rover. I'd been wanting one of them for the longest time.

We'll see. I thought.

Jo-Jo dropped me back off at the Thunderbird and drove off. I turned the key and the damned battery was dead again. It took me an hour this time to find someone selfless enough to want to spend their time giving me a jump. Once the car was started I was on my way.

SHANTEL

I had thought I saw Keno driving some piece a shit car. I didn't think he would drive something like that but it looked a lot like him. I had Tarika chasing this car down for about two miles now. Finally on Century and Yukon, we got stopped at the red light along side Keno. I was in a silver BMW, about ten years old with dirty windows. He didn't recognize the Snicker colored female driving or the kid in the back seat, but this brown paper bag complexioned passenger was his chick forever. We'd barely dealt with each other much in a few years but I'll always be his bitch. My name is Shantel. I was his bitch, he was my baby.

We pulled over into the shopping center parking lot which held a host of restaurants and stores like Red Lobster and Chili's restaurant. On the other side of Century was a Target and Home Depot.

I live in Keno's old neighborhood. I was something trifling from day one and I know it. Keno should have known better than to have a relationship with me at all to keep it real. At first it was just about the sex, it is always just about the sex in the beginning. I'm one of those females that you should just fuck and keep it moving. Okay you may fuck twice. I keeps it all the way real. Sorry to say that there are those kind of females out here and here I am, but I am hard to let go. I spent all of my money on weed and bottles of

Vodka. My body is soft and any man would love to lay up on it all night and day. My chest was almost flat but the tities were there, enough to make my naked body look sweet. My ass is supple and shaped great. The same way tall guys are built for basketball, I was built to be a stripper and I was good like LeBron. As far as sex was concerned, I was always game for any sexual desire Keno thought up. I had three holes that I knew how to use liberally.

Whoa!

I am a fiend for sex like only in a horny man's dreams. I couldn't get enough of Keno though.

Threesomes were no problem and to top it off I did whatever he said, no matter how perverted or illegal.

I held things with pretty hands and walked around indoors with pretty feet. I also had a swapmeet attitude that wasn't so pretty. I also kept Keno on a loose leash by being the ultimate party girl and by giving him money when he needed.

The driver was my stripping buddy Tarika, a underhanded chick that was always into something and her son was in the back seat playing with a PSP. Tarika was worse than me, when she gets loaded, like more than three drinks she'll go and go until she passes out.

Me and Keno looked at each other.

"What's up Baby?" I said to him once the filthy window came down. "I heard you was about to be getting out. You on your way to my house right?"

"Nah, but I will later though. You still stay in the same spot?"

"Don't play! You know if I would've moved you'd know."

I was there for him forty percent of the time so he gave me the love I seemed to be desperately missing in my life. I classified as an alcoholic, mostly cheap liquor, White Zinfandel and cheap Vodka or Gin shots. Weed was a must.

Keno told me, "Bye" but before we pulled off I asked, "I'ma see you tonight right?" then I handed him a key to my door.

"Of course girl. You know I can't live without you."

"Funny thing about a mouth, It'll say anything." I replied.

Just then a guy walked up trying to sell incense. He asked me if I wanted to smell his new flavor just as he noticed Keno in the other car.

"Get the fuck on Legit!" Keno said through his teeth.

He almost ran.

Us girls laughed.

"Momma I'm hungry." Tarika's son said.

"Shut the hell up. Ask yo daddy for some food, if you can find his ass. You always asking for something. Look what you've done to my life. Look what you've done to my stomach. I can't even charge what I want to charge for this body. You just worry about getting your ass in the bathtub when we get home and don't turn on my damn hot water neither."

Tarika was interrupted when her BMW got hit from behind by a little Spanish lady in a little white Chevrolet car. Tarika's son looked out of the back window. Tarika had done sooo many insurance accident scams that now that she had a real accident she didn't want to be involved.

She let the lady go with no fuss. The lady walked back to her car with her license and insurance card in her hand looking at the damaged quarter panel on Tarika's car.

CHAPTER THIRTY-SEVEN

TANYA

As I inconspicuously crept to the door I heard, "Oh, fuck me Daddy!"

"Whose pussy is this girl?" Malcolm said.

"Yours, all yours." The girl purred

"We gonna get that money?" he asked.

"Yes Daddy, I will steal it for you. Anything for you Baby."

The only problem was that she was the type to say anything while she was getting fucked good. But while she was sober Malcolm couldn't ever get her to actually do it. Everytime he got her to say it he only could hope she meant it.

I could smell the maple syrup that Fatima stole from the restaurant in the air. I was getting sick to my stomach. A lotta questions were running through my mind instantly.

What money does he want her to steal?
Is he using a condom?
How could she smile in my face?
Is it because I won't suck his dick?
Does he eat her pussy then kiss me?

I lightly pushed the door open. Peeping through the crack, my eyes grew as big as quarters and I gasped and fell back. I saw Malcolm and Fatima, fucking. I had to cover my mouth.

Malcolm and Fatima were going at it like an X-rated reality show. They were both covered in syrup. It was all over their faces and bodies.

Wet anger rolled down my face. I sat on the floor and restrained myself while contemplating my next move as Fatima's moans filled the house.

Suddenly, rage overtook me and I wished I was at home to get Malcolm's gun out of my panty drawer and kill him with his own gun. I got up and went to the kitchen, grabbed a steak knife and started toward the bedroom.

I bursted through the door like a madwoman, I held the knife up above my head and went toward Malcolm.

"Arrrrrgggghh!" I screamed.

Fatima jumped off of Malcolm's dick and ran to the corner clutching the sheet, she covered her naked body. They both looked at me like I was the crazy one. I was now standing on the bed, holding the knife down to Malcolm's throat as Malcolm braced himself against the headboard. Fatima sat nearby with her hand over her mouth. I would handle her in a minute. Fatima was supposed to be my friend. I thought we were like Thelma and Louise. And Fatima would do this to me?

"Tanya, Baby I-I can ex-explain." Malcolm stuttered.

"What is there to say? I saw it all."

298

The room smelled of sex, syrup, weed, sweat, and alcohol all mixed together and I wanted to regurgitate my Big Mac.

I pushed the knife down a little harder on his neck and Malcolm's eyes nearly bulged out of his head.

I then thought of Ma and my future and couldn't do it. I couldn't go to jail for killing him, he wasn't worth it. I threw the knife aside, turned and smacked Fatima down to the floor then went out the door.

Malcolm and Fatima were on my heels but I didn't want to hear nothing they had to say. They didn't exist anymore.

By the time I made it to my car I was hysterical. I started the engine, put the car in gear and drove off. Malcolm jumped in front of the car naked, balls swinging, trying to stop me. Once he saw that I wasn't going to stop he tried to jumped out of the way but it was too late. I crashed into his leg and he fell back. The leg didn't break. I looked in the rearview mirror and saw Malcolm on the ground. I also saw Fatima run over to him and lean over to see if he was hurt.

"That Bitch." I grumbled.

I was in a state of total disbelief and shock. All the years we'd known each other meant nothing to Fatima because she'd betrayed me in the worst way. Fatima didn't care about me at all. Fatima only cared about Fatima and getting her pussy wet.

My cellphone consistently rang but I ignored it because I knew it wasn't anybody but one or both of them. Pain had turned to rage. Not caring to look, I threw the phone into my purse.

Back at Malcolm's house Anthony Hamilton's music filtered through the small apartment while he thought about Tanya. Tanya was a cool female as far as he was concerned but she wasn't trying to go along with his scheme to come up on millions.

His love of money and his greed made him carry on an affair with Fatima.

For months Malcolm had been begging Tanya to embezzle money from TSL Investments but it wasn't working.

Fatima was his only hope. His only option for the money he only dreamed of having someday. He saw himself living lavishly, driving through the hood in a Bentley and all the guys on the block stopping and taking notice of him. He wanted to be the H.N.I.C. Those aspirations made him go after his next option, Fatima. It was an opportunity made in heaven. He could tell she was feeling him because whenever she was around she'd give him that look, the look of lust and want. The biggest hint was how she'd always dress very provocative when she came over Tanya's house. Tanya didn't even suspect anything. She didn't know her girl was so heartless, so callous. Tanya trusted Fatima and Malcolm knew it.

One day Fatima passed by Tanya's house and saw Malcolm's Toyota truck. Fatima knew Tanya's schedule so she knew Tanya was at work when she went by in the middle of the day. She blew the horn. Malcolm came out with no shirt on.

The neighbor was on his knees tending to his garden in the front yard. He had red stains on his shirt.

Fatima and Malcolm exchanged hellos. She got out of her car and stepped up to Tanya's porch. Malcolm allowed her to enter. It was on from there.

Now Malcolm was sitting in his living room alone hoping things went well with Fatima. It was over with Tanya, he'd failed his task and lost his allowance. Malcolm dropped his head in his hands as an Anthony Hamilton song played in the background.

CHAPTER THIRTY-EIGHT

KENO

I went to the apartment where Crystal was. The baby was crying but it didn't faze me. It seemed that I had connected with somebody who was about his business like I was, and obviously prepared.

I sat up in the bed and drunk a couple beers then rolled on top of Crystal and fucked her for a quick ten minutes then rolled her over and laid her on her stomach and stuffed two pillows under belly. Her ass was raised high in the air. I spread her knees and squeezed on my dickhead as I manuvuered in between her pussy lips. After only a couple pumps her hot wet pussy and soft round ass made me burst an amount deep inside her. I fell over on my back. She stayed comfortably in the position she was in, ass up. Cum coated half of my dick. Cable was on, the movie Ocean's Eleven was playing, I couldn't help but think about the night of the come up. My thoughts were totally consumed with coming up until I fell asleep.

Crystal got up to use the bathroom about midnight. She dropped some thick stinky turds into the toilet. She opened the bathroom window to let the night breeze circulate through the bathroom and air it out. She heard gunshots and then she heard some people scurrying through the back parking area of her building.

On the other side of the fence there were always a bunch of thugs hanging out, slanging, smoking, drinking, etc. There was always trouble too. She was used to it, she went back to bed. That night me and Crystal and the baby slept good.

The next morning Crystal saw yellow tape and police officers through the same window. One of the youngsters had gotten shot and gave up the ghost in Crystal's assigned parking space. It's a wonder how some people can see terrible things and still be good people. Crystal didn't seem to have a malice bone in her body.

When Saturday came I was ready to set something off. The thought of it had built up in me since the subject was brought up. I anticipated the conversation. I played with the thought of doing something that could get me out of my rut.

It is scary to do crime, the ramifications can be terrible if you are caught but the thought of being broke is scarier. The only thing that I didn't know was, what Sonny had up his sleeve. Anyhow, I was ready to roll out but the ole Thunderbird wasn't, so Jo-Jo had to pick me up.

We took Van Ness south straight down and went to Sonny's house. We pulled into the garage the same way we did the first time. Sonny came out the back door and got into the back seat of the car again the same way. He was Black and Mild scented. This time he had a folder in his hand.

He said, "Whut it do? I see yall ready to get paid and shit. Aight that's what it is then."

Sonny opened the folder and took out the first sheet of paper. He handed it to me and said, "That's the spot we're going to hit tonight. It's an underground After Hours strip club on Florence and Figueroa."

"Hit how, robbery?" I asked as electricity surged through my body.

"Yes sir." Sonny answered.

I took the paper and looked at it. It was a hand drawn diagram of the whole block the place sat on. Sonny had Jo-Jo's car drawn on the paper so we could see where he wanted us to park. Stapled to it were two pictures of the front of the place taken in the daytime. It didn't look like a club at all. It looked more like a store that had been closed down. He handed me three more photos. They were of a hot little young female. She was brown skinned and thick. In each picture she was hugging a different guy.

Sonny said as we looked at one photo, "The big dark skin guy with the thick mustache is the owner. The other two are security."

The two undercover security guards floated around inside and mixed with everybody else.

Sonny told us, "At any given time you might see the guards near the stage flirting with the girls and throwing money and drinking just like anybody else but one thing for sure and two things for certain. One is that they won't be drinking liquor and two is that they will have big guns under their shirts."

I said, "The bitch is fine. Who is she?"

Sonny said, "That's a chick I know. She's down for whatever. I use her for a lot of different things. But when I don't have nothing for her to do or if I don't deal with her for a while then she'll go find someplace to strip. But her loyalty is here." I thought of Shantel. "Anyway this last picture is of the guy that's going to be in the front. He determines who gets in and searches everyone."

"We getting searched?" I asked.

"I just said he searches everyone, didn't I?"

"So how do we get passed him?"

"Relax, you sound like you worry too much. My girl will have the guns inside waiting for us. Here, look at this." He handed me another sheet of paper. It was hand drawn. "This is what the whole layout on the inside looks like."

I studied it then said, "So what time we gonna hit it?"

He messed my head up when he said, "About four o'clock in the morning."

It was six p.m. in the evening at the moment.

I said, "The only place I can think of that would be open and have money in it at four in the morning would be a casino."

"Well think of it as the smallest casino you've ever seen but one thing for sure and two things for certain. One is, we gonna be paid by sun up. And two is, this is just practice for the big hit in a couple weeks."

Sonny gathered up all of the papers and photos and said, "Be back here at two a.m. sharp." and got out of the car. He stopped short, "Oh and dress nice. Button ups and shit like that." he said then continued on into the back door of his house.

Jo-Jo looked at me with that same dumb smile. He didn't say anything. Both his hands were on the steering wheel. A tattoo of a cobra and a dagger showed on the back of his hand. He took me back to the Thunderbird and I went around to my boy Mike's house by the airport. A couple of the homies was over there just chillin', smoking weed and drinking. They were mourning one of the homies who got caught off guard the other night, some enemies came through the neighborhood in a limousine, and when he walked up to the car, they started shooting. He ran and got shot right in the asshole. There was no bullet hole but he was shot dead.

Mike was arguing with his girl about everything from spending too much money at Chuck E. Cheese to letting the grapes spoil in the refrigerator to her not letting him kick their son's ass when he calls Mike a bitch. The child is only three years old and doesn't say much but he knows who to call a bitch and who not to.

I was anxious so I took a hit of the weed to calm my nerves. The inhale was deep, the exhale slow. I've been out of the loop for far too long and Sonny was my chance to get in where I fit in. I couldn't wait. Matter of fact a lot of people were already starting to look like something to eat, even the ones I knew.

CHAPTER THIRTY-NINE

SHANTEL

My phone rang three times before I answered it, "I only fuck with real niggas.net hello?"

"You stupid, Shantel girl, what you doing tonite?" Tarika asked.

"Shit, I was gonna do the usual, shake my ass for some money on Florence but I ain't gonna go tonite, I'm staying in. Keno told me not to go there, he supposed to be coming over." I said with a super cute grin.

"I know some ballers that need some girls for a party tonite." Tarika interjected.

"Yeah? Is they paying upfront?"

"Yeah, what you think?"

"Bitch don't even try to play. We don't always get paid upfront."

"Haha you right but these guys is gonna give us a hundred each just for showing up and it's supposed to be a bunch of ballers up in there tonite."

"Well, if Keno aint here by eight then I 'm wit it."

"Alright we in there then cause Keno's ass ain't coming. I'll pick you up after eight. Oh, guess what? I got approved for my Section 8. God is good."

CHAPTER FORTY

KENO

I had left Mike's house around nine p.m. and went to Shantel's house. I tried the key she gave me. It unlocked the door. Shantel wasn't there but the bed had a stack of over due bills on it. The economy was bad and seemed to be getting better and worse at the same time somehow. Strip clubs and restaurants always seemed to be full while at the same time more and more people were getting laid off.

Guess it's true what they say, "Pussy and food will always sell. They're economy proof."

Maybe Shantel went to chill out with her friend Tarika. I thought as I took a leak in the toilet.

That's something she said she did often, chill with Tarika. I left and went to Crystal's apartment and did the-family man-thing, steadily thinking about the come up.

At 12:30 a.m. I got up, took a quick shower and got dressed in some jeans, some colorful Nike sneakers and a soft light colored fitted shirt and left the apartment.

I didn't have a gun of my own but I needed one just in case me and Sonny got into it about the money afterwards. So I drove around until I found an older security guard patrolling a shopping center. I parked around the corner and walked back. As I approached the guard I started asking for directions in a funny accent. It wasn't English, it wasn't Spanish, it wasn't French, it wasn't anything the guard would recognize. I couldn't speak any other languages so I just threw some foreign words together and said airport and airplane a couple of times. I had an innocent and lost look on my face until the guard got within my reach. I had totally brought the guard's defenses down.

Boom!!! Bam!!!

I gave the old man a two piece without the fries, extra large on the shake!

The old man fell back but before he crashed to the ground I pulled the man's gun from his holster. Forty-five seconds later I was in my car and driving down the street with a .38 revolver in my hand.

That's how we always did it when we were younger. Sometimes it would be a couple homies. One of them would distract the guard and the other would run up from behind and put the guard in a full Nelson choke hold and then I would just lift the pistol from its holster.

Now I was ready.

CHAPTER FORTY-ONE

SHANTEL

When me and Tarika walked into the mansion we were in awe at what we saw. We knew we were going to come up big with any baller that would kick it in a house like this. The ceilings stood up high. There were four columns in the atrium. It was all big boy status. The bar was fully stocked and we noticed. Tarika asked for a shot of Patron for her and me after being in the house for only two minutes.

The men smiled in unison, knowing what kind of women they had on their hands. One of the guys named Marvel rushed to service us to get some liquor into our system. It didn't take long for the party to get started. There were five guys and only the two of us girls.

Marvel's phone beeped, it was a text message.

1 message from Katrina.

It said, Hello Marvel

He text back.

Marvel: Yo Katrina what's up baby

Katrina: Im at d therapist rght nw bt all I cn thnk bout is u fckn me. I wnt u 2 put tht 11 inch dildo n my asshole n fuck me wth tht big ass dick u hve wit dem hairy balls hangin

Marvel: I aint comn out there no time soon. I got ma thing goin out here in L.A. I got tht good green sticky Cali weed. I'm in my partner's mansion rght nw they got some strippers over here n shit

Katrina: Oh. U don't lke my pussy no mo? I wanna suck on ur dick Marvel

Marvel: I'll hit u up 2mor

Marvel put the phone down and took some ice cream out of the freezer and got back into what was going on with us. After things got going good, one of the guys took Tarika towards another room. She took a gulp of another shot of Patron on her way out. They fucked and came back. When they came back in, I aint gonna lie, I was jealous at Tarika possibly walking away with more money than me. So I took a swig straight out of the bottle, grabbed Marvel's hand and led him up the stairs and into the master bedroom.

Marvel set down the cup of ice cream he was eating on the night stand and unbuttoned his belt, took off his pants and laid back on the bed with his feet still on the ground. The first thing I noticed was his hairy legs and hairy butt cheeks. His balls were so hairy I could not see them but the liquor had me in a cool state so I got on my knees in between his feet, dove in and swallowed his dick. Then I jacked him off a little while I licked his hairy nut sack. He loved the feeling I was giving him. He told me to hold up a

312

second while he repositioned himself. I lifted my head up and he scooted all the way back to the head of the bed and put his back on it. I climbed onto the bed and put my mouth back on his dick. He leaned over to the right and put my right hand under his left ass cheek then leaned over to the left and put my other hand under his right ass cheek. He held my head and guided me as I bobbed up and down. I was on my knees so my ass was high in the sky. After a couple of minutes a lot of saliva developed. He pulled my head back and wiped off his dick and put his dick back in my mouth. He reached over my back to my ass. He grabbed one ass cheek and pulled me closer, he gave a pelvic thrust at the same time, shoving his penis deep into my throat causing me to gag. He then took the other palm and rubbed the saliva off of his hand and onto my pussy. He repeated the process again taking more saliva out of my mouth and rubbing it on my pussy.

My phone rang. Marvel lifted one ass cheek to free my hand so I could answer it. As I continued sucking I pulled my phone out. It was my mother, I put it on speakerphone.

I sucked Marvel's dick as I talked on the phone with my mom. My mom kept talking and I kept managing the dick sucking and the conversation. It helped a lot that

Moms barely took a breath. I just said some uh huhs and yeahs, periodically.

Marvel put ice cream on his dick and watched me lick it off. I kept licking and talking to my mother about my son's school behavior.

After the second time Marvel had smeared my spit on my crack, another guy walked in. He saw me face down ass up and gave Marvel an upward nod with both of his palms up silently asking, "What's up?"

Marvel gave him the thumbs up signal and secured my hands under his butt cheeks. He took my head back into his hands cupping my ears so he thought that I couldn't hear the second guy. The second guy stripped near the door and wasted no time. He slipped the rubber on as he approached the bed. It was an XL Magnum condom and it still barely covered the extent of his fully engorged dick. In a flash he was on me. He put the shin part of his legs on the back of my calves so that I could not move my legs. With the help of my saliva lubrication he pushed his fourteen inch dick right into my pussyhole. I tried to react but my hands were weighed down under Marvel's butt. The second guy just grabbed two handfuls of my ass and went to town. He fucked me hard. He fucked my whole pussy. He was digging so deep we were bouncing up and down as he stroked. My hips served as fuck handles. He fucked me too hard for me to continue sucking

Marvel's dick. I began to yell that I was cumming. This excited Marvel so much that he began to spew cum. He pulled my face close and bust globs of sperm all into my eyes and up my nose. At the same time the second guy released his load into his condom.

Omg! That was good!

Marvel liked me, I took it all and didn't complain and so he gave me $100 extra and his number. He said I reminded him of some bitch named Katrina. Me and Tarika got our $100 for showing up as we were put out.

We went to pick up our kids from the babysitter, gave her twenty dollars each and went home. When Tarika dropped me off, we gave each other a pound and put our index finger to each other's lips in our vow of secrecy and parted ways.

CHAPTER FORTY-TWO

MARY JAY

It had been a week since I talked to Milky, when his girl had him buggin'. I had already set the trap with that talk about a deep tissue massage, that only translates into one thing with men.

SEX!

The insinuation is enough to cloud men's minds. I knew he would call. I didn't think it would take a week but I knew he would call. I bet you can guess that I was not sitting by the phone waiting either. There are so many drug dealers out there and so little time. When Milky called he tried to act like everything was peace, I went right into my act.

"You just now tryna call somebody back? It's been a week. What if I already solved the problem I had? What if somebody already scratched my itch... I mean massaged my back?"

"I'm sorry baby girl I had some business to take care of."

"Uh huh, me too. You sure your girl didn't make you stay home?"

"What girl? I ain't got no girl."

That's what I was expecting him to say.

"You ain't got no girl? You ain't got no girl? Well where you at?"

"I'm at home by myself."

"Well what's your address? I'm bout to come see you."

"Well... umm... I'm sitting in my car in the driveway. I was getting ready to make a run. Tell me where you at. I'ma come see you after I make my run."

"Milky where you live at?"

"By Alliso Village off first street."

I knew where he lived. The street he said was kinda close by his house. I started to lie and say I was close by and I was on my way but I wasn't anywhere near there. He said he was already in his driveway. Fuck it! I told him to meet me at Starbucks at the 3rd st Promenade in Santa Monica in two hours. He agreed, happy that I eased up about coming over and blowing up his spot. Little did he know I had ran his license plates and knew where he lived with his wife. And I knew he was moving drugs, marijuana to be exact and worst of all, I was already tired of playing with his lying ass but I did find him physically attractive. I wanted to see his dick, maybe even try it out before I canceled his membership in the game. I wore no make-up, put my hair in a ponytail and slipped into a t-shirt and jeans, two and a half hours later I was sitting on a bench on third street with my third cup of

Carmel Macchiato from Starbucks in my hand and watching the alluminum man entertain for tips from whoever strangely enough found him interesting. I could feel the double shot espresso whizzing through my system like streams of cool water and hyper-activating my metabolism when my cellphone rang. It was Milky asking me where I was. He said he was in the five story parking structure connected to the mall up the block. I guided him in to my location next to Mr. Reynold's wrap. Me and Milky walked the Promenade for about an hour. I just wanted to waste his time. The Promenade was basically an outside mall. I was just taking it slow I wasn't in a rush. I knew what his future held, maybe I was letting him savor the atmosphere.

He asked me, "How's your back?"

I almost said, "How is it supposed to be?" then I remembered what I had told him. "Oh it's still in need of attention, maybe you can fix me... it, I mean."

When I said that, is when I knew I would fuck him.

He said, "Can we take care of that right now?"

I said, "I don't know. I think you have a woman, your too fine not to."

I kept contact with him while we walked for two reasons. One to fuck with his head, make him think we had something going. Two, because I could feel when his cell phone vibrated in his pocket. He told me to stop trippin' because he was a bachelor but here he is with his phone on vibrate because his wife is calling him. I led us into a sex shop and we looked around for a bit. I picked up this dildo that was huge, looked like it belonged on a horse, a big horse. I had to hold it with two hands. My first thought was to joke with him and tell him if he wasn't able to compare with it then we couldn't have sex. My second thought was that it would surely backfire on me and make my pussy seem like it was open like the ocean. Instead I just said, "Damn!" marveled at the size and put it back.

I saw some black leather stiletto low cut boots with a pocket on each side to fit a condom. The boots was part of an outfit complete with handcuffs and a whip. I liked them so he bought them for me. He also picked up some anal beads. Ain't no dick going in my ass but beads I can do. While he was deciding which beads he would have the most fun stuffing and plucking out of my ass. I acted like my phone battery was dead and asked him for his. About ten minutes later I came out of the restroom and handed him his phone back. As we were leaving I told him I was ready to go to his house, he said he was too tired to drive all the way home, like he really lived that far. Telling him "I'll drive" flashed through my mind real quick but I really couldn't see how that would do me any good right now, knowing his wife was there.

I suggested we get a room and we went to his car. I told him not to start the engine, that I just wanted to lay back in comfortable seats of his Aston Martin in the quiet garage. It was so quiet he felt like he needed to say something and when he started to I went Pulp Fiction on him and told him to enjoy the comfortable silence with me. After five minutes, right before the comfortable silence got to him his phone rang, rang out loud because I had taken it off vibration mode and unbeknownst to him, put it on speakerphone.

He pushed a button and put it to his head and said, "Hello".

When his wife answered back, her voice was loud and clear. He snatched the phone back to look at it, meanwhile she was still talking "Who the hell answered your phone a while ago asking me if I was your girl!"

He was busted!

She kept talking, "I said his girl? I'm his wife…"

He looked at me in shock.

"…Marcus! What the hell is up with that?!"

He was too shocked to respond. I was sitting there with my arms crossed and my-you ain't shit-look on my face.

He got his head right and took control and cut her off midsentence. "Ay! I don't fuck witchu no more! Why you keep calling me!"

She sounded more shocked then he did.

"What... what do you mean? We live together..."

He cut her off. "Listen Bitch, I'm tired of you stalkin' me and shit!"

This is a dog ass mother fucker! I thought.

She said, "Is somebody there in front of you? Who are you showing out for?"

"Showin' out?! Look man, I'm wit my new girl man. You ruining my life. You gonna have to get a grip. It's been over a long time." he said looking at me for acceptance, by now his wife was crying.

She yelled out, "You just left here two hours ago!"

"Man, listen man, don't call me no more!"

Just when she was saying, "You son of a bitc..." he hung up.

I wanted to shoot his scanless ass but I just said, "Bitches is crazy huh, let's go."

He opened the glove box and grabbed a nice blue steel 9 shot Smith and Wesson 9mm and placed it under his seat, then we were on our way. I told him to drive me around the corner to my car and then follow me. I decided to keep it simple and go to a motel.

I took the interstate 10 east to the 405 south passed up Venice Blvd and exited Washington Blvd. I swung around and got back on heading back north and got off on

Venice. The off ramp let us off before we actually got to Venice Blvd. It let us off with the decision of making a left or a right on Sepulveda Blvd. Left to Venice Blvd, right to Washington Blvd. Directly ahead across the street was the entrance to the Sea Breeze motel.

To the left and right of it was a string of competitors, we were way on the Westside so they were decent. I drove in and passed the window of the office. I went towards the back and tucked my car between two others while he paid for the room.

CHAPTER FORTY-THREE

KENO

Jo-Jo was pulling up to Sonny's house at the same time I was. I parked in front and got in the car with Jo-Jo and we drove down the driveway to the back. The garage was open, the house was dark, the air was quiet.

As usual, in the first minute Sonny came out of the back door.

He got into the backseat. He looked normal, like a regular 9 to 5 working class guy, with jeans and a button up shirt. He had on a nice expensive watch. It was the type that you couldn't tell if you didn't know because it wasn't gaudy and had a slim leather band.

I knew this cat in the car with me and Jo-Jo had made lots of things happen, probably had a few dead bodies under his belt.

"Let's go." Sonny said.

Jo-Jo backed out of the driveway and they drove to the place, which wasn't that far away from where we were. We parked down 73rd street in the same spot that was on the diagram. There were a lot of cars parked up and down Florence Avenue. Lots of ghetto action happened on Florence. It is indeed a main artery of the city's ghetto. I left my gun in the car and we walked around the corner, the first thing we saw was the big ass man from the photo searching a man half his size. Jo-Jo was still limping from when he almost broke his ankle.

As he searched us, we could hear, "No one else" by Biggie, 112 and Mase.

One's dead, 112 played out and one's a rapper gone preacher then a preacher gone rapper or somewhere in the middle.

I saw a gun poking out of the security's waistband as he searched Jo-Jo. Sonny was acting really weird, like he had never been to a strip club before, actually like he had never been on a night out. He was happy in a geeky way. Even made the security laugh and tell him not to spend his whole check inside.

We walked in and the place was kinda small. It was kinda dark with the lights kinda limited mostly to the stage where two girls were kinda fucking each other with a thick ass double dick dildo kinda thing.

They made me hard immediately. I went closer to the action right away. There was a lot of money on the stage and money all over the girls and no $1 bills. I saw $20s, and lots of them.

Those two girls did things that I never saw before. And the girls after them did even more. I noticed a couple of doors in the back where guys kept taking girls. I positioned myself by the doors so that I could see what was behind them the next time they opened up.

Both rooms only had a couch and a stack of towels on the floor.

I hadn't spoken to Jo-Jo or Sonny since we had gone in but I had seen both of the other guys on the photos.

I looked at my watch. It was 4:15 a.m. Just when I started to think about when we would be setting it off, suddenly, my phone started vibrating in my pocket. I looked at it. It was a text message from Jo-Jo forwarded from Sonny.

It said, Fwd: fllw da gurl wit da white purse n2 da rm on da rght. Get a gun. Thn position urselfs nxt 2 da 2 men u saw n da pics.

It took us five minutes to get that done. I was one foot in front of my man with my hand in my pocket, gripped on the pistol handle. I watched Sonny throw some money on the stage. It was the girl he knew. I couldn't tell how nasty she was on the picture but she was on stage doing some wild stuff. Sonny walked out through the front door. I didn't know what Sonny was doing but I was already strapped so I stayed close to my man. I could see that Jo-Jo was staying close to his man too. Suddenly, everybody heard a loud noise even over the music.

Boom!

The big man from outfront fell through the door backwards and landed flat on his back so hard that the building shook. Everybody jumped in fright and looked. Big man's eyes were staring at the ceiling. He had blood puddling up out of a hole in the middle of his forehead. At first everybody was shocked frozen staring at the big guard for a second, then we all noticed Sonny step in and close the door behind himself. The two undercover men started to spring into action. I gave the one behind me a elbow to his nose. It landed square on target and busted his nose so bad that blood splattered onto my face.

Jo-Jo drew his gun on the other one. I pulled mines out. Sonny's was out already and he was blocking the exit.

He hollered, "YALL KNOW WHAT IT IS! WE WANT IT ALL OR SOMEBODY GONNA CATCH FIRE ON THEIR ASS! ALRIGHT, FUCKIN' EVERYBODY UP AGAINST THE LEFT WALL NOW!"

He pulled a sheet out of his shirt that was wrapped around his waist, flipped it open onto the floor in front of everybody and said, "Alright, everybody is to walk over the sheet and drop all your shit, money, jewelry everything, except your car keys then stand on this wall on the right. One by one! Now lets go!"

326

Everybody was so shocked at what they had just saw happen to the security guards that they were willing to do anything they were told to ensure that they could get out of here alive and unharmed. This included the hardcore gangsters too.

Once everybody made it to the other side of the room, I took the adjacent corners of the sheet and tied them together then did the same with the other two corners. When I was done I grabbed the laptop off the DJ booth and snatched all the cables out of it and I headed right out the front door. I didn't know what else Sonny had in mind if anything, I just stepped over big man and exited the joint. Jo-Jo and Sonny were right behind me. We made it to the corner without anybody trying to follow us. We got to the car and took off into the night.

We split up the money and jewelry in Sonny's garage on the hood of the car.

Sonny said, "It just goes to show that when you decide to do something. You can do it, Right!"

After we divided it all up we gave each other dap and a look that was an unspoken vow of secrecy, we went our separate ways.

Sonny went into the back door of the house, Jo-Jo went to the left and I went to the right. When I got to my car I noticed that my rear tire was really low, like it had a slow leak.

Damn!

Jo-Jo was passing and saw that I was having car troubles so he stopped, rolled his passenger window down and said, "What's wrong?"

"Man this fucking piece a shit ass car been fucking pissing me the fuck off! I got a flat. Fuck this shit! Man can you take me home? I'm buying some new shit in the morning. Fucking punk ass car!"

Jo-Jo laughed and took me home.

SHANTEL

"Damn girl..." Tarika began talking as soon as I picked up the phone, "...you seen the news?"

"No."

"Guess what happened last night?"

Before I could answer Tarika said, "Big Josh got his brains blown out in front of the club and a gang of guys ran up in there and jacked everybody for all they shit." Tarika the hood news reporter said.

"You Bullshittin'!" I said.

"I'm sho fuckin' glad we didn't follow our first minds and dance up there last night." said Tarika.

"We would've been in that muthafucka probably half naked and shit."

We laughed.

CHAPTER FORTY-FOUR

MARY JAY

Milky got the motel room key then parked his car. He went into his trunk for a bottle of Ciroc Vodka and walked over to my car. I was messing with the pocket on the side of the boots that he bought me. I put 'em back in the bag with the other stuff and got out of the car. When we got in the room he took the ice bucket off the table and went outside. The room had a hot tub so I turned the faucet on to fill it up with water and kicked my shoes off. He came back in with a bucket full of ice and a couple of cans of cranberry juice. That spelled trouble and he didn't even know it. I had withdrew myself from the presence of alcohol purposely because it always turned situations messy for me, always messier than intended. Not yet has it personally got me caught up but I knew there was a big potential and with the juice, I could drink a whole bottle of Vodka like water.

I turned my back to him and said, "I don't think I want to drink anything." I checked the water temperature in the huge tub.

"Ah come on, you gotta loosen up. The alcohol will relax you so I can give it to you good. The massage I mean."

"I don't know."

You know how it be, I really wanted some but I didn't.

"Just a little bit, one cup."

"Okay, one cup."

"Alright."

He went to the table and made the drinks. In the meantime I undressed and got in the water. It was full of suds because I emptied the whole two lil bottles of bubble bath in it and had the jets on.

Milky brung me my drink and got in with me. Before he could get comfortable I was telling him to refill my cup. He got back out, dick swinging. He made me another cup and gave it to me. I took a sip and sat it down. I felt warm inside. I moved to his side of the tub and sat in his lap facing him. We weren't talking, I was just looking into his eyes. My right hand was being mischievous under the water rubbing the tip of his dick on my clit. Then suddenly, I just got up and got out of the water. Suds were sliding down my body. I walked into the bathroom to get a towel. He stood, I told him to be cool and sit back down. He was watching my every move as I bent, reached and seduced him in the way I ran the towel over my body. I felt the liquor swimming through my head. That feeling that makes me want more. I downed the rest of my cup then I put the stiletto boots on. I grabbed the whip out of the bag and snapped it in his direction.

"Stop playin." he yelled.

"Boy don't be so scary. It could get worse than that."

I walked over to the table with the Vodka and the juice on it. The heels of the stiletto's had my calfs and my ass looking good. I took a nice swig of the Vodka and then another one.

Whoa!

Then I chased it with a gulp of cranberry juice. I took another swallow of the Vodka and told him, "Come 'ere."

He got out the water so fast I laughed at him.

"You a impatient ass freaky ass lying ass punk."

The liquor was starting to take over. I could tell because that was my first time verbalizing about his lies.

"Yeah and you gonna love all my asses once I put this meat in you." he said holding on to his thick chocolate dick.

My pussy throbbed.

Before he came to me he went to his pants. I thought he was getting a condom but he came up with a pack of about an eighth of an ounce of powder cocaine, knocked some out on the table and made up four lines. He snorted two lines right quick and left two.

Now he was playing with fire!

I chose coffee to substitute my cocaine usage. The caffeine didn't amp me up as much, it was working for me. Now he had two lines sitting on the table for me.

I said fuck it!

I was gonna fuck him and fuck him over anyway so now I might just over fuck him. I snorted the two lines. My nose tingled. I held my head back a minute, sniffed back in the drain.

Booyow!

My head felt like a hot air balloon lifting up in the air and at the same time like a carousel because of the liquor. Before I knew it I spun and snapped the whip at Milky again. It stung him on his chest.

"Ouch Bitch!"

"Bitch? Okay I'll be your bitch but you a pussy with your pussy ass."

He was pumped up too because hc had alcohol and cocaine in his system too. He grabbed me by my arm. I dropped the whip. He pulled me onto the bed and got behind me. Before I knew it he had pushed his dick up in me. He had a tight hold around my arms and body, banging me. Banging the shit outta me! He made me cum after only about ten of his thunderous strokes. He found out I liked it rough. He grabbed me by my hair and pulled it hard as he slammed into me doggystyle.

Pow! Pow! Pow!

Like he was a jockey trying to win a horse race

"You like that don'tcha Bitch!"

"Yeah!" I growled as I threw my ass back on him. I clenched the sheet so tight it slipped from under the edges of the mattress. I got aggressive and began out matching him stroke for stroke. I was pounding my ass into his groin harder than he could pump my pussy from the back. I was completely under the influence of everything. After his upstroke he was ready to return a hard pump but I was already bashing back into him.

"Whoa!" he said almost falling off of this wild stallion but he was still tryna talk shit. "Yeah Bitch take this dick!"

I was on him though, bucking.

Pow! Pow! Pow!

I decided I wanted to get verbal too.

"Yeah gimme that dick you pussy ass punk!"

"Bitch you betta watch yo mouth!"

I was totally engulfed in it now, dripping sweat. Strands of hair was sticking to my face. He grabbed a fist full of hair and snatched my head back in an attempt to check my mouth and control my bucking.

"Ah yeah!" I growled again.

I reached my hand back and grabbed one of his butt cheeks and cocked one of my legs up like I was tryna slam his lower half into my pussy.

Pow! Pow! Pow!

"Get all this pussy, you pussy!"

I looked back and I saw his face was all balled up. He was mad because I was being too rough and I was disrespecting him, but I didn't like his personality. He had lost major points for dissing his wife like that. I know I had him on the verge of pulling his dick out of my pussy and putting his foot in my ass.

Pow! Pow! Pow!

With every thrust we inched further and further back.

Just when he said, "Fuck this shit! Stop!"

Bam! We fell on the floor.

"Damn Bitch!" he snapped at me. He was on his back.

I ignored him, reverse my straddle and faced him. I reinserted his dick but before I could take the first stroke...

SLAP!

He slapped the shit out of me. My head swung to the right. My sweat drenched hair flung sweat into his face. In a one, two motion I slid a razor out of the little pocket on my boot and slid it across his neck. It was so sharp he didn't feel a thing. Now that I was back directly facing him he grabbed me with both hands around my throat. I relinquished all resistance and exhaled as he choked me. I couldn't inhale any air I began to get light headed. All the while swiveling my hips and grinding on his dick. I started cumming. I wanted to moan but I didn't have any air in my lungs. I was staring at him the whole time, at the blood running from his neck and soaking the carpet below him. My body was shaking from cumming. It was one of my most phenomenal orgasms ever. I was getting ready to wrench his hands from around my neck when I felt them loosen. His adrenalin and anger was pumping blood out of him faster than water out of a busted fire hydrant. He lost his grip, he was suddenly weak. His arms fell to his side. My head fell onto his chest as I caught my breath. After a few minutes I climbed into the bed and went to sleep.

At six in the morning I got up. He would never get up again.

I picked up the baggie of cocaine and sprinkled some on the table, got his car keys out of his pocket, gathered my stuff, cleaned up all the traces of me around the room and left.

I went to his car and got that pretty blue steel 9mm from under his seat. I went home and switched vehicles. I got in my SUV and went straight to his house. I parked in the driveway behind an E500 Benz. I rang the doorbell and by the time his wife answered the door I was crying. She opened the wooden door but not the security bar door. I was trying to talk but I was sobbing too much for her to understand me.

She said, "Who are you and what's wrong? Why are you crying?"

I said something indistinguishable.

She said, "Huh?"

I said some more bullshit with one clear word like. "Marcus."

I heard her say his real name on the phone. His car and everything was in her name so I never found out his real name until she said it.

I threw some other words at her in the mix of crying like "pregnant" and "dumped me" and "he's not right"

Her maternal instincts kicked in and she opened the door and let me in. She was a petit little light skinned pretty woman. I walked in and saw that no one was in my immediate view. She had her back to me locking the door. I came out of my purse with the gun and chopped her hard on the back of the neck and broke it. Her face slammed into the door and she fell back on the floor paralyzed.

After a thorough search of the house I found $375,000 and 60lbs of weed. The good stuff from the Canadian side of the border. I had to make quite a few trips back and forth, loading it all up, stepping over her every time. She couldn't move or say shit. Her eyes just followed me every time I passed her.

I noticed the red light on the coffee maker so I helped myself to a strong black cup. I kicked back and drank a whole cup. I didn't think she wanted any so I didn't even ask. I left after that but before I could even drop the stuff off, my phone rang.

"Hello."

"What's up Ma what you doin'?"

"Who is this?"

"Sidney."

Oh shit! It was the drug dealer who lied about playing ball for Texas.

CHAPTER FORTY-FIVE

TANYA

My answering machine was blinking and said I had thirty messages, one from Jalisa, my Hispanic co-worker, and twenty-nine from Malcolm. After erasing the messages I went upstairs and showered. Today had been a long day and so much had transpired.

I stepped into the shower, the water washed the stress down the drain and I felt better.

After the shower I called Jalisa and told her everything.

Jalisa hissed. I had stood her up to have lunch with Fatima earlier. She was just as mad about Fatima's deceit as I was.

We talked a while longer and Jalisa told me she was on her way over. I could use a little company so I got up from bed, threw on a pair of shorts and a wife beater and kicked back in the recliner in my living room, we'd just hang out and watch movies for a while.

Jalisa rang the doorbell at exactly eleven o'clock.

"What's up girl?" I asked, giving her a hug. It was a long hug I thought.

Southern hospitality?

I told Jalisa to have a seat while I poured some wine. When I got back to the living room, I sat down beside my friend and handed her a glass, while I sipped on mines.

"You okay?" Jalisa asked. Her voice was filled with concern.

I was hurt by Malcolm's cheating but Fatima really really hurt me. I'd lost what I thought was a good friend in Fatima.

Salty water slid down my cheeks. Jalisa quickly wiped my tears.

It's going to be okay." Jalisa said soothingly.

She began rubbing my back and making her way down to my ass. Maybe it was just my imagination because Jalisa wouldn't try anything funny with me.

Jalisa coaxed me into laying my head in her lap. I cried until my sobs became mere whimpers and that's when Jalisa made her move. She began rubbing my breasts.

I jumped up and stared at Jalisa. "What the hell are you doing?"

"Tanya, I'm-I'm sorry I just thought you'd want to try something..." There was a slight pause. "...different, cause men ain't shit."

"And what made you think that I...? Look, Malcolm has hurt me deeply but I am not now nor will I ever be into women."

"All that's going to happen Tanya is that you will get hurt by another no good ass man and then another. Don't be like that. Let me…"

"Jalisa! You have to leave."

Embarrassment moved Jalisa's feet right out the door and I was glad too, because I had had enough of Jalisa also.

I climbed into bed and covered my head with the comforter and fell into a deep and therapeutic sleep.

CHAPTER FORTY-SIX

KENO

The day after the robbery I took a cab to a couple jewelry stores and pawn shops and tallied my gross to be a little over $15,500. And I still had the laptop. I helped Crystal and Shantel out by paying up all the bills that they were behind on. That was a little over $1,500 which left me with about $14,000. I attempted to get Crystal's Thunderbird traded in with a couple thousand dollars for something more reliable but she told me not to do it, just to get a battery and a tire for it. She said when some real money came in then she could get the kind of car she wanted.

I paid $8,000 for a Ford F150 truck with black dual exhaust pipes. It was about ten years old but I looked great in it. I was ready to start looking for a better place to live but Crystal didn't want to. Crystal said that when things were really right then she would make the big move, maybe out of California, maybe even out of the country. Until then she'd stay where she was. So I offered Shantel the opportunity to move. Shantel jumped at the opportunity to live some place better.

Me and Shantel looked for an apartment in the Dons. The Dons is in the hilly Baldwin Hills area on the west side of L.A. where all the street names started with

Don. Like Don Felipe, Don Tomaso, Don Miguel and Don Diablo.

Shantel got some applications and began the process. She found a nice place. They wanted her to put down a $1,000 deposit. I told her it was a go. I could get that much for the laptop.

I had put the laptop up for sale on Craigslist.com. I knew I could get more for it there than in my neighborhood.

I got a call the first day. It was a Chinese man that sounded interested until he found out that it was used. I made a deal with the man anyway that I knew I couldn't get around my way. It was a $2,000 computer. If it was new then I could get 60% to 70% of the retail cost. I negotiated $700 and we agreed to meet for the exchange at a coffee shop in Orange County later on that evening. It took me three freeways and forty minutes but that's always worth $700 any day. I got to test my truck out on the forty minute long drive.

The coffee shop was in the back of a small shopping center. When I got out of the truck I noticed a Chinese man standing to the side smoking a cigarette. When I looked at him he wasn't looking at me but when I turned my head I could tell that man looked back at me.

Most of the cars in the parking lot were obviously patrons of the coffee shop, I found that out when I entered.

This place was something different, so low-key on the outside but the inside looked like a strip club. The first three steps into the place there was a huge fish tank. Everyone had to walk around it to get in. Mostly every seat was taken by a room full of Asian men. A lot of them looked like the Asian gangsters you see in movies. Asian girls were walking around in clothes that can only be seen on strippers in a strip club. Clear high heels, tiny skirts and bikinis. I had left the laptop in the car but I guessed it was obvious who I was because Lee noticed me and raised his hand. I was the only black guy in the place. I went over to Lee's table. Lee was seated with one other guy. The guy Lee said was his son. Lee said that the computer was for him. Another guy walked up from behind me, said hi, introduced himself as Tooyung and took a seat at the table with us.

A fine ass Asian waitress came over and said, "Hi Keno Brown."

I was shocked! I looked closer to see the same Asain girl I had saved from them thugs trying to extort her on the street days before.

I said, "Whats up?"

She asked what I would be drinking. She was done up, much prettier than the day I saw her. I looked around. Everything about the place screamed prostitution. I swore

344

for the right price I should be able to fuck her in a back room somewhere but I just asked what kind of liquor they had.

I was informed that they only served coffee or tea.

I couldn't believe it!

I also couldn't believe there were no stripper poles. I didn't like tea so I ordered a coffee. She asked if I wanted it strong or medium.

I said, "Strong."

Lee said, "Give him a medium."

I said, "Nah, coffee don't taste good to me so if I'ma drink coffee at least I wanna feel it."

Lee said, "Trust me."

I conceded.

I got a few sly looks from around the place. I noticed they had internet and some computers at the tables with the booth seats. There were long blue horizontal lights in the corners of the room.

My coffee came in the middle of us conversing about me getting Lee more computers. I was telling him that I would see what I could do but I actually had no intention of getting more.

I drunk half of my coffee and was ready to get my money and go. I was about to say, "Lets do this." When the waitress came back over. She distracted me. She was thin and beautiful like a model. I looked into her eyes and told her so.

"You're thin and beautiful like a model." I said.

She smiled and said, "Thank you Keno Brown."

I asked her if I could take pictures of her. She smiled again and said, "Are you gonna pay me?"

I thought, *I knew these girls were hoes.*

Then she said, "I'm just kidding. I love to take photos. What do you want to do with them?"

"I don't know, I'll do a free photo shoot for you just so I can have some pictures of you, I guess." I said.

I wasn't a photographer but it was an idea that came to my mind so I said it.

She said, "Sounds good but I can't do that. If you're not going to use them for anything then I would pay you."

I immediately recognized the difference in her and the girls I was used to.She wrote her number on a napkin and wisked off. I got smiles from around the table. A few smirks from elsewhere in the shop. I was really ready to go by then. By the way, I was starting to feel wired from the coffee.

I said, "I'm done here." and stood up.

We went outside and to my truck. Lee gave me $700 in an envelope and I gave Lee the laptop. I went back to my part of town happy enough.

CHAPTER FORTY-SEVEN

"Who's the black guy?" asked Agent Steffans.

"Shit if I know." Answered Agent O'Brien.

"I didn't mean that literally. I know you don't know. I was just wondering out loud."

The two agents had been parked across the boulevard for two weeks watching the coffee shop. There was a murder investigation under way on Lee and his crime partner.

Lee is the brains and the other man is the martial artist killer. They were suspects in the robbing and killing of their Asian counterparts that were into illegal imports, diamonds, computer chips, etc. Anything that was small and worth millions.

The most recent murder Lee was being watched for, was of an established Asian businessman named Kim. They found him with his arms and legs broken and hands tied behind his back and dumped into the L.A. River. He also had two diamonds stuffed into his nostrils. It was a sign. He must have betrayed them some kind of way. The authorities had no evidence but knew Lee was involved so they hung around and watched.

"Whoa! Did you see that fine chick that just passed by the door inside that coffee shop? Now that's my kinda chick."

"I missed her, I was looking at that Chinese guy. He went over to the other side of the parking lot and now he's just standing to the side smoking a cigarette and watching the coffee shop."

He was from another law enforcement agency, undercover. The two agents in the van continued to spy on the shop.

Agents Steffans notes said:

...and thirty minutes later the black guy came back out with two Asian men. The black guy retrieved a laptop out of his truck, the Asian man handed him something and he handed a laptop to the older Asian man and left.

CHAPTER FORTY-EIGHT

MARY JAY

"It's kinda early ain't it?" I asked him.

I had left the motel early and got a jump on Milky's wife.

He said, "I guess it is kinda early. I just got in from the airport coming from O.T. (outta town) you know doin' what I do, and thinking about you."

"Oh really, you've had my number for a week you couldn'tve been thinking about me too much."

"No really, true story, I have. That's why I called you early, to catch you before you started your day. I'm hoping you can spend it with me. I got some peoples coming through then after that it's whatever you wanna do. I'm tryna get to know you."

My mind was moving fast. The back area of my Range Rover Sport was filled with weed. A police car was in the lane next to me. I had my window down because it was 5% limousine tint and that's illegal. The cop was smiling like the world was his and he just found out that I was in it. The air inside with me was pungent with the smell of weed.

I thought, *He has to be able to smell this shit. People at the bus stop are getting high when I stop at the light.*

I still had the phone to my ear, Sidney was waiting for an answer. I was processing the information he just gave me.

Back from outta town. Peoples coming thru.

I said, "To tell you the truth I got up early this morning to make some runs and I was going back home to climb back in the bed and take a nap and I probably won't be coming back out."

I stopped to let him respond. The cop was trying to get my attention. I smiled at him while I reached into the center console and got out a three karat diamond ring and slipped it on my left hand third finger.

Sidney said, "Where you at right now?"

I said, "Where you live?"

I raised my hand, palm facing me. The officer lost his smile and sped off.

"In Fox Hills." Sidney said.

"I'm on the 405 freeway south passing the interstate 10, coming from the valley."

I was lying I was really on the other side of downtown L.A.

He said, "You should stop by."

"I don't know. I'm kinda tired."

"We could just chillout right here if you want to."

"How we gonna chillout and you gonna be tryna put yuh dick in me?"

"Ahh Ma don't say it like that. I'm a gentleman. I'll be good."

"You want me to believe that?"

"Yeah I'll be good."

"Alright, what's your address?"

I told him I was going to make a stop at the mall, to give myself some time to unload my load. An hour later I was at his door with a light pink overcoat on and some open toe, four inch heels, both by Roberto Cavalli.

When he opened the door I let the coat drop right there on his front porch. His eyes bulged out like somebody over inflated his head with air. I stood there naked as a body in the morgue but a whole lot more sexy. The sunlight irredessed my skin like a new $20,000 caramel paint job. Sidney looked around to see if any of his neighbors were looking. We had one observer down a few houses.

Sidney said, "Get in here! That's a Pastor!"

I guess temptation had Pastor in a head lock and wouldn't let him turn his head. Sidney picked up my coat and I walked inside like I was on a runway.

He said, "You crazy. Fine but crazy and check it, you on the phone talkin' like you wasn't tryna have sex."

"I'm not." I said stopping in my tracks and sticking my arms out so he could put my coat back on me. "I just felt like doing that just then."

"Oh what, you the spontaneous type?"

"Hmmm, you mean like doing something you would've never expected?"

"Yeah unpredictable."

I looked around. "Nice house."

We were just inside the door in a big area with hardwood floor that preceded the living room.

The living room was sunken by two feet so it felt like I was on a stage. The color scheme in the living room had a lot of black and white going on.

Black Savonniere carpet, white furniture, white pool table, black que sticks in a white case on the wall next to it. The balls were clear the low balls had colored numbers and the high balls had black stripes with colored numbers. The pictures on the walls were four and five feet tall and they were all by a painter named Poncho known for using only black and white. They sat high on the walls under vaulted ceilings.

On one wall it looked like a chunk of plaster was broken out similar to the shape of California but somebody painted right over it. Right before I said, "I know somebody got their ass kicked for that fuck up." I realized it was done on purpose.

We walked passed the kitchen. It was full of stainless steel appliances. We stepped into the family room that was only separated from the kitchen by a breakfast nook. It was a big area furnished with a eighty inch L.E.D. television. A couch, loveseat, recliner and a coffee table that looked like it came from Italy. He went to the DVD component. The face of it was flush with the wall along with the other components. He put the movie Monster's Ball in and used the remote to scene select to the part where Billy Bob did to Halle Berry what I was sure he wanted to do to me.

His phone began beeping with the sound it makes when somebody with a similar phone sends an alert. He looked at the caller ID.

Evidently it was who he was expecting.

He answered it. "Where you at?"

"Pulling up the driveway to the back."

He looked at me and pointed to the massive selection of DVD's and told me I could find something I wanted to watch and pop it in. He said he had some business to handle for a little while then he walked through the house to the back. He went into the garage from the inside.

I heard the garage door raise up and a vehicle drove in. I thought about going out to my truck to get my gun but I knew he had to have a gun in the house somewhere, atleast a small pistol or something. I searched through the house as quickly as possible. I didn't care if I found a .22 caliber. All I needed was a bullet per person but I found a fully automatic with a full clip under his pillow. I went back to the door leading to the garage to eavesdrop on their conversation. I peeked in, it was two guys and Sidney, the same two guys that I saw with him at Aunt Kizzy's.

"How'd everything go?" the football player looking one said to Sidney.

"It was all good, that's why I told you I needed to double my order." he answered as he walked over to get a bag that he had on a table.

"This is $250,000." he said, opening the bag and dumping the money onto the hood of the black Denali they came in.

I had one of my hands in my pocket and felt the baggie of cocaine from when I was with Milky.

I took it out and said, "Fuck it!"

I dumped a little pile on the back of my hand and inhaled it.

The tall slender one with the pencil sized dreds got two bags out the back of the truck. He threw one near Sidney's feet.

"That's what you requested." The other bag he put on the hood and unzipped it. "Welcome to the future." he said. "Remember when G-Money introduced Nino to Crack Cocaine in the beginning of New Jack City? Well I'm G-Money and you Nino Brown but this ain't crack." he said pulling something out of the bag that looked similar to an asthma inhaler.

"What the fuck is that?"

This right here is P.M.E.D."

"P.M.E.D?"

"Yeah, Particle Medicated Epidermal Delivery device. I'm sure somebody will come up with a slang name for it soon enough."

"Aight I'm listening." Sidney said, pinching his chin with the knuckle of his index finger and thumb like he was in a college classroom during an important lecture.

"This is some new shit the pharmaceutical companies came up with for vaccinations. It blasts microscopic drug particles through your skin at, you ain't gon' believe this but, at 1500 miles an hour. It's microscopic so you don't feel it. It goes just right under the skin, too shallow to hit nerve endings so it's painless you need way less of the drug to get the same result but we don't lower the price, we quadruple the profit."

"How you get this?"

"Our connection been working with some Japanese mutha fucka's and Bam!" he raised it up, "We the new kids on the block."

"The new kids in hell maybe." I said, interrupting a little sooner than I planned. The cocaine in my system put octane in my plans.

They turned startled. I was standing in the door way with a Heckler & Koch machine gun in my hand.

"Who the fuck is that bitch?" the football player said.

Sidney was speechless, his jaw fell open, then fell to the ground. He was shocked that I was standing there with his gun in my hand and a serious look on my face.

Before he could pick his jaw up Boom! Boom! Two shots, one to the sternum and one to the heart laid Sidney down with only enough life in him to get "Ugh!" out of his mouth. The other two guy's arms flew up as they ducked and stepped back.

"Hold up Baby! You can have all this shit. I don't know what's up wit you and ole boy but we ain't got nothing to do with it. You can have everything. I been jacked befo'. Take this shit." Football said sweeping all the cash off the hood of the truck and onto the floor.

Tall Dred was moving slowly over to the passenger side with his hands halfway in the air.

"If anyone of you touch the door of that truck I'ma ventilate your ass."

I looked around and saw an extension cord hanging on the wall. I told Football to get it and tie Dred up. I told Dred to stand in front of the Denali and lay back on the hood. I told Football to tie his arms spread eagle to the side view mirrors I found some rope and threw it to Football. I told him to tie two lengths of rope to Dreds ankles and let it trail down to the front of the two wheels. After he set the second rope in front of the second wheel but before he could stand up I pumped a slug into the top of his head. I got into the driver's seat, put the truck in drive and pulled it up a couple of feet, rolling over the ropes and pulling Dred's feet under the front end stretching his body across the grill of the Denali.

"How do you feel?" I asked as I got out the truck.

"Like a fuckin' hood ornament! What the fuck is wrong withcu! If you gonna kill me just kill me then!"

He was bent backwards over the front end of the truck. I pulled up a chair and sat in front of him, his dick was right in my face. I undid his pants. I was so horny. I don't know if it was the cocaine or the killing. Murder makes me so horny. It makes my pussy wet.

I held his dick in my hand like it was a microphone and put my lips around the head. Unbelievably, in his uncomfortable position and extreme circumstance, his dick still got hard.

I deep throated him as it grew. When he was erect I stood up dropped my coat spread my caramel colored ass cheeks apart and backed up on him. I had a new toy for a minute. The dick was the perfect height and the truck had his body immovable.

Pow! Pow! Pow!

My butt slapped his thighs and belly.

Smack! Smack! Smack!

My legs started to shake. I held on to the chair and slow grinded my cum out until it ran down the inside of my thighs. I felt his dick stiffen. I looked back and saw the look on his face. His mouth was open. He was getting ready to bust a nut. I got off of him, turned around and sucked his dick viciously. He gushed cum in my mouth and I caught it all to the last drop. I hopped up on him, forced his lips open and spit it all in his mouth. While he coughed his own despicable substance out, I disappeared into the house.

About the time he was spitting the final remnants out I was back with a kitchen knife. I slashed the main arteries in both his legs. The whole time he was calling me all kinds of crazy bitches. I put the $250,000 back in the bag, grabbed the other two bags and walked out the front door like I was going on a trip. Daddy will be proud.

CHAPTER FORTY-NINE

TANYA

Malcolm had been calling me for a week but it was too late! I was moving on with my life. I sent up a prayer and climbed into the bed.

When the alarm clock sounded I could hardly get out of bed. That night was the most peaceful sleep I'd had in a while. I got out of the bed and went to the bathroom.

I had an appointment with my therapist. I showered and dressed in a pair of black slacks and a white silk blouse. I made a big breakfast of eggs, bacon, cheese and french toast.

No fucking syrup!

I ate and went to see Dr. Hunt.

Dr. Hunt had been talking to me about getting hypnotized. She told me that if I got hypnotized I could release things held in the recesses of my mind. Although she couldn't promise me that the dreams would disappear immediately, she was optimistic.

Dr. Hunt had told me to think about it and I was still thinking.

I sighed as I switched lanes and got on the expressway. I wondered if I would ever be able to forgive my mother. I'd cross that road when it came.

Traffic was jam-packed from bumper to bumper as I went through downtown and unfortunately there was no exit nearby to get off of the expressway. I cursed and elbowed the back of the seat.

I had to spend an hour with Dr. Hunt and after my appointment I had to get to work.

Traffic started to move again after ten minutes. My appointment was at 8:30 a.m. I looked at the clock and realized I was only five minutes late. I parked and sprinted across the parking lot into the building.

As I waited to be called I thumbed through the latest edition of Essence magazine. Katrina was there again waiting for her appointment. A light humming sound could be heard coming from Katrina's direction. Katrina's eyes were rolled up into her head and her mouth was open. She tried to be inconspicuous but it was hard to hide the fact that she was cumming. I just tried to ignore her, I opened the magazine.

When I heard my name I placed the magazine on a side table and walked back into Dr. Hunt's office.

I sat near the doctor's desk and straightened out a picture frame and a couple pens as we got ready for our session.

Eventually, I laid back on the chaise, closed my eyes and tried to cleanse myself. The doctor pulled the details from me as they came. I wondered if my issues had anything to do with me having a hard time dealing with and loving men. I broke down in tears. Some things I'd honestly forgotten about, but Dr. Hunt dug deep and began to pull those things out with questions. I found the therapy to be a great release. The doctor relaxed and comforted me to let it all out.

The doctor listened attentively as I recalled the major events, at least the ones I remembered, the ones that had changed my life completely. The people around me all played a pivotal part, from the hustlers to the prostitutes. I watched them, but thankfully didn't emulate them. I saw the hopelessness in the prostitute's eyes and greed in the hustler's. The stuff I'd seen all played a role in my difficult, rather shakey upbringing.

When I moved to Memphis I was in a shell, bottled up. Afraid to make new friends and didn't want too many people in my life. I was scared and scarred for life.

I opened my eyes and looked up at Dr. Hunt. She smiled then said, "You're making great progress."

I got up and went to the bathroom. When I came back I sat down and got comfortable again then the psychiatrist asked me about the person in my dreams. I thought and thought but no answer came. Dr. Hunt told me not to be so hard on myself. That I'd eventually pull it together with the proper guidance and help. She asked me about my mom.

"Tell me about your mother?" Dr. Hunt questioned.

"That Bitch, she's never been much of a mother to me!" was my bitter reply.

Any talk of my mother was like a sonic boom to my ears. I hated my mother and in my mind I had every right to hate her. She'd been nothing but cruel to me. I had always come second and even third to my mama's many boyfriends. Over the years I saw many men come and go in our lives, each time thinking the next would be different from the first. All of them were losers from the first on down. Leaching off my mama's little welfare check. I'd brought bad grades in because my home life was messed up. Cheryl only criticized and abused me more. No fond memories could be called upon from my childhood.

Except for Keno.

I took a few deep breaths, inhaled and exhaled as my thoughts gathered.

Dr. Hunt gave me all the time I needed, she was my therapist and her job was to listen.

"Tanya, take your time." she said.

Closing my eyes, I began. "My mother was a whore. For as long as I can remember she's been a whore, probably still is. I can never recall my mother being sober. She was always high or drunk. I guess sobriety just wasn't her thing. And I was left to fend for myself. Physically she was there most of the time, but emotionally and mentally she was detached from me. Her motherly instincts weren't there. We went days without communicating with each other because I had nothing to say to her and I guess she had nothing to say to me.

"She was never a good nurturer and the older I got the more I hated her ass, hated her for not loving me. I didn't ask to be born. I was just the result of an irresponsible moment. As a child I felt lonely. I was envious of my friend's relationships with there parents.

Me and Keno, our parents were good friends. Or should I say Junkie buddies. On a regular basis they got high together. Keno and I would play for hours. He was more like a brother to me. Whenever I felt out of place and needed someone he was there."

A smile pierced my lips as I reminisced about the good times I'd shared with him. At that moment my mind moved from unpleasant memories to pleasant ones. Then I wondered if Keno was alright and if I'd ever see him again.

When Dr. Hunt asked me more about Keno I blinked a few times, returning from my fond reverie.

"Keno was my friend. I trusted him. He was there, regardless. We had a lot in common and I guess because of our similarities we were cool together."

Memories of me and Keno danced around in my head. I laughed as I thought about the day we went to the park.

Jason had touched my butt and I was so scared my heart nearly jumped out my chest, but as usual Keno was as cool as an air conditioner. No one could put fear in his heart. He was a soldier. Jason was trying to get me but Keno wasn't having it. After Keno finished with him, Jason left me alone.

I looked at my watch. The session was over. I left and went to work.

I pulled up to my parking space near the entrance to TSL in deep thought. I needed to take a trip and visit the old neighborhood. Just maybe I'd be able to find Keno.

In one day I'd lost my boyfriend and two friends.

Honestly, I wasn't too torn up about losing Malcolm because he was being so adamant about me stealing that I was about to drop him anyway but I loved Fatima and thought of Jalisa as a close friend too.

I have to tell him to bring me my bank card today.

Behind the cloak of my office door I cried for my lost friendships. I couldn't cry long because I had work to tend to. A couple of transactions needed to be made and money needed to be transferred.

The ringing phone caught my attention, it was Sahara.

My sister was like my safe haven and I needed someone to vent to. I told her the whole story and she listened. When I was done Sahara was rendered speechless. Just like me, Sahara didn't know what to say or think about the situation.

The question that spilled passed Sahara's lips were, "You want me to whoop her ass for you?"

"No, she will definitely get what's coming to her. The Lord will handle her and that's why I'm not worried about it."

We chatted for a while longer and agreed to hook up around noon for lunch at our favorite Chinese restaurant near TSL.

I still had to give Sahara the bracelet I'd bought for her.

As soon as we got off the phone an emergency staff meeting was called. In the conference room, I was surprised to see Kimberly and Jalisa sitting next to each other. They were probably talking about me but I couldn't care lesser than I did at the moment. I had more important things on my mind, like what in the hell the meeting was about.

I sat by a new girl named Tianna. Tianna gave me a big smile and moved out the chair for me.

"Girl, that's a banging dress." Tianna whispered.

Tianna was nice enough but from now on I was definitely not making any new friends on the job. My new approach would be to keep my personal life personal and my work, just that, work.

Stephen sat directly across from me and I didn't miss the look in his eyes. Kimberly looked on with pure jealousy and a small smirk pierced my lips as the staff sat there whispering amongst themselves. I was in my own world until the President of the company stepped through the door.

Mr. Pennilton was always dressed to impress. Today wasn't any different. The silver silk suit he wore was tailor made. His Gucci loafers were shiny. He was tall, maybe 6'4" and had light skin. His hair had highlights of gray on the sides and was short, matching his trimmed mustache and salt and pepper goatee. He was very neat and well put together.

Mr. Pennilton rarely came to this particular location because he had several businesses and was a very busy man. He cleared his throat and began.

"I know you're wondering what I'm here for. Well, to stop all the whispering I'm here to promote someone."

Again the whispering began. They all were wondering who. He didn't leave them in suspense for long.

"Tanya Glass has presented everything this company represents. She exemplifies what we stand for, honesty, integrity and value. Today she'll be promoted to Supervisor."

Everyone gasped, including me. I couldn't believe it. Fortune was on my side. Everyone was clapping and congratulating me except Kimberly and Jalisa.

Mr. Pennilton looked over at me and smiled.

"Tanya, do you have anything to say?"

I slowly raised out of my seat and softly said with a huge smile, "Thanks so much. I am so grateful to be given this huge opportunity. I'm especially grateful for..."

"How did this bitch get the promotion?" Kimberly interrupted.

She stood with her hands on her hips. Stephen almost stood up to check Kimberly. I knew Kimberly didn't like what had just happened but I couldn't believe Kimberly had messed up my moment with that foul outburst. Everyone in the room turned to Kimberly, giving her their undivided attention. Kimberly was so jealous. Since she wanted all the attention they gave it to her, if only for a minute.

"That's no way to talk Kimberly!" Mr. Pennilton noted.

"I'm just saying, she's always taking my jobs. She didn't even apply for the position!" Kimberly snapped.

"No she didn't apply but she's who I want for the position." he said shrewdly.

"But…" she started.

"This subject is over and isn't open for discussion." he said.

Kimberly plopped down, sulking like a little kid.

Mr. Pennilton talked for a while longer before ending the meeting.

"Tanya, I want to talk to you for a minute."

When the conference room only held him and me, we took a seat at the table and went over a few assignments. I was still in charge of the resort project.

"Mr. Pennilton, why did you really pick me for the job?"

"Tanya I see something in you that I don't see in the other employees. Your work is always accurate and your expertise brings a lot of money to the company. I thank you for that and a promotion is one of the best ways to say thank you."

"I'm very thankful and surprised."

"I know you won't disappoint me Tanya." he said proudly.

CHAPTER FIFTY

KENO

On my way home from selling Lee the laptop I took the 5 Fwy to downtown L.A. and got on the 101 Fwy to Sunset Blvd. in Hollywood and stopped by a tattoo shop to get the second half of my tattoo finished. I had a sexy female demon coming out of my skin on my left arm. I wanted to put a sexy female angel coming out of my skin on the right arm.

I figured $300 would do it all.

This tattoo shop was kinda wild. All kinds of stuff went on there.

I saw two young cute girls, one was getting a tattoo on the back of her hand that said "I fly above." One was getting a tattoo on her foot that said, "Beautiful Liar."

I thought it was peculiar when I saw it. It seemed like she was telling the world that she couldn't be trusted.

Wow! What a deal breaker!

The young girl thought that one of the letters were wrong and she went off, cursing out the tattoo artist.

"Are you retarded? That ain't what I'm paying you to do."

He was trying to tell her that it was good but she just couldn't tell because ink and blood distorted the actual tattoo. They were going back and forth. The tattoo guy didn't want to wash her foot clean so that she could see the detail in his work. He knew what he was doing.

A guy who worked there and knew me very well said, "She acts just like your ass used to."

She looked at the man with a squint in her eyes and said, "Whateva!"

"Ooh she looks like you too."

"I don't look like him, he ugly." she snapped.

"Don't get smacked up in here lil girl." I told her.

"By who? You ain't my daddy!"

"Yo daddy need to put a belt to your ass."

"I don't know where he at and if I did he wouldn't be smacking me. Pimps do that to hoes."

I couldn't even deny it, she did look like me. I asked her the only thing that mattered at the moment.

"Who's your momma and what's yo last name?"

She didn't answer. She was really trying to ignore me. She thought for a minute then said, "Did you grow up in the Bottoms?"

The Bottoms is an area behind the low 100's between Prairie and Crenshaw. It was a Blood gang neighborhood, kinda designed like The Jungle (Baldwin Village) with apartments and twists and turns.

"Yep, but how you know that?"

"You used to have a green convertible low rider?"

The tattoo artists that knew me butted in and said, "I can answer that, hellz yeah he did. We used to be in that muthafucka boyee! Them was the days. We had plenty bitches!"

"Yeah, you my daddy." she said. "I'm sure of it. My name is Princess and this my "best friend" Danielle and since you my daddy you need to be paying for this tattoo."

The day I met Princess was the first day Danielle and her had hooked back up. They hadn't seen each other in a couple months. Danielle was a little older than Princess. Danielle was originally paying for the tattoo. She was half black and half Spanish. Danielle had a few tattoos as well.

Princess was sixteen and had been in the system for six years now. Her mother was a drunk and drug addict who got into a fight with her other babydaddy who pulled a gun on her. The neighbor called the police and Bam, Princess got taken.

CHAPTER FIFTY-ONE

TANYA

"Girl, Stephen asked me about you." The new girl Tianna said to me as if we were friends.

"Well what did he want? Tell him I'm not available." I said in a joking manner.

"Girl, a girl could never have too many men. Everyone should have a sponsor. Besides, Stephen is handsome and your man doesn't have to know about him. He said he sees you're moving up. He seemed excited for you. Here's his number, he said he wanted to take you to dinner to celebrate your promotion. He wanted to give it to you himself but he said he didn't know how long you would be with Mr. Pennilton. "

I took the number and thought about the idea of celebrating. The person I would have done it with was now out of my life and my second choice would be Sahara, sure why not Stephen, it would be okay, that's how coworkers and associates did it, right?

I was on cloud 9. On top of being promoted, Stephen was taking me to dinner. How nice!

Hopefully he wouldn't try to press sex from me.

Malcolm lucked up and had a good personality to go with his awesome looks so I was kinda taken offguard, so he

373

got in close to me although, technically, we never really had sex. Did a couple of pumps on a couple of occasions count? Stephen had nothing coming if he tried anything.

I took a long and warm shower before dressing in a very casual sun dress. I slipped my feet in a pair of black sandals. The clock said I had just enough time to put on a bare minimum makeup and pin my hair up. My grandma always told me simplicity was best and that's one of the reasons I didn't wear much makeup.

The doorbell rang at a little after eight o'clock. I was excited but I didn't want to show it too much.

I opened the door calmly and it was the neighbor. He looked a bit crazy. Kinda scared me.

"You wouldn't happen to have a pair of strong scissors wouldya?"

"Oh, you startled me! I thought you were someone else."

The neighbor stood there like, *Do you have what I want or not?*

I finally said, "Well let me check." while I tried to settle my nerves.

I left the door open and walked back into the kitchen and searched through a utensil drawer.

CHAPTER FIFTY-TWO

SHANTEL

"Am I gonna see you tonite?" I asked Keno over the phone.

"Nah, I got something I gotta do."

"Ah Baby, I want you to cum fuck me. It's only morning. You got all day."

"I'll probably see you tomorrow."

"Whatever."

I hung up the phone and texted Marvel. He couldn't get enough of me.

Marvel pulled into the parking stall where I would park if I had a car. I had the liquor and Marvel brought the weed. It was at the point where he wasn't paying for sex straight across anymore. I liked to smoke weed so the arrangement worked out fine. We smoked and fucked.

Marvel got into the bed and got on his knees, I laid on my right side and took his dick into my mouth. He started pumping his soft penis in and out of my mouth until it got hard.

I had my eyes shut but I could feel him watching me. We were total opposites.

He opened his knees and came down on his elbows. He put his stomach on the left side of my face and fucked my warm wet mouth. He stroked my mouth like a pussy for the first forty minutes before he exploded.

That's how I got stretch marks on my lips.

After he came in my mouth, we fell asleep.

When we woke up Marvel put his dick back into my mouth. He got me up on my knees, reached over and rubbed my pussy from the back. I had a flashback of the day at the mansion. I instinctively looked back to see if someone else was behind me. Marvel thought I just wanted to see his face. While I was looking at him he slid his rock hard dick back into my mouth again. He burst a quick nut and went to take a shower. I went to the kitchen, although it was after lunch time, I made breakfast. We relaxed with full bellys, smoked and fucked again.

As we laid there Marvel asked me, "What are your plans for the future?"

I shocked him when I said, "I plan on dying before I reached forty years old."

"Are you serious?"

"Yes, I'm serious. My life has been fucked up. I pray that God doesn't curse me to live a long life."

"You betta stop tripping. We could have a good life together until we're old. I ain't out here from Memphis for nothing. I got big things going on with some people. I just gotta wait until I get the word and then it's on."

"What are you talking about Marvel and who you out here fucking with?"

"Don't trip, you don't know him but he gets things popping."

"Whatever Marvel."

"My boy Sonny is straight. I got caught up on a move and he bailed me out. Shiiit I was getting out one way or another. I woulda told the police all they needed to know about his ass. I'm not even from Los Angeles. I'm from Memphis. I'm just saying."

I stood up, he took a picture of my naked booty with his phone.

"Boy you crazy. Now you got a special picture of me that ain't on Facebook."

We laid up and pillow-talked all night. He told me stuff he shouldn't have told me. You never know who knows who.

CHAPTER FIFTY-THREE

TANYA

I went back to the door and told my neighbor that I couldn't find any scissors.

"Thank you anyway." he said, already leaving the porch.

I closed the door.

Immediately the doorbell rang again. I was still behind the door. I quickly opened the door. Stephen was standing there looking nice in a pair of casual blue jeans and a collar shirt. His signature cologne tickled my nostrils. He watched the neighbor walk out of the yard before he turned his eyes back to me.

"You look good." he replied, peeking into the house as I stepped out.

Stephen led me to his black Cadillac Escalade. Ever the perfect gentleman, he opened the passenger door and I climbed in. Once he climbed in and fastened his seat belt, we were off. We conversed with small talk on the way to the restaurant. He told me he was taking me to a popular seafood restaurant on the east side of town.

The drive was pleasantly comfortable and we were there before I knew it. He climbed out before me and came over to my side and opened my door. I climbed out and he took my hand in his much larger one. We walked into the restaurant, I was all smiles and blushes. I wanted to tell him that I didn't want to move too fast with him but Stephen had a way of making a woman feel special, like she was the only woman in the world. The matre'd asked if we wanted smoking or non-smoking. Stephen looked to me for an answer. I said I didn't smoke.

"I don't smoke either." he said to me then told the matre'd no smoking and we followed him to our table.

Stephen pulled out my chair, I took in the ambiance of the place. It looked cozy and very comfortable. The lights were dimmed and soft jazz played in the background to add a hint of romance.

Stephen congratulated me again on the promotion.

"Thanks, I wish everyone could be happy for me."

"Don't worry about that, in life you should just try to do the best you can. Everybody isn't going to be happy for you and that shouldn't even matter to you. You should always just go for what you know."

I got lost in his words for several seconds. Then the waitress came over and took our order. She excused herself after taking the orders. I couldn't deny the tinge of jealousy that hit me when Stephen's eyes fell below the waistline of the curvaceous waitress on her way to the kitchen.

With our meal we had a few glasses of wine and everything went smooth. He conversed with me about life, money, relationships and got a clear understanding about my direction and was convinced not to try his hand at a relationship with me.

We were listening to some old school music in his truck on the way back to my house. I was so wrapped up in my thoughts of the times when the songs were new and I was a kid that I didn't even notice that we were in front of my house until he called my name.

"Tanya, I've called your name several times." he said.

"Oh, sorry."

My cheeks raised high. I told him what I was thinking about. It was about a time me and Keno went to the park with the neighbor in the neighbor's old station wagon.

After we laughed at the story Stephen walked me to the door and told me how good of a time he'd had with me. He decided to try and kiss me anyway. He leaned in but I declined. He asked if he could come in but I declined him again then gave him a half of a hug. He peeked into the house as I went in.

The neighbor watched it all through his window.

CHAPTER FIFTY-FOUR

KENO

I knew that money didn't last long so I decided to do a little something I had been wanting to do for a while that I never got around to doing.

I called up Sergio, I used to get my ecstasy pills from him. I used to have an ecstasy spot a few years back and I was doing pretty good until the head man went to jail and Sergio started acting funny on supplying the product. Sergio is Shantel's son's father but he and Shantel never got along. I always thought Sergio fucked me over due to jealousy. I'm always getting into it with my girl's baby's daddys.

One day Shantel and Sergio got into an argument and she yelled into his face that my dick was twice as long and twice as thick as his. The thought of my thick meat penetrating his babymama boiled Sergio's blood.

Sergio ended up giving me some bad shit and wouldn't take it back. He fucked me out of my money and things were never the same. I wanted to settle the score before the head man got out of jail because me and the head man were cool.

Time for get back!

I called Sergio up and told him that I had a few thousand dollars to spend. I told him that I needed to buy something for my people to sample. I told Sergio that I had some skateboarder white boys that had the underground rave circuit on lock and that they could run through a "boat" (one thousand pills) in a weekend. I could tell that excited Sergio. I told him to make sure it was right and that I hadn't forgotten that he owed me but after we got in good with the skateboarders then he could pay me a little at a time. Sergio liked the sound of that. I could tell Sergio's attitude perked up during the short conversation. We scheduled to meet again.

A few hours later we met in a shopping center parking lot. When I got there Sergio was there already and he had someone in his car with him. I was alone. He signaled for me to get in with him. I got out with a bag and got into the backseat of Sergio's car. As we did the exchange I ran down to him again the potential, then I left, leaving Sergio with the impression that the skateboarders were waiting on me.

I called Sergio the next day and told him that the skateboarders liked it and I needed the first "boat". I really wouldn't know if the first package was good or not because it was still at home in my closet.

We met in a different shopping center parking lot. Sergio was already there when I got there and his boy was with him again. I pulled up in front of him with the bag sitting on the seat next to me. I pulled over a little but still intentionally blocked the isle. I put my F-150 truck in park and signaled for Sergio to come to me. Sergio's door opened and he got out with a bag in hand.

When he got in my truck I laughed and said, "We bout to move a lot of shit as long as you can keep it good."

He gave me the package and guaranteed the quality. As I checked the package I went on and on about how we got things on lock until someone pulled up behind me and tapped on their horn. I could tell Sergio was ready to get his money and roll out so I reached into the bag and pulled out the .38 I got from the security guard and right when Sergio's mind clicked and told him that there was danger I pulled the trigger!

BOOM!

Sergio's mind may have still been calculating what to do when it exited the back of his head onto the passenger window. His companion must've been really looking hard into my truck because he jumped back in fright from the splatter! As the passenger door of Sergio's car opened, I discreetly pulled off. The person in the car behind me was none the wiser because my rear window was tinted.

I made a right out of the parking lot, made a quick left and a quick right. I put Sergio's seat belt on him, rolled the passenger window down to hide the blood and got on the 105 Fwy. I stayed in the right lane. After a few minutes I smelled the stench from the feces the dead body released in his pants.

Oh God!

Sergio had shit on himself! I started to think about CSI and DNA. I got off the freeway at the next exit and pulled into an alley off Central Ave. near the projects. I took the seat belt off. I slowed my speed, opened the passenger door and kicked Sergio out of the truck. I turned a couple corners and drove into someone's driveway, opened his passenger door wide and grabbed their water hose.

I washed off my window and door then I went to a vacant lot, got lots of dirt and threw it all over the truck inside and out. Then I took it to detail shop and told them I wanted every inch of it cleaned. Two days later, I sold it. It's always good when you can make money and fuck up somebody you don't like in the process.

I laid back feeling content and accomplished about something. For some reason my mind would wander on Tanya. I remembered how Tanya's friend's dad used to take us to the park. The dad didn't like our parents but he did like me and Tanya. He had that big station wagon with wood panels on the sides that we used to pile into. One day when we were at the park playing, a little boy named Jason felt on Tanya's booty. I punched him in the eye and ran. I smiled at the memory.

SHANTEL

"Bitch why you crying?" Tarika asked me.

"Lil Sergio's daddy got killed and robbed this morning."

"What, where at?"

"They found him in an alley off of Central. I had to identify his body because I'm the only family he got because of lil Sergio. It was terrible girl, his face was gone. I almost passed the fuck out."

"What you gonna do now?"

"About what? That man wasn't doing shit for his son no way. He would have me sucking his dick, thinking he was gonna gimme some money or do something for his kid but every time it never failed, I would just end up with a throat full of cum and a wet pussy. Girl he didn't give a fuck about nothing but himself and I really think Sergio's ass is gay cause he always be wanting to fuck me in the ass. What am I gonna do now? Same shit I been doing. It's still sad though." she said with authority then fell out crying again.

"I feel you girl. Well at least you could stop arguing with Keno about him thinking you still fucking with Sergio."

"Yeah you right. That shit has been stressful. I didn't think we was gonna make it this far. The baby is two years old now. If he would stay out of jail or come around more he wouldn't have to worry."

"It would be funny if Keno's the one that did it huh?"

"Ooh don't say that."

CHAPTER FIFTY-FIVE

TANYA

The next morning the sun poured through my window and I woke up feeling refreshed and rejuvenated. Talking to Stephen was like a breath of fresh air, although he was trying to get the booty.

I had an appointment with Dr. Hunt early then I would go to work. I wanted to wear something that wouldn't cause mixed signals with Stephen. I got the hint that he liked me. I dressed in a loose fitting grey skirt and grey silk blouse with matching pumps.

When my Blackberry began shrilling. I quickly snatched it up and looked at the caller ID.

It was Malcolm, Damn, when will he give up?

He'd been calling me for the past few days continuously. When I didn't answer he'd leave me messages on my machine. I didn't check them because I didn't care what he had to say. There was nothing he could possibly say for me to even consider taking him back. Our relationship was a done deal, embalmed and buried. Fatima had called me too, but I wasn't about to talk to her either. She along with Malcolm, going to hell with gasoline g-strings up their asses is what I wanted.

I went and met with Dr. Hunt.

After my session with the doctor she told me, "I've noticed that everytime you come in here you straighten out things like picture frames and pens on my desk and you're always fixing your clothes. That tells me that you are unconsciously masking things messed up in your life by keeping all the outer things in place. This disorder in called OCD for Obsessive Compulsive Disorder and Tanya, you're also suffering from PTSD which is Post-Traumatic Stress." Dr. Hunt confirmed.

The diagnosis sounded serious. I was about to object, even though I didn't know what that meant, I wasn't sick in the head, I hoped.

"Let me explain." Dr. Hunt said. She inhaled, and then began with her explanation. "Post-Traumatic Stress or PTSD is a very serious but treatable disorder. It comes because of not being able to handle something or somethings that have happened to you. Things you may have seen or experienced. Your nightmares are tell-tell signs of events hidden in your subconscious. There's this little voice in your head that's screaming loudly."

My eyes grew moist with tears. Dr. Hunt told me that things can turn out okay. She also informed me that I was suffering from some anxiety disorders, dissociative amnesia being one. With the proper treatment, I could overcome the disorders.

"Tanya, have you thought about what we discussed?" Dr Hunt asked.

She'd been telling me to undergo hypnosis. The doctor thought that would be a big step to getting better and overcoming my issues and fears. Hypnosis would help.

"Yes, I will do it." I agreed.

I left Dr. Hunt's office for work and felt like a huge weight had been lifted from me. My mind felt a little bit more at ease. Always optimistic, I was ready to get my life back on track. I left hopeful.

I pulled up to work and went straight to my office to manage the resort project. As I came closer to my office door I saw some of my things scattered about the hall floor.

What in the hell! I thought.

I stepped closer to the door and saw Kimberly coming out of my office. Her arms were loaded with my computer and wires. My insides instantly began to boil and smoke puffed from my ears. I had been trying to be civil towards her but this was the last straw. I was so mad I couldn't see straight.

"What the fuck are you doing?!" I asked, through clenched teeth.

The smirk Kimberly wore on her face wasn't making the situation any better.

I was a few seconds away from busting her in the face. I took a step closer to Kimberly.

Since you got the promotion you got a bigger office. I'm moving to this office. I was just helping you get your shit out of here." she said nonchalantly.

"Kimberly, I think you need to leave." I said, trying to gain some kind of calmness.

"I ain't going no damn where!" she said firmly.

Kimberly stood in front of me with my computer in her hands. I wasn't moving but Kimberly made a motion like she was going to make me move. Without warning I popped Kimberly in the mouth.

It was on from there!

Kimberly swung back but for a fat girl I was a little too fast for her.

I grabbed a handful of Kimberly's long blonde hair and wrapped it around my hand. I went to work on her.

Kimberly got one good slap in before she ripped my silk blouse. I was really pissed off now. The Christian Dior blouse I wore had cost me a pretty penny. Now I was really about to really whoop some ass. I began throwing blows at her until Kimberly kicked me in the groin. The pain was excruciating but that didn't stop me. I elbowed Kimberly in the ear.

Somebody must've called Patricia down to that floor because usually she never left her office. By the time Patricia, the manager from the HR department, broke up the fight. I had broken Kimberly's nose and busted her lip. Her blood was all over my torn blouse.

"Come with me please." Patricia said sternly.

There were things all over the floor. We immediately headed for the H.R. department. Patricia walked between us the whole way there. Patricia was a little taller than me. Maybe 5'6". Her skin was black and smooth like oil. She wore her hair cut really low and tapered on the sides.

I didn't feel like I was finished whooping on Kimberly and if I got fired I was going to really show Kimberly what I could do. Once we made it to the office we took a seat in front of Patricia. She gave Kimberly some tissue. Kimberly held it to her nose.

"Ya'll know the policies and fighting isn't acceptable so I'll have to terminate the both of you."

"What?!" I yelled.

I couldn't believe what I'd just heard. I'd just gotten a promotion and now I was getting fired.

"Pat, I really can't afford to lose my job and you know she started this." I whined.

Patricia looked from me to Kimberly. Her glasses were pulled down to the tip of her slim nose.

"Ya'll knew ya'll needed your jobs before acting a fool down there." she said angrily.

Kimberly couldn't say much because she was bleeding too badly.

"Patricia, with all due respect we know we messed up but please could you just give us a smack on the wrist or just write us up or suspend us. Just don't fire us. Can you call Mr. Pennilton?" I pleaded.

"I really want to help ya'll, I do. I admire women trying to come up in corporate America but fighting isn't acceptable. I don't want to fire you two. Especially with you just getting a promotion and all." she said to me. "but if I let you two slide, I'll have to let everybody slide. I'm sorry. I have to fire the both of you. Please clean out your offices and vacate the premises immediately."

CHAPTER FIFTY-SIX

KENO

A few days had gone by, I had sold all the X pills and made $5,000 so with that and the money from the truck sale I bought a Jaguar XK8. I liked them because they looked like Aston Martins but were less than half the price.

The first stop I made was on Don Tomaso Dr. to Shantel's new apartment. I used my key to enter. As usual she was in the bed, under the covers naked. Her hair was braided into small individual braids with brown streaks.

Eventhough it was nearly 12:00 noon, the room was dark. She kept it that way with thick curtains. She usually stripped all night so she slept-in most mornings.

I undressed and left my clothes on the floor on the side of the bed. I slipped into the bed and spooned up to Shantel's butt. Her skin was soft and feminine as any woman should be. Her warm temperature made my dick hard right away. I rubbed my hand up the crack of her butt. I pulled my hand back and put a little spit on my fingers then rubbed it on her pussy lips. The spit helped me enter easily but once I penetrated, her natural juices instantly wet my dick up. When I pulled back my dick was glazed like a Krispy Crème special. I pumped it back into her. She felt it reach deep inside. When I pulled back again she shivered. I pushed it back in and goose bumps appeared on her caramel skin. I tried to go slow but the low smacking sound made me pick up my rhythm. I started going faster and faster until the bed was shaking like a massive earthquake was in effect. As my balls tightened up my legs stiffened. My pumps got stiffer and more powerful until...

"Uggghhhh!!!!"

I busted a thick, intense load into her hot core.

My whole body relaxed until Shantel got up. She went and sat in the bath tub. A few minutes later I went into the bathroom, got a rag and washed my dick off in the sink and left. She was still in the tub when she heard my music going down the street. My dick still leaked a bit of cum out of the tip.

I called Jo-Jo to see what was going on with the come up. I was more confident in working with Sonny because Sonny knew what he was doing. And I knew Sonny was confident with me because I had handled my business. Jo-Jo told me he'd call Sonny and see what's up and hit me back. When he hit me back Jo-Jo said that Sonny told him it was a go.

I got a text message:

Daddy.Its ur daughter

Wutz up Princess? I text her back.

Princess: **Cum get me. I'm bored.**

Me: **Don't use that word in texts especially to** men. It implies sex.

Princess: **Whatever**

Me: **It does. Fa reals**

Princess: **But anyway. Come get your daughter Daddy, she wants to spend time with you and check you out.**

Me: **Where u at**

She text me the address then asked me: How long?

I told her I'd be there in a hour and was there in a hour and a half. Princess was posted in the window until she saw my silver Jaguar pull up in the driveway. She ran out and got in. We drove around the city, then ate lunch at Goss Seafood on Vermont and 62nd Street. The owner was talking about closing down. Princess hoped not, because the food was delicious. We left and I went by Big Will's old house. I just looked at the tree that took my car door off. Man I really almost got killed that day. I was Glad I was alive and able to drive passed two years later. I got on the 105 Fwy to the 710 Fwy, exit Rosecrans Ave. I made a right onto Long Beach

Blvd. and took Princess down a street I used to live on when I was small. We turned left on Peck Street.

A lot of memories lay in wait for someone from the past to come re-live. I showed Princess the house I lived in.

She said, "Dang that place is torn up. You lived there?"

"Well it didn't look like that then. I lived here in this apartment and my lil homegirl Tanya lived there in that apartment next door."

"You sure lived around a bunch of Mexicans, Daddy."

"Whatever, and don't be calling me Daddy especially in front of other people. I ain't known you long enough. Call me Keno Brown."

"Whatever. Boys get on my nerves." she said under her breath.

We sat and I told her stories about things that happened so many years ago on this street.

One day Keno and a little boy from down the street named Pee Wee were playing on his bike. Keno was sitting on the seat and Pee Wee was standing up pedaling. Keno tickled Pee Wee. Pee Wee wiggled terribly. Keno would stop tickling right before Pee Wee let the handle bars go. Then he would start back up again. One time he tickled Pee Wee too long and Pee Wee wiggled right into a pole. They both went crashing into the gate. Pee Wee's forehead cracked on the pole under the impact. He suffered from his injury and expired.

That was the first person that had ever died that I knew. Since then I didn't have enough fingers and toes to count them.

I told Princess a few more stories. Neither me nor Princess could tell you in between which story did a blue Cherokee jeep with tinted windows pass by.

CHAPTER FIFTY-SEVEN

TANYA

When I got back to my office I sat in my seat and gazed out the window for about thirty minutes. Quite a few co-workers and associates passed by the door to get a peek at me but no one dared knock on the door. After thirty minutes of disbelief I came to grips and began to clean out my desk. When I went to clean up the things on the floor I noticed that Kimberly had dropped her ID badge and thin gold necklace. I threw them into my box of stuff out of spite and finished gathering my things.

When I got home from being fired I flopped down on the bed, fell back and just laid there staring at the ceiling. I couldn't believe I had gotten fired.

When I began emptying out the box of my work things, I found Kimberly's work ID badge and the necklace. I still had them in my hand when I went to the kitchen to cook something. I threw them on top of the fridge and made a huge cold cut submarine sandwich with all the trimmings while I fried some potatoes.

After I wallowed around the house for a few days I decided to go ahead and take that much needed trip back to California.

Once I decided to go, I left. The next day I was at an L.A.X. airport rental car agency renting a blue Cherokee Jeep. I got a room for two days and two nights at a airport hotel on Century.

I napped the first night. The next day I ate lunch at Roscoe's Chicken and Waffles on Manchester and Main Street then I went to Compton.

I stood on the sidewalk of my old neighborhood, looking around and peeping out the scene. Plenty of real street violence went down on this part of town, but I wasn't about to get caught up in it. Mixed emotions began to stir in the pit of my stomach.

Nothing much had changed in twenty years except that some of the houses on the block looked old and unkept, while others appeared to be newly renovated. The weather was beautiful, sunny and warm. A couple kids were being typical children, playing the many childhood games I remembered playing. Tears glistened in my eyes. I shook off the thoughts from the past.

I noticed the Saturday rituals of the people from my old neighborhood. Fathers were out mowing the lawns and I suspected the women to be shopping or cooking.

The apartment building me and my mother occupied was delapidated. The local government hadn't torn the remains down so I walked through and checked things out. I turned and looked at the apartment complex. So many bad feelings flooded my mind, but I faced my fears. I took a deep, shakey breath and put one unsure foot in front of the other. Although it only took less than a minute to walk across the street to the complex, in my mind, it felt like much longer. I walked through the door. Apartment 7C was to the right. I pushed the door open and walked through into the small apartment. In my mind I heard the voices of ghosts.

Little girl, you can't run from me....

The voice was vivid and intimidating. Gasping, I turned toward the voice. It felt as if the walls were closing in on me. I had to get out of the building. I ran. Once the fresh air hit my face I took a deep breath then exhaled.

"Excuse me. You looking for somebody?"

Frightened, I jumped, but then I realized that it was a female outside talking to me. I turned around and saw a woman who strangely enough, even after so many years I recognized. Her name was Nina. Nina was one of Keno's cousins.

Time hadn't been good to Nina. Back in the day she was a truely fine woman, but drugs and alcohol had claimed her looks completely. Nina's once curvy body was just skin and bones now. She was a walking skeleton. Her hair was covered with a dirty blue hat so I couldn't tell if she still had all that long, pretty hair or not but judging by the looks of everything else, she probably didn't. Her cinnamon colored skin was dull.

"Nina?" I asked, looking at her through squinted eyes.

"Yes, that's my name. And you are?" she said.

"I haven't seen you in 20 years. I'm Tanya I used to live in here with my mother." I said, pointing to the building.

Nina thought for a minute then her eyebrows raised, she smiled and said, "What! Damn girl it's been forever, you look totally different." She was grinning like the Cheetos cat, showing her rotten teeth.

"Well yeah I guess, I was only ten then."

"What you been up to?"

"I've been working." I replied.

"I mean, where are you now? It seemed as if you disappeared into thin air."

I spent a little time telling her the basics. I didn't have to ask Nina what she'd been up to, I could look at her and tell that her days consisted of nothing but crack cocaine and alcohol.

I looked away, trying to hide the sadness in my eyes.

I couldn't resist, I had to ask about Keno. He was very much a missing piece of my puzzle.

"Uh, have you seen your cousin Keno, lately?"

"No."

Disappointment registered, but I did my best to hide my emotions. We talked a while longer before Nina told me she had to go. She started fidgeting so my logical guess was that it was time for her daily high.

"Nina." I called to her retreating back.

Nina turned to face me once more.

"Take care of yourself." I said.

Like a sad puppy, Nina dropped her head and hurried off.

I decided to hit up Eldorado Park in Long Beach, next door to Compton. You could always find this park filled with Compton natives. I walked over to the jeep, jumped in and pulled off.

I found a parking spot at the park and killed the engine. I closed my eyes, I kissed my two fingers and sent up a quick prayer.

I stepped out of the car at the park, I looked around. There was a family reunion going on. The smell of barbecue wafted through the air. As I walked through the crowd, a popular Janet Jackson song blared from the speakers. Kids were playing, running and laughing, while the adults were conversing and playing spades. There was a game going where two lines of people stood behind a yellow rope facing each other, the person in front of you is your teammate. They tried to throw water balloons to each other. The lines were put farther and farther back after every throw. Whose ever balloon busted were out and wet. Lol. It looked like fun.

The ambience was friendly and warm, inviting even. The huge banner that hung across two trees read,

Archer, Trap and Ewing Family Reunion.

The food smelled great. I acted like I belonged here. I walked over to a cooler and took out a soda, I turned around and...

"Keisha!" I squealed when I recognized my old childhood friend. I went over to the young woman who strongly resembled Sanaa Lathan. The only difference was that Keisha's hair was in a short and cute pixie cut. We embraced.

"Tanya, girl, where the hell you been and what the hell you been up to?"

Keisha and me lived on the same street. It was Keisha's father who used to take us to the park in the station wagon.

"I'm just working, I'm in Memphis so everything's good."

"I'm glad you're enjoying the south. I saw your mama a few days ago."

I was taken back quickly. Why did Keisha have to mention Cheryl?

Showing no emotion, I said, "Really?"

"Yeah I saw her."

Changing the subject, I asked, "What have you been up to?"

"Well, I've been married for five years and I have two beautiful kids."

We walked over near the grill and she introduced me to her husband, Kendric, and her two girls, Kenya and Kelsey.

We two chatted and ate for a while before exchanging numbers. I was about to walk off, but stopped in my tracks, and asked, "Oh, have you seen Keno?"

Keisha looked a bit puzzled, then thought for a moment before saying, "No, not in a while." she said matter-of-factly.

"Thanks." I mumbled.

"Don't forget to keep in touch." Keisha said to me.

I went to the Pike in Long Beach. It was completely redone. You name it they had it, movies, restaurants, rides, boats, bars and clubs. When I left there I drove by Kelly

Park in Compton, the one we used to go to when we were young.

As I drove around the city I paid special attention to every block, I didn't know where to begin looking for Keno but I didn't want to go asking around like a detective. Maybe our reuniting wasn't meant to be. Life was funny with its twists and turns.

Blinking away tears, I pulled out in the always to be expected L.A. traffic jams. Blaring horns didn't bother me. I'd tuned the rest of the world out to listen to my inner voice that said, *Go home.*

I drove through Compton one last time. I drove by the apartments I used to stay in. On the way up the street I rolled my tinted windows up, even though I was there intentionally, I wanted to separate myself from the feelings that were creeping. The houses were on the right as I headed east down Peck St. towards Long Beach Blvd. They looked different but still held the past just as strongly. I saw a nice silver Jaguar sitting across the street on the left.

CHAPTER FIFTY-EIGHT

KENO

When we left Compton, I drove to L.A. and went by a couple hot spots looking for a buddy of mine. I got a text from Shantel asking where I was. I text her back telling her that I was headed to 43rd and Crenshaw across the street from the Millennium.

We turned up into El Pollo Loco's Drive-thru and ordered some food. Princess dug into her food right away. I made a left on 43rd and a quick left into the alley. Just as much stuff went on in the back on this side as it did behind the Milliennium Barber Shop across the street.

I pulled up and went around to the back of the barbershops to look for my friend.

I saw a few of the local hustlers back there. I turned and saw Thugsta.

"Thugsta what you doing back here, don't you belong across the street?"

"Boy I go whereeva I please."

I asked him if he had seen Biz.

"Yeah I seen 'em a lil while ago but you know how that guy is. He be everywhere like..." and he made the sound, *Pyune! Pyune!* "Real shit, one night I was hanging out with him right. And we got the lowriders out and shit. The bitches is out. We chillin'. That night when I went in, my cousin was on his way out, bout to fly up to Seattle then drive up to Canada right. And I was drunk and I had some money so I was like, 'I'm going too right'. And it was nothing, we shot up there. It was easy at the border, we just showed our passports and shit. This is like a Thurday. Friday night I go to the club downtown Canada and I kid you not, this nigga Biz was up in there dancing with a bad ass white bitch. Dancing with the bitch like he knew the bitch, he did a few of 'em like that. In Canada my boy! Pyune Pyune!" He did a roadrunner gesture with his hand. "Speak of the Devil. There he go right there. See him leaned back with one leg out the car. That's one of his lil bitches car."

I walked over to give him the good news.

Biz stood up.

"What up!"

He had on a red Biz-e-Bee Apparel pullover.

We shook hands, the street way.

I said, "I'm ready to invest some money in your work. Yeah. How you like me now?"

"I love you for that but I'm already good. I did a couple of things, you know, a mil here, a mil there, and got it going. You know, I got my own brand out here." he gestured to his chest. "Everybody feeling it, everybody got it. See this hoodie right here."

"What! That's you? I got some of that shit at home. I was just about to ask you where you got that from?"

"I got it from me. It's moving." He pointed to his sweat pants. "These come out next year but they my last year sweats, get me? But aye that's good looking out. Lemme' finish hollering at her for a minute and if you gonna chill back here for a while, I'ma holler at you in a minute."

"Nah, I'ma probably dip. But I'm glad to hear it jumped off. Take it all the way. You'll be the new shit everywhere."

"All I can say is, get plenty toilet paper homie."

"That's what's up."

We thug hugged, I stepped, but hung around because Shantel was on her way and it seemed like she wanted to talk to me. I saw Legit at the end of the alley, looking down here with some incense in his hand.

Through the grapevine I heard about Mannish. He had been out a couple of months. He was already back in the swing of things. I heard he killed a nigga behind the Millenium named Q-Tip. I heard Thugsta was working for him and that Big Will was getting his product from him too.

When I got back into the car, Princess said, "Daddy... I mean Keno. First of all, I just want you to know that it's stupid that I gotta call you Keno. You my daddy fool. But anyways, are those two weed spots over there?"

"I see no evil, speak no evil." I said.

"Well I keep seeing some fly cars pulling up and one person always go in, no matter how many people in the car, only one person go in, and it's some fly cars parked back here. And them supposed to be stores right? But aint nobody never came out with no shopping bag."

I could only look at her, speechless.

We sat in silence and ate our tacos, watching everything.

Princess pulled a mini laptop out of her purse and went on Facebook.

Jo-Jo walked up to the car trying to get into the passenger seat. The door was locked so he looked in and saw Princess. I unlocked the door and Jo-Jo got in the back, the weed was loud on his clothes. We only chatted for five minutes before Shantel pulled up in Tarika's ragedy BMW. She drove up to my driver side window.

"Damn this is a nice car Keno. Jag and shit. I didn't know you got a new car, dang boy! I like that pretty ass silver too. You handling your bizness huh?"

"It is whatever you say like Jesus said."

"Which is why I came to talk to you. Do you know somebody named Marvel, well, you probably don't know him but do you know somebody named Sonny?"

That caught Jo-Jo's attention. He listened.

"Why?" was Keno's one word reply.

"Do you know him or not? Cause if you do you better be careful because Marvel told me…"

I realized that Princess was listening also. I didn't want her to know anything about my criminal life and I had no idea what Shantel was about to say. It sounded like a lot and I wanted to know what all she had to say but not right this second.

"Hold up…" I cut her off. "…I'ma be over your house in a lil while."

Jo-Jo opened his door and excused himself, "Yo homie, I'm gone. I got shit to do. I'ma see you tonite, check." then ran off to his car.

I introduced Shantel to Princess and talked to her for a few more minutes while I finished my food. When we were done I promised Shantel that I would be over to her apartment soon and started my car up. I pulled out in one direction and Shantel went the other.

Six gunshots rang out and found their destination through Shantel's car door and into her body. The car rolled into the street of Homeland and Crenshaw Blvd. and somehow stopped in the middle of the intersection. Before anyone ran up to see who it was and how bad it was, her life had already leaked out through the holes.

CHAPTER FIFTY-NINE

TANYA

I flew back home drained from the trip. My trip to Compton hadn't tied any loose strings. I still didn't have any answers and I was past frustrated. Today was going to be my visit with Dr. Hunt and I hoped the hypnosis would be successful.

I was thankful to be back in Memphis. Compared to L.A traffic, Memphis's was lovely.

I drove down Raines Road and took a quick left on Winchester Road. I parked where I always did and walked to the entrance.

Dry leaves and twigs cracked under my shoes. Dr. Hunt's receptionist greeted me and told me that Dr. Hunt would be right with me. Nervous energy tried to take me over. I hoped that after this visit everything would go back to normal. Taking a deep breath, I took a seat in the empty waiting room. No sooner than I'd picked up the latest edition of Popular Science, my name was called.

"Hey Tanya." Dr, Hunt greeted me.

I followed her down the hallway. We reached an office. Classical music played in the background, the room was dim. A white chaise and two chairs sat in the middle of the room. I looked up when Dr. Hunt introduced the man who occupied one of the chairs. I was scared of what my mind would say. I retreated, I wasn't prepared for this. I needed to go see Ma. I told Dr. Hunt that I had to come back another time and left quickly. I ran to my car. My hands gripped the steering wheel until my knuckles were white. I sat there for tweny minutes before I went home.

Before I got in the bed I checked my account and found out that my account was nearly empty and had been nearly empty for nearly two months. Sweat drenched my neck and back. None of my bills had been paid for months, mortgage or car note. Everything I had charged wouldn't be getting paid. I couldn't believe Malcolm could do this to me.

No way!

Yes way!

I fell into a slump. I moped around the house for a few days with no signs of life in my face. I couldn't believe I'd lost my job most of all. I had given TSL Investments years of my life and now it was all over. Thinking about Kimberly pissed me off and it may have been a good thing that I didn't know where Kimberly lived.

What was I going to do? With this recession it was hard as hell to find a job.

I staggered to the kitchen. I had a taste for some chicken noodle soup. It was in the cabinet above the fridge. I pulled a chair close and stood on it. As I reached for the can

I noticed Kimberly's work badge and necklace laying on top of the fridge. I got my soup and picked up the badge. I looked at it. Just like mines it had Kimberly's name and picture and ID number on the front and an electronic code on the back. I threw it onto the breakfast nook and went to the bathroom. Maybe a warm shower would make me feel better.

Talking with Ma always made me feel better so I figured I'd go see her. I wanted to tell Ma about my trip to Compton. I locked up the house and went to Memphis Hospital. Seeing Ma would lift me up a bit and hopefully I could lift Ma and get a confirmation on doing some aggressive treatment.

I ate some Mc Donald's to clear my mind before I got to the hospital. Every time something was wrong with me my grandma could sense it and I didn't want to make Ma worry.

The hospital smell wafted through the air and made me feel sick to the stomach. My last meal rose up in my throat and thankfully I was right near a bathroom. I ran into a stall and bent over right when my food was coming back out the top.

I searched for and found a drink machine, got a sprite, gulped an amount down and proceeded to Ma's room.

I walked into Ma's room and the bed was empty. I went to the nurse's station and asked, "Where is my grandmother? Is she taking tests? Will she be back soon?"

The nurse recognized me and knew who my grandmother was. She gave and uneasy smile and said, "She died."

"What!" I screamed!

A couple of alarmed nurses rushed over and found me on the floor. I was hysterical. I had broken down. Crying and screaming, screaming and crying.

"When?" I asked between outbursts.

"She passed away yesterday."

One of the nurses helped me to my feet and handed me the bottle of Sprite. I sat on a chair weakly.

Ma had passed away.

CHAPTER SEVENTY

KENO

Me, Jo-Jo and Sonny met up that evening. Sonny told me that the only thing I needed to do was back him up like I did the first night. That was cool for Sonny but I still really wanted to know how we were going to control a whole nightclub full of people and who knows how many security men. So I asked him again.

Sonny told me that it would be just as smooth as the first robbery except that it may take longer. I couldn't see it but fuck it! In a few hours we would be getting money. Sonny told me to go home and get fresh and ready for the club and that's what I did. I had that brown Biz-e-Bee Apparel outfit I had been looking for a reason to wear.

About eleven o'clock we came around the corner of the club.

The first thing I noticed was about ten U-haul trucks parked up the street before we turned the corner. The club was packed out with people lined up around the corner. High line cars were parked all along the front and valet was running back and forth. Jo-Jo parked the car up like half a mile and we walked back to the club. It seemed like there were even more people out front by then. At this point I still

416

didn't know who the hell was performing, but obviously the person was popular.

Sonny was friends with the man at the front with the guest/vip list. When he saw Sonny he said, "What's up homie?" gave him a dap and a hug and asked, "How many wit you?"

Sonny said, "Two right here and I got two more coming."

"Alright, fasho. Just tell them to get at me and say your name."

"They already know."

With that we headed to the door, a man bumped me and had the audacity to look at me for an apology. I noticed but just continued on towards the entrance. Then he said, "Aye!" I already knew what was next. Either someone bowed down or it was clash time.

"My fault." I said and didn't skip a beat through the doors into the packed club. Me and Jo-Jo followed Sonny through the club. Sonny put on a green neon glow in the dark wristband. I got my ass squeezed a couple of times by a couple of hot bitches. One girl actually ran her hand across the front of my jeans. I grabbed her hand and pulled her close. She was pretty. She put her tongue in my mouth. I accepted it with pleasure. She must've taken an ecstasy pill. She was the kind of girl a guy would hang with all night if he

SOMETIMES IT IS WHAT IT IS

thought it would yield him even just a kiss. I felt fortunate and hoped my luck would continue through the night. We followed Sonny to the far right to a couple of doors.

"They're locked now", Sonny said, "...but they won't be soon."

We maneuvered to the other side of the club and watched some women for about thirty minutes. Then the lights started to flicker and somebody came out on stage and started speaking into the microphone. Sonny went to the bar. After about two minutes I saw the bartender hand him a couple of drinks and I didn't see Sonny hand the bartender any money.

Sonny came back with the drinks and said, "Here, have a drink and get ready for some action."

The artist came out and the crowd went wild. Oh my God! I wished someone went wild for me like that. I was feeling the liquor. I was now ready for anything.

CHAPTER SEVENTY-ONE

TANYA

I ran out of the hospital and took off in my car. Nauseous waves went through my stomach. I took a few deep breaths and swallowed the spit that had crept up my throat. I pulled over and threw up on the side of the highway.

I dropped my head in my hands and began to sob.

What am I going to do?

I made it home and dove right into my bed and wet my pillow as I fell asleep. I dreamed...

"Please stop!" she said, as she was fondled.

No matter what she said, the pain of being penetrated wouldn't go away. The young girl was being violated, but couldn't do anything about it.

"Spread your legs," the voice boomed.

She didn't want the grimey character on her, she didn't even want to be touched. His body was rough and cold. She was made to lay back on her bed with her legs spread eagle while the monster had his way with her. When she felt a sticky, wet tongue in between her legs she squirmed and yelled, "Stop!" again.

"Shut the hell up!" the voice barked.

She cried in silence because for her, life would never ever be the same. His tongue delved in and out of her as she lay there motionless. What had she done to deserve this? For fear of getting popped in the mouth, she didn't say anything else, she just laid there. After about ten minutes of licking it stopped and she was rolled over...

I jumped up out of my sleep and wiped off the sweat. I didn't have anywhere to go so I stayed in.

I felt terrible, so many things were wrong. My stomach pained me again. I looked at the date on the calendar and almost fainted. My period was late. I'd never been late before in my life.

"I can't be pregnant. I can't be pregnant. Malcolm never got that far, unless he is a premature ejaculator or something." I said to myself as I paced the floor. I wasn't ready for motherhood and I sure as hell didn't want to have Malcolm's baby.

Wait, maybe I was overreacting for nothing. I tried to calm down. I wanted to talk to Sahara but was too ashamed. I'd told her how much of a sorry man Malcolm was and now I was possibly pregnant by him? I would be a damn fool. As I thought I realized that I could have the answer I needed really easy in less than twenty minutes. There was a store right around the corner that sold pregnancy tests.

The phone rang, I grumbed and grabbed my cordless phone. When I saw a bill collector's number on the caller ID I didn't even bother to answer.

I buried my face in the pillow and cried for Ma. The sorrow kept me down but the throwing up kept me getting back up.

Damn, I got to do something, I thought, climbing out of bed.

I looked in the mirror at my body. Suddenly, the urge to throw up overtook me. I ran into the bathroom and emptied my stomach.

I spent two days in bed then decided to find out for sure if I was pregnant, if not I would need to see a doctor.

When I stepped out the door of my home, the thing that I dreaded to see the most, a notice of default was posted on the door. I took the notice and threw it on the breakfast nook.

I lost Ma, I lost my job, Malcolm stole my money and now a notice of default was on my door. He had me thinking he was just taking care of little business, just a few hundred here and there. He'd stolen well over $50,000.

I would wait no more, I was going to take a pregnancy test. When I stepped out the house the driveway was empty.

Damnit!

My car was gone!

OMG!

What in the hell is going on?

Although I wanted to play dumb I knew my car had been repossessed. I loved that car! Tears clouded my eyes as I stepped back into my house and I called the finance company immediately. They told me where I could go to retrieve my things.

I called Sahara and on the first ring she answered.

"Hi Sahara." I said, "I need you to come over."

"I'll be there in an hour." Sahara said without hesitation.

There was a ring of the doorbell about 45 minutes later. I was greeted by my beautiful sister. Today Sahara was dressed in a simple white tank top and a pair of khaki pants. She had her long and wavy mane pulled up in a high ponytail with a ponytail clip.

"Hey girl!" she said.

"Hi." I said weakly as Sahara stepped through the door and took me in a warm embrace.

We went into the living room and I told her all about my situation. Sahara told me not to worry about it. Sahara had two cars and she told me she'd let me drive her black Maxima until things got better. I thanked her profusely because right then I needed someone in my corner. I picked up a glass off the counter and took a few sips. Really I was trying to buy a little time. I didn't want to tell her about my missed monthly friend, I really didn't want to be pregnant. Maybe if I denied it enough, it wouldn't be true. But the truth was hard to deny. There was a reason why I was throwing up.

"Tanya, why didn't you tell me you were having money problems?"

I hunched my shoulder. I was embarrassed and I didn't want to drag anybody into my problems. I was too independent for help.

I took a deep breath then exhaled and said, "Sahara, I might be pregnant."

Sahara's expression was unreadable so the color drained from my face.

"Are you sure?" Sahara asked?

"Well, uh, yeah. But I haven't taken a test yet."

When I expressed my feelings to her, Sahara grabbed my hands and gently squeezed them.

"You don't have to be embarrassed when it comes to me. We are family and you know you can share anything with me. Please let me help you."

She pulled out her checkbook and I immediately stopped her. I was very adamant about not taking money from her.

"Sahara, please, I don't want your money. Although I'm having a rough time right now it will get better. As a matter of fact I need to pick up a small check for some monies owed from TSL. Can you take me?"

"Of course I'll take you Tanya. Are you ready now?"

"Yeah, let's go."

We left and headed to TSL. When we pulled up Stephen was standing in the front smoking a cigarette.

I spoke, "I thought you didn't smoke?"

"I would've stopped for you."

"Whatever." I laughed and went inside.

When I exited the building Stephen was walking away from the car, from talking to Sahara.

When I got in the car I asked, "You met Stephen?"

"Yeah I just met him."

"He's cool huh?"

"Yeah, he was just talking about you."

"Oh yeah, what did he say?"

"Just a little of this and a little of that."

"You got secrets now?"

"Maybe. Nah, he asked me how you were handling things. He said he wanted to bring you something. He said he had a surprise for you. He wants me to help him."

"What is he gonna do? What did you tell him?"

"I said okay."

We laughed and went back to my house.

CHAPTER SEVENTY-TWO

KENO

Half way through the artist's set, right in the middle of all the hype, the music went dead, the artist's microphone cut off and then about ten seconds later the whole place went black. There must've been a few lights on the stage because I could see the artist being rushed out the back.

I felt a tug on my arm and Sonny's voice saying, "Come on!"

I couldn't see him but I could see the wrist band Sonny wore. We followed Sonny to the far right of the club where the back doors were. I could hear people getting disgruntled and asking, "What the fuck is up with the show?"

We slipped through the doors and I almost shit on myself when I saw a masked gunman in a pair of coveralls. I quickly regained composure figuring the gunman had to be with us. Then I noticed two other masked guys with coveralls standing to the side, looking like they were waiting for instructions.

Just then Sonny said, "You two go out and get in the U-haul trucks." he said to Marvel, "You get in the one right on the other side of this door." to the other he said, "Get in the first one around the corner and be ready to put it here when this one leaves." Marvel and the other guy both nodded and exited.

Sonny looked at me and Jo-Jo and said, "Hurry up, put one of these on and pick up an AK47 Rifle." He was pointing to a pile of one size fits all coveralls in the middle of the floor with one hand and to two assault rifles leaning against the wall with the other hand. We hurriedly followed directions as we could hear the music kick back up inside the club. Then it stopped, then started again, then stopped, then started again. Then someone on the loud speaker said, "We're going to have to ask everyone to exit the doors on the right."

Then the music came back on. We pulled our masks over our heads, grabbed the weapons and Sonny killed the lights in the room we were in.

Suddenly, one of the doors opened and people started pouring into the room with us. The whole place was in total darkness and the music in the club was blasting again. I saw the door shut and the lights in the room come back on. There were four of us, one in each corner of the room masked up and armed. Everybody's gun was drawn but mines. I quickly pointed mines. Some women screamed. Some men screamed too. It was easy to understand why. Sonny began to speak, with the door closed his voice was clear enough.

"ALRIGHT!" he yelled. "I'ma say this once, anybody disobeys I'm shooting. STRIP! Leave everything you got on the fucking floor and put on one of those jumpsuits in the middle of the floor. Only thing you can keep are your keys. NOW MOVE!"

One man said, "I aint..." and before he could get the rest of his sentence out, one of the gunmen shredded his flesh with about fifteen bullets real fast. A girl on the side of him dropped too. No one could tell if she got hit or fainted but obviously everyone understood how easily they could die in the side room of a club. Everyone got undressed so fast you would think their clothes were on fire.

Tits, dicks and ass was everywhere. They got dressed in the coveralls just as fast. Everyone was rushed out the exit. Once the door was opened we could see that a U-haul had been backed all the way to the door and a small ramp leading up into the back. After they were loaded into the truck like cattle I was told to secure the latch. The whole thing took about three minutes. And then the next rush of impatient people came through the door. The music in the club was still going off and on. After the door shut, the lights inside the room came on again and the first thing everyone saw were the two bloodied bodies on the floor and the gunmen looking as menacing as possible. All Sonny had to say was "Strip! Or end up on the floor. Put on a jumpsuit. Keep yuh keys." It seemed to go even a bit faster with this group. Guess the bodies helped. The next truck was in position and they were loaded in and wisked off.

After it all, we loaded up all the clothes, purses and jewelry into a bunch of trash bags and rolled out in the last U-haul truck. I got out of the truck at my Jag. Sonny told me to circle the block and get a look at what things looks like then to meet him at his house.

Things were chaotic as to be expected, because when everything was going down there were still a lot of people in the front still trying to get in who had no idea what was going on.

When I got to Sonny's house, I pulled to the back as we usually did. I figured Sonny was slick for getting rid of the U-haul so fast. I waited for a while but Sonny never came out of the back door.

After about ten minutes my patience ran out and I got out of the car. I figured maybe somehow I had gotten there before them. I walked to the front and looked down the street. The street was quiet as a cop behind bars. Another five minutes passed and Sonny still hadn't shown up. I tried the back door of the house. It was unlocked, I went in. The house was empty.

And by the looks of it, it had always been empty.

CHAPTER SEVENTY-THREE

KENO

I went home hot as a drag racer's tail pipes about Sonny skipping out on me with my share of the money. Over the next few days me and Crystal got into a few arguments because I was on edge. I cursed and threw things around.

Crystal couldn't take it no more. She screamed and said, "You need to check that shit at the door. You're always dealing with shady people. You need to tap on yuh brakes playa and slow all that hollering down. I got about five hundred dollars, if you feel like you gotta have some money in your pocket you can have it! I gave you another chance at life, to feel good again, to be making moves and getting money. You up in here hollering and throwing shit because you got played. You lucky your ass didn't get killed messing around. Take this money and get the fuck outta my house until you get your mind right."

I wasn't listening to none of it except the part when she said, "I gave you another chance at life." that repeated in my head.

Bitch aint gave me no fucking chance! What chance she give me?

I was too messed up about Sonny skipping out on me with my portion of the money. I figured it had to be at least $250,000 on my cut with all the iced out jewelry that was thrown on the sheet on the ground. I swore to exact my revenge when ever I saw Sonny.

I left the $500 Crystal offered me on the table and stormed out of the apartment and burned rubber in my Jag halfway down the street.

I heard my phone beep.

It was a text from Princess: Daddy did I leave my phone in your car?

Me: Lemme C. I text back then reached over and felt under the passenger seat.

I found it. When I looked at the display it had Princess kissing another girl. I pushed a button on the phone and her instant message screen came up.

A note said, I love you Danielle, your baby Princess.

I was speechless. I told her I had found the phone but I never mentioned my startling discovery.

Princess hung up the phone, kissed Danielle and told her that she didn't have to buy her a new phone because her daddy had found it.

In the meanwhile I had to put my twos and fews together. I had come up on another laptop so I called Lee and Lee told me to meet him back at the coffee shop. I went and after we did the transaction, Lee asked, "You steal these things or what?"

That kinda caught me off guard, almost pissed me off so I didn't answer. Lee waited. I waited.

Lee said, "I ran the serial number on that last one and it came back stolen. I bet if I run this it will come back stolen too."

I still didn't have an answer for him. After a few moments he said, "If you don't mind stealing then maybe you come with me and steal big."

Lee got up and started walking towards the door. I followed. When we got outside, Lee kept walking.

I said, "Hold up. You wanna do something now?"

Lee said, "Now, interesting word, of course now. No matter what time it is or where you are in this life, there is hardly ever a better time then Now. Get into your car and follow me." he said as he continued to walk.

Lee got into a pearl white colored Porsche Panamera sedan. It was a four door car and had a 4.8 liter 500 horse power V8 Turbo engine. I got into my car and followed Lee out of the parking lot. We got stopped by the first light. I was right behind Lee then a motorcycle pulled out of the same parking lot and came up behind us. It was Lee's partner. The white van with the detectives in it stopped behind the motorcycle. When the light changed Lee pulled off and then me. The motorcycle stalled, it didn't move and so the van wasn't able to move either. The light turned red.

I followed Lee onto the freeway and we drove to the westside of Orange County where there were warehouses and factories. We pulled into a parking lot. Lee pulled over and motioned for me to pull up next to him. Lee handed me a clipboard, a pair of glasses and a walkie-talkie through the window. He tossed a pistol into my lap. He told me that his partner was on the way with a truck. He said that we could get started and by the time I had things under control that his partner would be there with a truck.

I was thinking, *What the fuck is he talking about! Here I am with a fucking gun, a walkie-talkie, a pair of glasses and a fucking clipboard. What the fuck is going on?* So I asked, in an irritated tone.

Lee said, "It's obvious that you steal. But you steal small. We are going to steal big right now. I can see in your eyes, you kill before. Maybe you kill for small things. Maybe you don't have to kill here but if you do, you kill for big payday. You go inside that warehouse. You find one man, he in charge of counterfiet electronics computer shipment. You in and out. You fool him with glasses and clip board. When he put his guard down you put your gun up. Put him somewhere out of site. He make trouble you shoot him. That place have three hundred thousand dollar of laptop. Okay you go now, in. My partner soon come."

Lee really didn't have to say anything else. I felt like Lee had read me like the directions on a box of instant oatmeal. I just got out of the car and went straight into the building. Everything went basically how Lee said it would go except that I did indeed have to blow noodles out of ole boy's head. His brains hung out like a busted can of Spaghettios.

When I went inside, the place was like a big maze made up of boxes of computers. I walked through slowly with my glasses on, clipboard in hand and gun in the front of my pants. I found an office to the side.

I called out, "Hello?"

Someone said, "Yeah, I'm in the office."

I followed the voice and found a white dude standing near a desk. He was about 6' 3" 150lbs. with a swag that said "Distributor" by day "Rocker" by night. He was on the phone. I set the clipboard down and raised the gun up. His jaw dropped. He was speechless. I walked up and put my finger on the End button on the phone and hung it up. He was still shocked. On the way in I had seen cameras so I asked him for the tapes and he ignored me. I wasted no time, I gun butted him in the forehead and he dropped to the ground and hollered out.

I told him, "Right now I see a two for one special, your merchandise and your soul."

He took me for a joke and grabbed my legs to tackle me down. As I was falling back I rammed the gun barrel into the top of his head as hard as I could, hard enough to crack his skull and I pulled the trigger at the same damn time. His mouth fell open and brain matter and blood poured out like vomit. His body jerked up straight so I didn't fall. I summoned Lee on the walkie-talkie and searched for the video tape. I got it and we loaded up the truck with everything Lee pointed out. There were 2,000 counterfiet Apple computers. And when it was all said and done Lee paid me $75,000. He said the $300,000 worth of stuff was really worth 70% so he gave me half, although $75,000 wasn't half but I was happy with it, no complaints. My pockets were fat, my hard work paid off.

I was feeling much better. I put that with what I had made on the ecstasy pills and my pockets were all nice. It was a big difference in how broke I was not too long before. I put a $20,000 down payment on an Aston Martin. tan paint job with French Vanilla ice cream color interior, tan rims with chrome accents.

CHAPTER SEVENTY-FOUR

TANYA

I felt miserable as I drove around in Sahara's Maxima. I had made some runs around town then headed home. As I sat at a red light, suddenly I had a hallucination. It was Ma, right in front of me. It scared me almost into a cardiac arrest. But Ma talked to me as if everything was normal. Ma had on a head scarf and her skin was radiant. Ma sat in the passenger seat and told me that she died alone and disappointed because I left town without a word. Guilt flooded my veins. I tried to explain that everything was going wrong at the same time and I couldn't think. I tried to tell Ma that nothing was more important than her but I felt like a whirlwind was making my decisions for me. Every time I spoke, Ma finished half the sentence in sign language. Then Ma told me. Not to stress it because it was all temporary. That everything physical was temporary. Ma told me that I had more problems to come and more decisions the whirlwind would make for me as well. We talked about everything from my bad dreams to my being fired and my breaking up with Malcolm.

Ma told me how happy she was for me for finally dropping 210lbs of dead weight, (Malcolm).

Now if I could only drop some weight around my waist. I thought.

"Yeah Ma, now I see what you were talking about. I'm so sorry for not listening to you."

"Experience is da bes teecha Tanya."

I simply smiled,

"Wen you gonna gimme a lil great gran' baby?" Ma asked.

I wondered where that question came from. Ma didn't know how close she was to getting her wish.

"Don't you think I am too young for that?" I asked.

"Nonsense, I was sixteen wen I married an' nineteen wen I started havin' children."

"Things were different back then."

"Well, yeah, I caint argue wit you on dat. Times was ruff back then but we didn't take anythin' fa granted. Though money was low, half da time we was thankful fa being alive and healthy."

I knew what she was telling me was right.

"How's your friend Fatima?"

Rolling my eyes, I sighed.

"Ma, me and Fatima ain't friends no more."

"Since when?" she inquired.

"Since about a week ago."

"Oh!" was Ma's subtle reply.

Ma's husband had a stroke over his other woman's house. The other woman was her closest cousin. She battled with loving and forgiving people and trust issues.

Then just as suddenly as it appeared, the vision disappeared. I reached but nothing was there. I headed home with red eyes and wet lashes. Rush hour traffic was always the worst. When traffic hadn't moved for five minutes I grew frustrated. I let out a slew of curse words and maneuvered through traffic, an emotional wreck I was.

I couldn't believe I had had an experience with Ma. This was a bit much for me to handle. Too many things were coming at me from different directions. I got home and fell to the living room floor and cried. What was I going to do now? I pounded the carpet until I was tired and fell asleep right there on the floor. As I slept, saliva dripped from my mouth. My dreams continued...

"Bitch, shut the fuck up."

Her cries went unheard and soon her piercing screams became pure whimpers. She didn't have anymore to give. Physically she was tired. After a while the pain subsided but she was still crying. She'd been robbed of something she could never get back, and there was no one to protect her. After a few pumps it was over. He pulled out, a milky and sticky substance spilled on her stomach. He finally let her go and immediately, she ran to the bathroom and curled up in a corner. It hurt between her legs so she thought a nice warm bath would ease the pain. She ran some water and sunk into the bath tub, she closed her eyes.

CHAPTER SEVENTY-FIVE

KENO

Anybody that puts money into your pocket becomes your new best friend and Lee was mines. I found myself hanging out at the coffee shop a lot more often until Lee exposed me to another spot that had nice women that kinda just hung out with you for tips. It was a lot different than the strip clubs I was used to. These girls didn't strip. They weren't expected to fuck but they might go home with you for a thousand dollars a night.

After a couple of visits to this place I was put up on a scheme. There was a guy named Cho that Lee had been watching. Lee told me that Cho was a former business partner of his former business partner Kim. The only reason Kim was Lee's former business partner was because he was dead. Cho was Kim's former partner only because Cho robbed Kim and killed him.

Lee was small potatoes compared to Kim but Lee vowed to set Cho up and avenge Kim's death. Kim was found with jewels stuffed in his nose. It was Cho's signature. Lee knew someone had misinformed the feds that Lee himself was involved and Lee knew the agents were lurking. I couldn't help but think that Lee had found the perfect assassin and scapegoat in me.

The next morning I stopped by Princess' to give her the cell phone. When she saw the Aston Martin she fell in love with it instantly.

"Take me for a ride Daddy... I mean Keno." she asked.

"Aight, you can go with me to hook my car up today. Let's ride."

During the ride across town I saw an old lady trying to cross the busy street, I pulled over, left my driver door open and engine running and ran back and took my time helping the old lady safely across.

Princess couldn't believe it.

Mister Help Everybody and shit. Where he been all my life?

Afterwards, we spent the whole day on Venice Boulevard and La Cienega Boulevard. First stop was Globe tires to get some 24 inch rims. I let Princess pick them out. Then across the street to AAA Mufflers to get a K&N air filter, a performance enhancement chip and dual exhaust. When the car was done I took La Cienega northbound up to Pico made a left and pulled into Twin Dragon restaurant for some great Chinese food. Despite her constant pleas I didn't let her drive. The saltwater fishtank was a good look. It made me think about the tank at the coffee shop where Lee hung out which was four times as big.

We were seated on the opposite wall of the tank.

"Daddy... I mean Keno, aint that the father from that show on HBO?"

"Who? Oh him, yeah, that's him."

"You got your digital camera?"

"Yeah its here in my jacket. You gonna go take a pic with him?"

Just then the camera flashed.

Papparazzi in effect.

"Dang that was like a sniper shot. Why didn't you just ask him to take a picture with him?"

"I don't know."

When we were leaving the restaurant Princess refused to get into the beautiful fast car if she couldn't drive it. I said no because she didn't have a license and not much driving experience but she wouldn't let up. I told her to get in the passenger seat or be calling a cab. She out stubborned me and I agreed to let her drive herself home.

Why oh why did I let her take the wheel?

She pulled off and burned a little rubber in the process. She was going southbound on La Cienega, she passed the 7-11 on the right, she was doing good! She swerved a couple times but got the car under control.

Ten minutes later she got a text message and looked at it. It was Danielle, her "best friend." She was at a red light so I didn't say anything. I looked up at the remodeled Kaiser Hospital. Princess returned the text before the light turned green. A couple minutes later her phone beeped again, she was going 40 mph she looked at the text. I looked at her. She had gotten real comfortable real fast behind the wheel. She began to text back as she drove. We passed Globe Tire shop. As she went around the bend on La Cienega Blvd. just past Venice, she veered over a little too far over the double yellow lines and into the lane of the opposing traffic.

I had just cracked my lips to yell at her about watching what she was doing when.

SMASH!

BAM!

BOOM!

A Ford Pick-Up going the opposite way crashed into the driver's side of the Aston Martin, crushed the rims and flipped us over. The car flew up into the air about twenty feet and flipped over twice towards the sidewalk. It landed on top of a parked car.

The man who Princess crashed into was okay, just a little disorientated. He got out of his truck, trying to see if we were alright. As soon as both of his feet touched the ground he got hit by an old lady in a Buick!

BOOM!

SMASH!

BAM!

The old lady cried as she held him until he died.

CHAPTER SEVENTY-SIX

TANYA

I finally made it back to Dr. Hunt's office ready and willing to continue with the hypnosis. I was called into the back immediately,

"Okay Tanya, let's try this again. This is Dr. Kramer, he will be the one to hypnotize you. Come and lie back on the chaise."

I did as I was told. I laid back on the chaise while Dr. Hunt took a seat in a chair.

I relaxed the best I could and took a few more deep breaths. Dr. Kramer took over.

"Tanya, I'm going to ask you to close your eyes and relax."

I looked over to Dr. Hunt and she gave me a head gesture, letting me know it was alright to do as Dr. Kramer was telling me. Dr. Hunt pressed the recorder on her smart phone. I closed my eyes as Dr. Kramer continued.

"Tanya, I'm going to take you back. You are going to re-live some of your past."

Dr. Kramer pulled out a pendulum and told me to focus as he swung it back and forth before my eyes.

"Tanya, I want you to focus on my voice okay?" he asked.

"Yes." I said lowly.

"Okay fine. I want you to go back to as far as you can remember."

I was silent for a while.

"Ten years?" he asked.

Silence.

"Twenty years?"

Silence.

"I want you to go back to the time that you have blocked out of your mind all these years."

Silence.

More silence.

Eventually, I spoke.

"I was only ten years old I was in the kitchen to get a drink of water. I was.... I was thirsty. I guess he heard me. Maybe he was waiting for me. He crept up behind me and... and... "

Silence.

Tears brimmed the edge of my eyes. They were ready to spill out and roll down my face, but I tried to keep my composure as best I could.

"Go on." Dr. Kramer urged.

"He hurt me. He snatched my panties off!"

"Who is the he?" Dr. Kramer asked.

My face teared up. I was so upset.

"Dr. Kramer, please repeat the question." Dr. Hunt said.

Dr. Kramer nodded his head. "Who is the "He" that you are referring to Tanya?"

In my mind the lights were dim but the silhouette was taking long and purpose filled strides to the light. The figure had on a long, white t-shirt that draped off of his boney shoulders.

Shoulders that looked so familiar to me. The figure grabbed me. I jumped.

The face became clear. clearer. Clearer. Clearer!!

I jumped again.

Dr. Hunt and Dr. Kramer had to hold me from bolting out of the room. They sat me back down.

"Oh no! Nooo! It was him! It was him!"

"Who?!" Dr. Kramer asked.

Belligerently, I yelled, "My Father!!!"

"Your father? What else do you see?" Dr. Lambert asked.

I was cringing. My eyelids were closed but my eyeballs were moving rapidly under them. I was seeing much more than I was speaking of. I started swinging my head from side to side, my eyes were twitching, I began sweating. My body went limp.

Dr. Hunt told Dr. Kramer to bring me out of the hypnosis. Dr. Kramer snapped one time and I came out of my trance. My eyes slowly opened. I looked around the room. I looked at Dr. Kramer then Dr. Hunt then back to Dr. Kramer. Dr. Hunt hugged me and told me everything would be okay.

She asked me how I felt.

I answered in a whisper. "I don't know."

The doctor played back the recording for me.

My head hung low.

I said in a low voice, "There was always something I didn't like about him. The way he looked at me or maybe it was the way he touched me, small gestures." I was staring at the carpet. "Once he rubbed me on my back and I almost jumped out of my skin. It felt too, I don't know, too sexual, I guess, now that I'm older. That night my mother was passed out. As usual she'd had an alcohol and drug binge. She'd passed out in the room. He must've heard me because as soon as I got into the kitchen and opened the refrigerator door he was behind me, grinning, showing those filthy, yellow teeth. He was high, I could tell by the look of his eyes. He began chasing me and tugging at my shorts. I tried making him stop, but he wouldn't. I lost my balance and fell and... and..."

And I didn't want to talk anymore.

CHAPTER SEVENTY-SEVEN

KENO

Princess' head went through the windshield. Her skull cracked and her neck was broken. Since I didn't have on my seatbelt I was slung out of the window and broke my fall in a nearby bush.

The driver of the pick up truck was dead. It wasn't long before an ambulance rushed to the scene and into action. It was decided that if they could stabilize Princess they would fly her to a specialist in Tennessee for brain surgery.

CHAPTER SEVENTY-EIGHT

TANYA

As the sun poured its way through my bay window and onto the floor in the living room, I began to awaken. Emotionally and physically I was weak. The phone rang.

"Hello." I said weakly.

"How you doing?" Sahara asked gleefully.

"I'm okay. I'm going to stay in today cause I'm not feeling up to getting out." I said, a bit saddened.

Sahara asked me if I'd mind her staying with me for a few days.

"You know I don't mind but what's going on? You are one who revels in having your own space."

Sahara fidgeted a little. Suddenly, she looked uncomfortable. She loved me but didn't know how to tell me what she knew. She fought for words.

"I-I'm having problems with an ex boyfriend." she lied. "I need sometime away from it all. He won't be able to find me over your place." she sputtered.

"Is it Corey again?"

"Yeah." Sahara lied.

I know she wanted to be truthful with me but she was scared. I didn't pry, I safficed with the bit of info. She was the only person I had and if I lost her I'd be miserable.

Sahara told me she'd be over later on. With that we hung up the phone.

I took a deep breath and heard Ma whisper my name. I looked up and saw another illusion. Ma was standing in the corner, wearing a long white gown.

"Cheryl is coming to see you."

At the mention of my biological mother's name, my whole demeanor changed.

"I didn't raise you ta hold grudges. You have ta try ta forgive in this life. Now, Chile, I'm not asking you ta forget, but the Bible says "Don't let the sun go down with hatred in your heart." Your mama has gotten help and I think you should at least talk ta her. Please, think about it Ladybug."

"I will think about it."

"That's all I ask, Chile. That's all I ask."

The vision disappeared.

Ma just didn't understand the connection between me going to a psychiatrist and Cheryl's drug love.

CHAPTER SEVENTY-NINE

KENO

I couldn't go to Memphis with Princess for the surgery because I had the biggest lick in my life set up with Lee for the next day.

This was something I knew would get me out of the rat race for good. The lick I'd been waiting for all my life, even better than the one Sonny promised.

It was a Friday afternoon, Lee and his son and me went downtown to a big building. We knew Cho was there because his Phantom was in the parking lot. Through Kim, Lee knew one thing for sure about Cho and that was that when he was in town and at the bar then business was shortly to follow. He would have at least a million dollars from his transaction. They had no way to know what his product would be because he was the type to deal in many different high priced things. But surely Cho's never faltering routine was to have fun with the girls, handle his business then head out of the country.

Later on that evening we tracked Cho to a ten story brick building in downtown Los Angeles.

We laid back in the cut and waited. I took my time eating a Club sandwich and drinking a huge 7-Eleven soda.

Cho was known to arrive earlier than who ever he was meeting and would stay behind and count all the money. When the black big body Benz pulled up I got goose bumps all over. I felt like I had to take a piss. We watched two white guys walk inside. They both wore black suits and one had an attache' case in his left hand.

It didn't take long, it had been maybe fifteen minutes when the two white guys came back out and climbed into the Benz. When they left, Lee, his partner and me quickly rushed into the building. We had no clue what floor Cho was on so we quietly took the stairs and scoured every floor. I wished I had taken a piss before we entered the building. Ten minutes later we heard voices as we crept up the stairs to the tenth floor.

Lee came through the door first. With a black .380 Berretta held low in his right hand he yelled, "Choooo!"

Cho looked up in surprise with the last stack of bills in his hand he had just picked up out of the money counter. His movements were slow as he placed the money into the attache' case with the rest and closed it really slow.

He picked it up by the handle as he spoke calmly. "Lee. It's been a long time."

Guess he figured he was going to talk his way out of his situation. He did have his gunman at his side. I just squeezed and fired to eliminate that safety net Cho thought he had. I aimed straight for the center of Gunman's face to blow a chunk out of the back of his head but Gunman turned his head in a flash. It was a quick move but I squeezed twice and when Gunman was returning his head he caught the second one. It ripped through the bridge of his nose and took out his right eyelid. He dropped in excruciating pain. I fired four more shots into Gunman's body. Cho jumped at all six rounds I fired. It seemed as if Cho was the one getting shot. Lee walked up to Cho, back slapped him with the gun and Lee's partner pulled a gun out from inside Cho's jacket. Lee told me that I could go wait in the car. I figured in reality it was a personal matter, so I got out of there.

I sat in the car for a couple minutes until I couldn't hold my pee in any longer. I scanned the area for a quick spot to release before I pissed on myself and the car seat. There was an alley behind the building. I pulled out of my parking place and swerved into the alley. I thought I saw the same black big body Benz pass the alley in my rear view mirror, but I wasn't sure. Only thing I was positive of was that my bladder was about to burst. I pulled my dick out and let it go.

I couldn't have been there for more than the time that it took to get out of the car, pull my dick out and drain about eight ounces onto the already piss-stained concrete

451

behind a dumpster, when all of a sudden I heard a man's screams coming from over my head.

Then BAM!

A man's body slammed onto the top of the dumpster I was behind. Blood, dust, dirt, flies and stank flew into the air and engulfed me. I was immediately disgusted. I looked and saw Lee splattered on top of the dumpster with his head hanging over the edge, eyes glued on me, no blinking or nothing. I couldn't believe it. I thought to myself that I shouldn't have left Lee. But Lee told me to. Lee let out a sigh and blood spilled out of his mouth and nose. I probably would've thrown up had my attention not gotten diverted by the sound of a briefcase crashing to the ground and a shower of hundred dollar bills raining down above me. I quickly looked around and determined that no one on the ground was around or in earshot of what had just happened. I heard another sigh escaped Lee's mangled mouth. My first thought was to scrape up as much money as possible as quickly as I could and dash out of the alley and into the wind, so that's what I did. I started grabbing money and just stuffing it in my pockets until they were full then into my shirt until I looked fifty pounds fatter. I kept stuffing until it got ridiculous. There were too many bills. Still no one was coming so I picked up the briefcase and started stuffing money into it. After I gathered up all the money I jumped into the car and took off down the alley and around the corner.

No sooner than I hit the corner I crashed into a white van head on.

BAM!!!!

The impact was so great it threw the car backwards, spun it around and knocked me unconscious.

I awoke into the face of two federal agents trying to open the car's driver door. The same two guys in the Big body Benz. That jolted me awake. The windshield had a big dent in it, probably the size of my excruciating headache. Frightened to death I smashed on the gas. The car didn't move. The engine didn't even rev. I thought quick and turned the key, the engine turned over but didn't start. The agents started yelling and pulled their weapons. I ducked down, turned the key again. One agent fired a shot, the glass blew as the motor came to life. My foot was still depressed on the gas fully and the car was still in drive so it jerked into action and hauled ass down the street. I felt heat in my chest and wetness on my shirt immediately. My adrenaline didn't let me worry about that right then. I turned two more corners and entered the freeway. I did 100 mph up two exits and got off and got back on the opposite way and did the speed limit. I had gotten away with a briefcase full of money.

A smile crept up at the ends of my lips. About four miles up the pain started in my chest, it became unbearable fast. The whole front seat was wet and red. I blacked out doing 65mph.

CHAPTER EIGHTY

TANYA

Where you at? said the text Sahara sent.

I'm headed home. I texted back.

Stephen is not right. Sahara texted.

Huh? I text back.

No answer.

An hour later, I pulled up to my house and saw Sahara's car in the driveway. Her lights were on and the engine was still running but I didn't see Sahara anywhere.

That's strange. I thought.

I walked around the car a few times then called the police. Two detectives got there within minutes. They cut the engine off of Sahara's car and took my statement.

"Ms. Glass, can we take a look in your house?"

"Sure, why not?" I said, hunching my shoulders. "But Officer I think someone may have abducted her from here. She was meeting me. I mean I just talked to her about an hour before."

They looked at me incredulously, they didn't believe my story. I showed them my phone and they rambled through my call log.

Another police cruiser pulled up and two officers got out of the car and walked around to the back of the house. While they were still back there another car pulled up and went into the neighbor's yard on the left. Yet another group of police officers drove up and began slowly scouring the block. The two cops that were in my yard hopped over the brick wall that separated my back yard from the neighbor on the right.

After ten minutes an officer yelled from the left, "Over here! I found something!"

Beneath some beautiful white and pink flowers, two fingers pierced the dirt of a shallow grave. Everybody dashed to the back yard. An arm up to the elbow was found, then another body part and another. The officers kicked the door of the house in but no one was there. A disgusting stench infiltrated their nostrils. A pair of bloody cutters stood in the corner of the kitchen.

A Dodge with the neighbor and another man in it stopped halfway up the block. There were a lot of officers, ambulances and media in front of his house, he reversed.

The next morning the police were still next door digging. I was barricaded inside my house, I drunk coffee and watched the news. I had called Sahara's phone all night to no avail.

As I sipped from the mug I flipped through the channels watching different news stations.

Breaking news just in." the anchorwoman said. *"It seems as if we've found the body of another young unidentified woman. She was thrown in the Mississippi River. A young man was fishing when he saw what appeared to be a mutilated body. We don't know any other information and police aren't giving us much either. Not until they find out whom the woman is. The one thing we do know is that she has a tattoo on the inside of her wrist of a half of heart and a bracelet of a half of a heart also. This is Shamoi Owens with channel 5 news.*

My mouth was wide open as I watched. I was extremely nervous. I couldn't believe what I'd just heard. I couldn't believe any of this was going on in my life right now. I went and got into the car, maneuvered through the yellow tape and cars in front of my house and just drove around aimlessly. Ma appeared in the passenger seat.

Ma said, "Tanya, go ta my house, there's a surprise fa you."

"What do mean surprise? I can't take anymore surprises!"

"I hope you won't be too mad at me when you see."

"Are you listening to me? I can't take anymore! What are you talking about?" I yelled.

Ma didn't say anything else, just sat there and looked forward at the road.

I just drove.

I noticed that Ma was crocheting a quilt and the quilt had different photos on it, some of me when I was a baby, some during my childhood, some adolescent and college years, some of me and my mother. I noticed that me and Cheryl looked just alike in the face when she was younger except that she wasn't fat.

"Before da drugs she was a very loving and attentive person." Then Ma said nothing else for a while. She looked like she was getting her thoughts together then she said, "Your mama was a beautiful baby with a head full of black curly hair. She had a smile that would light up any room. She wasn't a fussy child. As a child she made very good grades. She was just an all 'round joy ta have. Boys was a calling my house all da time but all through high school your mama was a good girl. 'Erthang changed when she met dat Ron Ron. I thought it twas jus a phase she was going through. Then he got her inta dem drugs and that's when she began actin' strange. My baby was goin' to be a nurse and he took that away from us."

Ma didn't say anything else about her daughter. That subject was still touchy, although Cheryl'd been off drugs for a while now. Ma looked over at me with a sigh and smiled.

When I got to Ma's house I went over to the passenger side to help Ma get out. Ma was hesitant to get out then I remembered it was just a vision.

The vision appeared on the front porch of the house in the blink of an eye.

"I jus want da bess for you." Ma said.

I could barely hold myself together but I looked at Ma strangely and said, "Okay, now let's go in the house."

I reached for the door handle and Ma disappeared.

Suddenly, the door opened.

"Hey, I just whipped up something to eat." Cheryl! My mother said.

The hairs on the back of my neck stood up. I took a few deep breaths. I knew Cheryl was there to try and cash in on Ma's possessions. It was showdown time. Me and Cheryl would go to war before the day's end.

"Hey Baby." Cheryl greeted me and went to hug her only daughter. I stepped back and looked on in disbelief.

"Tanya, come on in the house please." Cheryl asked.

Ma stood behind Cheryl with begging eyes.

I knew I needed to go in for a minute and see what Cheryl was up to. But I wasn't interested in having dinner with her. I went and sat at Ma's oak table, Cheryl walked over to me, trying to make conversation.

"Hey Baby." Cheryl said smiling.

I turned up my nose, looking Cheryl up and down. Ma was right, she did appear to be off drugs. She looked clean, but she was still pretty skinny. She was 5'7" a little taller than me, with short hair. Her light colored skin was smooth and she wore a nice pair of camel-colored slacks and white button down blouse.

"Don't say shit to me!" I spat.

Cheryl was oil to my vinegar, we didn't nor would we ever mix. I hated her and didn't think I could ever forgive her. I turned to walk away. I just needed to get away, maybe go to the living room to cool off a bit. When Cheryl grabbed my arm I exploded.

I turned around and faced the woman who was supposed to protect me, who was supposed to provide for me. I was close up in Cheryl's face, she could smell my mouthwash.

I slapped my mother with the back of my hand.

Swack!

Cheryl's wig flew off of her head. I'd been waiting for this opportunity for quite some time and now I was ready to give Cheryl all she asked for.

"You know what, you are a poor excuse for a woman! I was raped by your sorry ass man but you didn't protect me because you were too busy thinking about your next high. Then you shipped me off to live with grandma. I hate you!"

Cheryl held her face and backed up. I was pacing the tiny space.

"I didn't ship you off. They took you from me and your grandma told them that she would take you so that you wouldn't be in the system. I didn't know what happened. You were always so damn smart with me. We could never talk about anything."

"And do you know why I acted like that, Cheryl?"

I took a deep breath and took a seat at Ma's oak table. For a minute I was wrapped in my own thoughts. Cheryl looked over at me.

"I've been having fucking nightmares?" I said, looking away.

"I was sick. I wasn't in my right mind. Yes, at one point in time only drugs mattered to me. I wasn't thinking about you, but I wasn't thinking about myself either. I mean, I wasn't thinking about effects the drugs would have on my body. I wasn't thinking about losing you Tanya. I'm sorry but that was so long ago and Ron Ron is dead now, so why is any of this relevant?"

"Fuck You!" I shouted. I dropped my head in my hands and sobbed like a baby. I was crying so hard I was trembling.

I looked at the vision of Ma just standing there looking on like a quiet spectator.

Ma finally said, "In dis life da only way you will prosper is ta love your mama an' forgive her or at least try. Forgiveness is a gift ta yourself. I know your mama wasn't dere fa you in da pass, but she's tryin ta be now. Juss let 'er be dere fa you an' love you. Please Baby try fa me." Ma pleaded.

I had always been a sucker for my grandma. I'd never been able to tell her "no" but this was about to be the first time.

I walked out of the house and drove home. When I pulled up to my house I could see that the crew had mostly left and the rest were leaving. I was met by two police detectives.

"May I help you?" I asked cautiously. Nervously I shifted my weight knowing it wouldn't be good news.

One of the officers took off his hat and said, "We have a few questions to ask."

The detectives followed me into my house and the three of us stood in the kitchen.

"The last time I heard from her was a text message." I said.

"We want to rule you out as a suspect in her abduction and that's why we are talking to you. Can we see the text?"

"I showed it to the officers yesterday. Wait a minute, a suspect? You think I'd do something like that?" I asked.

"We just want to get to the bottom of this. You called the police over here yesterday with her car in your driveway and now she was found dead."

"Why would I do this to her? I cared for her. We are sisters."

The officers listened attentively but they still asked me about fifty more questions. Finally Detective Linders handed me a card with his name and number on it.

"Please call me if you can think of anything else." he said.

I walked both men to the door.

I locked the door and leaned back on it. I stood there for a few moments, long enough for the detectives to leave my house.

After that I didn't leave the house for two days, I hadn't spoken to anyone. I finally went to the grocery store and when I came home and went into the kitchen, I noticed a drinking glass where the plastic cups were designated. I would never do that. Then I noticed broken glass on the floor from the back door. I looked up and saw the back door was ajar. I pulled out my cell phone, looked at the card the detectives had given me. I had only dialed the first three numbers when I heard Stephen's voice saying, "Don't do it.

I'll have to kill you too." as he descended the stairs slowly and deliberately.

"Stephen, what are you doing here? What is this?

"Shut up and sit your fat ass down on the couch."

I could only see his silhouette, I couldn't tell if he had a gun in his hand or any other type of weapon. I walked slowly to the couch with my cell phone still in hand.

"What the hell is wrong with you Stephen, what do you want?"

He stepped into view twirling Kimberly's badge on his index finger. "What does everybody want? I want my turn. The come up. I tried to work you a few different ways but none of them seemed to work and tonight is the last night for me to earn forty eight million dollars so as they say, drastic times call for drastic measures."

"Is that what this is about, the investment money at TSL? Well in case you didn't get the memo I don't work there anymore."

He leaned against the wall at the base of the stairs. "I know, I was there remember? Don't worry about that though, I've got all that part figured out. All I need is your access code and some of your know how, in exchange for your life of course."

"You would kill me Stephen?"

He crossed his arms. "Well now it's gotten to that point. At first I tried it the nice guy way. The real power is behind the throne. I sent Malcolm to seduce your puggy ass but he has feelings like a bitch. He made love to you and ended up getting an allowance instead of making you see the great big picture. No one in their right mind would possibly continue to work for five figures a year when in the palm of their hands they hold the key to eight digits, just a couple clicks of a button away. Well it's okay because if you don't want it I know someone who does, yours truly."

I stood up! "You killed Sahara?"

"Yeah, she's another dummy. All she had to do was convince you to do this. I tried to do this as civil as possible, believe me, coming in here and hurting you was not on the top of my list, it was on the list, if necessary, just not on top, I prefer no blood shed."

I took two steps forward. "You son of a bitch!"

His eyes bucked. I would step no closer.

He began slowly walking around the living room. "You can call me what you want but tomorrow, if you're alive you'll be calling me a multi-millionaire. Even Kimberly could've made things easier but jealousy fucked her up. She's been my bitch for over two years now, that's how I got the job at TSL. I've been plotting on this company for some time now. When you got that last promotion I knew you

465

were the one I needed to keep close. When I told Kimberly I was going after you she tripped out and ended up almost fucking everything up. Put black dick in a white bitch and things get crazy. Either things get real good or they get real bad.

Maybe you should've just let me in when I took you out, I can only think that maybe we could've came to a better arrangement than this one." he stepped close to me.

He looked me directly in the eyes and said, "Oh well, now that you've been brought up to speed. Lemme' tell you how the rest of the story goes. We are going to wait until after midnight because the scheduled pay out is for tomorrow's date. Everybody in the building will be gone, then we're going to use Kimberly's badge to get into the building. Once we're in, we'll go the President's office and log in. I know that six people in the company have access to the accounts, you being one of them. I have already opened an offshore account which you will be transferring all of the funds to, all that information is right here." he said, tapping on his jacket pocket. It's all gonna work out, trust me, the plan is fool proof." he said, "If you don't design your own plan, you fall into someone else's. And guess what they'll have for you? Nothing."

Wow! This son of a bitch really had it all worked out. If he did it just how he planned he really would be able to steal all the money.

He interrupted my thoughts by saying, "We have a few hours to kill and I know your big ass is hungry so why don't you go into your favorite room and cook us something to eat. Oh, lemme have that cellphone." he said extending his hand.

He sat on the couch and watched me over the breakfast nook as I worked around in the kitchen with shot to hell nerves.

He set a knife down on the coffee table. It was a nice size knife, not too small not too big. It was the same knife he had cut Sahara's neck with he said.

After I cooked up some fried chicken and potatoes I sat the plate down in front of Stephen and headed to the bathroom. He got up and walked behind me.

"Excuse me!" I said. "I'm going to use the toilet."

"I'm going with you. You only have a couple hours left and until then I won't let you out of my site. Take it or leave it."

"How about if I decide to leave it?"

"Then I'll hog tie you and stick you in the car trunk until midnight."

"Okay you win." I spoke as I lifted my dress and sat on the toilet. I was thankful that I only had to urinate.

I didn't have on any panties. He noticed but it didn't turn him on. He watched me wipe myself then get up.

When it was time to leave he instructed me to get dressed in all black. We went upstairs and he commanded me to sit on the bed while he went through my closet and pulled out some black clothes.

He threw me a pair of black jeans and a thick black blouse. He wanted me to dress in front of him. I was apprehensive. I picked up a bra off of the dresser, put it on then put on the blouse. I needed socks so I walked over near him. He put the knife to my neck as I bent down to open the bottom drawer of the dresser. I grabbed a black pair of socks and sat on the hardwood floor and put them on. I stood back up and got the jeans off of the bed. Every move I made he was there.

"I need panties." I said as I walked over to the armoire. He could only imagine the bloomers such a big momma would wear. That was something he really didn't want to see. He stepped back a little so I could get my panties.

It was a one, two move then time stopped and sped up at the same time.

BOOM!

BAM!

The gun Malcolm left in my drawer fell to the floor. My hand vibrated from the shock of the blast. I'd never shot a gun before but the bullet went straight through Stephen's right lung. He fell back against the door and slid down. He tried to curse at me but blood filled his lungs quickly. He coughed up some blood and died with his eyes open, no doubt shocked at the instant turn of events.

By now it was 12:20 a.m. and my first thought was to call the police and tell them everything. Then I thought about how they were accussing me as if I myself had killed Sahara. What if I couldn't convince them of the truth about Stephen and ended up in prison. No, I had to re-think this through. I had already lost my car and the foreclosure of my house would be coming soon. Maybe I could do it myself, steal the money and pay my bills. Maybe I would just take the money and leave. I didn't have anything or anyone to keep me in Memphis anymore.

Stephen's idea and plan was pretty damn good but I didn't know if I could live with myself if I did it.

I decided against it. I picked up the phone and dialed the detective's number. I looked over at Stephen's dead body. A vision of me in jail clothes flashed before my eyes. I hung up the phone and ran out of the house. I wished I had time to think about it, at least a day or two but unfortunately or maybe fortunately, tonight had to be the night. I dug into Stephen's pocket for the account information then went into my kitchen drawer for some latex gloves. I found them, got into the Maxima and drove off.

CHAPTER EIGHTY-ONE

KENO

I was busted and booked and my charges were incredible. I was charged with Cho's and Gunman's murder. I was also charged with Lee's murder. I was charged with possession of unscrupulous funds for the half of million dollars that was turned in.

Lee's partner and me were in a holding cell together.

He told me, "I'm getting out, you're getting a life sentence. My father is a diplomat of China. In court they'll negotiate for me to do my time in China because all the dead were Chinese and they'll release me to the Chinese Government but I won't do any time. You'll get blamed for everything. It's too late now but if you ever get out. Look me up, your lawyer has my lawyer's info. That job on Cho was small potatoes. It was personal for Lee. Look at him now. That's why there's no room for emotions when you're getting money."

I was nearly speechless. I almost said something then I shut back down and just nodded my head.

"I guess it be like that sometimes." I said to myself.

We spent the day in court. Crystal was there. She looked nice. I wanted to tell her where I had some money stashed, felt like me and Shalleen all over again. The sheriffs

471

didn't allow any communication between the defendants and the public. So it was damn near impossible for me to tell her all I wanted to. I tried and the deputy officer told me he would put whoever I was talking to out of the court room if I continued. Crystal didn't care. She mouthed me some words from the audience. I couldn't understand her so she repeated.

No comprende'.

She repeated.

The court officer said, "Hey you Miss. No talking with defendants." and he walked to the other side of the court room. She repeated and repeated until finally I read her lips perfect.

You ain't neva gonna change. I won't be coming to visit you. Pardon my back.

then she got up and walked out of the court room, never to deal with me again.

When it was all said and done, I had a life sentence and Jin was ordered immediately deported to China. Jin was the only prisoner on his father's diplomatic jet.

CHAPTER EIGHTY-TWO

TANYA

I parked the Nissan at a distance, sat and staked out in front of TSL, my old job. I knew everyone's routine so it wouldn't be hard for me. The lights cut off around 10:30 p.m. It was dark.

Cautiously, I got out of the car and went to the back entrance. Using Kimberly's card I got in successfully and went up to the fifth floor and went to the huge office and went straight for the computer. I was thinking of only one thing, getting into the resort account and disbursing the funds to an account offshore. When I accessed the accounts goosebumps popped up on my skin.

Could I actually do it? Could I really steal all of that money? What if I did it and got caught for it? Or if I got away with it, would my conscious make me give it back?

One more click of the mouse and it would be done. This would mean I'd be passed the point of no return. I clicked down on the mouse and the money was transferred to the account offshore.

I leaned back in the huge office chair. "I did it!" I said almost in a whisper.

I wanted to run out of the building and not look back. I peeped out of the office and when I didn't see anybody coming I took the back staircase which took me down to the first floor. I went out the back way undetected. Life had just gotten better.

Breaking News

I stared at the results of the pregnancy test. This determined my future with or without Malcolm. Having a baby and being single was not what I ever invisioned for myself. My breathing quickened, big balls of sweat rolled down my forehead. I willed my trembling body to be still.

The pregnancy test came back negative!!

Ma didn't raise me to be somebody's babymama.

The ringing cellphone caught my attention so I grabbed it.

"Hello." I said tersely.

It was Jalisa. I rolled my eyes upward.

"Girl, Kimberly robbed the company!" Jalisa shrieked. "It's on every major news station."

"I don't work for TSL anymore, and yes, I know."

"How are you doing?"

I just hung the phone up. I sat it on the bed of the hotel and walked out.

The news broadcast played in the background as I left the hotel room. They said Kimberly had stolen $48,000,000 by transfer and her ID number was linked to it all. As they talked about the theft and the company I smiled. Mr. Pennilton, the president of the company, was doing an interview with channel 5 news and his face looked like he held the weight of the world on his shoulders. There was footage of Kimberly being led out of her house in handcuffs.

CHAPTER EIGHTY-THREE

KENO

"Yeah man," I said. "Crystal had picked me up from the bus station, fresh off the bus from prison. That same day the grocery store we went to got robbed while I was in the parking lot. And just thirty days later I was back in jail looking at a whole heap of charges. That punk ass chinky eyed public defender did me in and got me a life sentence and they let that lil Chinese bastard go back to his country." I was saying this as I stared up at the sheet metal under the top bunk in my jail cell.

"Man, that was some hell of a shit you went through in just one month. I wish that was me." My cell mate said.

I said. "I spent a lot of money and one thing I know for sure is that you may not get all that you pay for but you will pay for all that you get. Fredrick Douglas said that."

"You could say that again."

I gave a crooked smiled at the thought of it all and got up from my bottom bunk, took a piss and said to my cell mate, "Yep that's how it all went down and how I had $1,000,000.00 in my hands then ended up in jail again eventhough them agents only turned in half. But at the end of the day, I wouldn't change nothing if I could. Except for Princess having that accident, yuh know."

"Did she survive?"

"Yeah she did. She's much much better now."

"That's good. One of these days I'ma tell you how I ended up in here." Cellmate said with a half grin, half frown.

I looked over at the stack of books on my locker. They were the same ones that Ole Mack had introduced me to. The 48 Laws of Power sat on top.

I got back into the bed and fell asleep. I fell asleep thinking about Tanya and the last time I had seen her.

Flashback:

As Tanya bathe in hot water trying to scald Ron Ron's terrible essence off of her, Ron Ron laid back on the couch with his hand in the front of his pants. A knife arched down from over the back of the couch with much force and punctured Ron Ron's belly button. It went through his body and chipped a piece of bone off of his vertebrae. Ron Ron screamed and scrambled off of the couch and crawled to the wall.

"I swear to you she was coming on to me! Please Son! She was flirting with me with those little clothes she wears. I swear to you Son!"

It was only a couple weeks earlier that my mother had let the cat out of the bag. It was a secret she had held on to out of respect for Cheryl. I was the result of a weak moment, the result of manipulation from a womanizing, sick pedophile crackhead. Ron Ron had fathered me and Tanya.

"You're going to hell old man! No more secrets. I'm ashamed to call you my father." Keno said as he stepped closer. "You shoulda stuck to smoking crack with Cheryl."

Stick! Stick! Stick!

Keno went blind with rage and couldn't stop. Keno stabbed Ron Ron 81 times.

Emergency vehicles and police cars were blocking the driveways of half the block. The ambulance parked in front of little

476

Tanya's house was being loaded with Ron Ron's dead body. The neighbors gasped when he was wheeled out uncovered.

The police car pulled away from the curb. Tanya ran outside and ran down the street behind the police car. Keno was the only person in the world she knew she could trust. A friend she could rely on. As Tanya stood there and watched the police car until it disappeared, blood trickled down her leg.

Keno did the only thing he could do. He watched Tanya out of the rear window as he smiled with no regrets and dropped a tear at the same time.

I had thought about that day often. The sound of the bell, telling the prisoners that it was time for chow, began ringing. I got up, got dressed and put my shoes on.

I walked down the dry dingy tan colored hallway. I traveled in a trance, not wanting to admit that maybe jail was where I was destined to live from the beginning. I raised my head when I heard my name called by a familiar voice.

I looked up and saw Jo-Jo passing down the hall in a line movement. I jumped out of line and ran up on Jo-Jo and punched him in the mouth. We began to scuffle until the guards broke us up. As they pulled us apart I got a final kick into Jo-Jo's ribs.

Kapooya!!

Jo-Jo lunged at me but the guards held him. Me and Jo-Jo were cuffed and taken directly to the SHU (Special Housing Unit).

Guess who was my celly? My favorite ole timer Mack! He was getting out soon. After all these years of coaching his daughter Marijka, who prefers to call herself Mary Jay, they had made some progress. She finally made the right connection

477

with the right Defense Attorney, Paul Downing. She had gotten up enough money by taking it from those who were poison to the black race. Mack was scheduled for an appeal and during his appeal he would be able to bail out and the bailbondsman had already been retained. He doesn't know his daughter is a freak though.

I was in confinement for a week before I was able to go to the gated off recreation area. There me and Jo-Jo saw each other again. He was in a 10' by 10' just like me but about 4 cages away.

I shouted out, "You bitch ass Mutha-fucka."

"Whatever faggot, we can get it on again anytime, check."

"It's on! Everytime I see either of you faggots!" I yelled.

"I know you mad but I got burned too, check. I don't know how you got locked up or how long you been locked up but I been here since the night we hit the club, check. I never made it back home, check. That bitch Crystal and Sonny set me up."

"What the fuck you talking about?"

"Just what I said, check."

"You ain't said shit!"

"Check it out Keno, this is what happened..." he told me about a meeting. "This is how it all started. Sonny, his baby momma Crystal..."

"His baby momma Crystal?"

"Yeah, Sonny's baby momma Crystal and…"

"What Crystal?"

"Your Crystal. Yall Crystal. That's not your kid, check. So Sonny's baby momma Crystal and me were sitting on the floor in the empty house on Van Ness after we finally finished loading up the U-haul truck. I said to Sonny, 'That's fucked you lost this house Sonny. You know you should've called me sooner. I'm sure we could've done something to get the money up, check.'"

Sonny said, "It's cool, on to the next one. But I do have a couple of things I've been looking at. But I need at least two down muthafuckas I can trust to have my back."

"Well you know I'm down for whatever, check." Jo-Jo said.

"I know but I need one more person."

Crystal said, "I know someone who is down as hell Daddy. He been doing ill shit his whole life Baby. He aint scared to do shit."

"Who is that Babygirl?" Sonny asked.

She said, "This guy named Keno."

I said. "I know him, he from the Bottoms."

She continued, "I used to talk to him right before I met you. He's been locked up for about two years but he about to get out like tomorrow." Crystal said.

"How you know, you been writing him?"

"Yeah I check on him every now and then Baby. He thinks were still close. He even thinks your baby is his."

"What?"

"I never told him that, it's just that after he got locked up, one day we got in touch after a few months and I was already pregnant by you. I told him I was pregnant and he took it the wrong way. Don't even worry, I don't want him. I just know you be needing soldiers sometimes. Only thing is that I can't be the one to hook yall up but he will help you get the job done."

"Aight Babygirl, that's what's up, we gonna use him then."

"Okay I can pick him up once he gets off the bus from prison tomorrow."

"Send me and Jo-Jo a text message telling us you got him and Jo-Jo can go from there. What size he wear? There's some clothes in this bag that might fit him, give them to him. It's some panties in there you can have too."

Jo-Jo finished telling me the story. "The next day she picked you up. She sent me a text telling me that you were in the car with her. I waited an hour then I called her phone and asked for you. I told you that fake story about getting into it with my girl and getting arrested. Remember, yall were on the way to the supermarket? Matter of fact, we set that up. Crystal was the look out on the inside. I got charged for that too when I got arrested. Them two soft ass niggas that got caught, snitched on me. Both of 'em!"

I was silent for a second, then I said, "Shantel is dead."

"I had to. Her boyfriend Marvel too. He talked too much."

Her boyfriend Marvel? I didn't even ask.

Jo-Jo said. "Don't you know who my homeboy Mannish is?"

"Yeah, why?"

"He just got shot up by his crackhead sister's man at a motel."

"Ahh that is fucked up! Is he alive?"

"Yeah he's alive."

By the time Mannish and Ty reached the motel Ty had decided that his mother was dead to him. He didn't even want to see Shawna.

"Ay yo Man I ain't getting out."

"Aight. I'll be back then." Mannish said, getting out of the vehicle and going up and knocking on the door next to 111. On the door was just a 2 and the bottom piece of a 1 on it.

Shawna opened the door then stepped out of the way. Mannish walked in. A man snuck from around the back of the building with a pistol in his hand. Moving quickly he ran up behind Mannish. Ty saw something moving fast out of the corner of his eye and looked.

"What the fuck!" he said to himself grabbing the door handle of the truck to get out. Before he could barely exit the vehicle three shots caught Mannish off guard. Two bullets came out of his chest and one blew out of the side of his jaw. He slammed face forward into the floor.

Ty ran into the room with his gun drawn. Shawna sat on the bed frozen. The killer was on his knees digging through Mannish's pockets.

481

"Mutha fucka!" Ty screamed. Travis, Shawna's husband looked up. Ty looked him deep in his eyes and unloaded his clip into the both of them, Travis and Shawna.

"Now you could be a better mother." Ty told her.

I guess cum is thicker than blood. Ty thought to himself.

He dug into Mannish's pocket and took out the Hacienda Hotel room key. Ty pulled off in the Range Rover as the sirens in the distance were getting louder.

Something grabbed Ty by the shoulder. He was frightened, he looked and no one was there. He had second thoughts. Maybe he had jumped the gun. Maybe Mannish wasn't dead. Ty was just too used to running from the scene. He looked into the rearview mirror and saw that the sirens were from a Firetruck passing the motel. He made a U-turn and headed back.

I was happy our lil yard time was up and it was time to go back in lock up. Jo-Jo had told me plenty. I needed to lay down.

CHAPTER EIGHTY-FOUR

KENO

Two years passed but in prison the days began to run into each other to the point where weekends and weekdays were no different. Holidays were nothing special. Christmas day and Valentine's day were just days.

"Mail call." echoed outside the cell door.

Five months earlier I had gotten a letter from Tanya. She was inquiring if she had gotten the right person. The letter said for me to write back if I was the right Keno Brown. I wrote back, happy as hell! Wrote her a ten-page letter then she sent me a letter that filled me in on much of her life but the last page was something I couldn't deal with, knowing that I would never get out. I never wrote her again.

I was on my bed reading a book when I heard,

"Mail call!" again then a letter was slung under the door of my cell.

It was a letter from the Asian girl from the coffee shop with a picture of her standing next the Public Defender that helped the system railroad me. She said the Public Defender was her uncle and that she was helping him clean out some boxes and ran across the Keno Brown file.

The letter went on about how she told her uncle how she met me and how I saved her life. The Public Defender promised her that he would do some research and see how he could help me get out. Four months had passed and this letter was telling me that I had a court date the following Monday at 8:30 a.m.

The arresting cop had gotten in trouble, a scandal. That could help me. She said that her uncle could get me back into court and before a judge but the only bad news was that the final decision was still up to the judge. She said the Public Defender did some researching and found a black judge that could hear the appeal. Just cross your fingers and hope for the best.

A favor for a favor.

Monday 8:30 a.m.

Court Day

All rise presiding Judge Solomon Alexander Sweetwater. When the judge entered the courtroom my heart jumped thunderously and warmed my chest instantly.

The judge continued to step more into view. I looked the judge in the face and sure enough it was the same person I had known as a kid.

Huungh! The judge drew in a breath in shock when he looked at me. Shock seemed to sit on his face for a few seconds.

When the judge spoke he was not normal, he was stern, he was improvising. He said, "Another blackman before my bench. I'm disgusted!"

He really wasn't disgusted. Because of what the boys at school did to him when he was younger he liked destroying young black thugs. He lined them up and sent them up the river for as long as he could. Lil man that pulled the gun on him came in front of Judge Solomom Alexander Sweetwater for shooting someone and Solomon sent him up the river for two life terms. People remember bullies. And me, he never forgot what I did for him either.

"I smell a rat. I have thoroughly reviewed this file…" He was lying. "And this has a set up written all over it. I believe this man may have had some involvement but he could not have controlled everything that the prosecution say he did in the file."

The judge said that because he knew that the detectives always did put extra lies in their reports.

"I want more defendants and until then I'm throwing this case out and I here by order the defendant released immediately."

On my way out of the court room the judge said, "Good Luck." to me. And that was it.

A favor for a favor.

CHAPTER EIGHTY-FIVE

<u>KENO</u>

I stepped back into my cell with the biggest smile on my face. My celly knew what that meant. He knew I had gotten released. We talk for a minute then Cell mate hopped up on his bed to give me room to pack.

After several minutes Cell mate realized that it was sobbing he heard. He said, "You crying Keno?"

"Tears of joy man, tears of joy." I said in a half whisper.

"Pull out that letter I gave you five months ago that I told you I didn't want to see again but not to throw away.

Cell mate got up, went into his locker, pulled out a folder and pulled the letter out.

The letter was from Tanya. The last page that tore me apart said,

I'll say again that it is sooo wonderful to hear from you. There is still sooo much that I want to tell you face to face about the things I've been through. I've shed so much weight I look fantastic, I'm so happy about that. Some stress I've suffered since a kid actually affected my eating habits and kept a lot of weight on me. It's funny, I've been fat all my life but the last time you saw me I was slender and I will be slender if you ever see me again. Happy to say I made it through all the madness, I am retired and well off now. I'm on Seychelles Island, 1,000 miles off the west coast of Africa. Not the main island Mahe', I'm on Praslin, one of the satellite islands. You would love it where I am. You wanna know something else that's crazy? Out of 115 islands I have some neighbors that are from Los Angeles. They're great. Their names are Sonny and Crystal. It's a couple, with a young child. I want you to meet them.

The End!

Coming Soon!

Be Like That Sometimes Part 3

www.bebpub.com